THE RECIPIENT'S SON

Also by Stephen Phillips

Proximity: A Novel of the Navy's Elite Bomb Squad

STEPHEN PHILLIPS

THE RECIPIENT'S SON

A NOVEL OF HONOR

NAVAL INSTITUTE PRESS

ANNAPOLIS, MARYLAND

This book has been brought to publication with the generous assistance of Marguerite and Gerry Lenfest.

Naval Institute Press
291 Wood Road
Annapolis, MD 21402

Library of Congress Cataloging-in-Publication Data

Phillips, Stephen
  The recipient's son : a novel of honor / Stephen Phillips.
     p. cm.
  ISBN 978-1-61251-116-0 (hardcover : alk. paper) —
ISBN 978-1-61251-169-6 (e-book) 1. United States Naval Academy—Fiction. 2. Naval education—Fiction. 3. Self-realization—Fiction. 4. Fathers and sons—Fiction. 5. Medal of Honor—Fiction. 6. Annapolis (Md.)—Fiction. 7. College stories. I. Title.
  PS3616.H475R43 2012
  813'.6—dc23

                              2012020767

∞ This paper meets the requirements of
ANSI/NISO z39.48-1992 (Permanence of Paper).
Printed in the United States of America.

20 19 18 17 16 15 14 13 12   9 8 7 6 5 4 3 2 1
First printing

Book layout and composition: David Alcorn, Alcorn Publication Design

In memory of Monsignor John Frances Laboon, S.J., Captain, USNR (Ret.)
and the United States Naval Academy Class of 1943

Acknowledgments

Many people helped in the development of this manuscript. I would like to extend sincere appreciation to Molly Agundez, Brian Castner, William Hubbard, Michael Huete, Tom Kilkenney, Will Lagasse, Steve Maffeo, Carol Parkinson, Rick Russell, Kurt Schick, and Kevin and Rebecca White.

I would also like to recognize my family, who supported me through the whole process from writing to publication: my brother, Tim Phillips; my parents, Stephen and Maureen Phillips; my wife, Christina; and my sons, Stephen and Zachary.

PART I
SERVICE SELECTION

1

SERVICE SELECTION NIGHT

FEBRUARY 13, 1992
2030
BANCROFT HALL, ROOM 7412

He tried to study, though there no longer seemed to be a point to it. The stereo blared, plus the commotion in the passageway distracted him. More important, the young man knew most of his classmates were now out in town celebrating. He stared at a book on political philosophy, waiting for his number to be called.

It was Service Selection Night for the Class of 1992 at the United States Naval Academy. Midshipman Lieutenant Donald Durago would soon take a momentous walk from his room on the fourth floor of Bancroft Hall's seventh wing down into Smoke Hall to select the ship he would serve aboard following graduation and commissioning.

The public address system drowned out all other noise as it reverberated across the thirty-three acres comprising the eight wings of the world's largest dormitory.

"Brigade, attention to announcements. Midshipmen with class rank numbers seven hundred to seven seventy-five report to four-one for service selection. I say again, midshipmen with class rank numbers seven hundred to seven seventy-five report to four-one for service selection."

The mids jokingly referred to the last hour of this auspicious evening as "Surface Selection" because the only assignments available were for surface ships or Marine Corps ground billets. The coveted aviation billets and nuclear power slots had all been selected hours ago by classmates with better academic and military standing. Durago imagined the top half of the class whooping it up at all the various watering holes in Annapolis, the submarine selectees buying drinks with their nuclear-power bonus money. He surmised the last remnants of those high enough in the class to select naval aviation were donning their newly issued leather flight jackets before heading into town.

There would be no money or leather for a mid of Durago's standing. Still, there was something he hoped for—orders to a very specific ship, a destroyer still under construction in Pascagoula, Mississippi. Unlike those who selected a ship already in the fleet, the mid who picked Durago's ship would not even receive a ship's ball cap.

Looking at the clock again, Durago reminded himself that its availability this late in the evening was a long shot. *I'll probably get a "food ship,"* he thought to himself.

The Academy's radio club disc jockey interrupted a tune by Def Leppard with some color commentary.

"Hey there, Brigade, just got a call from Midshipman First Class Mark Moore. Marky can't decide what to select so he wants us to have a call-in vote! That's right, call in your votes and we'll all decide his destiny! Now, for those of you left in the hall, realize Mark has but two choices left—Surface or Marine ground. Caller, state your name."

"Tony, from Third Company. Mark, go Marine. You'll like the haircuts."

"Okay, one vote for Marine Corps. Keep 'em coming, Brigade."

The public address bellowed again.

"Brigade, attention to announcements. Midshipmen with class rank numbers seven seventy-five to eight fifty report to four-one for service selection. I say again, midshipmen with class rank numbers seven seventy-five to eight fifty to four-one for service selection."

Durago got up from his desk, retucked his dress shirt, and donned his service dress blue jacket. He put on his cover, the hat worn by midshipmen that was similar to that of a naval officer. Then, by habit, he checked himself in the mirror.

As he clicked open the heavy wood door to his room, Durago looked at the black nametags fixed at eye level.

D. R. DURAGO '92
14th Company Commander

J. D. WARREN '92
3rd Battalion Drill Officer

He smiled to himself briefly.

The passageways were charged with excitement. Talk of "who selected what" reverberated off the polished tile floors and the hospital-white walls. The Brigade of Midshipmen realized that Service Selection Night was as important as graduation and commissioning. It marked what each midshipman would graduate to, what he or she would become.

Three Plebes, freshman midshipmen, were affixing warfare devices next to the names of the first class midshipmen, the "Firsties," or seniors in 14th Company who already selected. Thompson, Hall, and Ritter had the wings of a naval aviator next to their names. Potok had an atom symbol and a surface warfare pin for nuclear-surface. Mann had the "Budweiser" eagle, trident, and flintlock pistol designating him as a SEAL-select. Nguyen, Kohl, Lagasse, McClure, and Wilson, all future Marines, had the Marine Corps' eagle, globe, and anchor, or "EGA," next to their names. James "Slim" Warren, Durago's roommate, had both the wings of a naval aviator and the EGA, designating him as a Marine Aviation selectee. Other companymates would have the devices denoting submarines, surface, supply, intelligence, and naval flight officer placed next to their names.

As Durago strode down the passage, several underclassmen gave words of encouragement.

"Get some, Donny-boy."

"West Coast, man, think of Subic."

"Don't take anything in Earle, New Jersey."

Captain Robert Oberly, United States Marine Corps, the 14th Company Officer, was standing outside his office in the main passageway on the top floor of seventh wing. The hallway was wide enough for the whole company—3 platoons with 3 squads each, totaling approximately 110 midshipmen—to stand in formation.

Durago noted as he made his way toward the captain that few of his classmates were left in company area. It was another reminder that the chances of getting his ship were slim.

Oberly was in his greens. Though he did not have any campaign ribbons above his left breast pocket, an anomaly of assignments and deployments on the West Coast, all of the mids thought he was a great leader. Fourteenth Company would have more than its fair share of Marine selectees because of Captain Oberly's mentoring.

"Don, would you give me one more chance to convince you to join the Corps?" Oberly called out as Durago approached.

"Sir, you know I admire the Marine Corps, but I've realized it's not for me."

"Well, that's too bad. You're the only one that got away, then. Still, I bought EGA tie clips for all my charges who go Marine Corps. I bought an extra one with you in mind."

"I'm flattered, sir."

"The decision isn't made until you sign on the line."

"I'll think on it all the way down to Smoke Hall, sir."

"You do that."

When Durago stepped onto the deck a floor below, the mate of the deck looked up from his post. He smiled and nodded at Durago. Sensing recognition, he nodded back. Then he strolled down the hallway, past another set of Plebes marking the warfare selection of the Firsties in 13th Company. Finally, he stopped outside room 7312. He knew he could not pause too long, so he garnered one last look before continuing on.

The service selection process actually began in the offices of the Commandant of Midshipmen on the first deck of the fourth wing of Bancroft Hall, commonly called 4-1. Only the desks labeled "Surface" and "Marine Corps" still had officers sitting behind them. Durago signed the required forms at the "Surface" desk then walked toward Smoke Hall.

On the way there he stopped in the rotunda, a cathedral to naval service where Smoke, Bancroft, and Memorial Halls all join. Durago emerged from 4-0 just as two classmates stepped through the leftmost of three bronze doors at the main entrance of Bancroft Hall. The largest, center pair was verboten. By tradition, only Naval Academy alumni were authorized to use that portal. Though his two classmates had just selected their ships and were heading to the officers' club to celebrate, they would never brazenly break tradition.

Turning from the entrance to his left, Durago stopped a moment where the marble floor met a wide granite staircase rising to Memorial Hall, set between its twins that descend to Smoke Hall below. Looking up toward Memorial Hall, Durago thought of all the names enshrined there, names belonging to young men who once lived in Bancroft, who were part of the Brigade. Memorial Hall was always a reminder, a symbol of why the Naval Academy was different from Harvard or Stanford or Duke.

Some of you are going to die. Heroically, tragically, slowly, or quickly. . . . Some of you are going to die in the service of your country.

Down in Smoke Hall, the line moved slowly toward a vast tote board covered with placards displaying the names of all the ships available for selection. Each mid approached the board in order and removed the name of the ship he or she wanted to serve aboard. Some chose based on ship type, some on geographic location, still others on the date that they had to report aboard.

From the end of the line, Durago could see that most of the remaining ships were auxiliaries and amphibious ships. Midshipmen with a higher academic standing selected orders to most of the coveted *Aegis* cruisers and destroyers hours ago. The workhorse auxiliaries and the troop-carrying amphibious ships were less glamorous, less desirable. Durago remained silent as the line moved. He strained to see if his ship was still there.

Twenty minutes later, Durago hustled down the narrow steps at Bancroft's entrance and across the tan brick of Tecumseh Court. He looked across the court to the grounds that separated where the Brigade lived, prayed, and attended class. A steady stream of his classmates meandered like a line of ants in front of him, walking past the bronze bust of an Indian chief, a replica of a ship's figurehead that was the courtyard's namesake.

Midshipman lore holds that Tecumseh is the "God of the 2.0." Those who pay proper homage and respect to the idol will garner fortunate results on their examinations. On more than one occasion, Durago had tried to throw a penny into the Indian's quiver and had rendered him a left-handed salute. He especially appreciated the war paint emblazoned on the statue before each football game. Durago smiled, recalling that Tecumseh was depicted as Batman during the past season.

Light from the academic buildings along the Severn River to his right, the modern looking Chauvenet and Michelson Halls, bathed Stribling Walk, the path from Bancroft to the classrooms beyond. Following his classmates toward the officers' club, he noticed as he approached the Naval Academy Chapel that some were turning back, that the clan now moved to his left, toward the Superintendent's office and Gate 3 out into Annapolis.

"What's up? No good at the O-Club?" Durago asked no one in particular.

"Nah, they ran outta beer already," one of his classmates reported.

Durago noted that several of his classmates were visibly intoxicated. One or two had their covers tilted back on their heads. Several ties hung loose.

Figuring that he missed his roommate heading out into town, Durago knew where to go next. He and Warren had a standing plan for such occasions, a specific location in town where they would "escape and evade" in the event of separation.

As Durago entered the pub on Main Street, Slim discerned immediately by the look on his face that his roommate's hopes were realized.

"Holy shit, Don, you got it!"

"Yep!" Durago was beaming.

"Well, how the fuck? Why was it . . . ?"

"How should I know? Either nobody wants to go to Pascagoula or they don't want to be on a pre-commissioned ship for two years, waiting to join the fleet."

"Well, hooyah, brother! Congratulations! I don't know what to say, man."

"How about buying your roommate a beer?"

"Sure, sure. Have you told anyone?"

"Nah, man, let's not go there. By the way, nice jacket."

When they returned to 7-4 just after midnight, much of the company was engaging in fraternity-like revelry. The first class midshipmen were all in various states of intoxication. The underclasses, especially the Plebes, were enjoying a little fun at their expense. As they walked from the company officer's office down the center passageway to their room, Durago and Slim could see the Plebes shaving Lagasse's head. McClure and Wilson, already shorn, stood by and laughed.

"Guess you're next," said Durago. "You gonna fight 'em, or just give in?"

"Oh, they're gonna have to earn it," Slim replied.

Suddenly, one of the Plebes saw Slim striding toward his room.

"There's Mister Warren! Get him!"

A train of six Plebes, the last with a pair of electric clippers, barreled toward them. Durago stepped to the side to avoid the melee. Slim fought valiantly but was soon dragged to the ground, then to the closest electrical outlet, and held down so that a stripe of hair could be mowed off the center of his scalp. Durago saw his roommate laughing, not only at the humor, the silliness of how he knew he must appear, but at the triumph, the unbelievable joy of earning the right to become an officer of Marines. Then he thought again of his own prize, a private one known only to Slim and him. He wondered if he would ever share it with anyone else.

Alcohol fogged his nightmare, but his heart palpitated as it always did. When Durago woke, he was panting and he had bitten his tongue again. He calmed himself and then noticed that it was pitch black. He frowned inwardly, realizing that he was on the floor of his locker again. A wave of shame came over him, a feeling similar to his embarrassment at wetting the bed in childhood. Reaching over with his hand, he slid the door open and rolled out onto the floor as he had done countless times before.

A sliver of light skated under the door, joining a bluish glow coming through the window as the sun started to rise. As he stood up, Durago looked over to his roommate. Slim appeared to be fast asleep, but as he slipped into his rack he heard Slim roll over.

"I heard you."

"Just now?"

"I heard you going in, too . . . decided not to wake you."

"Probably for the best," Durago said as he pulled his blue wool blanket up to his chin.

"Did you cut yourself?"

"Not this time."

"Is this going to keep happening?"

"Ease off, man. I just got his ship last night. That's what caused it."

"I'm talking about when you're on the ship. You ever gonna get any sleep? Or what about your stateroom mate?"

"I dunno."

Durago sensed his roommate wanted to respond to his last remark but decided to refrain. After a few moments of silence, he was able to return to sleep.

2

QUANTUM MERIUT

MARCH 8, 1992
0530
CLEMENTS CREEK

A diesel's low rumble brought the sleeping woman to full consciousness. It was joined by the clapping of water as the yacht's hull pushed through the incoming tide. She opened her eyes just as the vessel passed, noting a solitary man at the helm. Across the stern was the name *Beautiful Swimmer* in bold black, red, and gold that suggested the Maryland state flag, above a smaller, more subtle font that read "Crownsville, Maryland."

A layer of dew that an hour or so before was probably frost covered her sleeping bag, the sail bag under her head, and the rest of the sailboat's forecastle. The front hatch was open, but no sound emanated from the berth below. She looked aft, past dock lines faked out on deck and the mast, to the cockpit. Seeing it was empty, she assumed everyone else was still asleep. *Asleep, hell. They're passed out,* she surmised. There had been a lot of drinking the night before.

At some point during the previous evening, Jan Meyer had realized it may fall to her to sail *Quantum Meriut* back to its slip in Eastport. So, she stopped imbibing and retired to the dark spot on her boat's bow to avoid the unwanted advances of Steve Stone and Doug Tripp. It was Tripp that she was really worried about, but Jan had no doubt that with enough mojitos and the right moonlight, Steve would make a play. *Well, he'd have to strike out with Nina first.*

She wondered if Steve and Nina had in fact hooked up the night before. Unlike her and Tripp, both were civilians, sailing bums Jan met one summer in college when she was big into offshore racing. Since then she had graduate to open-ocean cruising. For two years after college she sailed vessels belonging to the rich and famous, from Bar Harbor or Martha's Vineyard to Baltimore or Annapolis, and eventually on to Fort Lauderdale, Key West, and the Virgin Islands.

Now she had her own boat, a "hole in the water to throw her money into." When Jan first told her friend, Nina did not believe her.

"No, really, whose boat is this?"

"Mine."

"Bullshit."

"I'm serious."

"You can't afford this. You gotta sugar daddy?"

"No, a job . . . and now a mortgage."

"Whoa, you're serious."

"I am. I've saved up and got a little inheritance, which allowed me to put a nice down payment on the *QM*."

"And what does that mean?"

"*Quantum Meriut*? It's a legal term that in general means, 'What one has earned.' But it kinda goes deeper than that. The Latin is used because the concept doesn't translate well into English."

"Huh."

Jan could tell that Nina had lost interest. Her curiosity about how her friend had suddenly become a boat owner was satisfied.

Of course, the name had real meaning for Jan. The forty-three-foot Beneteau embodied one of the two life goals she developed in adolescence. As a teen, Jan had fancied herself a Robin Lee Graham, "the boy who sailed around the world alone," and fantasized about slowly circumnavigating the Earth, taking in all its majesty and making lifelong friends along the way. Her naval service provided the means for Jan to go to law school, while using her savings as a down payment for the boat. As a result, sailing around the world was, at a minimum, postponed a few years. Jan was already starting to realize that after paying back the Navy with her valuable time, she would face a real, grown-up decision—take off, becoming an aquatic nomad like Steve and Nina, or follow Tripp into a high-powered law firm and pay someone else to sail her boat from Bar Harbor to the islands.

Maybe I'll stay in the service, become 'Admiral Meyer.' It's got a nice ring to it.

Jan recognized that this conflict came to the surface regularly these days. While in college, and especially in the sailing scene, she had been surrounded by wild, free spirits. She always seemed to be more rational than her friends, worried about appearances and consequences. Deep down she thought the real choice before her was a life where she was happily adrift, or one of regimentation.

I need to be daring sometime, impetuous, to find out what the rush is.

Realizing this decision would not be made today, Jan unzipped the sleeping bag and rose, draping it over the lifelines to dry. Then she headed aft, feeling a little sore from her slumber on the deck. *Why do I always do this?* she thought. *Shit, it's my damn boat.* Jan decided next time, rather than avoiding berthing arrangements where the potential for sex increased, she would simply claim the stateroom as hers alone, then lock it behind her.

Peering down the hatch near the center of the boat's bow, Jan saw Tripp plopped in her bed below. She realized again that she was glad she had avoided him. There was potential, but several times over the weekend he did things that made her feel uncomfortable. Deep down they both knew this weekend would determine if their friendship would turn into a romance. By noon on Saturday, Jan decided it would not. By Saturday evening she was going to give him another chance, but this soon died under the weight of Tripp's arrogance.

There had been a time when Tripp had real potential. One of the first people she met in Annapolis, Jan immediately saw that he was as smart as he was handsome. She appreciated that he was interested in her as a whole person. Jan knew she was a head turner. In fact, Nina often joked that if Jan were taller she could be a model. "One of those 'hangers,' but with a nice rack," Nina had said once. But the military uniform was not flattering. Since Tripp met her wearing navy blue, Jan was sure he really liked her for her brains first.

Initially, Jan figured that after completing his commitment Tripp would leave the Navy for a law firm or lobby in D.C., where he could make gobs of money. Later she discovered he was seriously considering making the Navy a career, something she found endearing. In fact, he told her that he decided to pursue a master's through the Naval War College program offered to officers on staff. "Just to keep my options open," he had said. He convinced Jan to sign up with him.

As the only JAG officers in the class, the two studied together to understand some of the subtleties of the curriculum that came easier to line officers. After getting somewhat closer and going on a couple of dates, Jan noted that Tripp became a little aggressive when he drank. *It's not that he's a wild man, it's that he becomes an asshole, one I don't feel safe with.*

When she hopped in the cockpit, Jan heard someone moving in the cabin. Peering down below, she could see Steve was making coffee. Rather than descend and force a morning greeting, she decided to sit in the cockpit and enjoy a little more quiet.

Jan looked aft to the ladder she had installed on the open transom on *QM*'s stern. It was much stronger, sturdier, and deeper than most boats' swim ladders, designed to hold the weight of a diver with all of the equipment. Jan could now dive from *Quantum Meriut* to sightsee, spearfish, or, most important, repair *QM*'s hull, rudder, and running gear. *Still gotta get a few open water dives, gain some experience,* she thought.

Though the water was probably pretty cold, Jan considered slipping down the ladder for a morning swim, but now that the power boat was gone, the creek returned to its early morning slumber. Jan decided not to disturb it further, and instead she simply sat and listened to morning birdsongs while following an egret as it plied the shallows for breakfast, bobbing with each step.

When they had moored *Quantum* the previous night, the shoreline had been bathed in darkness, so not many details had been visible. Now Jan saw several houses tucked into a deciduous forest, each sixty or more feet above the shoreline. Most of the waterfront was lined with a seawall of treated wood, braced in place by creosote-covered pilings. The high-tide mark was noticeable owing to a dark-colored growth of barnacles and moss. Reeds and grasses were growing in some places, making the river look mustachioed.

Every property had a pier with at least one boat moored next to it. The whole creek was narrow enough to denote the path from its source to the Severn River, but wide enough and with enough turns to give a sense that it meandered and provided more than one sheltered spot to anchor for the day or to lay up for a night or two.

Quantum Meriut gently tugged on a buoy labeled "PROPERTY OF THE U.S. NAVY," like a mare on a hitching post. *Screw it, I'm in the Navy,* Jan thought as she looped *Quantum*'s bowline through a padeye on the buoy's top the night before. The last of the sun's rays revealed a number of these moorings dotting the cove. Now, in the morning light, Jan counted twelve. *The Academy must shelter their boats in here during bad weather.*

Knowing the weekend would be over in a few hours, Jan thought the foursome had had a good time and she felt relieved, liberated by the fact that she did not develop any romantic entanglement with Tripp.

Nina emerged from the cabin. Jan shot her a quizzical look.

"Were you with Steve last night?"

"No," Nina said quietly. "We slept in that double berth aft, but we didn't . . ."

"Oh," Jan replied knowingly.

"I mean, it's no secret that we've hooked up before, but we're really just friends. What about you? I thought you and Tripp were an item."

"There was potential, but not now. I dunno, something happened this weekend in fact that has just turned me off."

"He got real drunk last night . . . and for me to say that is saying something."

"Good morning, ladies," Steve said as he stepped into the light. "Coffee?"

After a breakfast of eggs and coffee, *Quantum Meriut* got under way. Tripp never emerged during the meal or the preparations to return home. Once they cleared the creek, Jan asked Nina to take the helm.

"Sure, babe. You gonna check on Tripp?"

"Yeah, and I think we'll put some sails up."

Descending below deck, Jan first entered *Quantum*'s main cabin, which served as a galley and living area. A small navigation table with the boat's radio set was at the foot of the ladder just to the port side. Wordlessly, Jan slipped past Steve standing on the starboard side of *QM*'s cabin, where all of the cooking implements, storage, and a refrigerator and freezer sat. Opposite this nautical kitchen on the port side was a booth-like dining area. The table could be dropped and the back cushions placed on it to turn it into a double berth if there were a large crew on board. One of *Quantum*'s two heads—the nautical term for a bathroom—was aft, tucked between the navigation and dining tables serving two cabins farther aft that lay under the cockpit. To starboard was a single berth, to port the double where Jan surmised Steve and Nina had kept each other warm the night before.

Jan slid open the hatch to the forward V-berth, the master stateroom, complete with the boat's second head, that normally served as her bedroom. She waited a moment to see if Tripp would stir.

"Tripp, you okay?"

There was no response.

Jan reached over the bed, grabbing a pair of tortoiseshell Wayfarers and a Tilly perched on the shelf just above Tripp. She hung the Ray Bans around her neck on a lanyard and plopped the Tilly on her head.

Then she went to the head and grabbed sunscreen from the medicine cabinet, applying it liberally, especially on the back of her neck and face.

"Nina says you want to put some sails up," Steve said as he ducked his head into her cabin.

"Yeah, it looked like there was a little wind in the river, and we're not in a rush, are we?"

"Hey, I came to sail."

"Cool. I think we need to put up the number one."

He motioned over his shoulder toward the hatch leading to the open air. "Why don't you go up on deck? I'll pass up whatever you need."

Jan regarded Nina when she was back in the cockpit. "You good on the helm?"

"Totally."

Jan quickly removed the ties along *Quantum*'s boom and raised the mainsail. Then she went forward and peered down the hatch into her stateroom, which also served as the boat's sail locker. Tripp had not moved. She saw Steve enter the space.

"Is he breathing?"

Canting his head a moment, Steve replied, "Yeah, he's alive." A look of horror came over his face.

"What?"

"He farted."

"That doesn't mean he's alive," Jan said as she tried to stifle a laugh.

"I'm alive," Tripp murmured, "but I wish I was dead."

Steve pulled the jib Jan requested out from under the berth and handed it to her through the hatch. She clipped it to the riser and pulled hand over hand, raising the sail as Steve fed it through. In two minutes the sail was full and *Quantum Meriut* accelerated a little more toward the Severn River Bridge.

Four hours later, *Quantum* was moored in her slip at a small marina in Eastport, across from the Annapolis Harbor, Ego Alley, and the Academy. The sails were down and secured, the boat had a pair of umbilicals that allowed it to receive water and electrical power from the pier, and a majority of the gear was stowed. Steve and Nina said their goodbyes and promised to check in periodically to see if Jan needed crew or company.

Jan went back down below and began to configure her boat for the work week, when it would serve more as an apartment than a sailing vessel. Tripp stirred, then dressed, and worked his way to the dining table. He looked like shit, but this also seemed to render him harmless.

"Do you want me to drive you home?" Jan asked.

"No, I'll manage."

Jan waited a moment, thinking Tripp would then leave, but he stayed put. She went back to stowing some items and setting up her creature comforts. Tripp was so quiet and still, she almost forgot he was there.

"Jan," he finally called out with a pitiful tone, "I'm sorry. I'm sorry I had too much to drink last night. I'm especially sorry because I thought we had something going."

Jan wanted to let him down easy.

"We did, Tripp, but . . . you know . . . it's just not going to work."

Her fellow officer raised his chin, almost defiantly, looking directly into her eyes. "Well, why not? What happened?"

"Tripp, I don't want to sound like a cliché, to use the whole 'We're better off as friends' bit, but I'm just not feeling it. I mean, I really, really like you. I think we really hit it off, and I value that. So, as we got to know each other more and more in class, I wanted us to go out. We did, and that was great. So I wanted more—which is why I invited you out on this weekend jaunt. But during this weekend I realized that we're incompatible in a way that makes a romantic relationship simply a bad idea."

"How?"

"Well, for one, you become a little aggressive when you drink. I got nervous on Friday night."

"Wait," Tripp said as he stood. "You just said yourself that you thought you wanted more. Well, of course I realized that. You were giving me all the signs. I thought that was why you asked me out here, and that's why I started making moves."

"And I get that. That's why I'm not angry, or totally creeped out. Still, I didn't like it. I guess it wasn't that you were making moves, it was the way you made them."

Tripp frowned. Jan turned to exit the cabin, to get into the open air where others could see her.

"So, stay if you want," she said. "I'm going to run some errands."

Tripp followed her out. "So, that's it. It's over."

"Tripp, don't you see, it's not 'over' because nothing got started.

We're just not meant to be. Please, let's not drag this out. Don't make this uncomfortable. If you leave right now we can both remember this sweetly—two friends who almost went down the wrong path. If you continue to push, this will feel very uncomfortable. It will ruin everything."

A light breeze shook the halyards on all the boats in the marina, causing a clanging that made Tripp wince.

"Okay," he said with an air of defeat. "I'm sorry, then. I guess I'll see you in class on Tuesday."

"You got it," Jan replied, and she smiled as if nothing were ever wrong.

3

SPRING BREAK

MARCH 14, 1992
0100
PANAMA CITY, FLORIDA

Two Jeeps headed south on I-95. The canvas tops on both reverberated with obnoxious rock music as the midnight highway slipped into memory. Jan Meyer searched for an anthem, something to provide lyrical encouragement as she felt the air getting warmer and warmer. If the sailboat weekend had gone well, she would have been on this sojourn with Tripp. Fortunately, they had only briefly discussed this diving vacation and never made formal plans other than reserving a spot on the dive boat. Now going by herself, Jan decided that because she never enjoyed the traditional college break, she would allow herself to go a bit wild in Florida, to misbehave a little while she still could without too many repercussions. She needed to cut loose from Tripp, cleanse the proverbial dating palate, and enjoy life the way Nina and her other sailing friends always seemed to.

Each time her mind went to seafood restaurants or a bottle of wine and a book on her veranda, she would stop herself. *No, it needs to be clubbing. Daiquiris. Dancing until closing time!*

She realized that going to the spring break capital of America by herself did not make for the best of plans. Jan hoped she would make a connection with some of the people she would be diving with. Maybe there would be a nice guy. *Shit, maybe I just need to get laid.*

Two mids in the second Jeep were thinking exactly the same thing, forming adrenaline dreams of drinking beer and chasing after the fairer sex. For one week, Midshipman First Class Donald Durago and Midshipman First Class James Warren would put behind all things military and academic. The trip marked a final respite, the pair's last retreat before leaving the Academy. Like for all men and women who graduate into service, it was not lost on them that their paths would diverge when Slim became a Marine flyer and Durago headed for a life at sea. Durago was particularly affected by their impending parting.

They first had become acquainted during Plebe Summer. It was a brutally hot Sunday morning in July 1988. The windows were open to all the rooms on 3-1, where Hotel Company, 23rd Platoon—the Plebes who would become part of 23rd Company—lived, trained, and endured together. Roomed alphabetically, Durago was with two other Plebes—Cutter and Dunfee—in a space originally designed for two. Cutter was gone, standing watch on 1-2 where the rest of Hotel resided. Durago and Dunfee studied rates, trying to quiz each other.

"Fifth law," Dunfee said.

"On the strength of one link in the chain—"

"Cable."

"I thought it was a chain," said Durago with derision. "We're supposed to be in the Navy and we're reading poetry."

"It's a system. Go with it."

"I don't get it."

"You don't have to get it," Dunfee said with an impatient tone. Durago realized they had this conversation before. Both of his roommates were growing impatient with him.

What's the worst thing they can do to me? Make me do pushups? he thought.

"Try it again, man."

"Try what?"

"It's right there in your *Reef Points*. 'On the strength of one link in the cable, dependeth the might of the chain. Who knows when thou mighst be tested, so live that thou bearest the strain.'"

Suddenly Slim was in the doorway.

"Warren," said Durago, "holy shit, man. You startled me."

"Yeah, we don't chop on Sundays until after noon. Kinda quiet around here."

"If only we could get some sleep. I'm frickin' exhausted," said Dunfee.

"What are you guys doin'?" Warren asked.

"Developing a sense of irony," replied Dunfee, "while trying to get Durago boned up on his rates."

"Well, listen, I'm going to Mass. Either of you guys Catholic? Or just wanna go? We can go to Ninety-Two hour after."

"Not me," said Dunfee. "Scotch-Presbyterian."

"I'll go just to get out of the hall," said Durago.

Durago put on his white jumper top, and then looped the black neckerchief under the flap on the back, centering the knot at the center of his chest. He then put on the combination cover, keeping the shiny black brim two fingers above the bridge of his nose and aligning the gold anchor right down the center of his face.

"Squared away," said Slim.

Finally, Durago tucked his *Reef Points*, the Plebe handbook, into his waistband. Plebes were required to have it with them at all times. Also, he may have a moment to study.

"You Catholic?" Slim asked as they walked across Tecumseh Court toward the Naval Academy Seal, the statue of Tecumseh, and Stribling Walk.

"Yeah, but I've not been confirmed. My mom put me in boarding school in sixth grade. We kinda stopped going to church then."

"That's cool. I've been kinda hot and cold myself for the same reason. My folks shipped me off to military school in sixth grade."

"Yeah? Which one?"

"The Marine Military Academy in Harlingen, Texas."

"So, you back on track now?"

"We'll see. I mostly wanted to get out of the hall too. Plus, then there's Ninety-Two hour."

"Yeah. What is that?"

"A hospitality thing. Donuts, coffee, parents, sponsors, and, I've heard, a few girlfriends."

As they ascended the steps into the U.S. Naval Academy Chapel Durago asked, "You got a sponsor?"

"Nah. Don't see the need. I've been away from home for so long on my own anyway. I kinda thought that's for public school kids—first time away and all that."

"Yeah, my thoughts exactly."

It had been a long time since Durago had attended Mass. He had to mimic Slim's movements. However, once he got started on the standard responses, they came back to him.

Ninety-Two hour was hosted in several places. Mids attending the 0900 Mass were encouraged to go to Michelson, just across from the chapel. The crowd filing across the Yard was predominantly Plebes. There were a few first and second class midshipmen—the"upperclass"—some with red name tags that identified them as part of the Plebe Detail. Others had black and gold nametags—mids who were in Annapolis for training or summer school. Mixed in with the crowd were several families. Durago could almost tell by the body language which were sponsors and which were there to see their sons or daughters. Though Plebes were forbidden to date, it was clear that more than one young lady was there to see her sweetheart.

"Dude, I think Mann is dragging that chick. If he's not careful, he's gonna get fried."

"What?" asked Durago.

"Fried, man . . . put on report."

By "dragging," Mann was in effect escorting the lady in question. If she was his best girl, Mann would proclaim that she was his "grease girl."

Durago was still not used to the lingo. It especially amazed him how many things that sounded bad at Navy actually had positive implications.

"Come by after and I'll give you the gouge."

"The what?" Durago had replied.

"The gouge, man. The knowledge."

Midshipman Fourth Class Brendan McDougal had joined them at Ninety-Two hour.

"Hey, guys, saw you at Mass. I thought Durago was gonna fall asleep."

"Me, too," said Durago. "In fact, I'm going for more coffee."

Once he was out of earshot, McDougal said, "Warren, did you drag him out here?"

"Yeah. So?"

"He's a head case, man. I think he's next to go."

"Nah, he's alright."

"He doesn't get it. I mean, the guy hasn't figured out the system yet," McDougal said, as if he were enduring his third Plebe Summer.

"I dunno," said Slim, "I think he's just not fazed by it. And I don't mean like he thinks he's too cool for school . . . it's like the yelling and PT and all isn't a big deal to him. He almost comes across like a prior."

"Maybe," McDougal replied as Durago returned.

"Yeah," Durago said, "That's gotta be Mann's girlfriend. Cute, too."

After Plebe Summer, Slim and Durago had been fortuitously thrown together in a four-man room. They elected to remain together as "Youngsters," the term for sophomores at Annapolis, and remained roommates ever since. The two developed a bond that they both sensed was even closer than those normally formed in the crucible of a service academy. Their friendship solidified through a mutual understanding of boarding school upbringing and lukewarm familial relationships. Slim had a cold, distant connection with his family, just this side of being estranged. Durago never really had a father, and his mother passed him off to a prep school and then departed to the next life before they could ever resolve the conflicts borne of her absence. Without siblings, Slim became more than Durago's best friend; he was the brother Durago never had. In fact, James Warren was the only person that Donald Durago was able to relate his personal trials and tribulations to—a confessor who let him know he was normal. With one relatively minor exception.

If Slim was Durago's closest compadre, Master Chief William Strong, a retired Navy diver, was his greatest mentor. Master Chief Strong's last assignment was ashore, mentoring midshipmen at the Naval Academy. During Durago's Plebe Year he became one of Strong's special projects—one that the master chief deemed a success story. In fact, Strong took such a liking to the kid that he pushed him to join the fraternity of underwater warriors. So, with a little manipulation, Strong directed Durago into the challenging screening process and scuba curriculum at the Navy's dive school in Panama City, Florida, the summer after his Plebe Year. Not to be outdone by his roommate, and with an eye to potentially joining Marine Recon, Slim also endured scuba tryouts and dive school.

During the previous summer period the pair returned to Panama City to train at the Naval Experimental Diving Unit as part of the Academy's human-powered submarine team. The sub, bearing the name of "Squid," was designed, built, and ultimately powered and maneuvered by midshipmen, the latter specifically by Durago and Warren. Durago pedaled, driving a gearbox that ended with a nozzle-protected propeller.

Slim steered two dive plans on the boat's fiberglass nose. Weeks of training at the Academy led to two weeks in the inland waters of Saint Andrews Bay. Then they joined twenty or so other subs for the second international competition of both design and performance hosted in Riviera Beach, Florida.

Though he retired before their summer at EDU, Strong remained an important team mentor—especially important now that he lived in the cradle of naval diving. Strong stayed connected to the Brigade by extending an open invitation to all mids to dive aboard his sixty-four-foot dive boat, *Strong Diver.* Thus, while the roommates' nights were set aside for collegiate-level debauchery, daylight would find them underwater, breathing compressed air and chasing denizens of the deep.

The mids arrived at their hotel early in the morning. After a quick check-in, they ran to an all-night breakfast place and wolfed down pancakes and eggs. They returned to the hotel ready to satisfy a need for sleep, but the light on the room's telephone was on. Durago saw it first.

"Slim Jim, did you tell anyone where we're staying?"

"Yeah, my folks. Why?"

"Look at the phone."

Slim sat on the bed and picked up the phone. He dialed the front desk. Then he dialed another number while Durago took a shower. When he emerged, Durago noticed that Slim looked upset.

"Dude, what's wrong?"

"My sister got in a car accident. She was driving to Vail with some of her sorority sisters and they slid on some ice or something."

For a moment there was silence. Durago did not know how to react. He had never met Slim's family, and he was less in tune with the family dynamic than his roomie.

"Damn, Slim. Well, is she alright?"

"Well, I guess she's going to be okay, but it's serious. My folks want me to come home."

Durago sensed that their spring break plans had just evaporated, that despite his relationship with his family, Slim would go to his sister's bedside.

"So, you'll be leaving then?"

"Yeah. Listen, I want you to take the Jeep."

"Oh, shit, Slim, I can't do that. You need it—"

"Listen to me a second, okay!" Slim barked.

Durago sat down and Slim took a deep breath. When he spoke again, Durago could hear emotion in his voice. He knew it was not directed at him.

"We'll go to the airport and I'll get a ticket on standby or something. I'll see my sister, do whatever I can to pay my dues, and I'll fly back to the Academy from there. I want you to stay here and enjoy the break. You can scuba dive with Strong and do everything we planned. I'm sure if you go to one of the clubs here you'll find some guys from the Academy who we know. Even better, you might even hook up with a chick."

Durago could tell now that there was a purpose to Slim's state of mind. He wondered if there was more to this family crisis than met the eye. Plus, there were subtleties to Slim's family dynamic that, despite their closeness, Durago knew he could never understand. The tension in Slim's voice reminded him of the last time they had a serious argument. It was Army-Navy.

4

ARMY-NAVY

DECEMBER 7, 1991
1600
VETERANS STADIUM

Every Army-Navy game is momentous. Many suggest that it remains the last remnant of purity in college football. Perhaps it is the recognition that the players are in it only for the game. Many used their skills on the gridiron as a vehicle to get into college, but it was with an ultimate goal of service, not scholarship. Such a choice is fully embraced by the two student bodies, and all alums. Thus, like no other athletic team, the mids and cadets truly represent their respective schools. This extends even beyond the alums, as any veterans can lay claim to the game when they see future leaders darting down the field with the "Screaming Eagle" of the 101st Airborne or the "Jolly Roger" of Fighter Squadron 84 sewn on their shoulders, a reminder that those on the field will soon rely on each other in battle.

The sibling rivalry between young men in such circumstances is simply unequaled.

The matchup in December 1991 would be memorable for a number of reasons. The Mids faced the Black Knights with a 0-10 record. Morale within the Brigade was decidedly low until a group of Firsties kicked off Army-Navy week by absconding with all four Army mules, including their saddles, blankets, and other accoutrement. Kidnapping the mules was a coup of epic proportions, a feat never before accomplished and likely never repeated.

In contrast, the cadets often shanghaied Bill the Goat. Navy's mascot was borne of the fact that in the age of sail, midshipmen were responsible for the ship's complement of livestock. Stealing the ornery creature was not a daunting affair. A group of West Pointers simply drove down with a truck or a van from New York to the farm in Gambrills, Maryland, where Bill resided six days a week. Sometimes they had to overpower one or two guards, but the goat usually found himself paraded through halls on the Hudson during the first week of December.

During the mules' week of captivity, many mids posed for photos with them in Tecumseh Court. Members of the football team donned full pads and uniforms, then gripped the leads to two mules, flexing and mugging for the camera, tugging the animals in a manner that emphasized their subservience.

The whole week was capped off with a Thursday night pep rally and bonfire on Farragut Field. After the bulk of the Brigade gathered in the dark, the superintendent, commandant, head coach, and one of the team captains all arrived by mule. The mids roared with delight as their leadership trotted through the crowd toward the flames.

Equally triumphant was the mids' march-on right before the game. As the Brigade took the field the cadets, already in the stands, began to shout, "Oh and ten! Oh and ten!" This was quickly silenced when the Brigade fired back with, "We got the mules! We got the mules!"

Durago made sure to take in all the pageantry of his last Army-Navy: the military flybys, the skydiving, the patriotic music. Navy won, 24-3, achieving 43 wins to Army's 42, with 7 ties. Durago stood respectfully as the defeated cadets sang their alma mater. Then he cheered with the rest of the Brigade and half of the stands as the Navy team walked back across the field, some arm in arm with Army's team.

As they reached the sidelines next to the Brigade, the stadium grew quiet for Navy's alma mater.

> Now college men from sea to sea,
> May sing of colors true,
> But who has better right than we,
> To hoist a symbol hue?
> For sailor men in battle fair,
> Since fighting days of old,
> Have proved the sailors right to wear,
> The Navy Blue and Gold.

Half of the stadium then joined in with "Beat Army!"

After "Blue and Gold," Durago followed Slim and shuffled with the rest of the mids out of the stands and toward the exits. They had dates waiting for them. Slim was seeing June, a girl from Wilson, an all-women's college two hours north of Annapolis, just over the Pennsylvania border. He introduced Durago to one of her friends, named May.

"You're kidding me," McDougal had said. "You guys are dating a set of chicks named May and June . . . are they twins? Damn! You dudes gotta dress that shit up in some Catholic school outfits and take happy snaps."

"They're not related," Slim said.

"Still, May and June. Next you'll tell me they gotta sassy little sister named April and a hot mom named December. Shit, I gotta figure out how to get that in the Log."

Slim thought there was real potential for his roommate and May. Durago dated, but Slim knew he was often distracted and purposefully never let anything get serious. He hoped that over this long weekend Durago might really be able to connect. So, at his suggestion, the foursome got a hotel room and planned to spend the weekend in Philadelphia after the game.

Slim turned around and whispered to Durago, "Dude, can you drive?"

"Yeah. Why?"

"I was taking hits from Mann's flask and I'm buzzing a little. Plus, I'm fucking exhausted after the drive and the game . . . I might even sleep on the way to the hotel."

"You're gonna fall asleep on me? Make me have a three-way with the girls?"

"Nooo . . . I'm not gonna leave them alone with you!"

Durago noted that Slim had a lilt in his voice that he did not perceive during the game. They continued following the crowd out of the stadium. Durago heard various proclamations for post-game debauchery that equaled a Viking conquest. Several 14th Company Plebes had become particularly ratey after exchanging the shoulder boards on their calf-length wool bridge coats with first class midshipmen in the company—an important tradition that transformed them to seniors during and, most important, after the game. Durago remembered Army-Navy of his Plebe Year as the last bit of freedom before a long winter of confinement. He, Slim, Potok, and Mann had found their way into a bar in downtown Philadelphia. They were served beers in rapid succession, paid for by vets and alumni. Then they made their way to Penn, where Mann had a friend from high school. More alcohol was consumed, and the mids tried to connect with some of Penn's coeds, but to no avail.

This year will be more successful, Durago thought as he looked to the two young women waiting for him and Slim on the ground floor of Veterans Stadium. They were both very attractive. They were dressed fashionably, yet appropriately, for the game in ski parkas and corduroys that were fitting, almost like tights. Each wore leather boots with a low heel and earmuffs instead of winter hats, ensuring that their hair provided an outward mark of femininity.

"Let's go quickly," June said as Slim and Durago approached. "I'm soooo cold."

May put her arm in Durago's and drew him near. "Great game, huh?"

"Yeah, it was," he replied.

They made their way past tailgaters draped in black, blue, and gold. Mids and cadets mixed together throughout the parking lot like salt and pepper spilled on a countertop. The air was filled with ethereal concoctions as steam emanated from coffee and hot chocolate, mixing with hot breath in the cold air and smoke from portable grills. More than one tailgater combined fans from Annapolis and West Point. Durago saw a mid and a cadet standing next to each other that were unmistakably brothers.

As they turned down the row of cars to where Slim's Jeep waited, Durago saw a familiar group gathered on the corner. They were Naval Academy graduates, not yet old, but clearly middle aged. Men who were just starting to succumb to gravity and time. They rallied with a few spouses, holding cups full of equal parts warm liquid and alcohol and standing around a flagpole bearing a gold banner with navy blue numbers that read "'67."

To include "Navy" or "USNA" would be helpful but unnecessary in this forum. The numbers' color implied their origin. They also sent a clear message, something automatically implied and understood by all who passed by, whether from Navy or Army, for their own class number reflected similarly.

We were junior officers in Vietnam. We screamed over clouded airspace, plodded on the oppressive gun line, zipped through the brown rivers, and slogged through humid jungles. We led and commanded through the Cold War and the proxy wars of the Eighties, patrolling beneath the

North Atlantic for Soviet submarines and scanning Beirut's cityscape for terrorists and kidnappers.

To the class itself, the numbers provided immediate memories that were more personal, only known or fully remembered by them as a class, as if they were a singular creature.

We've swum to Baltimore. Kennedy gave us amnesty.

Just as Durago looked away, Slim nearly knocked May over as he reached and grabbed his arm.

"Dude, Sixty-Seven . . . you gotta go over there, man. I'll go with you."

"Slim, don't," Durago said icily.

"So, don't say anything. We'll just drink some beers and let them flirt with our months."

May looked peeved. "Sliiim, I told you not to—"

"Nah, man," said Durago, "the girls are cold . . . let's go."

"Don, this is your destiny."

"Stop, Slim, just stop," Durago said more firmly.

The anger in Durago's voice cut the air. Surprise registered on the girls' faces.

"What's going on?" asked June.

"Slim's a little . . . drunk. It's cool, though. Let's get something to eat," Durago replied.

"No . . . no, Don, listen. This is it, bro! It's frickin' Army-Navy, Blue and Gold, man! Listen, you gotta—"

Durago spun on his heel, wrenching himself out of Slim's grasp, and trotted away.

On the far side of the parking lot was a line of blue-and-white buses with gold lettering on the sides that read "U.S. Naval Academy." A number of mids, mostly Youngsters, filed onto the first one in line. Durago got in line, found a window seat, laid his head against the window, and closed his eyes, trying to calm down. He opened them again as the bus started to move. Looking through the crowd, he saw Slim with May and June in tow. Slim looked upset, the girls bored and frustrated. Durago was nearly seething with anger.

Six hours later, he returned to the darkness on 7-4. He dropped his cover, scarf, and bridge coat on his rack, opened his closet, and without taking off his service dress blues, rolled in and lay on its floor.

Pausing only a moment, he then closed the door as he had hundreds of times before. Durago was uncomfortable, but within a few moments he was asleep.

He was sitting at his desk tying his running shoes the next morning when Slim returned.

"You're back early."

"You're still talking to me?"

"Oh, I'm still pissed, but I've calmed down some."

Slim glanced knowingly at Durago's rack. "Sleep much?"

"I slept fine, thank you. But now I need to go out for a run to work out the kinks."

"How's your tongue?" Slim said, looking to the sink.

"Fine."

"Don, I'm sorry. I was a little drunk, and—"

"That's no excuse. It's this simple: we're roommates. You're supposed to understand. I get you. You get me. You broke that rule. Don't ever fucking do that again."

"Yeah."

Slim sat in his chair without taking off his uniform. Durago sensed he needed to say more.

"What?" he asked accusingly.

"June broke up with me."

"Ah, so that's why you're back so early."

"She was pissed, and they both wanted to know what was going on. I wouldn't tell them, so she asked me to drive them back to Wilson."

"Wow, well, I'm sorry you broke up, but I'm glad you didn't compound this."

"I know. So, we looked around for you for awhile before I figured you took the bus back. We went around that damn parking lot two or three times, even returning to the . . . well, the tailgater—I thought wrong, I know—and the Jeep, thinking we were just missing you. Anyway, I finally sobered up enough and drove them home. June would not let it go the whole way back. Neither would May.

"Finally, I got them back. May just went to her dorm. June broke up with me right there in the parking lot. 'Trust issues,' she said."

"Fuck her. Did you explain to her that we developed a 'trust' in each other that you were trying to salvage?"

"Yeah, she didn't get it. Chicks, huh?"

"Yeah . . . so, I'm sorry. I'm still pissed, but I can see that you've suffered for your sins. I'm going for a run. When I get back, this matter is closed."

"Cool, brother."

5

DIVING

March 14, 1992
1030
Aboard the *Strong Diver*

Durago agreed to go along with Slim's suggestion. He decided to get a few dives in and hit the clubs at night. But, deep down, he suspected that before the week was over he would head back to Annapolis. *Won't be the first time I spent a lot of time alone in the hall.*

As he jumped from the passenger side of his Jeep, Slim said, "Remember, no WUBAs."

Durago blanched at the term. It was an ugly word, an acronym that had once officially meant "working uniform blue alpha," but it was transformed in the Brigade to "women used by all," a derisive term directed at female midshipmen. It did soften over time as some female mids embraced it, stealing the word as other minorities have done and almost using the word with pride. As a result, to imply the negative, "fuck" had to be added when used to cut.

"That fucking WUBA fried me for being late to class."

Political correctness eventually erased the term. This was solidified by changing the name of the uniform to "working winter blues." Thus, any vocalization of "WUBA" would represent a violation of midshipman regulations. Durago recognized this as a positive aspect of the movement sweeping the country, especially college campuses. It now shamed him to think of how easily he—how they all—had bandied this term about. He knew that Slim's use of the term meant his roommate was fragmented, that demons he suppressed during his Plebe Year were emerging with this trip. So Durago pretended not to hear him and simply headed back toward Panama City Beach.

Durago slowed a little on Thomas Drive as he passed the Naval Diving and Salvage Training Center, where the Navy trained Explosive Ordnance Disposal, RECON Marines, and military salvors to operate underwater. The NDSTC curricula spanned the whole spectrum of diving, from scuba to surface-supplied air to mixed gas, re-breathers, and even saturation diving systems. Looking toward the main entrance, the quarterdeck, brought back a flood of memories from his scuba class two summers before—especially of pool week, the most challenging part of the course. Durago remembered swimming slowly, counterclockwise along the bottom perimeter of the training pool with Class 89-75-scuba. From the surface, he and the other midshipmen looked as tranquil as koi, until chaos ensued as one by one the diving instructors "hit" the students, imposing problems on them that mimicked the maelstrom of a crashing wave or a ship's prop wash.

Air was always the first thing to go. Durago recalled the high-pitched hissing sound as the valve on his tank was shut. Then his regulator was pulled from his mouth and tied in knots around the first stage. This also had a recognizable squeak as the rubber hose was torqued down upon itself. Next, his mask was ripped off, then one or both of his fins. All the while, Durago closed his eyes, tucked his chin into his chest, and gripped the shoulder straps that held his tank on. If the instructor was able to separate him completely from his source of air, Durago would fail the problem. Finally, the yanking of his waist strap signaled the rolling and tumbling would begin. It was like an underwater wrestling match, except the student could not fight back.

It was about this time that vertigo and lack of air would cause panic to seep into Durago's brain. He tried to focus on remaining calm, to ride out the spinning and bouncing by planning his first reaction once the subaquatic torture ended. *Your air is on your back. Soon he'll be done and it will be just you and your precious tank of air.*

Once satisfied with the havoc he created, the instructor left for the surface. Durago then had two minutes to safely remove the tanks, untie the regulator, restore his air, gather his equipment, and return to a prepared condition. Failing the problem meant a trip to the surface, and a scolding. Two or more such trips and the candidate might be expelled from the course. Real panic, like bolting for the surface, could also cause the student to be dropped, but it usually led to them resigning, a drop on request or "DOR." Those who controlled their fear and were able to work through the problems, escaping the wrath of their underwater nemesis, got to experience such turmoil over and over again, both alone and with a buddy. By the week's end the survivors were completely confident in their ability to calmly work through any diving casualty or equipment failure, with or without the benefit of oxygen.

Just before the bridge over the Grand Lagoon, Durago saw the Panhandle Dive Shop on the right-hand side. As he got out of the car, he could see *Strong Diver* moored at a pier behind the shop. When planning the trip, Strong had explained that he acted as the primary charter captain for Panhandle and helped out in the shop, but the two were partners rather than one business.

The dive shop was like many others—an open plan laid out for retail sales. Just inside the door to the left was a long wall where a variety of masks, fins, snorkels, and knives hung on display. The floor had four or five clothing racks that held wetsuits and skins of various thicknesses. One rack contained buoyancy compensators, or "BCs"—vests that divers wear to carry their tanks that employ internal air bladders that allow them to stay neutral underwater and float on the surface. The wall on the far side was similar to its companion near the entry, but it held regulators, weight belts, and spearguns. Scuba tanks lined the floor below. Durago noted Strong behind a counter in the center of the back wall, talking to a very attractive woman. Strong looked up and nodded. Durago sensed that the woman was on the manifest for tomorrow and that Strong was checking her certification while she signed waivers. She was shorter than Durago, with auburn hair cascading to just between her shoulder blades. Her tight t-shirt and board shorts, coupled with shapely and muscular legs, suggested physical fitness. Durago decided he wanted to meet her. As he moved toward the counter, he could hear Strong.

"Great. Well, we have a fine selection of fins over on the wall there. Try 'em on for size and we'll hook you up."

"Thanks."

She seemed to notice Durago as she turned on her heel and headed for the display wall near the front of the store. With no obvious beau nearby, Durago immediately asked Strong, "Is she with someone?"

"Yeah—you. Like you, she had a partner who backed out. So, I put you together. You owe me big time, son."

"Yes," said Durago, looking back toward the door, "I do."

Jan casually noticed the shop owner talking with the next customer, the one he said she would be partnered with. He was clearly a few years younger than she, college-aged but confident. She selected a pair of fins, tucked them under her arm, then stood next to a display that allowed her to watch the two. *They know each other. I wonder if the younger guy's a diving instructor.*

Both men looked in her direction almost simultaneously. Jan pulled a knife from its hanger and focused on it until they looked away. When she looked back, the younger one was definitely checking her out. He was classically handsome, with dark hair and an athletic build. Jan saw again that he seemed sure of himself. It wasn't the frat boy, cock-of-the-walk attitude she loathed—yet expected to see throughout this week—but a composed nature that she found attractive.

The next morning Durago pulled Slim's Jeep pierside, across from *Strong Diver*. Grabbing his dive bag from the back seat, he slung it over his shoulder and headed for the brow. He noticed moored just next to it was a smaller vessel, *Week Diver*. Durago smiled as he realized the origin of the name.

Strong Diver's design was perfect for close, offshore diving. It had a wide beam emphasized by an open deck that spanned the back two-thirds of the craft. A fully enclosed cabin covered the front third, through which Durago could see the cockpit and a passage belowdecks. He recalled Strong telling him that it had a small stateroom, galley, and head below—enough to live on for short periods of time. As he stepped on board, Durago noted bench seating running both sides of the deck. Single scuba tanks lined each bench, so that the divers could attach their BCs and set up all of their gear. When it came time to dive, they could simply sit into their equipment while slipping on their BCs.

Master Chief Strong slid open the hatch, emerging with a cup of coffee in his hand.

"Welcome aboard, sir. Stow your gear anywhere you want. Grab some coffee. We've got you, your new partner, and a small university class today."

"*Week Diver?*" Durago inquired.

"Yeah. I couldn't resist the name. I bought that one a few months back. It's a twenty-eight-foot Parker, perfect for shorter trips or smaller groups. Plus, now I can run two groups at once. My only real problem is getting someone to crew it. Marcie's working on her license, but it's more than that—she needs experience. I suppose I'll find someone from the dive school who's about to retire to help me out."

Another black Jeep pulled in the parking lot next to Slim's. A woman wearing an oversized blue sweatshirt and an Orioles cap got out. As she extracted her own dive bag, Durago recognized her as the woman from the dive shop.

"That's her, isn't it?" he asked.

Strong looked up. "Yeah, that's her," he confirmed. Strong turned and disappeared when Durago's partner started up the gangway.

"Can I lend a hand?" Durago called out.

"No, thanks. I've got it," she said.

"I'm Don Durago. We're gonna be dive buddies. I've put my gear in the back there, so if you like, you can set your stuff next to mine."

"Super."

She set her bag down, then extended her hand. "I'm Jan Meyer."

"Nice to meet you, Jan," Durago said as he shook her hand.

"And you."

"So, I guess like me you're here for spring break."

"Something like that," she said. "You alone?"

"Yeah. I came down with my roommate, but he got called away for a family emergency. Have you dived in Panama City before?"

"Actually, I'm new to the sport. I just recently got certified. This will be one of my first open water dives. How about you?"

"I'm still relatively new myself. I got certified two years ago, but I've only been in the water a few times. I've been on a couple of trips with the scuba club at school. Then I did a few dives over summer break."

"Well, then, I'm sure I'm in good hands."

As Jan smiled at him, Durago noticed her blue eyes. He studied her face for a brief moment, taking in her beauty. It was then that he realized that Jan was a few years older than he, maybe four or five years out of college. It did not emanate from her physical appearance, but from her demeanor. In this brief encounter, he could see that she possessed a strength, a part of her presence that suggested maturity and confidence derived from years of independence. He guessed that she would be kind, but would not show any interest in a college senior.

As the university group arrived, Durago and Jan set up their gear together. He checked all of his equipment meticulously to ensure he had everything he needed, that his first stage and BC were properly connected, that his mask was clear. Finally, he tested his regulator. If he were diving with Slim, Durago would have blatantly rummaged through Slim's gear to make sure he was set. Slim would never be insulted because he would be busy tinkering with Durago's gear. Instead, Durago eyed Jan's gear casually to ensure she had everything set up properly.

Jan went below deck to change. She put on a green, athletic bikini that showed her figure well, yet tastefully covered her body. Looking in the mirror, she turned and inspected herself. *Yeah, this will work,* she thought. *I look good, but like I'm serious about diving.*

When Jan returned, Durago felt like he was seeing her for the first time. Several of the other males on the boat also looked at her. *Damn, she could be a swimsuit calendar model,* he thought. He noticed how her dive booties accented her beautifully sculpted calves. She had a tight tummy, and toned arms. Jan stood next to Durago and bent over to strap the knife on the inside of her ankle. *This view could send a priest to the confessional,* Durago thought.

"So, where do you go to school?" Jan asked as she stood up. She flashed him a smile, but he could not decide if it was flirtatious or a little condescending.

"Uh, the Naval Academy."

"You're shitting me."

"No, in fact, in part that's why I'm here. I went to the Navy's dive school here in—"

Jan wore an undecipherable look that stopped Durago mid-sentence.

"What?"

"I work there."

"Excuse me?"

"My name's not just 'Jan Meyer'; it's 'Lieutenant Jan Meyer.'"

"Oh, okay . . . ma'am."

"Stop. Let's not have any of that here. Listen—" She paused, biting her lip as she thought, *You can still enjoy this.* "It's spring break," she continued. "Clearly we both came here to escape the Navy for a while. So, let's just forget all of that and have a good time, okay?"

"You got it." *Well, that's it. This definitely won't go anywhere.*

Durago followed Jan down the anchor line to the bottom. He felt like James Bond trailing Domino in *Thunderball*. The visibility was about six feet; beyond that, the water turned into a green haze. As the wreck came into view, Durago could see from its lines that it was just as Strong described—a tugboat sitting perfectly upright. They were approaching from the bow.

Before they splashed, Durago suggested that Jan lead through the whole dive, especially because this was her first wreck. Several varieties of fish darted around the air-breathing invaders, but none were particularly interesting.

From time to time Jan turned to confirm Durago's presence. Each time their eyes met, she recognized something. *He's actually watching me . . . watching out for me, not just checking me out.* It comforted her that the young midshipman was looking to her as a diving partner. *Okay, so he might be getting a peek or two, but it's flattering. If this were Tripp, he'd want me to follow him, darting all over the place.* She decided it might be worthwhile to spend more time with him on the surface.

Similarly, Durago thought the dive was even better than taking a date to the movies. Not only did he not have to talk, he could study her as she finned gracefully through the water. They slowly circled the tugboat three times in thirty minutes, trying to avoid the other divers. This meant they saw a better variety of fish, which kept their distance but were not spooked away by just the two of them. Finally, they ascended and stopped at the ten-foot marker that Strong dropped beneath the hull and waited for two minutes. It was an added safety precaution to ensure they off gassed enough nitrogen to prevent the bends.

Back on deck, they rinsed and disassembled their gear.

"Thank you for diving with me. I think I actually felt better going with someone who has some experience—and a Navy diver at that." Jan said.

Is she serious, or being condescending? "Sure. It was a good dive, wasn't it?"

"So, what's the plan now? You going out tonight?" Jan asked.

"Nah. I'll probably take it easy. I'm thinking about diving again tomorrow."

"Yeah? Me too. Why don't we talk about it over dinner? You up for some seafood—my treat for getting me through my first wreck dive?"

"Oh, hell yes."

"Then it's a date."

Durago nodded silently as he thought, *She just said "date."*

Durago picked Jan up four hours later. Though she was wearing a simple sweater set, miniskirt, and loafers, she looked really appealing. Durago tried to hide any expression of this on his face.

"The dive shop just called me," she said as she got in the passenger seat. "The boat broke down this afternoon, so they won't be going out tomorrow."

"Oh, man . . . that's a bummer."

"Well, yes and no. Now we can go clubbing after dinner," Jan said with a devilish grin. "You are twenty-one, aren't you?"

"Yes, ma'am."

"Good. Then I won't be completely corrupting you this evening."

Over appetizers they talked again about the dive, reviewing and reliving all of the things they saw. As the waiter put a plate of mahi mahi in front of Durago, Jan asked, "You know the dive boat captain, don't you? Was he one of your scuba school instructors?"

"No, actually, I know him from the Academy. He was one of my enlisted advisers. But it was through him that I found out about the dive school. Master Chief Strong was a Navy diver and encouraged me to come through the school during my Youngster Cruise."

"So, what led you to the Academy?"

Durago held his breath a moment. When he exhaled he replied, "Well, Jan, that's a long story . . . and this is going to sound like a cliché, but basically, I had nowhere else to go."

"What about your parents?"

"Really not much to tell there, either. Let's just say my folks shipped me off to boarding school. I never knew my father, and my mother passed away before my senior year of high school. So, I'm kind of an adult orphan."

"Oh, I'm so sorry," Jan said as she reached across the table and grasped Durago's hand. "I've said the wrong thing, haven't I?"

"No, no, it's okay . . . it's a natural question, right? Look, my mom and I . . . we had a weird relationship. See, she was a workaholic and pretty successful . . . and, as I said, she sent me to a boarding school. I didn't go home much. I basically messed around, worked as a life-guard. So, I guess in some ways, going to the Naval Academy is just an extension of that life, the boarding school thing, you know?"

Durago shoved some rice in his mouth, then sipped his Sam Adams, hoping the silence would allow a break in the subject. After sharing as much as he was ready to share, he reverted to a technique he employed often when the subject of his lineage arose, and asked a question in return.

"How about you? Why did you join the Navy?

Jan shared that although she had been at the Naval Academy for almost three months, she was still becoming attuned to the Academy and the Navy. She had finished law school and then signed up for the Navy, which in turn paid her school loans. She was pushed through a quick officer indoctrination course designed for lawyers, doctors, and chaplains. Jan had been in uniform less time than Durago, yet she was a lieutenant junior grade.

Through the dinner conversation Durago noted that they both became more comfortable with each other. He realized that he was genuinely enthralled by Jan and was not put off by her rank, and per-haps even a little puffed up by the fact that an older woman seemed interested in him. As they left the restaurant, she grabbed his hand and tugged him toward the passenger side of the Jeep.

"You should open the door for me," she said.

As he closed the door, Jan looked right into his eyes in a manner that implied invitation. There was a spring in his step as he strutted around the Jeep to get behind the wheel.

The music in the club was so loud that they could not really talk. But they had a good time dancing. Durago went back and forth to the bar to get them drinks. At one point he looked toward her from the bar while he was waiting. Some guy was trying to pick her up. She was obviously giving him the brush-off. Durago read her actions. She clearly wanted to be with him.

He drove Jan to her hotel and walked her up to her room. She opened her door, then turned around, put her arms around his shoul-ders, and kissed him. A long kiss.

"I need some sleep. Call me tomorrow?"

"I will."

Durago thought to himself as he drove his roommate's Jeep back to his hotel room, *Slim is never going to believe this.*

Then he realized he might not ever tell his roommate about Jan.

The next morning, Durago was awakened by the phone.

"Good morning—did I wake you?"

Durago looked at the clock. It was 1000. "Yeah, you sure did."

"Well, get up, we're going to the beach. I'll be out front in forty-five minutes."

"Aye, aye, ma'am."

As soon as those words came out he regretted them. How would she react? Did he want to remind her that he was still a midshipman?

"And if you're late, I'll put you on report," she quipped.

Fortunately she shared his sense of humor.

Durago showered quickly, donned a pair of Jams, and flew down the stairs to the parking lot. He removed the top from Slim's Jeep. Jan got out of her own Jeep as he was taking the doors off. She was in a yellow bikini this time and was wearing a baseball cap. Her hair was tied back in a ponytail. Jan hopped into the seat next to him and shot him a smile.

"I know a great beach at St. Andrew's park. You drive and I'll direct you there."

When they got there, Jan laid out a large beach blanket for the two of them. She slipped off her sandals and lay on her stomach.

"Would you rub suntan lotion on my back?" she said.

This has gotta be a dream, Durago thought to himself.

They had a great day. The beach was secluded, so there were not many people. They spent the afternoon sunning themselves and talking about nothing. By dusk there was literally nobody else on the beach. Jan rolled over and placed her arm on Durago. He looked up. Again, she smiled at him.

"Are you ready to go back?" he asked.

"No," she said, "let's stay a little longer."

She slid her hand to his face, pulled him close, and kissed him. Durago rolled onto her. He kissed her passionately.

"Now . . . " she gasped, "let's go back now. My place."

6

ACCUSATIONS

 March 20, 1992
1810
MD Route 2 South

O ut of habit, Robert Oberly looked to his left as his Ford Bronco approached the U.S. Naval Academy Bridge. It never ceased to amaze him how, just like its mission, the architecture of the Naval Academy seemed to strike the right balance of military heritage and academia. It was all columns and cannons, prows and prose. As the Yard grew larger in his view, he realized that he was experiencing the same dread that many mids would encounter in less than forty-eight hours as they descended toward the bridge. He laughed inwardly at the Brigade's name for this stretch of highway—"Oh, Shit Hill," implying that as the Academy came into view after a weekend or holiday, the mids would cry, "Oh, shit!"

Oh, shit, indeed, Oberly thought. The young Marine officer knew that duty could call him at any minute, but he had a hard time imagining why he was summoned back to the Academy late on Friday of the Brigade's spring break.

Slowing almost to a stop as he turned left and passed through Gate 8, the company officer nodded when the Marine sentry saluted. As he stepped on the gas he heard a guttural "Oorah!" After only a few weeks at Navy, Oberly received such a greeting every time he entered the Yard, signifying that the guards recognized him, or at least that his truck belonged to a fellow Marine.

Oberly noted as he continued along the Severn River toward Bancroft's seventh wing that the Academy seemed like a ghost town: no profs, no officers, and no mids. The few people he did see were either ground crew working overtime to spruce up the place as spring continued to unfold or tourists snapping photos of their taxpayer-funded granite and glass.

Pulling into the small parking lot nestled between the fifth and seventh wing, Oberly noted that three other company officers' cars were already there, in addition to the battalion officer's Volvo. Oberly wondered if his Bronco was tall enough to crawl over the hood of his superior's sedan. He imagined the roof caving in with a satisfying crunching sound, followed immediately by the windows popping out, sending shattered glass across the tarmac. He decided to simply pull into the spot next the commander's car instead.

Oberly had learned quickly that he and Commander Gordon were at opposite ends of the leadership spectrum. As a Marine infantryman, Oberly emphasized leadership by example. He demanded the respect immediately owed to his position from his men, but then worked to solidify it through his personal performance and competence. Gordon, a submariner, seemed to focus on management through rules, regulations, and standard operating procedures. Oberly was driven to serve and mentor his Marines, now his midshipmen, enhancing and honing their abilities so they could tackle any assigned mission. If successful, he should earn the privilege of promotion and the opportunity to guide even more Marines. Gordon seemed to feel promotion came at the expense of his charges, that by highlighting their flaws and removing the weak he would build a team that would lift him to the next level of command.

I'd look for the one lost sheep, Oberly thought. *Gordon would see it as thinning the herd.*

Though it was after normal working hours, Oberly knew that Gordon would expect all of them to don their uniforms. Not wanting to lose any time, he took the elevator up to 7-4, zipped into his office, and put on his service dress. He was in the battalion officer's conference room on 7-0, notebook in hand, five minutes before the appointed meeting.

All the company officers were present, with the exception of Manuel Santiago—like Gordon, a submariner. Lieutenant Thom Schwartz, the battalion's third submarine officer, was seated at the conference table sipping coffee. It was Schwartz who had called Oberly in. He looked like he had spent the better part of the day in the office. Oberly appreciated that Lieutenants Santiago and Schwartz did a lot more work for Gordon than the other company officers. Gordon naturally reached out to officers from his own community. They both knew the extra attention and responsibility was a blessing and a curse. Gordon's impression of their performance here at the Academy could have an enduring impact on their careers in the "silent service," good or bad.

Third Battalion also had two surface warfare officers, or "SWOs." The 13th Company Officer, Lieutenant Ned Breedon, had served on the USS *Kidd*, a destroyer originally built for Iran. Ironically, both of his deployments had been in the Persian Gulf, one during the Tanker War, Operation Earnest Will, the second during Operation Desert Storm. Oberly knew that, like many of the other officers, Breedon was working on his master's degree. Breedon hoped that after his tour at Navy and Department Head School in Newport, Rhode Island, he would receive orders to one of the newest *Aegis* cruisers or destroyers.

The second ship-driver, Lieutenant Marc Sinclair, had also served in the Persian Gulf conflicts, but on the minesweepers *Affray* and *Enhance*. While Breedon seemed poised for transition to the Navy's newest combat systems, Sinclair seemed more traditional. Oberly sensed Sinclair was not impressed with phased array radars and gas turbine engines. He probably preferred a 5-inch gun on his forecastle and a set of D-type boilers or a suite of thrumming diesels below his feet. Contrary to his own service etiquette, the Marine admired the fact that Sinclair seemed unconcerned with military protocol and practice. The guy was often direct, blunt, and unflappable whenever Gordon growled at him. Oberly surmised that of all the sailors in the room, Sinclair was actually the most competent.

Despite a large officer community, there was only one aviator in the group: Lieutenant Commander George "Fabulous" Ferren, an F-14 pilot straight from central casting. The tall, svelte, blonde-haired, blue-eyed flyer claimed that a flight school instructor once tried to paint him with the moniker "Ferret." "But he couldn't pull it off. I'm just toooo fabulous," he had said. While Sinclair brought brutal honesty to the group, Fabulous provided the levity. He was even able to crack up the commander from time to time.

Oberly walked up to the aviator, pouring himself some coffee from a stainless steel pot. "Hey, Fab. What's up?"

"Don't know, Marine, but apparently Thom's been working this thing all day."

"And it can't wait 'til Monday?"

"I know, brother. I've got two airline stewardesses cooling their jets in my swimming pool right now. I seriously hope this is a simple heads-up for an inspection on Monday afternoon or something."

"You guys ready?" Schwartz suddenly asked. "If so, please take your seats."

Jeez, we're being real formal with this, aren't we? Oberly thought.

After everyone was seated around the conference table, Schwartz got up, went to the commander's office connected to the conference room, and knocked on the door.

"Sir, we're ready," he called out.

Gordon opened the door to his office. The four officers remaining at the table stood in a respectful but casual form of attention.

"Please, take your seats."

Oberly noted that Gordon had goined weight. There was a roll of fat around his waist, and he thought Gordon's trousers looked like they were not fastened underneath the buckle bearing the silhouette of an *Ohio*-class submarine.

"Gentlemen, thank you for coming in so late on a Friday. I've asked you to be here so I can share some information with you before the Brigade returns on Sunday. Most of you probably recall that we had a performance board for Midshipman Third Class Whorton just before the break. The recommendation of the board was to separate Miss Whorton."

Oberly remembered the case. Less than two weeks before, they all had concurred with the recommendation to "separate"—to kick Whorton out of the Academy for sustained poor performance. She had barely made it through Plebe Year and was struggling even as a Youngster. At the board itself, Oberly thought she seemed autistic.

"Whorton's parents got involved when they learned of the board's decision. First, directly through the Commandant's Office, then through their congressman."

Oberly thought the way Gordon said "the board's decision" made it sound as if they all shared equal responsibility. Oberly had agreed with the decision, supported it, but Gordon encouraged separation.

"The end result," Gordon continued, "is that we are now going to investigate the possibility that Whorton has endured undue harassment that led to her poor performance."

"Harassment?" Breedon said out loud. "Really?"

Oberly remembered that Breedon was Whorton's company officer, as the commander replied, "Yes, Mister Breedon, harassment."

"Sir, we can't really believe this. I mean, we all saw the documentation. We went overboard to ensure that Whorton was getting a fair shake."

"I'm not so sure," the commander replied. "In fact, I blame myself partially. I should have known better, especially in our current climate of reforming this institution."

Oh, no, here we go again, Oberly thought. He braced himself for another of Gordon's diatribes about how their mission was to change the culture of the Brigade. Fortunately, Breedon cut him off.

"Wait, sir . . . we were using that very argument to get rid of Whorton. One of the tenets you've preached is removal of those who are not up to snuff to strengthen the whole institution and, thus, the Navy. If Whorton were a Plebe, maybe we'd be able to point to harassment, but in this case we focused mostly on the fact that she could not perform as a Youngster, a time when she is not under the spotlight."

Oberly heard Breedon's voice rise in pitch as he continued registering frustration. It was clear that he felt that this was an affront to his own leadership, and a recognition that mids in his company would be implicated.

"Remember, sir, not only did her poor performance include failure to get out of bed for muster, and failure to show up to appointed duties such as watch, class, and drill, she was also caught drinking in the hall."

Oberly joined most of the officers in nodding affirmation.

"That . . . the drinking . . . that really sealed it for me," Oberly agreed. "Sir, that was simply beyond the pale."

Sinclair also chimed in: "Sir, we were all surprised she got in here in the first place, remember? We even joked that she was like Rain Man."

Sinclair's comment brought the room to silence. Oberly noticed that Breedon relaxed a little with the recognition that he and Sinclair came to his defense, pointing out that they had all agreed that Whorton was unsuitable. Though not as vocal, the others seemed to be in agreement as they looked to their superior for a response. Similarly, Gordon scanned the faces of his company officers a moment.

"Gentlemen," he said, "there have been serious accusations made regarding midshipmen in this battalion harassing one another. We have already seen this before and we will not let it slide. My concern is that everything we saw in Miss Whorton manifested itself due to the harassment she received starting during her own Plebe Summer."

Oberly sensed Gordon looking at him with that comment.

"We owe it to Whorton—"

"—and her parents and congressman," Breedon chimed in.

"Enough, Mister Breedon!" Gordon snapped. "We owe it to Miss Whorton," he continued, "to fully investigate to ensure she got a fair shake, and to root out any remnant of bad behavior and bad seeds we may still have in the battalion.

"Now, Thom will pass to each of you a synopsis of the case, plus a review of the conduct cases in your company."

Oberly furrowed his brow as his fellow company officer—referred to by his first name, rather than rank and surname, because he was a submariner—passed him a folder.

"For example," Gordon went on, "Captain Oberly and Lieutenant Sinclair both have midshipmen among the accused who served as squad leaders for Miss Whorton. Naturally, the bulk of the offenses are within Thirteenth Company."

Oberly opened his folder and saw a charge sheet with Durago's name in the opening paragraph. Then he looked over to Breedon, who had a stack of about ten folders in front of him.

"These initial charges are leveled after Thom conducted an initial investigation today. Because none of the accused are in his company, he is formally bringing the charges. The next step will be to inform your midshipmen next week, shortly after their return. We are appointing Midshipman First Class Antonelli as the midshipman investigating officer. Antonelli is in Thom's company and is a submarine warfare selectee."

Imagine that, thought Oberly.

"After Antonelli's investigation, I'm sure we'll need to bring this at least to our level."

Oberly thought that Breedon looked like he was going to puke.

7

ACCUSED

MARCH 26, 1992
1410
BANCROFT HALL, ROOM 7412

The first week back, all Durago could think about was Jan. To try to distract himself, he listened to all his companymates' tales of revelry outside the Academy's walls. Two Youngsters set out to ski in Germany and Switzerland by hopping on a Military Airlift Command space-available flight. Instead they ended up in Honduras, ski parkas and all. When asked, Durago only talked of scuba diving and only vaguely mentioned meeting a girl. When in class, Durago daydreamed. He tried to think of Slim and his family, even murmuring a prayer or two, but his mind would always return to his last conversation with Jan.

By Friday of spring break, Durago had begun to wonder what would happen when they returned to Annapolis. He could tell that Jan was not sure how to broach the subject. She finally did, awkwardly, over Chinese fortune cookies on Saturday evening before their return. Durago replayed the conversation over and over in his mind, trying to discern its meaning.

"We need to talk about this week," she started.

"Yeah?"

"It's been a lot of fun. I really like you. But I'm also worried about how it would look back at the Academy."

"You don't want to see me again."

"I did not say that and I am not saying that. I just want you to understand that this was spring break. Once we head north . . . I think this is over."

I think this is over?

"Listen, Don, I don't want you to get an idea that I just throw down with anyone. I also don't want you to think I'm cold. So, here's my phone number," Jan said, handing him a postcard with an aerial shot of Panama City. He flipped it over and saw a number written neatly on the reverse.

"So, if you need something . . . someone to talk to, a JAG . . . call me."

"Okay," Durago said with a lump in his throat.

Jan smiled at him once more, then said, "Have a safe trip back," as she slid out of the booth.

Back in Annapolis, Durago worked hard to resist the temptation to call Jan. Deep down he realized that although Jan did not want to use the word "fling," it was what he represented, and an illicit one at that. He suspected that Jan's offer was genuine, but for legal assistance, or advice, not romance. Perhaps the offer was for her own dignity, so she could create in her own mind the notion that romance was budding, but that it fell flat because of their relative positions—something simply not to be. Still, he wondered what would transpire if they met in the Yard.

On Thursday, when he returned to his room after the last period, there were two notes on the two-man desk in the center of his room. One was from Slim, saying that he was on emergency leave for the rest of the week and would be back on Sunday night. The second was from his company officer, asking Durago to see him after class.

Shit, he thought, *I'm a Firstie and I still have come-arounds.*

Durago stowed his books and cover, ensured his uniform looked acceptable, and headed for the company officer's office. He noted that a number of the heavy wood doors that separated each room from the passageway were closed, indicating that someone was inside. During the day most of the doors remained open, indicating that the rooms' occupants were out, in class, or on watch. Each door had a lock that was never used, a statement on the Brigade Honor Concept: midshipmen do not lie, cheat, or steal. Infractions of the Honor Concept are handled by the Brigade in a self-policing forum that dismisses any violators. The honor system had all but removed theft from the hall.

The 14th Company Officer's office looked down the center connecting passage of the H-shaped wing. It allowed him to see almost everything in company area when his door was open. As he approached the office, Durago could see Captain Oberly talking on the phone. The officer acknowledged Durago's presence, but the mid decided to wait in the passageway.

It was known that Captain Oberly accepted the billet to the Naval Academy because he thought it would be a great opportunity to have an effect on the officer ascension to the Marine Corps. Not a grad himself, Oberly often found himself in conflict with officers that came from the Academy. Now that he had spent time in Annapolis, he understood them and their nature a lot better.

Oberly hung up the phone and waved Durago in.

"Good afternoon, sir."

"Mister Durago, please sit down."

The captain got up from his desk and shut the door. Durago thought that this was strange. His mind raced through the possibilities of what the company officer would want kept private. *The captain's acting like there's been a death—Slim Jim's sister? A professor's phone call regarding absentmindedness in class? Or had someone seen him with Jan?*

Oberly sat back down at his desk.

"Mister Durago, I have some news that will concern you. Do you know Midshipman Third Class Whorton?"

Durago's mind went immediately to a screwed-up Plebe he met two summers before. "Yes, sir, I was her squad leader during Plebe Detail. She's in Thirteenth Company."

Oberly paused and took a deep breath. "Well, Miss Whorton has brought up some allegations against you regarding harassment."

"What?" Durago was confused.

"It's true, Mister Durago. It seems she was about to be separated from the Brigade at a performance board. Apparently, she was a conduct case. After her board, a psychiatrist hired by her parents claimed that much of her bad conduct is some kind of reaction to harassment experienced here at the Naval Academy."

Now Durago realized exactly what was happening. He started out of his chair. "Sir, this is bullshit!"

His company officer held up his hand to stop him. Deep down, Oberly suspected that the accusations were fiction. In fact, Oberly tried several times over the past few days to squash the charges against Durago, to have them simply dropped before the process really got started. He noted that, conversely, Gordon seemed to like the idea that midshipmen from almost every company in the battalion were facing charges. Dropping Durago's charges would remove 14th Company entirely from the melee and solidify the notion that Whorton was an isolated case, an anomaly.

"When word gets out to all the companies in the battalion, it'll shake things up around here . . . keep all these mids on their best behavior," Gordon had said.

Oberly naturally took the opposite approach. He thought that, much like the charges against the mids he was having investigated, Gordon's actions bordered on harassment. Thus, Oberly wanted to be as protective as he could. There was simply no point in allowing one of his best people to get torn up over this, especially if the accusations were false.

When Oberly next spoke, it was in a very calming tone. "Mister Durago, I know this is alarming. You need to relax. I'm sure there's been a misunderstanding here. What you need to do is keep this under your hat. When the story gets out to the Brigade, the best way to protect yourself is to not talk about it to anyone other than the investigating officer. At this point, there are only allegations. There are initial charges, but nothing formal is filed yet."

Oberly paused again because he could see that Durago was visibly shaken.

"Midshipman First Class Antonelli, the battalion sub-commander, has been assigned as midshipman investigating officer. He will contact you in the next day or so. If you need any advice or counsel, I'm here to help. In any regard, keep me apprised of what is happening with your case."

"*Case*," Durago thought. *Suddenly, I'm a "case."*

"Mister Durago, I'm going to help you through this. I'm sure this will be over soon and everything will work out. I wish I could tell you more at this point. Any questions?"

Durago was really too shocked to think clearly.

"Uh, no, sir."

"Very well, then—you're dismissed."

With that, Durago left the office and closed the door. He went down the hall to the end of 7-4 and stared out at Farragut Field and the Chesapeake Bay. He sat there for a long time, watching two of the Academy's 44s practice tacking and raising and lowering sails. Still, Durago could not think straight. The only thing that was clear to him was that he wanted to be with Jan.

8

RUNNING

MARCH 26, 1992
2210
BANCROFT HALL, ROOM 7412

Staring at the ceiling that night, Durago hoped the storm would lull him to sleep, but after an hour he realized that he was too restless. Sleep was prevented by a combination of stress from the pending investigation and fear of the nightmare he knew was waiting for him. He rose and went to the window looking out toward the Severn. The drops of rain looked like dancing fireflies as they passed through the lights around Santee Basin. Rough seas tossed the Navy 44s back and forth against their moorings, so they looked like bucking broncos trying to break free of their stalls. Durago half expected to see Mickey Mouse, as The Sorcerer's Apprentice, atop the Robert Crown Sailing Center, directing the whole maelstrom.

The storm only distracted him for a few minutes. To burn off some energy and try to clear his mind, Durago decided to go for a run in spite of the rain. He donned a pair of running shorts, a t-shirt, and a water-repellant wind breaker. He knew he would be soaked in a matter of minutes, but it did not breathe well and so it would keep him warm.

From the seventh-wing parking lot, Durago headed toward Santee Basin, then turned left along Dewey Field. Looking over the river, the drenched midshipman noted that only the lights of the U.S. Naval Academy Bridge cut through the dark rain. There was little reflection on the water, giving the river an inky black appearance. Turning right onto the footbridge across Dorsey Creek, commonly referred to by its tributary, College Creek, Durago opened his stride. He remembered Master Chief Strong barking at him three winters ago.

"Let's go, Mister Durago, take the hill like you mean it! We're just getting started, mister."

"Hooyah, Master Chief!"

Now on Hospital Point, Durago ran on the inside of the quay to avoid some of the spray and to ensure he did not slip into the drink. Finally, he pumped his legs as he climbed uphill again, closing the distance with Gate 8. As he approached, he could tell the two Marines in the guard shack saw him.

"Oorah!" one yelled.

"Hooyah!" Durago replied as he pivoted on his heel and headed out of the gate, turning right toward the Severn and the naval station across the river from the Academy.

The crowd in the restaurant was starting to thin, so Jan decided it was time for her to leave. She sipped her wine as she scanned the room looking for Tripp and her National Security Studies professor, Commander Applegate. One she wanted to avoid, the other she needed to find. As she continued to survey the party, Jan noted that everyone eventually gravitated to their cliques. The aviators had their ties undone and were talking with their hands. The surface warfare tribe was howling at some sea story. Then there were the wives. Jan had met one or two of them, and they seemed nice enough, but she already had learned that military wives treat a woman in uniform differently. She still had not determined if it was condescension or jealousy.

Finally, she saw the commander near the bar, talking with Sheila Hagan. Her Naval War College classmate looked fantastic in her black cocktail dress, but it pissed Jan off when female officers wore civilian dresses to military functions. *Grades are already in, honey. Stop flirting,* she thought. Jan looked down to survey her mess dress. Not only did it make her look like a nun, it was uncomfortable. Gazing back at Sheila and Applegate, Jan sensed they were saying their goodbyes. She moved to thank her professor, as protocol required, when Tripp appeared out of nowhere.

"Hey, beautiful."

"Tripp, please."

"What?"

"Look, I need to go and you've had too much to drink again."

"Okay, so drive me home."

"Not happening. I learned my lesson last time."

"That's not fair. I didn't do anything wrong, did I?"

"No," Jan said firmly, holding her breath a moment, "you didn't. But, Tripp, we've been through this already."

"I think you just need to lighten up, relax. We can be friends, too."

Tripp's voice was a little loud. Jan sensed some of her classmates glancing their way, as if they thought a scene was about to develop. It was common knowledge that she and Tripp studied together, and were both JAGs, but since their weekend on *Quantum Meriut*, Jan had said subtle things in conversations to ensure people knew they were not lovers.

Normally Durago ran the obstacle course that threaded through the forest of the Annapolis Naval Station, but tonight he decided it was too dark. He may not be able to find his way, and if he did, he could not be sure-footed. The last thing he needed right now was a turned ankle, so he continued on the road, zipping through base housing, operations, and other parts of the facility that were unfamiliar to him. Looking to his watch, he saw that he had been running for almost an hour. It was time to turn back.

Wanting to avoid a scene, Jan smiled while lowering her voice.

"Look, Tripp, it's this simple. I'm going to go say goodbye to Commander Applegate. Then I'm driving back to Annapolis. You are going to get a cab or find someone to take you home. I'll see you back in the Yard tomorrow or Monday."

Tripp clenched his teeth and said nothing.

After saying her goodbyes, Jan headed for the door. The party had grown even smaller, and Tripp had disappeared. Another officer and his wife kindly shared their umbrella and walked Jan to her Jeep. She opened the door, hiked her skirt up slightly, and hopped in.

"You good, Jan?"

"I am," she replied. "Thanks, Bill. Thanks, Susie."

Jan closed the door, kicked off her heels, turned the engine over, and set her wipers to high. Shortly thereafter, she was in traffic heading back to Annapolis and had forgotten all about Tripp.

Starting up the U.S. Naval Academy Bridge, Jan sensed something was wrong. The Jeep seemed sluggish. *Am I losing traction?* Nearing the crest, she realized the right front side was sagging. *Damn, I've got a flat.* She pulled over to the right as far as she could, set the brake, and turned her flashers on. *Shit, this ugly-ass mess dress is going to be completely trashed.*

Pounding down the hill from the naval station, Durago could see the Naval Academy Bridge again. Just as he approached the foot of the bridge, he saw a Jeep pass in front of him. He recognized the driver as Jan. He saw her stop halfway over the bridge, pulling over and turning on her flashers. *Did she see me? Is she stopping for me?*

As the door opened he called out, "Jan!"

She looked back and closed the door. Durago slowed to a walk as he approached the driver's side.

"Don?"

"Hey, what's going on?"

"I've got a flat. What are you doing?"

Now Durago was right next to the door. They were talking through a small crack that Jan had opened in her window.

"Ah, I just went out for a long run—crazy in this rain, I know, but I just needed to get out. You're in mess dress. Were you at a shindig?"

"Yeah, a dining out for my war college class. So, listen, I'm really glad to see you. Normally, I'm all about doing this stuff on my own, but with the rain and my uniform . . . and you're already wet . . ."

"Change your tire? No problem."

Durago lifted the spare from the tailgate and grabbed the needed tools.

"Be careful," Jan called out. "Watch for oncoming traffic."

Durago had one tire off and the other on quickly. Tightening the lugs on the full-sized spare, the tire iron slipped and sliced his forearm. In the same motion, Durago fell and scraped his arm on the pavement.

"Ow! Damn!"

"Are you okay?" Jan called out.

Durago looked to his arm. "Well, I've cut myself, but it doesn't look serious."

Ensuring everything was set, Durago stowed the tools, mounted the damaged tire on the tailgate, and closed up the back of the Jeep.

Back at Jan's door he said, "All set. I'll send you a bill."

"Why don't you hop in?" Jan said. "I'll take you home."

"Nah, that's okay," Durago replied, motioning toward the Academy. "It's not far from here."

"No, I mean *my* home," Jan said. "Especially since you got cut. Let me clean and bandage you up. It's the least I can do."

Durago noticed Jan raising her eyebrows invitingly.

The two made small talk as the Jeep traversed the streets of Annapolis, to include a trip over the bridge from Spa Creek into Eastport. Jan asked about Warren; Durago asked about her class. They briefly reminisced about scuba diving. Durago recognized that Jan was in the driver's seat, both literally and figuratively, but he sensed a return to their physical relationship.

Jan turned off the Jeep's engine and then the headlights. There was enough ambient light from the lamps dotting the marina that Durago noted a pensive look on her face.

"Uh, have you changed your mind?"

"No, no," she said, "I was just waiting for the rain to let up a little. I'm sorry; I guess I got a little lost in thought."

"So, what . . . this is a romantic spot to bring someone—marina parking lot overlooking Annapolis and the Academy?"

"What? Oh, no . . . no. I'm gonna take you on board *Quantum Meriut*."

"A boat? Wow, okay, so I'm definitely getting laid."

"Excuse me?" Jan said with a laugh, dropping her chin as she looked at him.

"Yeah, you obviously don't want the neighbors to see me, so that means there's no pretense of innocence in your mind. You're gonna bandage me up, and then we're gonna throw down—on a boat, too. This has a whole 'Indiana Jones and Marion Ravenwood on the *Bantu Wind*' feel to it.'"

"What?"

"You've even got a pretty dress on and everything."

"I live here, you sonofabitch."

Now it was Durago's turn to be surprised. "What?!"

"I live on a boat."

"Oh, shit, this gets better all the time. I'm seeing a girl who lives on a boat?"

"Woman, asshole. You are so lucky that I realize you're kidding."

Once they were below, Jan did patch up Durago first. Then she gave a quick tour of the *Quantum Meriut*. It was fortuitous that it ended in her cabin.

Looking into the head Durago said, "You know, I'm pretty rank. I should shower."

"Go ahead," Jan replied, smiling. "Everything you need is in there."

Durago was surprised by the water pressure, and though it was a tight fit with the john, the water felt good.

When he was finished he called out, "Jan, you gotta towel?"

The door opened. Jan was there in a black silk wrap, holding a terry cloth towel. She grinned at him a moment, then began to dry him off. Before she could finish he scooped her up and carried her to the berth. He playfully pulled the belt open on her robe, then began kissing her on her thighs and stomach. Jan arched her back and called, "Oh, my . . . hurry!"

Durago stopped and looked in her eyes.

"I'm serious—I want you right fucking now."

As Durago positioned himself, Jan put one hand over her head to brace herself. The other reached to help guide him.

Instead of leaving the party right away, Tripp had stepped back up to the bar. Fabulous Ferren muscled in next to him.

"Hey, Jagman. A bunch of us are going to the Fleet Reserve. Wanna go?"

"Shuure," Tripp slurred, "Can I ride with you?"

"No sweat, man."

Within twenty minutes, Tripp was with Ferren and a number of his classmates on the Fleet Reserve Club's rooftop deck, overlooking Annapolis Harbor. By now ties were loosened and a few jackets were missing. Ferren wore a party shirt with print sleeves, a pattern of multicolored bears. Tripp thought it was a Grateful Dead logo.

Most of the club's clientele was enlisted retirees. One with a blue, ship's-style ball cap with the words "Korean War Veteran" joined them on the roof.

"Do you need another drink, Lieutenant?" he asked Tripp through nicotine-stained teeth.

"Sure, Senior Chief. Thanks."

The old sailor waved at one of the waitresses, who nodded back knowingly. Then the vet's thousand-yard stare returned as his mind went back to the Sea of Japan. "So, we're taking blue water over the bow and the screws are going air bound. Really not good for the line shaft bearings and MRGs . . ."

Tripp tried to listen politely with Ferren. He saw that Gillman, the SWO in the group, seemed genuinely enthralled. Walking casually away from the conversation, Tripp looked across the harbor to Eastport where *Quantum Meriut* was moored. The rain had let up enough that he could make out the boat. Jan's Jeep was parked nearby.

The rain had all but stopped by the time Tripp reached the end of Jan's pier. He hesitated. The logical side of his brain told him this was a bad idea. Then he decided he should at least see if Jan was still up. He could call out if a light was on; he would only come aboard if she asked him. *I'll tell her we kept drinking. I was close by, so I thought I'd see if she was up.*

As he got alongside, he heard a sound. *She is up.* Then he heard it again. He realized the noise was involuntary, a release, an exclamation. Jan was having sex. *Probably that fucker Steve!*

Tripp tried to spy, to see them. But *Quantum Meriut* was completely dark. He imagined Jan on all fours, Steve taking her from behind. *Damn, she's bleating like she's getting screwed by Batman.* He remembered that Steve had a nice body, a brawny build from steadying himself in rough seas and hauling sails. Lean, powerful. *Guy's got staying power, too . . .*

Tripp departed with a feeling of disgust and defeat.

9

A LEGACY

March 27, 1992
0300
Quantum Meriut

"Don! Holy shit! What's wrong?"

It was the dream again, the nightmare.

Jan's expression was not discernible in the dark, but she put as much distance between them as she could without leaving the bed, as if he were a threat. *What had he done?*

Durago tasted the blood in his mouth and felt the stickiness of it on his chest. He had bitten down on his tongue hard and had scratched his chest again. He lay back down in Jan's berth and began to calm down.

"Jan, I need your patience. This is going to take a while to explain."

"What is it?"

Durago recounted the meeting with his company officer and Whorton's accusations. He could tell that she was still confused. Then he told Jan about his father, the man he never met but constantly tried to emulate. As his tale unfolded, Jan inched closer to him. Then she pulled the covers around them both. When he told her about the nightmares that haunted him during times of stress, frustration, or grief, she put her arms around him, stroking his chest, and held him.

"So, basically, my subconscious is punishing me for not living up to my father's legacy." The defeated finality of his tone made it clear that Durago's story left him naked, empty, and vulnerable.

After a period of silence he looked at the clock on a shelf lining the bulkhead. It read 0345.

"I have to go."

"Don . . ."

"Yeah?"

"I can help you with this conduct case. The main part of my job is to give legal advice to midshipmen, even those who are involved in conduct cases. Come by my office this week and I'll see what I can do to help you."

"Okay, I will, Jan. Thanks."

"Do you want me to drive you back?"

"Uh, know what?" Durago said as he looked to his cuts. "I think the bleeding's stopped. I'm seriously in the mood for a swim. It's not too far."

"Know what . . . I'll take a quick dip with you."

"It'll be cold," he said.

"Refreshing," Jan responded.

She slipped on a bathing suit as Durago quickly put his gym gear back on, including his waterlogged running shoes. Following Jan on deck, he saw that the rain had slowed to a light drizzle, almost a mist. Jan lowered the ladder so she could get back aboard *QM* easily. Durago stepped off the stern and splashed into the water. Just as he was about to start swimming, he heard a splash behind him.

Jan surfaced right next to him. "Come here, sailor," she cooed.

He embraced her.

Jan whispered in his ear, "This ladder will be our little secret, our little sign. Whenever it's down, lowered in the water, you know I'm aboard. Okay?"

"I'll invest in a pair of binoculars."

PART II
PLEBE YEAR

10

SIMPSON

 NOVEMBER 17, 1988
1148
BANCROFT HALL, ROOM 4014

"Twenty-Third Company, attention to announcements!"

Sitting at his desk, Durago raised his head upon hearing the company mate of the deck. He had been dozing.

"Noon meal formation goes inside due to inclement weather! I say again, noon meal formation goes inside due to inclement weather! That is all!"

Durago looked across his desk at his roommates. They were all diligently studying their rates, the required Plebe knowledge.

Thus far, James "Slim" Warren was the only one of the four that Durago got along with. He was an easygoing Texan who, like Durago, came to the Academy from a private boarding school. Slim Jim spent his previous four years at the Marine Military Academy and was therefore already intimately acquainted with a regimented life. None of the pressures of the Academy seemed to faze him.

Brendan McDougal was Slim's opposite. McDougal was very high-strung and took everything about Plebe Year too seriously. He reminded Durago of a hyperactive Chihuahua. The other Plebes in the company called McDougal a "sweat"—a guy who was always worried about his performance, almost to the point of panic—yet he seemed to rank high in the upperclass' esteem.

Although they had been through Plebe Summer and six weeks of the academic year together, Durago did not know Moeller very well yet. None of them did. Moeller was rarely in Bancroft Hall during the day. When he was around, he spent all of his time sleeping on the floor in the closet. Plebes were not authorized to touch their rack, the nautical term for bed, between 0700 and 2000. It was poetic justice, then, that the Plebes in 23rd Company dubbed him "the Mole."

Durago looked at his watch. It was 1148. "Damn it!" he yelled.

He bolted upright and donned his cover. As Durago headed out the door, he tucked his chin into his chest in a "brace," locking his elbows at his side with his forearms parallel to the deck. It was a requirement for all Plebes to "chop" while traversing the passageways of Bancroft Hall. He darted out and made an immediate 90-degree right-face, squaring the corner. "Go Navy, sir!" he shouted as he turned.

The Fourth Class (or "Plebe") Indoctrination System Manual stated that each fourth class midshipman could be required to report to a third class midshipman fifteen minutes prior to breakfast, and to a second class midshipman fifteen minutes prior to lunch, for professional instruction and development. It was at this time that the Plebes were tested on their professional knowledge, their "rates." Midshipman regulations also stipulated that upperclass could require any Plebes delinquent in their knowledge to "come around" to their room at other times as they saw fit to enhance this professional development. Thus, the instruction period was termed a "come-around."

Durago knocked on Midshipman Second Class Walter Simpson's door at 1150.

"What?!" he heard Simpson call out.

"Sir, Midshipman Fourth Class Durago, reporting as ordered, sir!"

"You're late! Hit a bulkhead!"

Durago performed an about-face, then a right-face. He took two steps and then performed another right-face. He was now facing the bulkhead just next to the second class' door. He hit the wall hard and performed another about-face, sounding off as Simpson emerged.

"Sir, Midshipman Fourth Class Durago, nine-two-two-three-one-four, Twenty-Third Company, Second Platoon, First Squad, Beat Army, sir!"

Simpson stepped into the passageway. Durago vehemently disliked his second class. *This guy's a pain in the ass,* he thought to himself. Simpson held a section of masking tape rolled up inside out. He taped himself off in preparation for the noon meal formation, brushing and tapping himself, removing all lint from his navy blue uniform with the adhesive.

Nobody liked Simpson, not even his own classmates. He was a fastidious prima donna whose uniform appearance was always immaculate. Added to this, Simpson's blonde locks gave him a "Hitler Youth" appearance. This theme carried over into his demeanor—Simpson was famous for inventing new and imaginative ways to harass the Plebes.

"Give me your pro book," Simpson demanded.

Durago removed his cover and pulled the six-by-eight-inch professional book from it. The Plebes were required to learn new professional material from this book each week. They were even tested on the knowledge every Saturday. The Naval Academy placed a lot of emphasis on its professional knowledge, which separated it from other academic institutions. Failing a chemistry quiz or two went nearly unnoticed at the Academy; maybe it would draw a comment from the professor. But fail two weekly professional quizzes and the Plebe went to a Battalion Performance Board, which could result in separation. Durago was already sensitive to this term—separation—a more personal and severe definition of expulsion. It was not enough to simply kick someone out; it was made clear that you were no longer *one of us.* You were *separated.*

Simpson flipped to the current week's section in the book. "Okay, Durago, what's the topic this week?"

Durago stared ahead blankly.

"I'll give you a clue: it's a ship."

"Sir, the topic this week is the *Ticonderoga*-class ship."

"Cruiser."

"Cruiser, sir."

"Try again."

Durago visibly sighed.

"Am I pissing you off, Durago? Do you need to be somewhere?" Simpson said with disdain.

"No, sir."

"Well, then stop rolling your eyes in exasperation. In fact, do you have a Form Two in your cover?"

Midshipman regulations stipulated that any midshipman could be brought up on disciplinary action submitted to his chain of command via a Form Two. There was a standing order throughout the Brigade that all Plebes maintain a Form Two in their cover to ensure that any upperclass could easily "fry" the Plebe, put them on report. In fact, the Plebes usually filled the paperwork out themselves at the upperclass' bidding.

"No, sir."

"No?!" Simpson said incredulously.

"No, sir."

"Why not?"

"No excuse, sir."

"Tell ya what—bring around a Form Two for disrespect and another for failure to obey an order. *Capiche*?"

"Yes, sir."

"Honestly, Durago, you're the only Plebe I've ever known who's had to bring around a Form Two for not having a Form Two."

Simpson threw the pro book on the deck and began inspecting Durago. He talked as he scrutinized Durago's appearance.

"You're a piece of work. You're late to come-around, you don't have a Form Two, and you're pissed at me when *you* don't know the pro topic this week. On top of that, your cover has smudges on it, your haircut is unsat, your belt buckle looks like shit, and your shoes aren't shined. What did you tape off with, anyway . . . a cat?! Cripes, the only way I know you edge-dressed your soles is that there are black marks all down my passageway."

Simpson stood close in front of Durago so that they were eye to eye. Durago smelled the sharp medicine smell of Simpson's mouthwash.

"Get that brace in there, Durago. What are you, a girl? Get it in. I wanna see chins. Hell, I'd fry you for the constellation of zits you got on your face, if I could. You been bathing, Durago?"

"Yes, sir."

"Well, good, 'cause guess what, buddy? You are in the hot seat today. Brooks is going to be all over you, and you are not ready. Damn, you don't even know what the topic is!"

"I'll remember, sir."

"You're screwed and I got no sympathy. Rig it."

Durago brought his arms up and placed both thumbs on his chin. He folded his fingers behind his neck, touching the tips, "rigging" his brace. It hurt.

Simpson picked up the pro book and held it out in front of Durago. "Touch 'em."

Durago kept his hands in position and brought his elbows together, grasping the book with them.

"Don't you dare drop it, Durago."

Simpson looked up and down the hallway. Plebes could be heard chopping throughout company area, returning from their come-arounds. Durago's breathing became labored. *Why am I here?*

As if he read the Plebe's thoughts, Simpson leaned even closer to Durago and whispered, "Durago, you don't even wanna be here, do you? I'll bet you got applications in to some pansy Ivy League, don'tcha? Well, I suggest you go. Yep, if I was you, I'd think about quitting. We don't want you here."

Simpson stepped back and surveyed Durago again. He shook his head in disgust. "Unrig."

Durago dropped his arms with a "Beat Army, sir!" His pro book slapped on the deck.

"Shove off."

"Aye, aye, sir."

"And clean my deck."

"Aye, aye, sir."

Durago picked up his book and chopped back to his room.

11

NOON MEAL

 NOVEMBER 17, 1988
1220
SMOKE HALL, KING HALL

The herd of midshipmen filled Smoke Hall. They moved to the back of the hall and down two sets of stairs, descending into King Hall, the Naval Academy wardroom.

Like its counterpart, Bancroft Hall, King Hall is the largest dining room in the world. Fully 4,500 midshipmen, the entire Brigade, can sit and eat at once during the academic year. Each table in King Hall is built to seat an entire squad. Two people sit at the head and foot of the table, four on either side. The wardroom is supported by an enormous staff, and it requires its own dairy farm.

Midshipman Ensign Brooks sat at the head of the table belonging to 23rd Company, 2nd Platoon, 1st Squad. Sharing this position was Midshipman in Ranks Smith. At the other end were two Youngsters, midshipmen third class that Durago recognized had been Plebes just a few months before. All the Plebes sat to Brooks' left, the upperclass across from them on Smith's right. In this way, the Plebes could be effectively berated throughout the meal.

Durago sat in the "hot seat," directly to the squad leader's left. It would be his job to ensure all upperclass at his end of the table had their glasses full, that they got seconds on demand, and that they did not bother his classmates. He could effectively set the tone of the meal for his classmates. *Shit-screen for a day,* he thought. To make the event more interesting, Simpson chose to sit directly across from Durago. Thus, Durago knew he would get attention from both directions.

"Durago!" Brooks called out.

"Sir!" Durago snapped his head and looked squarely at the upper-class next to him at the end of the table.

"How are you coming with your pro knowledge this week?"

"I'll find out, sir."

"Wonderful. What's the topic?"

"Sir, the topic this week is the . . ." There was a pregnant pause.

"Don't tell me you don't know."

Durago felt himself turning red with embarrassment.

"See, I told you," Simpson said from across the table.

"Sir, the topic this week is the *Ticonderoga*-class cruiser."

"Ball one. What are the weapons systems on the *Ticonderoga*-class cruiser, fore to aft?"

"Sir, the weapons systems fore to aft on the *Ticonderoga*-class cruiser are: Mark forty-one VLS forward; five-inch, fifty-four-caliber gun forward; two twenty-millimeter close-in weapons systems port and starboard; harpoon missile canister; Mark forty-one VLS aft; and five-inch fifty-four aft, sir."

"Strike one."

Simpson looked down the table at the other second class. He held his arms out, gesturing toward Durago. *See, I told you guys; Durago is screwed up.* Durago noticed the other upperclass at his end of the table were shaking their heads in disbelief.

Brooks' voice got softer, reminding Durago of a guidance counselor. He knew that Brooks was trying to be a mentor. "This isn't hard, Durago. Think about what you said and try again."

"Durago!"

He snapped his head again, looking directly ahead at Simpson, keeping his eyes forward, or "in the boat." "Sir!"

"Aren't you going to offer me more to drink?" The voice came from Midshipman Second Class George Gladstone, Simpson's roommate, sitting to Simpson's right. Durago was almost flummoxed that he was demanding service. Gladstone had a reputation for being even-keeled. He had rarely, if ever, demanded anything of Durago.

"Mister Gladstone, sir, would you like more orange drink?"

"Obviously."

The Plebe quickly scanned the table for the telltale blue carton with gold striping and the Naval Academy seal emblazoned on it. He grabbed it and handed it to Gladstone.

As Gladstone poured, white milk mixed with the orange elixir.

"Dammit, Durago!" he said. "You did that on purpose!"

"No, sir. Sorry, sir."

"Yeah, you are sorry . . . give me your glass."

Durago handed over his empty, unused glass. Gladstone stood up, looking down the length of the table for the carton of orange drink. Durago listened a moment to his classmates being grilled by Simpson.

"What's the second general order of a sentry?"

"What is the range of the five-inch, fifty-four?"

"Tell me about the GE LM twenty-five-hundred engine."

"Durago—*Tico*, try again," Brooks said, shoving a forkful of salad in his mouth.

"Sir, the weapons systems on the *Ticonderoga*-class cruiser are: five-inch, fifty-four-caliber gun forward; Mark forty-one VLS forward; close-in weapons systems port and starboard; harpoon missile canisters; Mark forty-one VLS aft; and five-inch, fifty-four-caliber gun aft, sir."

"Swing and a miss. Are you guessing?"

"No, sir."

"McDougal!" Brooks yelled down the table to McDougal on the other end.

"Sir!"

"Weapons systems on the *Tico*—go."

"Sir, request permission to not bilge my classmate."

Brooks smirked at McDougal's attempt at classmate loyalty. By showing up Durago, he would be "bilging" him.

"Do you know it?"

"Yes, sir!"

"Then you've already bilged him, haven't you? Why do you know it and he doesn't? Correct me if I'm wrong, but not only is Durago your classmate, your companymate, and your squadmate, he's your *roommate!*"

The table was suddenly silent as everyone looked to McDougal, who had a frown on his face.

"Give it to me," said Brooks.

"Sir, the weapons systems on the *Ticonderoga*-class cruiser, fore to aft, are: five-inch, fifty-four-caliber gun forward; Mark forty-one VLS forward, twenty-millimeter close-in weapons systems port and starboard amidships; Mark thirty-two torpedo tubes port and starboard amidships; Mark forty-one VLS aft; five-inch, fifty-four-caliber gun aft; and harpoon missile canisters aft on the port side, sir."

"And McDougal knocks it over the bleachers. Good one, McD."

"Thank you, sir."

"Don't thank me, McDougal. Are you a kiss-ass? Are you a smack?"

"No, sir."

"McDougal, what's different about hull numbers forty-seven through fifty-one?"

"Sir, they have Mark twenty-six launchers fore and aft instead of the VLS."

"Correct. Durago, know where your mistake was?"

"Sir, I put the harpoons amidships instead of aft."

"And what else?"

"I'll find out, sir."

"Weren't you listening to McDougal? He just told you the answer!"

Durago just stared at his squad leader.

"I don't know which one pisses me off more: the one who knows his stuff and won't share it, or the one who doesn't seem to care enough to try," Brooks said to no one in particular.

"Duurrrrraaago!"

"Sir!" he said, facing Simpson again.

"My glass is empty! What's your problem, boy? Pay attention!"

"Aye, aye, sir."

Back in the room, Durago slid books into his bag. He heard McDougal chopping down the passageway. He stepped into the room and immediately uncovered.

"Don, I'm sorry."

"Don't worry about it."

"Seriously, let me help you. We'll spend some time tonight studying this stuff."

"Sure, whatever."

"Don'tcha want to get these guys off your back?"

Durago shrugged.

McDougal looked frustrated. "You don't really care about this stuff, do you? What the hell are you doing here, anyway?"

Without thinking, Durago responded, "I dunno."

"What's this?"

"Huh?"

McDougal handed Durago a piece of paper. It was a note from Simpson.

> *Durago,*
> *This room is UNSAT! You will have an inspection*
> *on Saturday at 1000.*
> *Midn 2/c Simpson*

"Great," said Durago. "When is this guy going to leave me alone?"

"As soon as you stop giving him a reason to shit on you!" McDougal blurted.

"Yeah, but on a Saturday morning?"

"Simpson's got the duty. He'll be able to shit on us all weekend long."

12

Absent

Midshipman Lieutenant Kevin O'Rourke loved being the 23rd Company Commander. He felt it was a bigger leadership challenge than being a battalion or even the brigade commander. In his mind, the Brigade Staff was really figureheads, liaison with the Naval Academy faculty and staff. As company commander, O'Rourke was on the deckplates. He had to earn and maintain the respect of his peers, as well as the respect of the subordinate midshipmen in 23rd.

O'Rourke entered the office of Lieutenant Commander Brown, the 23rd Company Officer, for his daily meeting. Brown wore the wings of a naval aviator. He spent most of his career flying the largest helicopter in the Navy's inventory, the MH-53E Sea Dragon. Similar to the CH-53E Super Stallion, the Sea Dragon could be used for heavy lift but was primarily intended for mine-hunting and sweeping. O'Rourke liked the guy because he was calm and fair in dealing with the mids.

"Hi, Kevin."

"Morning, sir. How'd the meeting with the battalion officer go?"

"Fine, nothing new. Listen, I've looked at some of these Form Twos, and I'm going to let you adjudicate most of them."

"Okay, sir."

"Am I remembering that you want to talk about one of the Plebes?"

"Yes, sir. In fact, most of those report chits are on him."

"Durago."

"Yes, sir."

"I figured it was a Plebe Year thing. I've noticed Simpson messing with him in the hall."

"Yes, sir. Simpson is hard core, a flamer . . . mostly because he caught a lot of attention himself when he was a Plebe."

"Is Simpson violating regulations?"

"No, sir. I mean, I don't agree with his leadership style, but he isn't breaking any rules, per se. He's . . . he's just one of those hard core guys, sir."

"So what's the story on Durago?"

"Well, sir, . . . and this is where Simpson perhaps has it right . . . Durago doesn't really show any motivation to be here. The upperclass in Brooks' squad, even the Youngsters, say that he isn't engaged; he won't play the game."

"This is not a game, Mister O'Rourke."

"Roger that, sir. My point is that he exerts no effort. Let's compare him to Hall. Hall is screwed up, but he's trying. His upperclass feel like they can work with him. He's dumb, but he's motivated."

"So how do we motivate Durago? Somebody, somewhere, decided this kid belonged here. Tell me how we're going to bring him around."

"I've already thought of that, sir, and I have a solution."

"Yes?"

"Washington."

He never imagined that going to class would be an escape. Durago had always been a good student, but he really had not enjoyed school. At Annapolis it was different. The upperclass left Plebes alone when they were in class. It was like he was in another world. Or was it that Bancroft Hall was the parallel universe?

When in class, Durago felt normal. Often the only indication that he was still at the Academy was that everyone around him wore uniforms: the same navy blue shirts and trousers, ties tucked between the second and third buttons, accented by gold name tapes and insignia, and white covers when outdoors or in some type of military formation. This illusion started to fade during Durago's last class period each day. As time ticked toward the end of his fifth-period class, Durago began to get a sick feeling in his stomach. He was not looking forward to going back to the hall to face the onslaught of Simpson and the other upperclass. It reminded Durago of riding on the bus when he was in grade school and the neighborhood bully often picked on him.

The professor droned on about covalent and ionic bonding. Durago half-listened and took notes. He had completed a chemistry course at Collfield Academy, so he knew that he would earn a "B" in this course with no effort. If he studied he would get an "A."

The bell marking the end of class sounded. The midshipmen in the lecture hall all jumped and scrambled to leave.

"Don't forget, quiz on Monday!" the professor called out.

In a moment Durago was the only one left, plodding along, trying to put off the inevitable return to Bancroft Hall and the clutches of the upperclass. Some days, he would take most of this last period of the day, some of the only free time he had in his week, to meander back to Bancroft. Suddenly, he paused. *I gotta stop this. I need to change this up, do something different.* Durago looked at his watch and decided that he would go to study in the library, Nimitz Hall. That way he could postpone returning to company area while improving his grades. He felt a little better.

Durago sat in a study carrel on the second floor of Nimitz, next to a window that overlooked College Creek, reading his naval history book. Like much of the Academy, Nimitz was built on reclaimed land. The building was slowly sinking into its neighboring estuary. Academy legend held that the Army Corps of Engineers team that designed and built the library had not accounted for the weight of the books. The jokes about this architectural snafu went both directions. Either the Corps of Engineers was incompetent, or the team had played a great practical joke on the Navy.

Durago read about the sinking of the *Maine*, which precipitated the Spanish-American War. Durago remembered from his *Reef Points*, the Plebe Summer predecessor of his pro book, that now the foremast was not a half-mile away, near the point of land where the Severn River started to mix with the Chesapeake. *Maine*'s aftermast stood as a memorial at Arlington National Cemetery, earning her the distinction among the Brigade as the "longest ship in the Navy." Durago thought about life aboard a dreadnaught at the turn of the century. Suddenly, he heard a *boom*. He looked up, and then heard several in succession. *Boom . . . boom . . . boom, boom, boom.*

It was a drum. Scanning down the creek in the direction of Worden Field and the red-brick housing known as "Commander's Row," Durago noted the Naval Academy Drum and Bugle Corps marching toward the parade deck. He could see that several companies were already in position, lined up and looking as still as permanent fixtures from five hundred yards away.

Parade practice.

Though it was unnecessary now, Durago looked at his watch. The sick feeling that he was working to postpone now rushed into his stomach. He had lost track of time and failed to return to the hall in time for practice. He was going to get fried again—this time for UA, "unauthorized absence." To try to bolt back to the hall, grab his rifle, and join them now would be impossible. Durago watched the Brigade as the mids continued lining up on the field.

The mids seemed to move only from their hips down, legs snapping and feet pounding with each beat of the drum. As each company turned, the company commander would call out, "Guide online!" Shifting his weapon from shoulder arms to port arms, the midshipman in the front rank on the extreme right would then run ahead to a plate in the grass that denoted where the company was to form. The company would then "guide" to that position, so that when it stopped the guide was back in his position in the front row.

Look at them, Durago thought. *Straight, even, regimented.* From this distance the navy blue uniforms and white covers made the Brigade look like chocolate cake with white icing.

Durago sat back and sighed. The sickness in his gut rose to his throat. He felt like crying and swallowed hard to prevent his emotion from running out. As he watched the Brigade go through all the steps for a formal parade—rehearsing and repeating sections under the tutelage of Captain Sharpe and two or three Marine noncommissioned officers he did not know—Durago realized that Simpson and McDougal were right: he was not one of them. They all got it. They knew why they were here. He knew *how* he arrived at Annapolis, but he did not know *why*.

"Brigade, seats!" Simpson stationed himself across from Durago and started in right away. "Durago, you take the frickin' cake, man."

Durago smirked at Simpson's comment.

"You think this is funny?"

"No, sir."

"What're you smiling about?"

"No excuse, sir."

"No . . . I really wanna know."

Durago noticed that all of the mids at the table were silently listening for his answer. It was clear that everyone in the company was aware of his absence. It appeared they all surmised it was not a legitimate excuse, but an entertaining faux pas—a story to be relayed to classmates and friends. *"Dude, you'll never believe this Plebe in my squad. He is so effed up."*

Evening meal had a strange dichotomy. On the one hand, it was the most formal affair of the day. All midshipmen were required to don service dress blues for evening meal formation and the subsequent repast. This meant switching their navy blue class uniform for a white shirt with a navy blue necktie and double-breasted jacket. Gold-braid stripes on the lower sleeve of the jacket replaced the gold collar devices signifying rank. The uniform was complete with ribbons and warfare devices. Many midshipmen had jump wings from airborne training or a scuba pin from attending dive school during the summer. But seeing a mid with jump wings and two rows of decorations usually denoted real time in the fleet.

Contrasted with the more formal attire, some of the Brigade was noticeably absent for any variety of excused evening activities, from sports to club activities. Additionally, by this time of the day, minds were starting to focus on studying. As a result, the Plebes drew less attention during evening meal because many upperclass wanted to simply eat and depart for their rooms or study hall. Sometimes they went entire meals without any banter with the fourth class at all. Before it even started, Durago knew this meal was going to suck. At a minimum, Simpson was going to go ballistic because of Durago's absence from parade practice.

"We're waiting, Durago."

"Sir, I thought the Brigade looked like cake."

"What?!"

Now Durago grimaced with embarrassment. "When I saw the Brigade marching onto Worden Field from Nimitz today, sir, I thought it looked like chocolate cake with icing. That's why I was smiling at your comment, sir."

Simpson's jaw dropped. Some of the mids at the table were laughing.

"Durago," said Smith, "you some kinda poet? I think maybe you belong over at St. John's. What do you think?"

"No, sir."

Durago almost winced at the insult. Annapolitans sometimes remark that within their city limits, the nation's most liberal and most conservative institutions of higher learning sit side by side. Literally across King George Street from Navy, St. John's College follows a "great books" curriculum. The school has no majors, no assignments, no exams. Students read the great works of Western society and discuss them with professors, called "tutors."

Smith was relentless. "They've got a heck of a croquet team over there. Do you know the difference between a Johnnie and the homeless?"

"No, sir."

"Johnnie's got a Frisbee."

All the mids joined in the laughter now, except Simpson. Durago was particularly embarrassed that Smith was deriding him. Like Gladstone, the Firstie had a reputation of being very relaxed. It made his mockery all the more painful.

"Just think, man . . . tie-dye shirt . . . grow some dreadlocks. It could be your scene, man."

The laughter rose. Durago noticed that even his classmates could not help joining in on Smith's joke. Recognizing that they were laughing not only at the joke but at the premise that Durago was more suited for St. John's than Annapolis, his shame radiated again. He squeezed his mouth tight, trying to keep from crying.

The food arrived, giving him a reprieve. He worked with his classmates to pass things around the table and ensure the upperclass had all of their needs met. Simpson took a couple of bites of mashed potatoes. Thinking perhaps the onslaught was over, Durago started to eat. After one forkful went into his mouth, Simpson spoke up.

"Durago, it's this simple, man. You are at the United States Naval Academy. You had to go through some shit to get here, and yet you don't seem to want it. You don't even care enough to be on time to the most simple of evolutions. The only conclusion that I can come to is that you never applied in the first damn place. I think your daddy did . . . is that what happened? Did your daddy get you in here?"

"Yes, sir."

"He ain't the only one, Simp," Gladstone interjected.

"Fuck you, George."

Simpson dropped his fork and looked Durago directly in the eye. "Bring around a Form Two, Durago, for unauthorized absence. You're making this very easy for me. In fact, the only way it could be easier is if you just quit. What do you think? Wanna be a Johnnie?"

"No, sir."

"I don't think they have to show up for class or anything, man . . . think on it."

"How does that jodie go?" one of the Youngsters asked.

"'I wanna study Che Guevara . . .

"'. . .I'm a left-wing kinda guy.

"'. . .I wear socks with my sandals,

"'. . .all my shirts are tie-dye.

"'. . . I don't take pens to class,

"'. . .I don't take written tests.

"'. . .I don't want a real degree,

"'. . . so I went to S-J-C.'"

Now it was Simpson's turn to smile. Then he shook his head and got up from the table, leaving most of his meal unfinished.

The four roommates stood nervously, waiting for Simpson to inspect their room. They had spent Friday evening and Saturday morning covering every possible surface and facet of cleanliness imaginable. The personal lockers were open for inspection. All shirts and underwear were folded in precise, six-inch-wide squares. Socks were rolled together and had "smiles." The grey tile deck was stripped with a razor blade and waxed—twice. All racks were pulled taut, with hospital corners and blankets folded just so. Hanging clothing was placed very neatly in the lockers with same uniforms together, left to right, black to white. The books on the two-man desks were lined up with all spines even, left to right, tallest to smallest. The mirrors were spotless. So were the sink, the windows, and the blinds. They were ready.

Simpson startled them when he stepped in the door, despite the fact that they were waiting for him. The roommates popped to attention and sounded off, led by McDougal. "Sir, Midshipman Fourth Class McDougal, nine-two-one-four-two-three. Room four-zero-one-four standing by for inspection, sir."

Simpson said nothing. He stood in the door and scanned the room. *He can't find anything wrong,* Durago said to himself.

The second class picked up a black sock from the desk. He stepped in the shower and rubbed it on the marble wall. It was covered with soap scum. He dropped it on the desk, giving Durago a look that said, *"One."*

Next he opened one of the desk drawers. He pulled the drawer out and set it on the table. Then he reached in the drawer's now-empty slot and pulled out a handful of dust and dropped it on the desk.

"Two."

Simpson produced a penlight from his pocket. He got on his knees and shined it onto the floor under the desk. "Mister Durago, look at this deck."

Durago broke from attention and joined Simpson on the floor. The deck under the desk was filthy.

"It's dirty, sir."

"Wax the *whole* deck for inspection, gentlemen."

"Aye, aye, sir," the four said in unison. Their voices betrayed that they all thought it was a bullshit hit.

"Durago, bring around a Form Two for failing room inspection."

"Sir, I'm the Midshipman in Charge of Room; it's my responsibility," said McDougal.

"Understand, McDougal. Nonetheless, I directed Durago to be prepared for this inspection. He is responsible."

Slim began to protest. "But, sir, we all—"

"Enough, Warren. I admire your loyalty, but that's enough. Durago, bring around a Form Two."

"Aye, aye, sir.

The Plebes were now visibly angry. Simpson sensed this. On the way out the door he slid the door's bolt to the locked position and rubbed his finger on it. He held it up, showing them a black smudge.

"Four."

Slim slammed the door shut; Durago slumped in his chair; McDougal clutched his heart and fell on his rack in a mock death; and Mole slipped off his shoes, pulled a sleeping bag from his locker, and disappeared into the closet.

Slim shrugged his shoulders and said, "You know, Don, sometimes you have to laugh to keep from crying."

"That guy is a prick," remarked McDougal toward the ceiling. "And he's trying to run you outta here."

Durago said nothing.

"Know what, Donny-boy?" McDougal continued. "I think you're gonna let him."

13

THE BRICK

NOVEMBER 20, 1988
2200
BANCROFT HALL, 4-0

It was a Sunday ritual throughout the Brigade—"The Brick." None of
the mids knew how this tradition started, but none of them could set-
tle down to study until they found out who got The Brick, the award
given to the mid who had dragged the ugliest date over the weekend. It
seemed to be a matter of natural law that if you had a date with a dog,
it would get back to the Plebes.

As the upperclass came back from evening meal, the Plebes
dressed in their bathrobes or PT gear and began a conga line around
the 4-0 quadrangle. Nguyen was the first in line. He held The Brick—
a cinder block—on a pillow, as if he were presenting a crown at cor-
onation. The Plebes behind him chanted, "Who gets The Brick? Who
gets The Brick?"

Upperclass followed the parade. Many already knew who was to
be the honored recipient. They prepared to rumble the Plebes, an ille-
gal and very important part of the ritual.

The Plebes' chanting became louder, and their excitement rose
with each step. "Who gets The Brick?! Who gets The Brick?!"

As they got closer to the victim's room, it became a battle cry.
"WHO GETS THE BRICK?! WHO GETS THE BRICK?!"

The victim was Gladstone, Simpson's roommate. Suddenly, the
Plebes broke ranks and burst through the door. Nguyen tried to present The Brick with a formal speech.

"Mister Gladstone, sir, the Class of 1992—"

Gladstone vaulted out of his chair and tackled Nguyen, knocking him and The Brick to the floor. They began to grapple. Several second classes emerged from hiding places in the shower and closet, armed with buckets of water. The first seven Plebes in the room were doused. Hall, soaked to the bone now, scrambled and retrieved the trophy. He threw The Brick on Gladstone's rack, ensuring that he received it officially. Durago and four others sprayed shaving cream all over Gladstone's bodyguards and the whole of the room. A full-fledged rumble began.

With both classes engaged in combat, the battle spilled into the hallway. It would have appeared as a bar fight to an outsider. To a close observer, however, it would be obvious that no really tough blows were thrown. It was just a friendly way for all to release tension.

Unfortunately, the fun would not last. The mate of the deck came down the passageway. "Stop it, guys!" she yelled. "Come on, guys, stoooooop!"

She got no response. The mate realized that she was using the wrong words. "The OOD is coming!"

In an instant everyone looked up at her. She said it again in a calmer voice. "Everyone skedaddle. The Fry Guy is Officer of the Day, and he's in Steerage right now," she said, pointing to the student restaurant at the end of 4-0, beneath the rotunda, "—and he's coming this way."

Mids sprinted everywhere like roaches running from a kitchen light. Many disappeared instantly into the recesses of their Mother Bancroft. Someone had Durago in a headlock. He had heard the mate's call, and froze. When he was released, Simpson was standing in the room's entrance, looking directly at him. Simpson was in uniform, covered with shaving cream. His face was red and flushed. The second class was panting with anger.

The last of the rumblers filed out of the room, joining the escape. They could sense that Simpson did not approve of the Sunday night tomfoolery. Durago made no move to go with them. Simpson's expression told him that he was not excused.

"What's going on, Durago?"

"Sir, we gave Mister Gladstone The Brick, sir."

"You assaulted a superior officer."

"Sir, I—"

"Shut up, you sea lawyer."

"Aye, aye, sir."

"Who else was involved in this display of cowardice?"

"Sir, request permission to not bilge my classmates."

"Horsepucky, who else was involved?"

Simpson knew full well that every Plebe and all of Simpson's class-mates who were on 4-o during the rumble participated.

"Sir, I will not bilge my classmates."

"Then you'll be fried."

Gladstone looked up from his prone position on the deck. "Hey, Walter, that may not be the best move. If Lieutenant Commander Brown gets wind of this, a bunch of people will go down. I know in general he's cool, but he's not a grad and doesn't always understand this stuff."

Simpson looked back to Durago. "Fine. Well, then, Durago, unless you produce the names of all of your classmates who were involved, at 2230 you will march around Goat Court ten times."

"Aye, aye, sir."

"Now, shove off."

Goat Court was the square cutout in the middle of fourth wing. If mids ventured into the court, they could only escape through the windows of someone who pitied them. The week before the Navy–Air Force football game, an Air Force cadet on exchange was captured by some Plebes and tossed into Goat Court. Durago had joined the other mids in catcalls and mockery. The situation degenerated quickly, and soon the cadet was pelted with fruit, old milk, and garbage. As Durago sat down on his rack, he thought of that cadet.

"What's wrong?" queried Slim.

"I'm going to march Goat Court before lights out tonight."

"Why?"

"Simpson is punishing me for the rumble. He wants me to bilge everyone involved."

Simpson and Gladstone worked together to clean up all of the shav-ing cream in their room. "Next time you go hogging you need to tell me," Simpson teased.

"I didn't think she was that bad."

The roommates laughed together. The Brick now stood in the middle of their desk like a trophy on display. Following company tradition, Gladstone would tote it around in his book bag all week until someone else earned the block. He would undoubtedly assist the fourth class in finding his successor.

Gladstone spoke again. "You know, Walter, you have been dishing it out on that kid pretty heavy. There are a lot of other Plebes who would have broken down by now. "

"Maybe. Still, the kid doesn't get it. I get the impression Durago doesn't care about this place. He doesn't appreciate what it means to be here, or why he's here."

"Not everyone is a general's son—"

Simpson gave Gladstone a sharp look. He hated that label. Gladstone knew it, and continued.

"Or a grad's son, or lived in the Yard—twice."

"Okay, you made your point. My point is that the kid is a screwup and I'm gonna get him."

It pained Simpson that his desire to attend the Academy was genuine but everyone assumed it was at his father's direction. This frustration was made worse by the fact that Simpson hoped to become a submariner, something his father abhorred. Thus, while embracing a life of service and sacrifice, to include the Spartan life at Annapolis, his father saw only rejection and rebellion.

"My son wants to be a *sub*-mariner," he had heard the general say over the clinking of scotch-buttered ice at a barbeque the previous summer. "You know how it is with those gays—I mean guys. A hundred men go down, fifty couples come up!"

Life in a Marine Corps family was very demanding. Simpson grew up at a time when in order for the father to perform well, the wife and children had to perform well also. As an only child, Simpson sometimes felt like a houseboy, fetching beers or pouring drinks for his father's guests. His father always wanted him to excel so that Simpson's athletic or academic performance could be commented on whenever he came into view.

"You know, Walt made the varsity soccer team," the elder Simpson would relay in a tone that implied he had something to do with it. "We think the team could go all the way to state this year."

We? Simpson had thought when his father made that comment.

Of course, this was all history now, after his decision to become a submariner. The general either made a mockery of his son's career choice or did not mention it at all. In reality, Simpson's decision was not a rejection of his father, but an attraction to the leadership responsibility and challenges of undersea warfare. It was dubbed the "Silent Service" because, by and large, a submarine's crew was cut off from the rest of the world, literally blind and nearly deaf, while surviving in the harshest and most unforgiving environs. He imagined that he would one day rise to the highest-paid position in the U.S. Navy, that of commanding officer of a ballistic missile submarine. *Could there be any mission more important than maneuvering a 560-foot* Ohio-*class boomer toward Soviet waters, while trying to avoid their attack boats?*

Simpson knew he would get his wish. He had no problems excelling academically, a realm in which he was at the top of his class. Militarily, however, he did not do so well. He garnered more than his share of unwanted attention during Plebe Year, principally because he was a general's son. Then anytime he failed under this higher-than-average scrutiny, the blood in the water attracted all the sharks. Thus, Simpson became his company's shit-screen, filtering demerits from his classmates that led to poor conduct and military performance grades. This problem continued into his Youngster and Second Class years because, he was certain, he was held to a higher standard by peers and superiors alike. For example, Simpson was late one time getting back from a weekend at Wilson College, owing to an accident outside Hagerstown, Maryland. He got fried and served restriction—yet he knew of several similar cases where mids in the company were let off essentially scot-free. When he protested, Lieutenant Commander Brown said, "Each case is different, Walter, and this is how I'm evaluating this one."

At 2230 Durago propped open the window to Goat Court. He stepped through and shut it behind him. He started his march around the perimeter, hoping against hope that nobody would notice him. In his mind he calculated that, with his luck, he would make it down one length before the whole Brigade began to pelt him. Simpson was probably calling all the companies on Goat Court right now.

"My dirtbag Plebe is going around the court!"

Durago only walked past four windows before the next one in front of him opened. Mann popped his head out. He smiled at Durago and stepped through the window into the court. Potok and Hall were right behind him.

"What are you guys doing?" queried Durago.

"We're following you."

"What?"

Something caught Durago's eye. He looked across the court. Another set of his classmates was entering from the other side. "Guys, thanks, really . . ."

Suddenly, there was a call that echoed, "March, Plebes!"

"Oh, shit, someone saw us," said Durago.

"You heard 'em!" said Mann.

Mann, Potok, and Hall began marching around the quad, singing the Marine Corps hymn. Durago followed behind them. He felt better with the company. As they made their way around, more windows opened and more of the Plebes joined in. By his first full tour around, Durago could see that every Plebe in 23rd Company had joined them. The Plebes opposite him, led by Slim, started a different chant.

"'Ninety-Two, sir! Ninety-Two, sir!"

The onslaught began. The Plebes drowned out all verbal assaults easily, but then the garbage rained down. Durago first saw fruit being thrown at them. Someone in front of him was hit pretty hard in the head with an orange. He was smacked in the cheek with a wad of wet toilet paper. He did not know whether he should feel ashamed or if he should rejoice inside that his classmates were extending their loyalty.

As Durago passed around one last time, water poured down on him. He noticed immediately that it was warm and that it smelled of urine. He was covered with a bucket full of unflushed john. He stopped and threw up all of his dinner. An orgasmic cheer erupted throughout Goat Court, as if a lion had just taken down a Christian. Durago stepped through the closest window back on to 4-0.

Simpson was standing there.

"Good evening, Mister Simpson, sir."

"Durago, you stink. Go take a shower and do not be up after Plebe taps."

"Aye, aye, sir."

When he entered the room the lights were already out. Slim, McDougal, and Mole were already in their racks. Slim was verbally reliving the whole incident, blow by blow, with some exaggeration. They all were laughing hysterically. Durago stripped and entered the shower. When he stepped out and began to dry off, he noticed that his roomies were silent. Then he realized that someone else was in the room. He turned on the light above the sink.

"Good evening, Mister Durago."

It was Midshipman Lieutenant O'Rourke. Durago knew that the company commander was fairly well respected in the company, and he had a reputation for taking his billet as the senior mid in the company seriously.

Durago popped to attention. "Sir, Midshipman Fourth Class Durago, nine-two-two-three-one-four, Twenty-Third Company, Second Platoon, First Squad, Beat Army, sir!"

"Durago, what happened tonight?"

"Sir?"

"Is Simpson hazing you?"

Durago had learned several truisms while at boarding school. One was that you never ratted on someone, whether it was a bully or simply someone who you knew was violating school rules. Besides, he was sure that while Simpson came close, he never violated regulations when dealing with Durago. "No, sir."

"Fine, hit your rack."

"Aye, aye, sir."

Durago toweled himself off. He was donning his underwear when the door opened again.

"Durago, you never cease to amaze me," said Simpson, his voice dripping with disdain.

Durago stood at attention in the nude, with his underwear around his ankles. Under any other circumstances, all five men in the room would be laughing. Durago was too angry, his roommates too embarrassed for him.

"You are on report for being up after taps and for directly disobeying an order. Now hit your rack."

Durago did not say a word. He slid into his rack with his boxers still around his ankles. *I hate this fucking place.*

When Simpson left, McDougal spoke up. "Donny-boy, why do you put up with that guy? Why didn't you tell O'Rourke he was hazing you?"

"I dunno."

"Was it fun having shit dumped all over you?"

"Fuck you, Brendan."

"No, seriously, Don . . . haven't you learned anything yet?"

"I don't know."

Durago pulled his drawers up, rolled to his side, and looked to the light coming in from Goat Court. Through the window he could see upperclass walking casually down the passageway around the corner. Some were still in uniform, coming back from a late night of studying; others were in PT gear, t-shirts emblazoned with ships and jets, eagles and anchors. None of them were covered in shit or piss.

I do . . . I hate this fucking place. I oughtta get it tattooed on my frickin' chest: "IHTFP."

All mids endured times of difficulty. Several acronyms were used to display their frustration. Somone had scrawled "IHTFP" inside the cover of one of Durago's books. He spotted "FTN," or "Fuck the Navy," etched into one of the stalls in the head on 4-0.

Who has that underground company t-shirt? I need to buy one, he thought, remembering that several mids in 23rd Company had shirts that read, "BOHICA"—"Bend over, here it comes again."

14

WASHINGTON

DECEMBER 5, 1988
1005
BANCROFT HALL, ROOM 4014

It was not often that a Plebe was summoned by the senior midshipman in the company and the company officer. Durago looked again at the note placed in his room by the mate of the deck.

> To: Midn 4/c Durago
> From: CMOD
> Your presence is requested in the Company Officer's
> Office to meet with the Company Officer and the
> Company Commander at 1010.
>
> R/ Midn 4/c Potok

This was not going to be fun. Durago was still flushed and sweating from boxing class during his previous period. He looked in the mirror and thought about what Simpson had said.

"We don't want you here."

He realized that he had no idea what was making him stay, why he did not quit. All of his other classmates seemed to get it. After six months at Annapolis, he felt just as lost as he had felt on his first day of Plebe Summer. *Maybe I should quit,* he thought.

Durago opened the door to his room and snapped it into the door catch. He looked out into the passageway to see if there were any upperclass about. There were none in view. He emerged from his room and began to chop toward the company officer's office. Then he saw the mate of the deck coming toward him. The mate on duty now was a Youngster. All Plebes were required to know the names of all upperclass in the company and had to greet them by name.

Durago slowed as he approached him. "Good morning, Mister Johnston, sir."

"Hey, Durago."

He squared another corner by the mate's desk at the intersection of sixth and fourth wings, his foot making a loud smacking sound as it impacted the metal deckplate placed in the floor.

"Beat Army, sir!"

Durago picked up speed as he raced toward the rear of company area. The passageway in the "rear" of company area actually faced out into Tecumseh Court. It was home to all of the first class midshipmen in 23rd Company because it was farthest away from the battalion officer's office and closer to the company wardroom. The company officer had his office there in order to keep an eye on the mids, and also because it was farthest away from the battalion officer's office.

Durago squared his last corner in front of the office. "Go Navy, sir!"

The door was open. Durago stepped in.

"Sir, Midshipman Fourth Class Durago reporting as ordered, sir."

"Sit down, Mister Durago. Relax your brace."

"Aye, aye, sir."

Durago sat down next to Midshipman Lieutenant O'Rourke.

"Durago, Mister O'Rourke and I have called you in to discuss your performance," Brown began. "Academically, you're not doing too well. At the six-week point you maintained a one-point-nine. Not good, but not uncommon considering the stresses of Plebe Year. How do you think you'll end this semester?"

"About the same, sir. I understand the material, but I wrestle with balancing academics and professional knowledge. I won't fail any classes and hope to pull up one or two grades with good performance on final exams."

"Okay. Well, as you well know, your military performance is lacking. This is really why we're here. For some reason, you show a lack of discipline, a lack of understanding of what is expected of you, maybe even a lack of motivation.

"To add to these matters, you have a conduct record—mostly minor offenses, I'll admit. Let's see . . . I have here Form Twos for 'late to formation,' 'unsatisfactory room appearance,' 'failure to know Plebe rates,' and then there's this 'UA.' I understand you were in Nimitz and lost track of time?"

"Yes, sir."

Brown set the forms down, dropped his glasses on the desk, and looked up at Durago.

"Okay, so that's bad, but not really a UA, is it Kevin?" the company officer said, looking at O'Rourke. The mid nodded his head in agreement.

"It's probably more like 'missing formation,' right?" the aviator continued. "So, I'll emphasize—" he said, turning back toward Durago, "your biggest problem, son, is that you don't appear to be motivated to be here. Your upperclass express that basically you aren't applying yourself at all to becoming a midshipman. Poor performance professionally, conduct violations—albeit related to performance—plus lukewarm academics . . . it doesn't paint a pretty picture."

The lieutenant let a moment of silence encompass the room. It was interrupted only by the sound of a Plebe chopping down the passageway. "Go Navy, Sir!"

"Do you want to be here, Mister Durago?" Brown asked.

"Yes, sir."

"Well, Mister O'Rourke and I have identified you as a candidate for a performance board at semester's end if your performance doesn't turn around. Follow me?"

"Yes, sir."

"All of these factors have led Mister O'Rourke and me to a decision to place you in another squad. We want to give you a different set of mentors, and give you a new chance to demonstrate your potential as a naval officer. Are you receiving me?"

"Yes, sir."

"You will be in First Platoon, First Squad—Mister Templeton's squad. So, I've noted that you have these pending conduct charges, including the UA. I read your statements, especially the one regarding missing the parade practice, and have decided to send it and the other Form Twos back to Mister O'Rourke's desk. He will adjudicate the offenses. You two can work that out later. In the meantime, square yourself away, son."

"Aye, aye, sir."

"Dismissed."

Durago stood, did an about-face and chopped out the door. After he left, the lieutenant turned to the company commander.

"Kevin, go ahead and have Temp put him under Washington's scrutiny. Hopefully, he'll square this kid away."

"Roger, sir."

Durago's first come-around with Midshipman Second Class Raymond Washington went very poorly. His uniform was unsat, he did not know his rates, and most important, he failed to show up for it.

Instead, Durago was standing at attention by the mate's desk in the far corner of 4-0, waiting to perform his chow call. He was happy that he remembered "Mate's Desk/Noon Meal/Thursdays." The hall clock clicked, designating the hour.

"Sir, you now have five minutes until noon meal formation. Formation goes outside. The menu for noon meal is roast turkey, mashed potatoes, peas and carrots, tossed salad, cannonballs with hard sauce, lemonade, and milk. All hands are reminded to turn off all running water, electrical equipment, lock all lockers, and open all doors. Time, tide, and formation wait for no-one. I am now shoving off, five minutes, sir!"

He was impressed with himself for doing well on his chow call. Nobody stopped him. Durago was still grinning as he stood in formation on the light-colored brick of Tecumseh Court with the other midshipmen of 1st and 4th Battalions.

Then Washington approached him. Durago tensed as Washington inspected him and his uniform. The second classman was just under six feet tall and was built like a redwood. His hair was always cropped "high and tight," leaving only skin on the sides. Durago thought that his very dark and very clear complexion, coupled with his strong physique set in the navy blue uniform, made Washington handsome. Above his left breast pocket was a silver scuba pin, denoting completion of the Navy's scuba diving course. Below were gold jump wings, signifying graduation from the Army's parachuting school, followed by five more jumps required to be a naval parachutist. Thus, Washington was "dual cool."

"Mister Durago, I'm upset that you missed our come-around." Washington's voice dripped with the aristocratic South—a Virginian, Durago guessed.

"Sir, I was at a chow call . . . I—"

With a wave, Washington cut him off. He stepped around to Durago's left side and spoke with his lips right at Durago's ear. The second class whispered calmly but sounded very angry as he put emphasis on every word.

"Mister Durago, you will not speak unless you are instructed to provide me with a response. You will only respond with your five basic responses and the succinct answer to a question. You will never, under any circumstances, answer with an excuse. From this moment forth, you are my prisoner, and when in my presence you will behave as a prisoner of war. I will see you outside my door at twelve-forty-five."

With that, Washington fell in ranks. Several mids were still joining the formation. Without moving his head, Durago looked around to see if anyone noticed that he had, just slightly, wet himself.

Though he was "dual cool," Washington was not a prior enlisted Marine. In fact, there was little to no military experience in his family. He had heard that one uncle on his mother's side served a stint in the Coast Guard, but that was it.

Raymond Washington first had been exposed to the Marine Corps while on a bus ride to visit his grandmother in Morehead City, North Carolina. Only twelve at the time, he was a little nervous to be riding by himself. While in line to get on the bus, he saw a man in uniform. About twenty-five years old, the man had on blue trousers with a red stripe, a khaki shirt and tie, colorful ribbons affixed to his chest, and a white hat with a shiny black brim. Washington's mother always told him, and reminded him before he began this trip, that if he were in danger or need he should look for a person in uniform, even a postal worker. People in uniform usually had service to others in their ethos. They almost invariably would be able to help or at least find help.

The uniformed man sat up front, the seat next to him open. Washington sat in it without asking. Just after the bus got going, Washington inquired, "Are you a state trooper?"

"Excuse me?"

"A state trooper, a police officer?"

"No, I'm a United States Marine."

Today, Washington could not remember much of what they talked about, only that the Marine was kind and had treated him like a younger brother or cousin. Washington asked a lot of questions about life in the Marine Corps, about what Marines did and how they were different from the other services. He was impressed by the fact that Marines were considered to be more elite than the Army. The word "elite" was a vocabulary word he had learned recently in school, but it had been used to describe people of wealth. It resonated with him more as applied to a military force. By the time they reached Morehead City, Washington was hooked. He was going to enlist in the Marine Corps as soon as he graduated from high school.

"That's most important," the Marine had told him. "It's not actually a requirement, but the Marines really prefer that you have your high school diploma."

That gave Washington an extra boost. He always did well in school, receiving all "As" and "Bs." He figured he might even improve his grades with a little more effort.

As the bus slowed, the Marine reached into a small satchel sitting at his feet. "Hey, kid . . . I've got a gift for you."

Washington was beside himself.

"Here," the Marine said, "it's a book about Marines in the Vietnam War. Written by one of our own."

"*Fields of Fire*," Washington said aloud as he read the cover.

Thereafter, Washington became a voracious reader of all things Marine Corps. He read *Helmet for My Pillow* by Robert Leckie, *With the Old Breed* by E. B. Sledge, and *Battle Cry* by Leon Uris. Washington rented and watched movies such as *The Boys in Company C* over and over again. His mother never liked the fact that her son was exposed to such brutality. His father thought it was a phase, that war movies fascinated his son *because* of the violence—like some kids were into horror films—but that ultimately the violence would serve as a deterrent. In time, they both realized that their son was bound for the Marine Corps, and because his seriousness led him to a self-discipline that included working hard on his academics and staying out of trouble, they eventually learned to embrace the idea.

Then Washington found another book by James Webb, the author of *Fields of Fire*, entitled *A Sense of Honor*. Published only two years after Webb's first novel, this second was about the U.S. Naval Academy. By the time he put the book down, it was settled. Washington would not go to Parris Island or San Diego. He would go to Annapolis to become an officer of Marines.

Now that he was here, Washington had to work harder to earn good grades, but military life came naturally. He performed particularly well as a Plebe and was marked as one of the leaders in his class.

He joined the Semper Fidelis Society, connecting with prior enlisted and future Marines. It was during his Youngster Summer that Washington gave up his leave period in order to attend both airborne and scuba school before spending four weeks living the life of an enlisted sailor on board USS *Elliot*.

At 1245 Durago knocked on Washington's door three times. He then propped the door open and sounded off.

"Sir, Midshipman Fourth Class Durago reporting as ordered, sir!"

"Enter."

He bolted through the door and pushed it open so it locked on the door catch. Washington's roommate, Reardon, was sitting at the desk in PT gear, listening to his Walkman. He did not even look up at Durago's entrance. Within 23rd Company, the two were referred to as "the Odd Couple." Washington was squared away, disciplined, squeaky clean. Reardon was a lacrosse player. His hair was always just over regulation length, his uniform was slightly unkempt, and he often had an illicit day's growth on his chin.

Washington motioned toward his open locker. "In the box."

"Sir?"

"Get in the box . . . get in the closet."

Durago saw that there was a four-foot empty space below the last shelf at the bottom of Washington's locker. He crawled in. Durago's mind raced to all the Plebe daily rates that he crammed after his quick meal. The menus for the day; the number of days until Herndon, Ring Dance, and graduation; headlines from the *Washington Post*.

"Who is in your squad?"

"Uh, sir, Midshipman First Class Templeton, Midshipman First Class Porter, Midshipman Second Class Bradley . . ."

Then the pro knowledge questions.

"How many cells are in a VLS launcher?"

"Sixty-four, sir," Durago answered as he thought, *Why am I in this guy's closet?*

"How many carry missiles?"

"I'll find out, sir."

The game went on for a few minutes. Washington stayed on professional topics. Suddenly, without warning, he said, "Okay, that's enough for today. By the way, prisoner, you just gave me a ton of classified information. You are a traitorous fuck."

With that, he slammed the locker door. Durago sat in the dark. He had a sixth-period class. Was he going to miss it? Would Washington leave him here? Was this some kind of test?

He lost track of time. His ears began to ring. No sound came from the room. *Had five minutes gone by? Ten?*

Then the bells announcing change of class rang.

"Sir, request permission to shove off."

There was no answer.

Durago decided to take a chance; he opened the locker door. Nobody was in the room. Durago raced to his room, grabbed his books, and walked across the Yard as quickly as etiquette would allow.

15

COME-AROUND

DECEMBER 8, 1988
1930
BANCROFT HALL, ROOM 4014

At evening meal formation, Washington said, "Durago, come-around after dinner."

"Aye, aye, sir."

At the beginning of the academic year, the upperclass often held company-wide come-arounds after the evening meal. Technically, they could continue to mess with the Plebes until 2000. As their academic burden grew heavier, the upperclass dedicated the time from formation to lights out to study. So it puzzled Durago that he was asked to come-around. *Is he pissed that I left his closet?*

Nothing was said about what happened after noon meal. Dinner in the new squad was relatively quiet for the Plebes. The upperclass only spoke when ordering them to pass condiments. Durago sweated during the whole meal, though he was not sure why. *Maybe he's gonna put me in the hole again.*

When he got back to the room, McDougal was squaring away his uniform as if an inspection were coming up.

"Brendan, where are you going?"

"Come-around."

"With who?"

"With Washington, you idiot. We're all going to come-around with *you*."

"What?"

"Classmate loyalty, buddy. Are you ready?"

"Uh, I guess so."

"You guess so? I'm skipping thirty or more minutes of study hall when I should be getting ready for a chemistry test, and you *guess* you're ready?!"

"Uh, yep."

"Man, you take the cake, Durago. It's *your* come-around and I'm sweating it more than you. Fuck, man! I can't even remember the last time we did this!"

A few moments later, Durago was outside Washington's room. All of the Plebes in 23rd Company were there. Washington emerged from his room.

"My, my, what have we here?" Washington's southern drawl feigned excitement.

"Sir, Midshipman Fourth Class Durago, nine-two-two-three-one-four—" As Durago sounded off, all of his classmates joined him.

"Durago, it seems you've dragged all your classmates out here. Talk about classmate loyalty. I am sincerely impressed, Mister Durago. They must see something in you, Durago, if they're willing to join you out here. Is that what it is, Durago?"

"I'll find out, sir."

"Okay, I'll start with Mister Potok." Washington stepped to Durago's left in front of Potok.

"Mister P," he said enthusiastically, "what is the first article of the Code of Conduct?"

"Sir, the first article of the Code of Conduct is, I am an American. I serve in the forces that guard our country and their way of life. I am prepared to give my life in their defense, sir!"

Washington moved to the next Plebe.

"Good. Miss Kohl, second article, go."

"Sir, the second article of the Code of Conduct is, I will never surrender of my own free will. If in command, I will never surrender the members of my command while they still have the means to resist, sir!"

"Perfect, Miss Kohl, and a great performance on the soccer field last night."

"Thank you, sir."

"Moeller?" Washington snapped his fingers in front of Moeller's stoic face. "Mister Moeller, you awake?"

"Sir, yes, sir."

"Third article."

"Sir, the third article of the Code of Conduct is, if I am captured I will continue to resist by all means available. I will make every effort to escape and to aid others to escape. I will accept neither parole nor special favors from the enemy, sir!"

Washington made a big deal of walking past each of the Plebes who knew their rates, back to the spot in front of Durago.

"Okay, Durago, back to you. Fourth article!"

"I'll find out, sir."

Washington leaned in close to Durago. "I'll find out, sir?" he whispered.

Durago could feel sweat dripping into his ears.

"They know!" Washington screamed, gesturing toward the other Plebes. "Why don't you?!" he said, putting his nose right up against Durago's.

Doors began opening throughout company area, and upperclass looked out into the passageway. Several could not resist coming out and joining Washington. Within moments, 4-0 became an indoctrination Mardi Gras, an upperclass festivity. Suddenly Plebes all around Durago were being grilled, yelled at. Durago heard Simpson's voice through the others. Washington just stood in front of him, staring him right in the eye. *Look what you did*, his face accused. *Look at what you did to your classmates.* He did not ask Durago another rate.

As their suffering went on and on, shame welled up inside Durago. He realized that his ineptness was having an increasingly bad effect on the whole company. Finally, O'Rourke's voice boomed above all the yelling.

"Whoa! Okay, people, that's enough. We've all got to study. Everyone shove off, except for Durago."

The Plebes scrambled, quickly chopping back to their rooms to retrieve books, and then to get out of company area. Upperclass also quickly disappeared to their rooms and the company wardroom. O'Rourke approached Durago and Washington.

"Gentlemen, how's it going?"

"Fine, Kevin, no problems," Washington answered for both of them.

"Durago, let's get past this, alright? Better every day, got me?"

"Aye, aye, sir."

"Shove off."

After Durago left, O'Rourke and Washington stood in silence for a moment.

"Let's try not to drag the whole company into this, Ray."

"No problem, man. I'll have this kid squared away in no time."

"I know . . . I know you will—that's why he's yours. I also want you to know that it looks like he's going to a performance board before Christmas."

"Kev, I just got started."

"Well, he's got so many demerits from that asshole in Brooks' squad that it's too late. Still, from what I've seen, the kid just doesn't get it."

"He will," said Washington confidently. "He will."

That night the four Plebe roommates lay in their racks just after taps. They could hear the banter of upperclass coming and going from Steerage.

McDougal's voice broke the silence. "Man, that fucker Washington has fucking pissed me off! I can't even sleep! Personally, that fucker is going too far. I can't believe he made you get into his closet and you didn't stand up to him. I mean, Simpson is an asshole, but this guy is beyond! Hey, Don, you gonna rat on this guy?"

"I dunno." *I hate this fucking place.*

Out of the corner of his eye, Durago saw McDougal sit up in his rack.

"What the fuck, man, don't you have any sack?! You're just going to let him get away with this crap?! I'd go to Templeton or O'Rourke. They'll put an end to it."

"I'm not going to do that."

"Yeah, that's 'cause you don't have the balls. These guys are running you outta here and you don't even know it! How many demerits you got now?"

"I dunno."

"I'll tell ya what . . . you must have some kinda inferiority complex to let a guy do that shit to ya. Were you an abused child, Donny?"

"Shut up, McDougal, you're wrong," Slim said, sitting up as he came to Durago's defense. "It takes balls to endure what Don's going through. Only a pantywaste would go crying about it. Besides, what should he do? Fry Washington? You know how it goes. We all just have to take some heat, help Don out until Washington gets bored, and then things will get back to normal."

"You're wrong, Slim. There is no normal with Midshipman Fourth Class Donald Durago," McDougal countered. "He's been screwed up since he got here, and not because he's dumb, or confused, or over-whelmed. It's because he's fucking lazy. Durago's a slack. You guys want me to extend Don some classmate loyalty, well I'm tired of it! I'm tired of it because he doesn't fucking deserve it! I'm tired of going to come-arounds with him. I'm tired of enduring room inspections and marching through Goat Court when I should be studying. I'm tired of looking at you, Don, and wondering about some motivated kid at Michigan State right now who's wishing he were here, except you took his spot."

Durago now stared silently at the ceiling, looking at the light reflected there from the window. He heard McDougal lying back down.

McDougal's voice became relaxed again. "There is only one thing that grants me solace—Washington and the rest of them are not going to let up until they run Don outta here. If he has his way, we'll be visiting him at Saint John's by April. At least then, justice will be done."

Durago rolled over and pulled the covers over his head in an attempt to drown out McDougal.

"Why do you think they moved you, Don? Because they care about you? Because they wanna help you? Wrong. They're already set-ting you up for your next performance board so they can kick you out. A second squad leader and a second group of first and second class evaluators gives them more rope to hang you with. And like I said before, your problem, my friend, is that you don't want it bad enough. You don't care about any of this Plebe Year stuff. You only play this game because it's a nuisance to get fried. You're getting shit on—liter-ally, by the way—the other day you were *literally* covered in shit and piss—and you're bringing all this heat on the four of us, and I'm more upset about it than you are! Why the fuck are you here, anyway?!"

"I dunno."

"'I dunno, I dunno, I dunno . . .' You're right you don't know! You don't know why the fuck you're here and you're too lazy to quit. Why don't you just leave and take the heat off the rest of us who give a shit? Like the Mole here. Now there's a guy who gives a fuck! He doesn't take a shit without having a textbook or his *Reef Points* with him so he can study.

"Mole! Mole! Stop being so silent. Back me up here. What do you think?"

"I think it's time to get some sleep."

16

THE MASTER CHIEF

DECEMBER 9, 1988
1230
BANCROFT HALL, ROOM 4034

"**G**et in the box."

Durago dropped down and slid into the closet. The shelf was lower than before; he had less room to maneuver.

"How many engines are in the *Spruance*-class destroyer?"

"Midshipman Fourth Class Durago, nine-two-two-three-one-four, ten June, nineteen sixty nine, sir."

"Okay, now you've figured out the game. What is your Code of Conduct?"

"Sir, I am an American serviceman. I serve in the forces that guard my country and our way of life. I am prepared to give my life in their defense. I will never surrender of my own free will. If in command, I will never surrender the members of my unit while they still have the means to resist—"

"Wrong, wrong, wrong. You have to get it right word for word; otherwise, you have to answer your rates. How many engines on the *Spruance*-class destroyer?"

Durago paused.

"That's how this game is played, Durago. If you don't know the code, you gotta unload. Think of it as my version of torture . . . only friendlier. So," Washington said, clapping his hands in triumph, "how many and what type of engine is on the *Spruance*-class destroyer?"

"Four General Electric LM twenty-five hundreds, sir."

When the come-around was over, Washington closed the locker door again. This time, Durago had no afternoon class. He sat in the closet for a long time, hearing almost no noise through the thick, wood door.

Durago woke up when his right calf developed a charley horse. He yelped and tried to move so he could reach down and massage it. There was no room. Suddenly the locker door opened. The light blinded him momentarily.

"Durago, what the hell?!"

It was Reardon, Washington's lacrosse-player roommate.

"Uh, good afternoon, sir."

"What are you doing in the closet, you moron?"

"Sir, I was directed by Mister Washington to get in the box."

"Did he tell you when you could get out?"

"No, sir."

"Well, I'm telling you—get outta here. I'll square things with Washington."

"Aye, aye, sir."

Durago got up and bolted back to his room.

Durago rapped on the battalion conference room door three times. He opened it smartly and strode in front of the conference table. Lieutenant Commander Brown, the five other company officers in the battalion, and the battalion officer were at the table.

"Sir, Midshipman Fourth Class Durago reporting as ordered, sir."

Only the battalion officer spoke.

"Midshipman Durago, you are being placed on performance probation. Your company officer and battalion enlisted adviser will keep me apprised of your progress. You will not be granted Christmas leave due to your conduct violations; you will be under the charge of Master Chief Strong for the duration. Any questions?"

"No, sir."

"Dismissed."

A light breeze from the Chesapeake Bay darted up the creek and spun among the boats moored in the marina's floating piers. It lifted the smell of dead fish and brackish water, ran over the seawall, and then spilled through the vessels sitting on blocks in the yard.

They're like Sirens in a salon, Master Chief Strong thought as he surveyed each of the boats in various states of repair or neglect. Some simply needed a hull scraping to remove barnacles and other sea life, followed by a new coat of bottom paint. Others clearly needed major overhaul. Strong was told the craft he was looking for was in good shape, but it had been sitting for a long time waiting for a new owner. *Must be in the back,* he thought.

As he got out of the truck, the smell became str°°nger. Two grey cats skittered across the gravel lot, chasing each other. *This smell is probably heavier than catnip,* he mused. *They're probably high.*

Strong worked his way around, looking for a dive boat with *Sea Quest* emblazoned on the stern. He found it nestled between two of the warehouses close to the water. There still did not appear to be anyone around. He looked back to the parking lot and noted that his Dodge Ram was the lone vehicle.

Looking at the forty-six-foot craft, Strong felt a mixture of sadness and excitement. This boat marked the end of a naval career and the beginning of retirement. For twenty-eight years, Strong had sailed all of the world's oceans and major seas. He started as a deck seaman on USS *John S. McCain.* He came on board just as the former destroyer escort was refitted with guided missile systems and earned the designation "DDG," for "guided missile destroyer." When *McCain* plied the waters off Vietnam, she served in the Pacific Fleet, commanded by her namesake's son, Admiral John S. McCain, from his headquarters in Pearl Harbor, Hawaii. The grandson, Lieutenant Commander John McCain, was physically even closer, enduring what would be five and a half years as a prisoner of war in the Hanoi Hilton. Strong always felt a sense of pride, a satisfying revenge as *McCain's* five-inch fifty-fours threw shells ashore at the call of U.S. Marines.

Boom, boom, boom . . . yeah, get some, Marines; get some, McCain. *Hang in there, Commander.*

Shortly after returning from Vietnam, a first class boatswain's mate took Strong and a couple of other seamen over to a destroyer tender to "cumshaw" some gear. Strong was not sure if they were begging, borrowing, or stealing the equipment.

"Strong, take this first load to the truck," the petty officer directed.

"Sure, Boats," replied Strong.

On his way back, Strong crossed the quarterdeck then headed aft. He emerged on the flight deck before finding his *McCain* shipmates. There were no helos on board, so a lot of sailors used the space to take a smoke break. Strong saw one group dressed in greens like the Marines wore. They all had a silver pin on their left breast, and their name tapes read "U.S. NAVY DIVER" instead of "U.S. NAVY."

Damn, that is too cool, Strong thought.

Within six months, Strong was sent to dive school. His first assignment after graduating as a second class diver was USS *Beaufort*, a salvage ship. There he learned about explosive ordnance disposal— EOD—when a detachment was brought on board for a salvage operation involving an F-4 Phantom that went down in 150 feet of water with ordnance on board. The EOD technicians had to render safe the bombs slung under the Phantom's wings, the explosive components of the ejection seats, and the nose cannon before the salvage divers could begin the process of raising the aircraft. Again, Strong was drawn in. Within eighteen months he graduated from the Naval School Explosive Ordnance Disposal in Indian Head, Maryland. The rest of his career was spent at EOD commands.

For Strong, this old boat represented a return to those diving roots he formed on *Beaufort*. He intended to ensure it was shipshape, then take it down to Panama City, Florida, the cradle of Navy diving and salvage since 1980. It would serve as the cornerstone of his retirement, which he envisioned as long day trips with scuba tourists, to include dive school students looking for a "hobby-lob," and evenings hoisting beers with Navy divers past and present at Down the Hatch, a bar across the street from the base owned by a retired master diver.

A ladder leaned against the vessel's hull. Strong climbed up and threw a leg over the rail. *Good deck space,* he thought. *I'll be able to get fifteen divers back here in comfort, and could probably fit twenty with no problem. Twenty-five would be a little tight, but doable.*

He went forward and entered the cockpit. Everything was in order, but he expected to install an upgraded electronics package. The engine compartment was impressive. The twin diesels looked like they were well maintained. He decided that if the price were right, he would buy the boat.

Looking at his watch, he realized it was time to meet with his midshipman. *What's his name? Durago?*

Durago looked at the plate on the door of the battalion enlisted adviser's office.

BMCM (EOD/PJ/SW) STRONG

He knocked three times.

"Enter!"

The battalion enlisted adviser's office was a midshipman room only last year. Upon the arrival of the enlisted advisers to each battalion, it had been converted because of lack of space. As a result, two of the two-man rooms in 23rd Company area had become three-man rooms.

"Midshipman Fourth Class Durago reporting as ordered, Master Chief."

The master chief motioned for Durago to sit down. Durago had seen Master Chief Strong before and knew he was a Navy diver and EOD technician. In midshipman terms, the guy was a total badass. The master chief was a definitive presence throughout the battalion. Drill, he was there. Formations, he was there. Intramurals, he was there. To most mids in fourth wing, he was more recognizable than the battalion officer.

"Mister Durago, I'm here to help you. We have a little more than two weeks to prepare you for the return of the Brigade. Not nearly enough. If you want to be here, I'll help get you on track so you can at least play ball. If you don't want to be here, I'll arrange for leave to be granted and you can go home. When you return from Christmas and New Year's, you'll have a month of checkout and then you'll be on your merry way." The master chief paused, then leaned forward. "What'll it be?"

IHTFP, Master Chief. I'm gonna quit. "I'll stay."

"Roger that. We'll start with a room inspection tomorrow at 0730."

At 0730 Durago propped his door open. Master Chief Strong was standing in the doorway. He stepped into the room.

"Sir, Midshipman Fourth Class Durago, nine-two-two-three-one-four, standing by for inspection, sir."

"Let's start with your closet. Bring me a pair of your white shoes."

Durago zipped to the closet and pulled out a pair of dress white shoes. He handed them to Strong. The master chief exaggerated an inspection of the footwear.

"The polish on these has turned yellow. Did you edge dress these this morning?"

"No, Master Chief."

"Why not?"

"We are now in winter uniform. I have not worn—"

Strong dropped the shoes to the deck. Chalky white shoe polish cracked and fell off them. "Is that an excuse I hear coming from your mouth? By the way, what do midshipman regulations say regarding footwear and formal inspections?"

"All shoes are to be edge dressed prior to inspection or formation," Durago said through gritted teeth.

Strong knew damn well that the implication was that shoes *worn* were to be edge dressed.

"Well, there you have it. Unsat. Let's look at the rest of the room."

17

COLLFIELD

December 23, 1988
1600
Red Beach

In the summertime Annapolis is very humid and hot. In the winter, it can be deathly cold. Nonetheless, Durago was out on the brick terrace behind 4-0 known as Red Beach. The freezing air stung his cheeks and ears. His toes were numb, making him focus more on his balance.

Durago's right arm was at his side, bent ninety degrees at the elbow. He held the stock of an M-1 Garand rifle in his gloved hand; it rested on his shoulder. He marched back and forth on Red Beach, keeping his eyes focused "in the boat." Durago marched constantly for forty-five minutes to complete a "tour." Toward the end of each tour, Strong would emerge from his office. Sometimes he had a cup of coffee in his hands.

"Keep your arm at a ninety! Stop bouncing!"

Durago frowned, trying to concentrate more on his form and foot placement.

"Great, now you shine up your act!" Strong bellowed. "'Integrity,' Mister Durago, 'is doing the right thing even when nobody is looking.' Are you a slack?"

"No, Master Chief!" He continued marching as Strong berated him.

"You know, if I lost Christmas break, I'd make good and damn sure that I was squaring myself away. You're just going through the motions! What do you think? Do you think that old master chief fucks with you a few days and then you get into the good graces of the United States Navy?"

"No, Master Chief!"

"I haven't seen a change, Mister Durago."

The master chief was silent a moment as the midshipman clopped through the cold, feeling more like a nutcracker than a true serviceman. "Alright, square yourself away," Strong finally said with defeat in his voice. "Be in my office in five minutes."

Durago chopped with his rifle back to his room. He locked it up in the rifle rack next to the door, then he removed his double-breasted wool reefer and gloves. *I'm going to quit*, he thought. *This is it. IHTFP. I'll quit, take some leave, get a hotel room, hit a few bars in town, pick up some chicks.*

He considered just strolling over to Strong's office. Durago hesitated, but then he chopped. "Beat Army, sir!" he called to nobody but himself.

Strong opened his door and scowled at him. "Get in here and sit down."

Durago sat across from the master chief.

"Son, let me ask you this. Why the hell are you here in the first place?"

Durago sat for a long time, staring into space.

Strong was about to break the silence when Durago blurted out, "Because my father died in Vietnam. I'm here because he won the Medal of Honor."

Strong sat back. His leather chair squeaked as he folded his muscled arms over his chest. "Are you shitting me? You're the son of a Medal of Honor recipient?"

"Yes, Master Chief."

"Boy, do you know what that means?"

"It means I applied to the Naval Academy and was accepted."

"Well, how did that happen?"

Durago sighed heavily, dropping his head and his shoulders. After a moment he straightened, and without stopping told Master Chief Strong his whole story.

Constance Durago had had no realization of the honor that Donald Senior bestowed upon her infant son. After his death, she fell into deep depression. When she eventually emerged, just over a year later, she coped by erasing as much of his memory as possible, including reverting back to her maiden name and legally changing her son's to match. Then she became a workaholic as she scrambled for partner in a blue-blood New York City law firm. Constance maintained a heady pace of work and social life, the lines of which became blurred by long hours, stiff drinks, and, her son suspected, an occasional foray into illicit drugs. This lifestyle demanded that Donald be shipped off to boarding school at the age of ten. Later, he realized his absence had an added benefit for Constance. It removed the daily memory of his father.

Thus, Durago was raised by Collfield Academy. His childhood memories were seared with school uniforms, dorm life, and intramurals such as rugby and lacrosse. Collfield did not have a swim team, but there was a pool. Durago became a lifeguard, which enabled him to use the facility for workouts and to store personal gear in the lifeguard locker room.

Separated from his mother through adolescence, Durago's real authority figures and mentors were teachers and coaches. When Durago did visit Constance on holidays and school breaks, she spent little time with him. His mother became more like a distant relative, an inattentive and unapproachable aunt. He played the role of unwanted houseguest while she avoided him, always engaged in work or play that did not include children or teens.

Naturally, Durago inquired about his father, especially in his younger years. His questions, his undying curiosity, never met with fruitful results. When he broached the subject, his mother would stiffen at once. Then she would quickly emit a mixture of sadness and a defensive anger, almost a fear, as she explained that it was not a subject to be discussed.

"I think the last time I asked her was right before she shipped me off to Collfield," Durago said to Strong. "The tone in her voice—it was unbearable. I mean, I could tell she truly was in emotional pain. After that, the subject was simply verboten." Durago reported that the only thing he was able to glean over the years was that Donald Senior was killed in Vietnam. Gradually, the realization that his mother would never speak of his father added to the distance between them.

During spring break of his sophomore year, his mother spent all of the first weekend at work. It was the last time Durago went home for any significant period of time. It was then that he realized that while they did not hate each other, he simply did not love his mother. Her career came first. Combined with Collfield, it enabled her to suppress the memory that she had ever been married to a young serviceman.

Then she died. Constance was diagnosed with pancreatic cancer in early March of Durago's junior year. It was quick. He buried her, literally and figuratively, only five months later, in July, between his junior and senior year.

Some of the students at Collfield had more than one private counselor to assist them with school applications. Most relied on the guidance counselors on the faculty, one of the perks for a school with such high tuition. Mrs. Budowski, Donald's assigned guidance counselor, had already taken him on as one of her special projects before the end of his freshman year. She volunteered before a judge to be his legal guardian until he turned eighteen. He could remain at Collfield because his tuition had already been paid, and Constance left him a small inheritance. Thus, in his senior year, Durago remained a permanent fixture at Collfield. He studied, worked as a lifeguard, and tried to figure out what he would do with his future.

It was the middle of February when Mrs. Budowski became the first person to tell him of his father's heroism. She came and got him out of class. "Donald, we need to talk about your college applications," she said, looking over her glasses at him. "Meet me in my office next period."

Twenty minutes later, he was in Mrs. Budowski's office. As he entered she said, "Donald, sit down. I have something exciting to tell you."

"Did the financial guy at Dartmouth reconsider?"

"Uh, no."

"What?"

"Donald, sit down. You need to sit down for this one."

Durago dropped his backpack on the floor and sat down. His guidance counselor sat on the front edge of the desk. She took her glasses off, folded them, and let them hang on the lanyard around her neck. She straightened her skirt, flattening it with her hands. Then she looked at him, pausing as if she knew this would be a momentous occasion.

"Donald," she said as if reading from a script, as if her words were practiced, "I took the liberty of talking to the Veterans of Foreign Wars about you."

"I don't understand," he said.

"I remembered that the VFW has scholarships for children of veterans. I spoke to Mike La Fleur, who runs their scholarship program, about your case. I explained that you were still waiting to hear from the Navy ROTC application process and that you applied for, but did not receive, a nomination to Annapolis."

"And?"

"He gave me some very interesting information," Mrs. Budowski said as she pinched her nose shut. Durago noticed her eyes were beginning to get teary and red. "I had to give him your father's name. I explained to him why he was Donald Fitzpatrick and you are now Donald Durago."

"Mom changed our names back to her maiden name."

"Right. He ... ah ... he checked his files to see if you were eligible for a VFW scholarship. You are, of course, but it seems that your father is ... was ... a Medal of Honor recipient."

"What?"

"That's right," she said, clamping her mouth shut a moment and gripping her knees in an obvious attempt to contain emotion. "He was awarded the nation's highest military honor."

"My father's a war hero? Wow ... I gotta call this guy La Fleur ..."

"I already asked all of the obvious questions. He really does not know anything past that."

There was a silence, and then Durago dropped his head and began to weep. Without a word, Mrs. Budowski placed a hand on his shoulder. He stood and she embraced him, holding him as he sobbed. "There, there," she said with a comforting voice.

Slowly, Durago regained his composure. He sat down, and Mrs. Budowski stepped behind her desk, taking her seat.

Durago asked, "What does this all mean? I ... don't know if I should be devastated or euphoric."

"It means that you have another avenue to apply to the service academies."

"You're kidding."

"The service academies accept all children of Medal of Honor recipients, as long as they meet the physical and academic entrance requirements. There is no requirement to apply for a nomination. It's awarded automatically. What do you think of that?" Now, Mrs Budowski was beaming.

In his youth, Durago had seen only one photo of his father. Now, years later, he could not recall any of his father's facial features. He did remember that his father was in a white uniform with dark, navy blue shoulder boards.

"I think I'm going to Annapolis," Durago declared.

18

NIMITZ LIBRARY

Master Chief Strong looked as if he were going to fall out of his chair.

"Whoa, okay . . . okay. Let me get this straight. Your dad died in Vietnam. Your whole life you know next to nothing about him because mom doesn't talk about it, and by the way, the two of you don't get along anyway.

"Suddenly, young Durago—the new pseudo-orphan, mind you—finds himself applying for colleges, despite the fact that he doesn't know how he's going to pay for it. Then your guidance counselor finds out that the service academies accept sons and daughters of Medal of Honor recipients basically sight unseen."

"Right."

"It's like a frickin' Disney movie."

"Yes, Master Chief, I guess it is."

"Well, then, we're gonna have to make sure it has a happy ending. By the way, how did your dad earn the medal?"

"Huh?"

"Durago, let me be blunt. How did your father die? He was obviously a hero. Was he a pilot? A SEAL? Didn't you find out? Aren't you curious about these things?"

"Of course I am. Mom obviously was no help. I also tried to get in contact with my father's family several times over the years, with no luck. I guess I'll find out someday . . ."

"Today," Strong said.

He pulled a piece of paper from his desk and jotted something down on it. "I'm surprised the VFW guy didn't know about this, or maybe he did and your guidance counselor got her wires crossed. I'm writing down a book title for you. It's called *Medal of Honor Recipients of the Vietnam War*. Go to Nimitz Library and look up your father. See what he did; find out why he's a hero. Then we'll really know why you're here."

As he strolled across Tecumseh Court, Durago violated regulations by putting his hands in the pockets of his double-breasted reefer. His turned-up collar, also against regulation, blocked the wind from his ears and neck. He sang to himself as he walked down Stribling Walk. *All the leaves are brown, and the sky is grey. I've been for a walk, on a winter's day . . .*

The Brigade believed *California Dreamin'*, the song by the Mamas & the Papas, was written about a stroll through the Yard during "the Dark Ages," the time immediately following Christmas break, because singer-songwriter John Phillips was once a midshipman. The Dark Ages at Annapolis is a time of little activity outside of academics. The cold keeps all but the most dedicated from exercising outside. The poor weather precludes any tourist gathering activities, like parades or formations. Much of the Brigade is sick and suffering from cabin fever. And the Yard is blanketed in a monotonous grey: the sky is grey, the buildings are grey, the squirrels are grey.

For Durago, the Dark Ages started early. He looked to the Naval Academy Chapel on his left as he reached the Mexican Monument in the center of the Yard. *Stopped into a church, I passed along the way . . .* Then Durago stopped himself. He considered heading to the chapel first, but suspected it was closed. He looked to the Herndon Monument a moment, just in front of the chapel but to the right a little, almost in line with the Superintendent's Office. Like many classes before them, the members of the Class of 1992 would scale the obelisk during Commissioning Week after a "dixie cup," a sailor's cover, was placed on top of the monument, which was then covered with lard. The Plebes would work together, performing acrobatics to form a human tower, so that one of their number could remove the cap— another "boat school" tradition to mark the end of their Plebedom. Legend holds that the one who removes the cover will be the class' first admiral. *Wonder if I'll be here for that*, thought Durago.

Though he was freezing, Durago continued his survey of the buildings around him: the ancient halls of Sampson, Mahan, and Maury across the Yard from Bancroft Hall, then the modern-looking Michelson and Chauvenet to his right. He wondered if these men were good midshipmen, or if any of them were fuck-ups like him. *Probably not; they probably all kicked ass.*

A gust of wind passed from between Michelson and Chauvenet, spurring him on. Looking in the direction of Rickover and Nimitz Halls, just beyond Michelson, Durago suddenly had an epiphany. He realized the frustration and inadequacy he felt over the past eighteen weeks was not about Plebe Year. It was because he needed to face the assignment that Master Chief Strong had just given him. This was an assignment that he should have completed of his own volition a long time ago. Durago felt ashamed that he had not yet mustered the courage to find out who his father was, to discover a part of his own definition and how his father's heroics led to his own acceptance to the Academy. It also boiled the indifference he felt toward his mother into anger. Denied a father, Durago was also denied even the solace in childhood that his father was a hero.

How many moments in my childhood could I have garnered courage from that thought?

Strong wrote himself a quick note about Durago's progress and his status as the son of a Medal of Honor recipient. He wondered why this fact never came out during the performance board. *But why would it?* he realized. *What difference does it make what a mid's nomination source was? Most of them receive congressional or senatorial nominations.* Strong recalled that there are also one hundred presidential nomination slots open to children of service members. *None of that is in their company-level performance record. It must be somewhere, but it simply isn't tracked here.* The enlisted adviser surmised that there may even be a code in the company record, but nobody ever looks to it. For most, it is an unremarkable fact.

Thinking more about Durago, Strong suddenly realized the young man may not react well to his father's heroic departure. *Would he break down? Would he freak out? Maybe there's some horrific reason they never told him what happened.* So, he just sent the kid on a mission that was a near equivalent to being informed of the unexpected death of a loved one without consulting a chaplain or a counselor.

"Shit!" Strong said out loud. Then the diver bolted for the door, grabbing his pea coat on the way out.

Durago opened the glass doors to Nimitz Hall Library and threw his cover on the floor of the lobby out of habit. A librarian looked up from the reception desk, surprised to see a mid during Christmas break. She noted his shivering.

"Cold today, huh?" she commented.

"Yes, ma'am," he responded.

It was not just the cold; Durago was now quaking from anxiousness and excitement. He bounded up the stairs for the second floor, then sat down at one of the computers stationed just inside the door and logged on to the card catalog. Durago typed "Medal of Honor" and took off his reefer while the computer worked on its newest challenge. After a few moments, several titles appeared. He found *Medal of Honor Recipients of the Vietnam War* and wrote the card catalog number on his palm.

Now the Plebe went down a floor to the second deck and scanned the stacks for the proper reference number. The shelves felt like a maze. Durago's anticipation mounted. The number on his hand became distorted from sweat. Still, he referred to it several times to ensure he was on track as he scanned through the stacks.

Finally, Durago found it. The book was on the shelf in both hardcover and paperback. Other books about the Medal of Honor with similar titles surrounded it. He pulled out a hardcover copy and sat down at the nearest desk. Durago opened to the index, and fate brought him to the Fs immediately. Falks . . . Fey . . . Fitzpatrick.

Fitzpatrick, Donald J., USN, 147–52.

Durago froze. A million emotions coursed through his soul. His chest and throat tightened. He felt excitement, anticipation, and sadness. He flipped through the pages, back and forth, twice missing the section detailing his father's award. Finally, he found it.

Lieutenant Donald J. Fitzpatrick, USN. April 20, 1946–December 12, 1970.

Citation: "For conspicuous gallantry above and beyond the call of duty while serving as an adviser to the navy of the Republic of South Vietnam October 15, 1970–December 12, 1970. While a prisoner of war, Lieutenant Fitzpatrick kept faith with his fellow prisoners. He resisted all efforts of his captors to extract classified information from him that was of vital strategic, operational, and tactical significance to U.S. and Republic of South Vietnam forces in the VI Corps area of South Vietnam. His resistance so infuriated his captors that he was summarily executed on December 12, 1970. Lieutenant Fitzpatrick's courage demonstrated the highest loyalty and honor to his country and is in keeping with the finest tradition of the United States Naval Service. Awarded posthumously this fifteenth day of August nineteen hundred seventy-one.

The citation was followed by a narrative written by the book's author.

Lieutenant Donald Fitzpatrick has the unique distinction of being the only military adviser to receive the Medal of Honor. He was serving his second tour in Vietnam as an adviser to the junk forces of the South Vietnamese Navy. While on a routine patrol with a flotilla of three patrol boats, called PBRs, his vessel came under heavy weapons fire from Viet Cong forces. Fitzpatrick directed the battle in a valiant manner. His flotilla sustained a fierce fight and suffered heavy casualties for a quarter of an hour. Lieutenant Fitzpatrick effectively directed use of U.S. Navy air assets, in the form of Seawolf helicopter gunships, to repel the Viet Cong.

A second ambush renewed the battle while the flotilla was evacuating wounded personnel in a helo medevac. Not much is known of the second struggle, except that Lieutenant Fizpatrick's boat was hit by a mortar and sank. The other two boats somehow fled to safety. No one was recovered from Lieutenant Fitzpatrick's crew, including another adviser who was reported as missing in action.

Fitzpatrick was captured by the Viet Cong.

The story of Lieutenant Fitzpatrick's captivity was later related to naval authorities by his fellow adviser and another crewmember who had been captured. The pair was moved several times in only a few days to various underground command centers and hideouts that dotted the countryside of SVN.

The Viet Cong realized that the advisers would possess information about the tactics of the Brown Water Navy, about their efforts to build and train the South Vietnamese junk forces, and about their preparation under Vietnamization. An NVA interrogator arrived from the north to gather intelligence from Lieutenant Fitzpatrick and his companions. Lieutenant Fitzpatrick was tortured in an effort to try to obtain information.

One night when he was escorted through an underground hospital room, he surreptitiously stole a scalpel. When left alone for a moment, he used the scalpel to remove his tongue. Thus, he was physically unable to give the Viet Cong information. There is also an unconfirmed legend that Fitzpatrick followed this act by carving the words "Sat Cong" ("Kill Communists") into his chest, replicating a tattoo common to the South Vietnamese junk forces. When his interrogators realized that Fitzpatrick was no longer valuable to them, they murdered him.

Lieutenant Donald Fitzpatrick is survived by his wife and son. He was a 1967 graduate of the United States Naval Academy.

Vertigo gripped Durago. Hot, salty tears flooded the pages of the book in his hands, and the ink of his father's heroics swelled. *Lieutenant Donald Fitzpatrick is survived by ... a son.* His legs gave out. Durago fell to the floor, curled up in a ball, and sobbed uncontrollably.

He was a 1967 graduate of the United States Naval Academy. No one had told him. In an instant, Durago's weeping stopped. He remembered that all graduates who are recipients of the Medal have memorials placed on the bulkhead outside the doors of their former rooms in Bancroft Hall.

Durago almost fell down the stairs. He burst out of Nimitz without donning his reefer and cover. Master Chief Strong was on the pavilion between Nimitz and Rickover.

"Durago, what the fuck?! Where is your cover?!"

"Naval Academy!" Durago shouted almost incoherently. "My father's a graduate!"

"Go then, go! I'll get your cover!"

Durago's elation was palpable. *His dad was a graduate?* Master Chief Strong thought. *What are the odds?*

"Two, within fifteen minutes of each other on Christmas break. Now, this is amazing," said the librarian at the circulation desk as Master Chief Strong approached.

"Yes, ma'am . . . except we're kinda here for the same reason."

"Well, he just left in hurry," she responded with a knowing air as she looked over her glasses at Strong.

"I know, ma'am. It's a long story, but I'm Midshipman Durago's battalion enlisted adviser, Master Chief Strong."

"Nice to meet you, Master Chief. I'm Marcie Week. So, what can I do for you?"

"Mister Durago was researching his father. I think if we look around we'll find his jacket and a copy of *Medal of Honor Recipients of the Vietnam War* lying around somewhere."

"Start on the second floor, Master Chief. If you don't return in a few moments, I'll come up to help you."

Strong soon returned. "Would you be willing to check out this book in Midshipman Durago's name?" he asked.

"I'm not supposed to do that, but in this case I'll make an exception," the librarian said with a wry grin.

Strong saw an opening. "How about dinner, then?"

"I don't date staff, either," she replied. After a pause she smiled broadly and said, "But again, I think I can make an exception."

During his race back to the hall, Durago did not notice the cold that had vexed him earlier. He ran on the terrace behind Michelson and Chauvenet Halls and into first wing. There was no method to his search. Durago ran up and down ladders, scanning the walls and empty corridors for the telltale plaque and photograph.

Quickly, but methodically, he raced through the odd-numbered wings: one, three, and five. Durago looked at citations for Commander Richard E. Byrd, Commander Lawson P. Ramage, and 2nd Lt. Robert D. Reem—boys who became men in Annapolis and later became heroes over the Arctic, in Pacific waters, and at Chinhung-ni, North Korea.

As Durago crossed the open terrace from fifth to seventh wing, the wind whipped at him from across the Severn River. He stopped and caught his breath, allowing the frozen air to revitalize his lungs and freeze the moisture on his face. Suddenly, he felt drawn to the seventh wing. Without hesitating, Durago entered the wing and headed up the first set of stairs.

It was the first room on the left at the top of the stairs. 7312. To the left of the door was a brass plaque with a copy of the citation he had just read from *Medal of Honor Recipients of the Vietnam War*. On the other side was a photograph of his father. For only the second time in his life, Donald Durago saw what his father looked like. He had nobody to talk to, nobody to share this moment. He felt immeasurably sad and simultaneously proud. His heart rejoiced that he bore a strong resemblance to his dad. *His dad.* Donald Durago could now think of his father as his *dad.*

He entered the room, a room that belonged to someone else now, two mids home on leave. He tried to imagine his father, a person he never knew, studying, laughing, living in that room. Now it meant something to him. After a few minutes, he wiped his eyes and stepped out into the passageway. Master Chief Strong was waiting for him there. He was holding Durago's reefer, his cover, and the book was under his arm. Strong held out the reefer and cover for Durago to grab. Then he handed him the book.

"Well, Mister Durago, now we can begin. Reveille tomorrow at 0600, followed by morning PT and quarters at 0730. Questions?"

"No, Master Chief."

"Hooyah, see you in the morning."

That night, Durago read the section describing his father's valor over and over again. Then he began reading the opening section of the book describing the Medal itself. He learned that awarding the Medal of Honor is governed by Titles 10 and 14 of the U.S. Code. Specifically, it is awarded for "action against an enemy of the United States, while engaged in military operations involving conflict with an opposing foreign force, or while serving with friendly forces in an armed conflict against an opposing armed force in which the United States is not a belligerent party."

Durago learned that there are three different designs, one each for recipients within the Departments of Army, Navy, and Air Force. Many of the medals are awarded posthumously. In these cases, they are given to the recipient's next of kin. *I wonder where my father's is,* he thought.

19

THE NIGHTMARE

 DECEMBER 25, 1988
0245
BANCROFT HALL, ROOM 4014

His head was throbbing. His hands were bound in front of him, so he reached up to feel if there was any blood coming from his skull. He felt lightheaded and dizzy. His vision was blurred and he could not think clearly. He was confused.

As he became more aware, he felt pain and soreness in other parts of his body. Not as if he had been exercising, but as if he had been in a car accident. At least he was breathing.

He had no concept of the passage of time. He could not think clearly enough to tell himself a story, to reminisce, or even to count. He could only survey his body with his mind. That made the pain worse. He tried to fall asleep again.

Then suddenly it came to him. He remembered his decision. Since it was already decided, his actions took a very short period of time. He removed the scalpel from its hiding place in his waistband, opened his mouth, leaned over, and deftly removed his tongue. It stung tremendously, and salty blood drained from his lips. The pain, however, was triumphant. He felt as if he had beaten his captors. He felt as if he had won.

One of the guards realized what had happened. He ran screaming, calling to the others. Now, it was only a matter of time. He took the scalpel and carved the outlines of his tattoo, removing the skin as if it were construction paper. "Sat Cong"—a last "Fuck you!" The blood ran down from the letters on his breast, mixing with the froth from his mouth.

The leader came into the room on the heels of the first guard. He said nothing. The last emotion he felt as the Cong raised his pistol was unbearable grief.

Durago felt a stinging sensation in his mouth. He started and sat up. His tongue felt as if it had been cut out. He moved to the sink and turned on the light. The digital clock read 0330. Durago spat blood into the sink and inspected his tongue in the mirror. It was swollen and definitely bleeding. As he looked at his reflection, he realized even more now than the previous afternoon that he would never be the same again.

His locker was open. Without thinking he turned out the light above the sink. He reached under the bottom shelf and pulled out the sweat gear and the laundry bag stowed there. Then Durago tucked his head and rolled under the bottom shelf. From his balled-up position, he closed the locker door. Before long, he was asleep again.

I can stand the cold, Durago thought. *I can stand being wet. But being cold and wet sucks.* Durago's grey issue sweats were soaked with Severn River, adding another five pounds to his weight. A strong wind was whipping in from the bay, slicing across the corner of Farragut Field, land reclaimed from the river and Spa Creek. Triton Light stood watch at this junction, flashing four times, then five, in honor of the Class of 1945. Durago shivered spasmodically as he pumped out four-count pushups, sounding each repetition only after completing two pushups.

The master chief called out, "One, two, three . . ."

"Twenty-two!"

"One, two, three . . ."

"Twenty-three!"

"One, two, three . . ."

"Twenty-four!"

"One, two . . . and halt. Recover."

Durago bolted to his feet. "Beat Army!"

"Back in the water; let's go."

Durago sprinted across the road, over to the Sea Gate, and skipped down the steps into the estuary. He was instantly numb.

"Hands in the air," called Strong. "Tread water like that for five minutes. Sing me a song while you're at it."

Durago silently tread water.

"Well, you gonna sing or not, sir? Time starts when you start singing."

Durago sang.

"Now college men from sea to sea may sing of colors true,
"But who has better right than we to hoist a symbol hue,
"For sailor men in battle fair since fighting days of old,
"Have proved the sailors right to wear,
"The Navy Blue and Gold!"

"Beat Army, sir!"

"A solemn hymn; hooyah! Good, very good, sir." Strong bent over at the water's edge and splashed icy cold water at Durago. "Now, in the name of King Neptune, John Paul Jones, and Davy Jones himself, I claim you for the United States Navy. You are now formally baptized into the realm of the deep. Hooyah?"

"Hooyah, Master Chief!"

"Now, outta the water before your song and situation make me weep for the young midshipman."

"Aye, aye, Master Chief!"

As Durago balanced himself on dry land, he cheekily asked, "So, is that it? Am I in the club?"

"Congregation, sir. But baptism is only the first sacrament. We've wiped the stain of civilian-ood from your soul. You still must prepare for communion with the Brigade."

"So, what's that mean?"

"It means, hit the shower. Quarters and room inspection goes at 0730."

Durago immediately broke into a run back toward Bancroft Hall. *I'm going to make this work*, he thought.

Strong maintained a busy pace throughout the break. Just like Plebe Summer, Durago lost track of the days, but now his focus narrowed to completing any given evolution and preparing for the next one. PT began each day at 0600. Room inspection was at 0730. The mornings were spent studying Plebe rates, naval history, or professional knowledge. Afternoons were taken up by marching tours, and then Durago and Strong went on a run through the Yard each day at 1600. They finished just before evening meal. Durago realized what Strong was doing. The master chief filled the whole day with lessons designed to make Durago a better midshipman, both physically and mentally.

It was snowing on New Year's Day as they jogged through the Yard. Strong quizzed Durago on Yard gouge as they passed each of the monuments or buildings.

"Tell me about Michelson Hall," the master chief demanded as they passed it on the seaward side.

"Michelson is named for Albert Abraham Michelson. It houses the computer science and chemistry departments. Michelson is an eighteen seventy-three graduate of the U.S. Naval Academy. He is recognized as the first to accurately measure the speed of light while a professor at the Academy, and the first American to win the Nobel Prize for Science."

"Good. Tell me about the monument in the middle of Stribling Walk."

"It's the Mexican Monument."

"Okay. So, what does it represent?"

"Uh, four graduates who died in the Mexican-American War: Hanson, Clemson, Pilsbury, and Schurbrick."

The pair ascended the bridge over College Creek. As they did, Strong spoke again. "Okay, I'm sending you on a mission. When we cross to Hospital Point, I want you to run up to the cemetery. Find the gravesite that has been there the longest—the oldest one, understand? I'm going to keep running. When you find it, catch up and report who it was and when he died."

"Aye, aye, Master Chief."

The next day Master Chief Strong conducted a room inspection, just as he had every day. He looked in all the same spots: the floor, the bookshelf, the closet, the rack. None of the four racks in the room had been disturbed for almost two weeks. Durago had taken to sleeping in his closet. He used an extra wool blanket he bought at the Midshipman Store and rolled up sweats as a pillow. By morning he was stiff, especially in the lower back and legs, but it felt good, like a penance to honor his father's sacrifice. He worked it out each morning with Strong during PT. Durago was pretty sure that Strong did not realize what he was doing.

The dream came several times, but only once in full force. Durago dreamed he was on a sinking PBR with three or four other sailors. For some reason he was in white works; the others were in greens. He fired a nondescript machine gun mounted on the patrol boat's stern in the direction of incoming and movement near the jungle shore. Then water came over the gunnels and all of the other sailors were gone.

Durago jumped into the water, swimming free of the boat. He tried to swim to shore but felt heavy with water. Suddenly, he was running and he could tell the enemy was right behind him. He stripped off his jumper, hoping to blend into the environment better with his tan skin. He slipped underneath a bush with thin, wide leaves, hoping to catch his breath. Sensing the enemy was near, he looked out from his hiding place. Suddenly his eyes locked—with Simpson's.

Next, Durago was in the bunker complex, standing at attention in front of Washington. His classmates chopped down the hall, but they wore jungle fatigues. As Washington asked him a question, Durago reached to where his *Reef Points* was normally tucked into his waist-band. Instead, he found a scalpel. He pulled it out and quickly cut out his tongue.

"Durago."

"Yes, Master Chief."

"Did you hear me?"

"Sorry, Master Chief. I'm not awake. I think I need another cup of coffee."

"In a minute, you can have a cup of mine. I—"

Strong paused. "What I was trying to say is, 'Why don't we take a field trip?' I got permission for us to go to The Wall."

"The what?"

"The Vietnam Memorial."

"Oh, yeah? I remember some kid talking about that in school. All the names from Vietnam are on it."

"Yes. Would you like to see it?"

"Huh . . . well . . . I guess. I mean, it's a wall, right? I figure the room here with my dad's photo and everything is the best way—better than just a name."

"Trust me."

"Okay . . . heck, I've never been to D.C. I'll love just to get out of the Yard."

Strong parked his truck in the vicinity of the Lincoln Memorial. He explained to Durago The Wall's setup as they approached it from that end. "The first to fall are listed in order starting in the center, moving outward toward the end here near us. Then it continues on that far side, by date, moving toward the middle. Thus, the first and last to fall are listed together in the center, creating a feeling of a full circle. So, look to the year your dad was . . . and he'll be there, in order. There are pencils and trace paper around if you want to make a rubbing of his name."

Durago stood at the narrow end, looking at the black triangle cut into the earth. Looking to his right, he saw the statue of three soldiers looking toward The Wall. As he surveyed the area, he noticed a pattern in visitors' behavior. As they approached, some spoke of the memorial, others of their plans for the day; but once they reached The Wall, they all grew quiet or silent.

Strong walked slowly, joining others who shivered both from the cold wind and the enormity of the sacrifice before them. Finally, Durago followed. He walked at a faster clip, hoping to catch up with the master chief, to find his father's name, and to move on.

Strong stopped a little more than halfway along the memorial. In silence he looked at a point on The Wall. Durago stopped next to him. "Do you see someone, Master Chief?"

"Yes, I see him . . . but I don't wanna talk about it."

Two panels further, Durago found his father's name. He looked at it for a few moments, but then he felt compelled to leave. He walked briskly to the end of the memorial and started strolling toward the Washington Monument. He was about twenty yards away when Strong called out.

"Mister Durago!"

Durago stopped and turned.

"How are you?" Strong said as he reached the Plebe.

"Okay . . . I mean, these last couple of weeks . . . it's overwhelming. I'm glad we did this, Master Chief."

"Sir, what do you think about contacting someone in your dad's class? Heck, I'll bet there's one or two in town that would sponsor you."

"Not interested."

"It'll be good for you, sir."

"Master Chief, if I don't make it, it'll shame him. I will never do that."

"Sir . . ."

"Master Chief, I don't wanna talk about it," Durago said, mimicking Strong's voice from a few moments before.

20

RETURN OF THE BRIGADE

 January 8, 1989
1530
RED BEACH

One minor advantage of being forced to stay in the hall over the break was that Durago had time to complete his assigned tours. He would be back in liberty status just as the Brigade returned. As he marched back and forth, Durago could see lights coming on throughout Bancroft Hall. The dull roar of stereo systems, Plebes chopping, and roommates telling stories of leave began reverberating between each wing. Durago replayed in his mind his morning meeting with Strong.

"Sit down and relax, sir."

Durago had sat in the chair he had occupied during their first meeting.

"Well, sir, you've come a long way in two weeks. And I mean a *long way*. You've changed like you've just finished your first ninety days in AA. I'm writing a report that recommends that you be removed from performance probation."

"Thank you, Master Chief."

"You still have a long way to go, son. I think now you have the direction you needed."

"Yes, Master Chief."

"My door is open anytime. Now, go finish your last tour."

"Aye, aye, Master Chief."

Again, Durago noted how different he felt, as if he had grown more in the past fifteen days than in the previous fifteen years. He sensed that he was more a part of the Brigade than he was a few weeks ago. Strong's lessons and discipline had allowed him to experience a metamorphosis. Durago was ready for Washington, or Simpson, or any other upperclass that might come after him.

But while the master chief helped Durago catch up on being a Plebe, his true rebirth came from his research in Nimitz and his subsequent visit to seventh wing. His questions about his father were partially answered, and miraculously, Durago was literally set in his father's footsteps. Now he would follow the path blazed by his father from adolescence to adulthood. *My mother is probably rolling in her grave*, he thought.

Slim, McDougal, and Mole all arrived on a bus from Baltimore-Washington International Airport together. The door to 4014 was propped open and the lights were off.

"He's gone," said McDougal.

"No, he's not," Mole responded. "Look, his clothes are still here."

"I told you he'd make it. Deep down, Durago's got moxie. Room looks fucking squared away, too," remarked Slim. "But where the hell is he?"

They all began stowing their luggage. Then Slim saw it. "Guys, look at the rifle rack."

One of the M-1 Garands was missing. Slim chopped out to Red Beach. In a moment he was back again. He began putting on his drill belt and bayonet.

"What are you doing?" asked McDougal incredulously.

"I'm going out there with him."

"Why, you're not on restriction? And besides, it's fucking cold out there!"

"Exactly."

Slim removed his rifle from the rack, then left. Without a word, Mole donned his drill belt, lifted his M-1 to "port arms," and followed Slim.

O'Rourke opened Washington's door. He was lying on his rack reading a book.

"There's something you need to see," O'Rourke said with a smile.

"What?"

"Check out Red Beach."

Washington strode out toward the double doors leading from the back of 4-0 to Red Beach. There was a crowd of upperclass, mostly Youngsters, standing in the doorway. As he pushed through them to see what they were looking at, he heard cadence being called.

". . . Left, right, left. Platoon, halt! A-bout-face!"

Despite not having drilled as a unit since the summer, the Plebes of 23rd Company moved together with the demeanor of the 8th and I, the Marine Corps Silent Drill Platoon. The fourth class company commander was giving the commands.

"For-ward march!"

Washington saw Durago in the formation. The Plebe looked different.

Durago had dressed with the fastidiousness of a debutante. He inspected himself in the mirror, a new habit. He looked perfect. There was not a speck of lint on his uniform. The knot in his tie was correct, with a small dimple under the knot. His white cover was spotless. His shoes shined like black onyx. Not a single rate raced through his head and he did not practice his menus. Durago did not need to. He knew everything.

The Plebe was amazed at how calm he felt as he turned the last corner to Washington's door. A new inner strength emanated from his being. He knocked three times and propped open the door.

"Sir, Midshipman Fourth Class Durago reporting as ordered, sir."

"Hit a bulkhead."

"Aye, aye, sir."

Durago performed an about-face, sounded off, moved to the opposite wall, and repeated the maneuver. "Sir, Midshipman Fouth Class Durago, nine-two-two-three-one-four, sir!"

Washington stepped out into the passageway. As usual, he appeared as immaculate and impressive as a military poster boy. "Get a brace."

"Beat Army, sir!"

"I'm serious, Durago, I want to see chins. Has Master Chief been soft on you these past few weeks? Get that chin in."

Durago struggled to squeeze his chin in tighter.

"You obviously need help—rig it."

Durago brought his arms up, pressing his thumbs into his chin, and wrapped his hands around the back of his neck.

"There you go. If you can't hold a brace, we'll simply rig one. Ready to dance now?"

"Sir, yes, sir!"

"What are the days, prisoner?"

He did not respond. Washington stared at him for a moment.

"What are the days, mister? Don't tell me you don't know any rates, either?"

No response.

"Days!"

"Sir, Midshipman Fourth Class Durago, nine-two-two-three-one-four, ten June, nineteen sixty-nine, sir."

"Did you learn something over break?" Washington paused, and then began pacing back and forth in front of, but keeping his eyes focused on, the Plebe.

"What is your Code of Conduct, prisoner?"

"Sir, the first article of the Code of Conduct is, I am an American. I serve in the forces that guard our country and their way of life. I am prepared to give my life in their defense. The second article of the Code of Conduct is, I will never surrender of my own free will. If in command, I will never surrender the members of my command while they still have the means to resist. The third article of the Code of Conduct is, if I am captured I will continue to resist by all means available. I will make every effort to escape and to aid others to escape. I will accept neither parole nor special favors from the enemy. The fourth article of the Code of Conduct is, if I become a prisoner of war, I will keep faith with my fellow prisoners. I will give no information or take part in any action which might be harmful to my comrades. If I am senior, I will take command. If not, I will obey the lawful orders of those appointed over me and will back them up in every way. The fifth article of the Code of Conduct is, when questioned, should I become a prisoner of war, I am required to give name, rank, service number, and date of birth. I will evade answering further questions to the utmost of my ability. I will make no oral or written statements disloyal to my country and its allies or harmful to their cause, sir!"

"Well, if it ain't the miracle of Christmas. You may make a midshipman yet."

Washington stood at attention in front of Durago and began inspecting him. He appeared to be pleased. "I have one more question for the prisoner. Do you know all of your daily rates today? Menus? Officer of the Watch... all that stuff?"

"Yes, sir."

"Your word is good enough for me, Durago. Unrig."

"Beat Army, sir!" Durago relaxed.

"Okay, so now I'm going to ask the most important rate of all."

"Sir?"

"What is your oath of office?"

Durago was silent.

"Durago, do you know your oath of office?"

"No, sir."

"Durago, in my opinion it is more important than the mission of the U.S. Naval Academy. Memorized by tomorrow morning."

"Aye, aye, sir."

"Shove off."

"Aye, aye, sir."

Durago started away from his position outside Washington's door.

"Durago."

"Sir?"

"Tomorrow, the fun really begins."

Heading for the next come-around with Washington, Durago felt very different. He was well prepared and focused to perform. Rather than a chore, he now approached his Plebedom as if he were training for the Olympics. Washington was his new personal trainer.

"Ready, Durago?"

"Yes, sir."

"Oath."

"Sir, I, Midshipman Fourth Class Donald R. Durago, having been appointed a midshipman in the United States Navy, do solemnly swear that I will support and defend the Constitution of the United States of America against all enemies, foreign and domestic, and will bear true faith and allegiance to the same. I take this obligation freely, without any mental reservation or purpose of evasion, and will well and faithfully discharge the duties of the office on which I am about to enter, so help me God."

"Perfect. So, you've probably figured out my priorities," Washington said. "Daily rates are fine, but I emphasize professional material. And not just the pro book material; you're gonna need to prove to me that you've absorbed all of the other pro knowledge, like the Code of Conduct."

"Aye, aye, sir."

"What are the general orders of a sentry?"

"Sir, the first general order of a sentry is to take charge of his post and all government property in view.'"

"Stop, stop, stop. You're wrong. It's got to be right, word for word, just like the Code of Conduct."

In his peripheral vision, Durago saw Simpson emerge from his room, only two doors down from Washington's. Durago watched him as he walked by, heading with the rest of the crowd starting to form up for noon meal.

"Durago?" Washington queried.

"Sir?"

"Are you listening to me?"

"Sorry, sir, I—"

"Responses!"

"Sir, no, sir."

"If you'd keep your eyes in the boat like you were taught, you wouldn't be eyeballing Simpson instead of listening to my instructions."

Washington stepped closer and lowered his frame, putting his face right into Durago's. He started to speak but was interrupted by the five-minute chow call. During the ten-second cacophony, Washington never blinked. Neither did Durago. He could feel sweat dripping into his ears.

"*I'm now shoving off, five minutes, sir!*" seemed to still be echoing in the passageway when Washington quietly said, "Don't pay any attention to that guy anymore. Got it?"

"Yes, sir."

"Now, shove off."

Durago chopped right for formation. He reminded himself that most of the company had changed positions with the new semester. O'Rourke was now his squad leader, Templeton was now the company sub-commander. A Firstie named Nelson, who Durago did not know much about, was the new company commander.

Once he reached the main passageway on 4-4, Durago noted that most of the company was already there. He found his place in 1st

Platoon, 3rd Squad, and stood patiently in the position of parade rest like all of the other Plebes. Washington stood two places to his right.

"Company, atten-hut!" Templeton called out.

Everyone stood rigid and silent as Templeton saluted Nelson. "All present or accounted for, sir."

"Very well," Nelson said, returning the salute. "Okay, everybody at ease," he said nonchalantly.

Plebes were still not able to stand at ease. Durago resumed the position of parade rest. Though he kept his eyes in the boat, Durago felt Simpson staring at him. Just in his peripheral, he could see the second class glancing over his shoulder from his spot slightly to Durago's left in 2nd Squad. *That guy is not going to leave me alone.*

At noon meal, Durago sat at the end farthest from the squad leader, but still across from Washington. Two Youngsters, Haney and Osagawa, sat at the foot of the table.

"Durago, what's the pro topic this week?" Washington asked.

"Sir, the pro topic this week is Soviet submarines."

"What subs are in the Soviet arsenal?"

"Sir, the subs in the Soviet arsenal are the attack submarines *Akula, Alpha, Echo, Foxtrot, Hotel, Kilo, Mike, November, Romeo, Sierra, Tango, Victor, Whiskey, and Zulu.*"

"Whoa," Haney chimed in, "you got the names right, but there are some other designations . . . Roman numeral designations . . . right, Durago? We covered this, this morning, right?"

"Uh, yes, sir. It is the *Echo I,* the *Hotel II,* there are *Victor I, II,* and *III,* and the *Zulu IV.*"

"Tell me about the *Akula,* Durago," said Washington.

"Sir, it is a Soviet attack submarine. Right now there appears to be only one in the class . . ."

21

THE MESSAGE

JANUARY 11, 1989
1430
BANCROFT HALL, ROOM 4007

T he message in his hand reminded Simpson of his heritage, a sharp, smarting pinprick that he endured almost daily, but at least weekly, since he entered Annapolis.

> *To: Midn 2/c Simpson*
> *From: Midn 4/c Moeller, 23rd CO CMOD*
> *Sir,*
> *General Simpson called. Please call him at your earliest convenience.*
>
> *V/R*

Even the Plebes know I'm a general's son.

It was the middle of the day, so nobody else was in the phone bank. After two rings Simpson heard, "Second Marine Division, this is a non-secure line, Captain Cameron speaking, may I help you, sir or ma'am?"

"Sir, this is Midshipman Simpson. I'm calling to speak to the general."

"Hi, Walt. The general told me to expect your call. I'll put you right through. Stand by." The United States Marine Band regaled Simpson with "Semper Fidelis" by John Philip Sousa for a few moments before his father picked up.

"Junior, how are you?"

"Fine, sir." It was never Simpson's business to inquire as to his father's condition or mental state.

"I'm calling to give you a head's up on our plans for spring break. Your mother's been after me to fit in a few more family vacations before you're commissioned. So, I've agreed to a Rhine River cruise with the alumni travel group."

"Sir, I had plans with Nancy."

"They just got cancelled. Your mother and I will be flying over early for some meetings with NATO. We're going to mail your tickets to you. Stand by for Cameron."

"Fuck!" Simpson yelled when his father's voice was replaced with "Stars and Stripes Forever." *Not only am I not going to spend the week with Nancy, I'll be playing the role of valet to my father and other flags on the trip.* Simpson looked to his watch and saw that it was now 1325. He decided to call Nancy and ask her to come to Annapolis so he could tell her in person.

Five hours later, a clerk handed them two room keys for a hotel on the Annapolis waterfront.

"Park the car, I'll head up and get settled," Nancy said flirtatiously.

Simpson could tell his girlfriend wanted to screw. He decided to wait before he gave her the bad news. He found a place to park her Volvo within a block of the hotel, then headed back in. The clerk and manager gave him a knowing look as he skipped across the lobby toward the elevators.

Closing the door behind him, Simpson noted immediately that the room was almost dark. Nancy had made sure the curtains were closed. Only the desk lamp was on, a spotlight on an opened bottle of merlot and a half-filled glass. The light faded to a glow around the rest of the room. When his eyes adjusted, Simpson saw Nancy standing in the corner, drinking the other glass of wine. She was wearing a pair of stilettos, one of his service dress blue jackets, and nothing else.

"Hello, sailor," she purred.

"You look like you're out of uniform, missy."

Nancy sat down on the chair, letting the jacket fall open. Simpson picked up the glass she had poured for him. He downed it in one gulp.

Twenty minutes later, Nancy was playing dress up again. This time she was putting on his oxford uniform shirt and boxers.

"I'm gonna need those back," Simpson said as he opened a second bottle of wine. He sat in one of the room's two chairs and put his feet up on the ottoman.

Nancy focused on herself in the mirror as she put her hair up. Then she turned, checking out her tight body, rubbing her hand over her firm stomach and looking over her shoulder at her ass. "So, besides this," she said, still looking at her reflection, "why did you want me to come down here?"

"We need to cancel our spring break plans."

"What?!"

Simpson watched his girlfriend medicate herself with two more glasses of wine as he explained what happened. She staggered a little in her heels now, nearly spilling the last of her second glass on his uniform shirt.

Nancy set the glass down and shook her head, dropping her gaze to the floor for a moment. He could tell she was furious. She hated whenever his family or the military impacted their lives. Suddenly, Nancy looked back for just a second. "Walt, I'm so tired of this shit. I love you, babe, but I don't think I can do this anymore."

Durago sat in the closet with his flashlight, studying the Soviet submarines. *It feels like I'm in a frickin' sub*, he thought. *This is good practice for the Rickover interviews.*

Hyman Rickover is the father of the nuclear Navy. He personally interviewed and selected every officer who served in the nuclear Navy, whether on surface ships or submarines, for almost thirty years. When they studied the U.S. Navy subs in the fall, Osagawa shared with the squad stories of these grueling affairs, which included everything from being locked in the admiral's wardrobe to being directed to "make me mad."

"So, the guy's like, 'Admiral, I can't do that.' The admiral calls in his aide and secretary and repeats, 'Son, right now, with these witnesses, I am ordering you to make me mad.' The mid picks up this real nice cutaway model of the *Nautilus* that the admiral has on his desk and proceeds to smash it into pieces. Of course, Rickover is furious. He kicks the guy out of his office, but when he gets back to Annapolis, there's a message waiting for him that says he's been selected."

Though the closet door was closed, Durago noticed the light coming from the passageway, followed by Simpson's voice.

"Where is he?!" the second class yelled. "Where the fuck is Durago?!"

Durago opened the door and rolled out, almost right onto Simpson's feet. As he rose to a position of attention, Simpson started in on him.

"You've done it now, mister. I'll have you doing tours and standing tall in Smoke Hall from now until Christmas. If you graduate, you'll be on restriction as an ensign."

Durago smelled alcohol on Simpson, and his words had just enough of a sing-song quality to suggest he was buzzing. It looked like the top two buttons of his shirt were missing, and that it was barely held together by his necktie.

"Shall I bring around a Form Two, sir?"

"You bet your bippy."

"Shall I put all three charges on it, separate by charges, or by offender?"

"'Scuse me?"

"Well, you and I are both up after taps and you've clearly been drinking underage."

Simpson stopped cold. Before he could respond with counterfire, Slim's voice emerged from the shadows surrounding his rack.

"Maybe I should fry both of you guys, since I'm a disinterested party who is witness to the offenses. Did you jump the wall tonight, sir, or were you drinking in the hall?"

"Slim," Durago said before Simpson could respond, "fry us if you like, but I'm also going to fry myself. I've turned over a new leaf since joining my new squad. I think I should demonstrate true accountability for my actions by frying myself. Why, I'd—"

Before Durago could finish, Simpson left the room.

"You really going to fry him?" McDougal asked.

"Oh, hell yes," Durago replied.

"Now that," said McDougal, "takes balls."

"Fuckers, go back to sleep," mumbled the Mole.

That Friday evening, Nelson stood in front of all the mids mustered in the 23rd Company wardroom. The upperclass lounged on fake-leather couches that all faced a large-screen television. The walls held a variety of photos depicting the Navy and Marine Corps. There was a *Perry*-class frigate plowing through turbulent seas, SEALS launching from a sub just below the ocean's surface, an F-14 fighter on final approach to an aircraft carrier, and Marines rappelling down a rocky slope. To meet the true definition of a wardroom—the officers' dining space on a naval vessel—there was a microwave, a refrigerator, and most important, a coffee pot. Durago thought that, other than having an actual dining table, it probably looked like wardrooms throughout the fleet, and undoubtedly there were thirty-five other copies throughout Bancroft Hall.

O'Rourke was there as Durago's squad leader. Simpson sat next to Midshipman First Class Smith, his squad leader this semester. Washington was present for two reasons: he was the new second class company commander, as well as Durago's second class. Templeton, the company sub-commander, was also there, mostly to support Nelson and act as another voice of reason, if needed.

"Okay, guys," Nelson started, "you know what this is all about. Here's how we're going to play this. Durago, you need to put in a request chit to stay up after taps. First, I'm awarding you ten tours for failure to use good judgment. Second, Washington is going to assign you some professional remediation. He'll determine the details. Questions?"

"No, sir."

"You're dismissed . . . get lost."

Without a word, Durago got up and left.

The upperclass all relaxed a little. Though from two different classes, they all had been in the same company for a year and a half. In general, the two groups got along well. It was for that reason that Nelson was able to defuse the situation by negotiating this internal, almost underground, punishment. Once he was certain Durago was out of earshot, Nelson started again with a sharp tone directed at Simpson.

"Walt, I think you're a Fascist prick and we all know you've got a hard-on for Durago. You're a dumbass for jumping the wall and drinking. But then putting these together and getting hammered and then going around to mess with the kid—after taps, mind you—totally unsat.

"Still, Smitty here tells me I've got you all wrong. He points out that Durago has done a lot of screwed-up things unrelated to being in your squad, and that, as a fellow squad member last semester, he thinks in most cases your wrath was warranted. He also pointed out that every one of us jumps the wall for a little unauthorized liberty now and again. This has made me a little sympathetic, and it's why I'm keeping all of this at our level. We don't want a fry war starting here between the Plebes and the second class. I've seen that happen, and nobody wins. In fact, the upperclass sometimes suffer more because we're held to a higher standard and have more to lose.

"So, here's what we're going to do. First, this Form Two, like Durago's, is going to become 'failure to use good judgment.' If any of this blows up, comes out later, nobody can say we didn't do anything about it. Second, the company has the battalion watch over spring break, and you're going to stay here and man it."

Simpson shifted in his seat with this statement. Nelson sensed frustration.

"You're getting a gift, Walter. If we send this forward as written, you'd lose a lot more than spring break."

"Fuck that," Simspon responded, realizing the general would be even less forgiving than his ex-girlfriend by losing his son's presence during the vacation.

"Walt!" Smith interjected. "I told you to keep your mouth shut."

"Are you done?" the company commander asked with disdain in his voice.

"He's done," Smith said with finality.

"Good. Next, the third part of your punishment; you're going to spoon Durago before the end of the week."

Nelson paused, waiting for another outburst. The other mids nodded their heads in approval.

"Fourth, with a father who's a general, and a Vietnam vet, there's something you should know about Durago, something I learned from Master Chief Strong . . ."

Washington thought about what he put Durago through as he walked back to his room. *The guy's dad was a POW and I was putting him in my closet.* He wondered if *he* should spoon Durago after making the kid endure that. Then Washington smiled, thinking of Simpson's punishment.

As the academic year neared its end, many of the upperclass would "spoon" Plebes, recognize them and end the indoctrination between them by introducing themselves by their first name. Some would actually introduce themselves by saying, "Hey, Matthew, I'm Mark." Others would simply surprise a Plebe by using his first name: "Luke, will you pass the potatoes?" This may startle a Plebe for a moment, but he would quickly respond, "Sure, John."

Thus, Washington thought Nelson's punishment inventive. First, it *really* punished Simpson. To spoon a Plebe so early in the year was unheard of. It would really put Simpson in his place. Second, it was a creative way to bring harmony back into the situation, to get Simpson to stop harassing the Plebe before it got completely out of hand. Washington also knew that Nelson's narrative about Durago's father had an impact on all of them, but it hit Simpson the hardest. The guy was wound so tight in part because he was constantly trying to live up to his father's high expectations. It was not easy following in the footsteps of a Marine general who had been a mega-striper when he was a midshipman.

"Sir, Midshipman Fourth Class Durago reporting as ordered, sir!"

"Russian subs . . . go."

"Sir, the Soviet submarines are the *Typhoon*, the *Akula*, the *Kilo*, *Sierra*, *Oscar*, *Delta*—"

"Stop, stop, stop," Washington said, waving his hands. "I'm confused already. What submarines are you talking about?"

"Sir?"

"You just spouted out four or five names in some random order. You didn't include the other designations, the Roman numerals indicating major modifications within the class, as Haney rightly directed. Did you and your classmates devise some odd pneumonic like, 'Go rub your balls with grease,' or 'Even red nuns have odd green cans?'"

"No, sir."

"Why that order then?"

"No excuse, sir. I just memorized them that way."

"Do you know them all?"

"I'll find out, sir."

"Listen, you need to learn these things in a logical manner so that you can someday present them in a way that is easily understood by others . . . seriously. You should be able to stand up in the wardroom and give a lecture on Soviet naval submarines right off the cuff. If you start memorizing them now by, say, smallest—the attack boats—to largest—"

"The boomers."

"Exactly. Then by newest to oldest—well, you'll be squared away. Plus, it's truly easier to remember them this way. I don't want you to memorize Soviet subs, Durago, I want you to *learn* them. This," the junior said, holding up a finger for emphasis, "is why this place is different. No commanding officer or executive from a defense contractor is going to ask you to derive shit at a cocktail party, in a wardroom, or during a watch. He may ask you, however, to expound on the capabilities of the Soviet submarine force. Do you get me?"

"I do, sir."

"Good. Well, then," Washington continued in his genteel drawl, "now I know what your punishment will be. You were studying submarines the other night, memorizing them, I'm sure. Now that I know you'll reform your habits and learn them, I want you to prepare a lecture for the whole company. I want you to present it Sunday night."

"Aye, aye, sir."

Washington looked to his watch. "We need to head to formation. Before we go, I have one other assignment for you . . . another part of your rehabilitation. I want you to find every submarine on the Yard. Not photos or paintings, but every actual submarine. I want you to prepare a report on them. Then present it to the company on the following Saturday. Questions?"

"No, sir."

"Get lost."

22

SQUID

 January 14, 1989
1430
Bancroft Hall, Room 4007

By mid-day Saturday, Durago felt ready for his presentation on Soviet submarines, so he started his second assignment, a search for submarines throughout the Yard. Realizing that he would not likely have much time during the week—he still had school work and new rates to study—Durago decided he must find all the subs during the weekend. By Saturday evening he had found only seven.

The most obvious was SS X-1, the mini-sub behind Lejeune Hall. X-1 evaluated the use of mini-subs for underwater swimmer attack. First, the sub would get close to or even enter an enemy harbor. Then, underwater demolition teams, or "UDT" sailors, predecessors of the Navy SEALs and more commonly called "Frogmen," could lock out of the sub through a hatch on the side of her hull. Remaining underwater, the UDT would find their way to a position beneath an enemy ship. The divers could then place limpet mines on the hull, rudder, or prop shaft. A time-delay fuze ensured the divers could return to the sub and quietly escape before detonation. The X-1 concept was short-lived for the harbor attack mission, so X-1 became part of the Naval Research Lab, where it evaluated the properties of sea water.

Next, Durago remembered that there was a set of dioramas that included a submarine in the vestibules of Memorial Hall. Durago first checked the vestibule on the left-hand side of the hall's entrance. The diorama there is commonly called "Ripley at the Bridge." It depicts Marine Corps captain John Ripley, Naval Academy Class of 1962, placing demolition charges under the bridge at Dong Ha on April 2,

1972, an action that thwarted the North Vietnamese Easter Offensive because the bridge was the only means for North Vietnamese tanks to cross into the south. *Shit, that took a monster set,* Durago thought. He wondered if Ripley had known his father, because they were in Vietnam at the same time.

Durago was drawn into the main hall, to the second of two places within the entirety of Bancroft Hall where his father was immortalized. The eyes of anyone entering the hall would be drawn to Oliver Hazard Perry's battle flag from the war of 1812 that immortalized his friend James Lawrence's dying words aboard USS *Chesapeake*: "Don't Give up the Ship." Just below this, a large plaque read:

DEDICATED TO THE HONOR OF THOSE ALUMNI WHO HAVE BEEN KILLED IN ACTION DEFENDING THE IDEALS OF THEIR COUNTRY WITH IMMORTAL VALOR AND THE PRIDE OF THEIR LIVES THESE PROVED THEIR LOVE OF COUNTRY AND THEIR LOYALTY TO THE HIGH TRADITIONS OF THEIR ALMA MATER BY INSCRIBING WITH THEIR OWN BLOOD THE NARRATIVE OF THEIR DEEDS ABOVE ON AND UNDERNEATH THE SEVEN SEAS THEY HAVE SET THE COURSE THEY SILENTLY STAND WATCH WHEREVER NAVY SHIPS PLY THE WATERS OF THE GLOBE

Below the plaque, encased in glass, were the names of all Naval Academy graduates killed in action. To the right side of the case he found the words "Vietnam War 1962–1973." He scanned down the names until he saw that "Donald James Fitzpatrick, '67" was included there with the other names.

After a solemn moment Durago refocused on his mission. *Submarines! Gotta find submarines!*

As he headed out, Durago entered the vestibule to the right as one ascends the stairs from the rotunda into Memorial Hall, opposite "Ripley at the Bridge." The diorama there depicts heroic action at sea, the capturing of the German submarine U-505 by USS *Pillsbury* (DE-133). During World War II, Captain Daniel Gallery, Naval Academy Class of 1921, led a task force from his flagship, USS *Guadalcanal*, that conducted antisubmarine operations in May and June of 1944. On June 4, 1944, the task force detected and attacked U-505, forcing it to the surface. *Pillsbury's* crew boarded the vessel after the Germans abandoned her to the sea. They obtained invaluable intelligence, including code books, and eventually salvaged the German sub as a war prize.

After taking detailed notes from the brass plaque below the diorama, Durago thought to go to Luce Hall, the building for seamanship, navigation, naval science, and leadership. *There'll be a sub model there*, he thought.

In Luce, Durago found several large, one-twelfth-scale models of surface ships, but no submarines. Next he decided to try Preble Hall, the Naval Academy Museum across the Yard from Bancroft Hall, near Gate 3 and Maryland Avenue. There he found five sub models: *Holland*, S-2, *Silversides*, *Albacore*, and *Nautilus*.

"How many subs have you found?" Moeller asked as the Plebes of room 4014 dressed for Saturday evening meal formation.

"Seven. There's the SS X-1 behind Lejeune, U-505 depicted in the diorama in Memorial Hall, and *Holland*, S-2, *Silversides*, *Albacore*, and *Nautilus* in the museum."

"What about Luce?" McDougal inquired.

"Believe it or not, they only have surface ships in there. I wonder if it's because everything we learn in seamanship and navigation has minimal impact on submarine—"

Suddenly it dawned on him. *There'll be models in Rickover.*

"You know what? I think I figured it out," he said aloud. "There's got to be a sub model in Rickover."

Slim, who had been adjusting his tie in the mirror, spun on his heel. "Oh, hell yes . . . why didn't I think of this before? They've got the tow tank in there. Remember?"

"Nah, man, I've got no idea."

"Yeah," McDougal chimed in, "you remember. We visited it on one of our tours of the Yard. In the basement of Rickover there's a long tow tank, like four hundred feet or so. It's used to test large ship models for naval architecture classes."

Durago looked dumbfounded. "I seriously have no memory."

"C'mon, how could you forget something as dramatic as that?" Slim asked.

"Watch," Moeller replied. "Don was probably mate of the deck when we did the tour. It's probably part of the reason he sucks—or used to suck—so bad at Yard gouge. He couldn't visualize it like we did because he never saw much of it in the first place."

"Probably right," Durago agreed, "but it doesn't matter now, anyway. I'm gonna make sure I search every nook and cranny on the Yard, so I was gonna eventually 'Message to Garcia' my ass into Rickover anyway."

"Whoa, 'Garcia!' Talk about a blast from the past. Maybe you were paying attention!" McDougal guffawed.

"A Message to Garcia" was a passage given to all Plebes on Induction Day. It was probably their first rate following their alpha code, company, and platoon. It told the story of "Rowan," who was directed to get a message to General Garcia somewhere in Cuba during the Spanish-American War. By legend, Rowan departed without asking for any guidance or information from his superiors.

At first, Durago did not get it. *Why didn't Rowan ask any questions?* Now he understood. The message to the Brigade was that leadership at times requires self-motivated problem solving. A minion asks for direction, a leader simply *does*.

On Sunday morning Durago found himself in the foyer of Rickover Hall, looking at a replica of the man the building was named after. Rickover's bust was not unlike Tecumseh's. His nose shined from mids rubbing it, a ritual of good luck before engineering examinations. The difference in patina from the rest of the statue made the protuberance seem exaggerated, like a nautical Jimmy Durante.

Just past the statue, Durago stopped. *Garcia, Rickover, Preble, Luce, Bancroft . . . Fitzpatrick.* He turned and stepped back in front of the depiction of the father of the nuclear Navy. Durago reflected that just as Rickover and Bancroft are recognized in the annals of naval history, in a small way, so was his own father. The name "Fitzpatrick" had earned a place of honor that was enshrined through his citation on 7-3 and his name in Memorial Hall. Long after *Medal of Honor Recipients of the Vietnam War* was out of print, his father would be remembered in the hall.

But he won't be remembered anywhere else . . . because I'm standing here with my maternal surname. Donald Durago decided in that moment that if he graduated from the Naval Academy, he would become "Donald Fitzpatrick."

Durago decided to search the whole building thoroughly, leaving the tow tank in the basement for last. Perhaps there would be a model somewhere in a classroom or hallway, another *Nautilus* or the latest *Los Angeles*–class attack sub. Durago went up to the top floor and did a complete tour around the building, looking in every classroom, nook, and cranny. He followed this same pattern, working his way down to the first floor. Satisfied there was not a sub to be found, Durago went down to Rickover's basement, the ground floor really, where all of its engineering labs were housed. Toward the seaward side, Durago saw two large metal doors that spanned from floor to ceiling. One was slightly open. He pulled on it, moving it more than opening it, and slipped through.

It was definitely the tow tank. The space seemed more than one story high once he was inside. *Did I come down two flights of stairs?* Durago wondered.

Here the lights hummed, and he heard other mechanical sounds, pumps and motors that worked hard for some effort. On all of the exterior walls were storage racks, large shelves that held ship models of various shapes and sizes. Some were fairly detailed and included gun mounts and antennas. Others were hull forms only. Some were in between—hulls with weights mounted on them. There was one submarine on a rack near the door. *There it is*, Durago thought. *That's a Los Angeles–class attack boat.*

The tank started at the center of the room. It had a launching well that looked only about six feet wide, then it opened to more than three times that size. Standing near the edge, Durago guessed it to be about fifteen feet deep. He scanned down its length, running in the direction away from the Severn. A series of working lights focused toward him were nearly blinding. Durago held up his hand to block some of the glare, but he could still make out only shapes. Some appeared human.

"Okay, bring 'em to the surface." The voice sounded like Master Chief Strong.

As he slipped past the lights, Durago saw that it was Strong. There were five mids, all working lines under his direction, that were lifting a seven- to eight-foot oblong yellow craft from the water. Two divers in the water on either side were guiding it.

"Up slowly, slowly," Strong said.

One of the mids pressed a button on a winch that payed in a Kevlar cable attached to lifting slings around what was looking more and more like a yellow submarine.

"What is that?" Durago asked. Nobody responded.

While the sub sat just below the surface, one of the divers next to it pulled a lever on the side. A hatch running about one-third of the length on top of the sub opened. Another diver emerged from inside the sub, followed by a second. Durago was somewhat surprised.

Washington.

Both divers looked up to the master chief as they pulled the regulators from their mouths. "How do you feel?" Strong asked.

"Diver on deck, diver okay," they said in unison.

"Mark time, one-zero-five-zero," Strong said as he hit the buttons on a set of stopwatches hanging from twin lanyards around his neck. "Pretty good, but let's go down to the end and run 'er again."

"Master Chief, what is this?" Durago asked.

"This, Mister Durago?"

"This . . . that submarine . . . with Mister Washington."

"That, Mister Durago, is *Squid*, the United States Naval Academy human-powered submarine. Mister Washington is the propulsor. We were wondering how long it would take you to find us."

Durago looked down to Washington, floating on his back in the tank. He smiled and nodded knowingly at his Plebe.

Durago stayed and watched the crew turn the sub and launch it again with Washington and the navigator inside. They were able to traverse most of the tank without crashing. Master Chief Strong explained that the sub was designed by some of the Academy's naval architecture students, was built by mids guided by the school's model builders, and would be raced by mids at the first International Human-Powered Submarine Races in Riviera Beach, Florida, that summer.

"Master Chief, I want in on this . . . this looks too cool."

"Good. But ya gotta go to dive school first, son."

23

SCUBA TRYOUTS

FEBRUARY 15, 1989
0430
FARRAGUT FIELD

The frozen ground beneath Durago's sneakers had a layer of frost that flaked off and turned to slush water as he stomped and shifted his weight in a vain attempt to keep warm. His shins ached from the running he had done over the last two days, but other than that and the cold, he was still in good shape. Looking to his left, he winked at Slim. *If I look like him, I'm gonna make it,* he thought.

The number of Navy diver "wannabes," mids trying out for a billet to the Navy's scuba school, dwindled each day. Almost one hundred mids from the 4th Battalion were there on Monday. This number dropped steadily that morning so that only sixty or so showed up on Tuesday. Some mids quit right in the middle of that first tryout session. One complained of an injury, followed by a second. Four more darted out of the formation and sprinted for Bancroft Hall like a perfectly coordinated prison break. The scuba cadre, mids who had graduated from dive school during one of the previous summers and who now ran the tryouts, ignored them. Instead, they "preached to the choir" that remained with fire and brimstone in their voices, yelling, "Close that gap! Close up my formation!"

Once the cadre got the running formation in step, they started leading the platoon in jodies, the running cadence that helped the mids breathe and kept them motivated.

"Got a dog, his name is 'Blue!'"

"Got a dog, his name is 'Blue!'" the mids in formation repeated.

"Blue wanna be a diver, too!"

"Blue wanna be a diver, too!"

Durago concentrated on the words, allowing them to distract him from the physical pain and stress.

"Give 'im a mask and four little fins!"
"Throw 'im in the ocean and watch him swim.
"Up from the bottom, much to my surprise!
"Gotta shark in his mouth and a gleam in his eye!
"I wanna be a Navy diver!
"Live the life of sex and danger!
"That's the life of a Navy diver!
"Left, right, right, your left, right, le-ooh!"

The sing-song cadence had the proper effect on Durago, but other mids dropped out continuously, a steady stream of resignation.

The candidates did not have to memorize the jodies, but they were directed on the first day to memorize "The Rat Song," an odd ditty that Durago could not connect to anything nautical, naval, or undersea in origin. Nonetheless, he learned it and now could sing it whenever demanded for the amusement of the scuba cadre.

Wondering how many wannabes would return, he noted the lights from Bancroft and Mitscher Halls silhouetting other mids emerging for the morning tryouts. Their sweats were waterstained and muddy, sagging and stretched from the day before. Durago looked down and smiled to himself, recognizing that his were the same. One by one, those who still had the heart to become Navy divers joined the formation for their battalion.

"Forty-two," Slim said to Durago. "Forty-two back today."

The scuba cadre emerged from Mitscher Hall all at once. Once the last of their number was through the doors, they broke into a run. Each wore a blue sweatsuit with gold lettering on the left breast and back. In the previous two sessions, Durago saw one with a skull and crossbones breathing a scuba regulator that read "Dirty Deeds, Done Dirt Cheap." Another depicted a diver wrestling a hammerhead shark and read "1/3 of the Earth is Land, the Rest is Ours!" Many simply pictured a scuba mask and hood, a depiction of the qualification pin awarded to graduates of the Navy's scuba curriculum, with "Navy Diver" in bold lettering.

When they hit Farragut Field the group split, with the cadre for each battalion heading for their charges standing in different locations on the field. The mids in each formation waiting for the cadre came to attention as they were directed two days before.

There were four mids running the 4th Battalion wannabes. Dieter, Jackson, and Collins were all Youngsters who had been in the wannabes' shoes only a year before. Each tried out, was selected, and, as part of their Youngster Summer training, completed the scuba course at the Naval Diving and Salvage Training Center in Panama City, Florida. They were led by Harrison, a Firstie who had been to dive school two years before and the previous summer completed a shortened, introductory version of the SEALs' Basic Underwater Demolition School called "mini-BUD/S." Harrison would probably enter BUD/S upon graduation, in pursuit of a career as a SEAL.

At first glance, these mids were all cocky. Durago soon recognized this attitude as confidence. *Like they can back it up*, he thought. *As if they don't have to prove anything.* He tried to imagine what that might feel like. He even started to picture himself a year from now as one of the Youngsters with blue-and-gold sweats hanging on a more defined build. Quickly he erased the thought, allowing himself only a glimmer of the potential future. *Earn it*, he thought.

As Harrison and the Youngsters stood in front of the formation, one of Durago's classmates from 22nd Company standing in the front rank reported, "Fourth Battalion, forty-two men present."

"Very well," Harrison replied. "That's good. I'm glad we're down to forty-two, but I need this number split in half. The fact that you're here this morning shows that you can hang . . . that you have the potential to be 'Strong Divers.' The weak are all snug in their racks this morning. So, from this point on, we're going to see who wants it more—who wants to be a Navy diver?"

"Hooyah!" someone yelled from the back of the formation.

"Hooyah, indeed . . . but I intend to have only twenty here on Friday morning for the diver PT test. If every batt had twenty mids, there will be one hundred and twenty trying out for sixty slots."

Harrison let that thought sink in a moment.

"Of course, I think about twenty of those slots are right in front of me right now. So, the rest of the Brigade will have to fight for the last forty, hooyah?"

"Hooyah!" Durago, Slim, and the others yelled back in unison.

"Okay, schedule this morning, gents, is in-place PT followed by pool PT, then a long run. We'll begin with eight-count body builders. Ready? Begin! One, two, three . . ."

The mids did eight counts, followed by flutter kicks, jumping jacks, and multiple rounds of pushups. Durago got into a mental zone, a place where he ignored the physical discomfort while focusing on the latest exercise. Just as he used the cadence while running, he concentrated on his breathing, hand placement, or carrying out the full range of motion. At one point, Harrison allowed the group to stretch and have a short breather. Durago noticed that there was only one other battalion on the field. He glanced at Slim, who looked back and grinned, mouthing *Hooyah*. Though he did not realize it, Durago drew a little more strength and endurance from his roommate's positive attitude.

"Okay, to the pool," Harrison announced. "Form up in two rows."

As they ran toward MacDonough Hall, Collins led them in another diver jodie.

"See old lady walking down the street!"

"See old lady walking down the street!"

"She got tanks on her back and fins on her feet!"

"She got tanks on her back and fins on her feet!"

As they repeated what Collins called out, Durago and the others sang loudly. Their voices echoed off Bancroft Hall, likely waking some of the Brigade. Durago liked the idea that simply his presence, the fact that he was up and trying out for scuba, showed he had more guts than most of the Brigade still asleep in their racks. *Mere mortals,* he thought, *can't hang.*

There was a strong smell of chlorine starting in the stairwell leading up to the pool in MacDonough Hall. Once on the pool deck, Durago and the others stripped down to swim trunks. The 4th Battalion cadre was joined by a group of mids who focused solely on physical training in the water, a great eliminator from day one. Some of the mids who were strong as an ox and fast as a gazelle lacked the ability to swim like a shark.

The session normally began with a five-hundred-meter swim in sidestroke or breaststroke. Once the candidates were sufficiently worn out, the pool cadre led them through crossovers, an exercise that demonstrated underwater confidence and efficiency. Four of the cadre wearing swim goggles treaded water as if it were their natural state, as calmly as sea lions or porpoises. In the leaning rest position, Durago looked straight ahead at the one in front of him, trying to shoot him a stern "Fuck you" look. The mid was an "impose swimmer," stationed there to harass Durago and any other mid who surfaced before reaching the other wall. Durago noticed that Slim was among the half of the 4th Battalion mids on the other side of the pool.

"Recover!" Dieter yelled.

"Hooyah!" the wannabes called out as they took to their feet.

"Go!"

Hearing the command, Durago and the others dove into the pool. As soon as the cold water enveloped him, Durago pulled violently so that he would sprint forward and go deep. He then stayed stiff, ramrod straight, so that he could glide as far as possible. The chlorine burned his eyes slightly, but he needed to navigate around the others.

This exercise on the first day was completely chaotic, with sixty-some candidates trying to negotiate across and around each other while resisting the desire to bolt for the surface. Durago felt that sensation building already, just as his momentum slowed. It did help that he was now near the bottom, almost ten feet below the surface. The additional pressure compressed some of the gasses in his system.

In one movement, he breathed out, disgorging the carbon dioxide that pressed on his upper chest, while sweeping his arms forward and back to his side again. He continued this motion with a flutter kick across the bottom of the pool. Hitting the side with his hand, Durago rose quickly and sucked in air desperately as he pulled himself out and returned to the front leaning rest, facing toward the pool.

Now, Durago listened. The only sound he heard was heavy breathing as he and the mids around him all tried to recover, and the *pat, pat, pat* of water dripping from his forehead and nose onto the pool deck.

Looking up, he saw Harrison and the others of the cadre conferring in the corner. Dieter spun on his heel and called out, "Eight-count body-builders, doing ten, begin!"

All the mids rose to their feet and began to count in unison as they performed the exercise. "One, two, three—one!"

When they reached ten, Dieter again called out, "Go!"

After a good thirty minutes of pool PT, the mids put their sweats and shoes back on and headed back outside. Harrison told them to emerge from the opposite side of MacDonough, adjacent to first and third wing and Ingram Field, and form again into two ranks.

"Forward at a double-time!" Collins called.

"Hooyah!" the wannabes responded, indicating they were ready.

"March!"

Within two steps, another jodie started.

"My girl's a vegetable!"

"My girl's a vegetable!"

"She lives in a hospital!"

"She lives in a hospital!"

"I'd do most anything to keep her alive!"

"I'd do most anything to keep her alive!"

Harrison led them toward Dewey Field and the Severn River, but then turned left, heading toward Hospital Point.

"She's got her own TV!"

"She's got her own TV!"

"They call it an EKG!"

"They call it an EKG!" Now the mids were trying not to laugh as they slogged through the cold morning.

"She's got an iron lung!"

"She's got an iron lung!"

Durago saw that lights were on in all of the classroom buildings, but there was no movement. The parking spots in this part of the Yard were empty, as probably nobody on the faculty had risen yet.

"I beat on it like a drum!"

"I beat on it like a drum!"

The mids passed the classroom buildings on their left, turned left behind Nimitz, and crossed the footbridge over College Creek. Then they turned right onto Hospital Point, following the running path the mids called an "outer." They were all still a little wet from the pool, so their skin was chilled by the February temperature. As they neared the picnic area at the base of the Naval Academy Bridge over the Severn, Durago sensed a hesitation, as if Harrison were considering something.

"Quick time, march!"

The platoon slowed to a walk. Collins immediately called a slower cadence. "Left, your left, your left, right, left."

Harrison led them right to the beach at the end of the Hospital Point seawall and the base of the bridge. "Pla-toon, halt!"

"Hooyah, PT in the mud!" someone yelled.

"Right-face!"

Now the platoon faced the river.

"Get in the water!" Harrison commanded.

Durago did not hesitate. When Harrison yelled "Go!" he was already moving, bolting for the brackish, brown liquid. He did a lifeguard's entry, a surface dive, while keeping his head up, like a graceful belly-flop. Then he ducked his head under.

The water was freezing. The shocking cold went straight to his bones, so he could barely discern the river seeping into the last semi-dry spots in his shoes and clothing. He felt like his muscles were seizing up as blood rushed to his core. His hands and feet went numb. Durago noticed that his back, especially the back of his neck, and his groin felt the coldest.

Two-thirds of the mids were in the water with him. Some exclaimed, "Shit, its cold!" or "It's fucking freezing!" but these comments soon turned into laughs and "Hooyah, cold water!" Then they started jeering those who hesitated, those who were still standing in the mud. "C'mon you pussies, get in the water!" someone said harshly.

Harrison looked to the fourteen or so mids still standing on the beach. "Gentlemen, get in the water now."

"Fuck that," said one of them.

"Fine, you guys are done," Harrison said with finality. "Stan, form them up and take them back to the hall." As they marched away sullenly, Harrison called to the mids in the water, "Recover; form on the beach; let's go!"

The mids reformed. Durago noticed that they all were shivering. Arms waved and jaws flapped like an epileptic seizure had hit the platoon. Harrison knew he had to get them moving. "On your faces! Twenty-five pushups! Begin! One, two, three—"

"One!"

When they finished, Harrison said, "Don't recover—roll. Roll on your guts, a log roll, that way!" he said, pointing toward the bridge.

The mids rolled, gathering mud and sand. The water in their clothing attracted every speck of anything solid on the beach. Once they were completely covered in muck and filth, Harrison finally yelled, "Recover!"

The whole platoon joined Harrison and the remaining cadre in laughing at their predicament. "Look at you!" he said. "This is an important milestone in your Navy diver career. This is what we call 'sugar cookies.' Hooyah?"

"Hooyah, sugar cookies!" the platoon agreed.

"Gentlemen, to be a Navy diver you need to be willing to be cold, wet, muddy, and sandy. Those who hesitated clearly did not have the mettle, the desire that you do. I think we're down to a good number. What . . . twenty-seven?"

"Hooyah, twenty-seven," Jackson agreed.

"Hooyah. Well, let's finish up with a run. We'll complete the rest of an outer, but first, 'The Rat song'!"

"Front leaning rest!" Durago commanded. The whole platoon dropped to the pushup position.

"Some liquor was spilled on the barroom floor and the bar was closed for the night—"

By the end of the first line, everyone had joined in.

"Then out from a tiny hole in the wall came a mouse in the pale moonlight!

"He lapped up the liquor on the barroom floor and back on his haunches he sat!

"And all through the night you could hear him shout!

"'Bring on the gosh-darn cat!'

"So, they brought out the cat and they had a little spat, and the cat whipped up on the mouse!

"The moral of the story is, 'You can't have a drink on the house!' Hooyah!"

When they started again, Durago was reminded of his runs with Strong only two months before. He realized yet again that he had come a long way in that time. He sensed that he had quickly proved to his superiors—to Washington, and maybe even Simpson—that he could handle the rigors of Plebe Year. His classmates seemed to appreciate that he was not bringing any more heat on them. But that alone was not enough for him.

Jogging through the housing area, Collins led them through a whispered cadence that had its origins with Marine Corps Reconnaissance. Waking company officers and their families would be ill advised.

"Swift."

"Swift," the platoon repeated when their left feet hit the pavement.

"Si-lent."

"Si-lent," they parroted, the first beat on their left, the second on their right feet.

"Dead-ly."

"Dead-ly."

In a normal tone, Harrison called out, "Road guards, post!"

Durago was second in line on the left-side rank, one of the designated "road guards." He sprinted toward Gate 8 and stood in the center of the road facing inward, blocking any potential traffic that might be leaving the Academy at this early hour while the platoon crossed the street behind him. One of his classmates did the same, blocking incoming traffic.

Looking across the vehicle bridge that crossed College Creek, he saw Dieter and the quitters, the mids who would not brave the icy Severn, walking back to the hall slowly. They were not even marching anymore; they simply meandered in their weakness, shame, and disappointment. As Durago looked at them, he realized that he was stronger than they. Some of them may have been faster, some able to lift more weight, but they did not have the heart, the will, to press on through difficulty. Suddenly, he felt like his ties to Annapolis were strengthened. For the first time since donning the uniform, he excelled, thrived, in an endeavor that most of his peers dared not even attempt, under which others folded. He no longer felt mediocre. Durago now felt that he demonstrated military moxie, and thus he was no longer an outsider.

After the 4th Battalion platoon passed, one of them called out to the gate guards, "Hooyah, Marine Corps!"

The Marine at the gate answered with, "Oorah!"

As Durago sprinted back to formation, he noticed even more that the cold and the physical pain he carried simply did not bother him.

24

COMMENCEMENT 1990

MAY 30, 1990
1230
NAVY–MARINE CORPS MEMORIAL
STADIUM

"From the Thirty-Third Company, Deborah Anderson."

A cheer accompanied by the clanging of a cowbell erupted from just behind where Durago and his companymates were sitting in the Naval Academy's football stadium.

"Thomas Wheeler," announced the public address system, followed by a similar cheer.

Each midshipman from the Class of 1990 walked up the ramp to the stage set up in the end zone, accepted a blue folder with the diploma and commissioning certificate, then shook hands with Vice President Dan Quayle.

Durago looked to the empty visiting side of the stadium. *Even in football, we remember service*, he thought as he reread the names of battles displayed in large blue letters, particularly "MEKONG DELTA," "THUA THIEN," "QUANG TRI," and "YANKEE STATION." *I wonder if someday there'll be battles that my classmates and I have fought in listed there.*

His thoughts were interrupted by Moeller asking him, "You all moved in yet?"

"What? Up to seven-four? Well, my shit's up there, but I'm going on cruise soon. I didn't unpack much."

"Me either. It's gonna suck up there—big difference in the walk from four-zero."

"Yeah, but nobody goes up there but the mids in Fourteenth Company. We'll be above the radar."

"I heard we're getting a new company officer—a Marine."

Finally, after the last folder was bestowed, Durago joined the crowd in anticipation as the newly commissioned officers rose to their feet. The president of the Class of 1991 stepped up to the lectern. The last of the crowd's chatter hushed with the realization that the two most senior classes were about to perform the Naval Academy's most recognized tradition.

The president surveyed Navy–Marine Corps Memorial Stadium to ensure everyone was ready. "Brigade, I propose three cheers for those who go before us! Hip, hip!"

"Hooray!"

"Hip, hip!"

"Hooray!"

"Hip, hip!"

"Hooray!"

Now the Class of 1990 started whooping it up and some of the audience started clapping with delight and anticipation, as 1990's class president stepped up to the lectern.

"Class of nineteen ninety, I propose three cheers for those we leave behind! Hip, hip!"

"Hooray!"

"Hip, hip!"

"Hooray!"

"Hip, hip!

"Hooray!"

With that, they all threw their covers in the air. It was as if a flock of birds took off at once. The jubilation was deafening. A herd of people pushed onto the field. Kids of all ages scrambled into the throng of celebrating graduates, racing to grab a midshipman's cover as a souvenir of the day. Durago worked his way toward the section where the 23rd Company Firsties had been sitting. He and his classmates had already slipped on the shoulder boards signifying that they were now second class as '91 and '90 carried out their ritual. Durago saw Washington high-fiving his classmates. Durago kept his eye on him and squeezed his way through the crowd.

By the time he reached Washington, the whole Washington clan was around him. Washington's mother and his fiancée were affixing the eagle, globe, and anchor, representing the United States Marine Corps, to his collar. His proud father photographed the moment.

Then his mother pulled out a Marine Corps officer's cover from a hat-box. As she handed it to him, he eyed Durago. Durago stepped up just as Washington put it on.

"Sir, may I be the first?"

"I'd hoped you would, Don."

Durago brought his heels together and assumed a perfect position of attention. Then he rendered the best salute he had ever given. Washington returned it in kind. He turned to his mother. "Mom, will you hand me that bag I gave you earlier?"

Washington pulled from the bag a plaque and handed it to Durago. On the plaque was a silver dollar and a set of gold bars. There was a brass plate that read "From 2nd Lt. Washington, USMC, to Midn 2/c Durago, USN. May 30, 1990. I'll see you in the fleet."

Durago was speechless. Washington's father snapped pictures as the two shook hands.

PART III
THE DETAIL

25

THE INVESTIGATION

 MARCH 31, 1992
1400
NIMITZ LIBRARY

Antonelli, the investigating midshipman, had asked Durago to meet him in Nimitz. On the third floor there were research rooms. Through the glass in one of the doors, Durago saw that Antonelli was waiting for him.

"How's it going?" he asked as Durago sat.

"How d'ya think?"

Durago hoped his classmate would give him a read on what was happening with the overall investigation. He and Antonelli had encountered each other in class once or twice during their tenure in the Yard but did not know each other well. Because Antonelli was a classmate, Durago surmised that he would not write a biased report, and that it would be fair.

"Ever been fried before?"

"Yes."

"Anything serious?"

"Somewhat. I was fried a bunch of times Plebe Year for performance stuff: failure to know rates, room inspections, stuff like that. They compiled to the point that they actually hurt my conduct grades and my overall class rank. But I've never been fried for a five thousand series or above, and I've never earned a black 'N,'" he said, referring to the unofficial varsity letter some mids earned for excessive demerits and restriction.

"Okay, good. So, here's how this goes. First, I'm going to ask some questions." Antonelli shuffled though some papers on the desk, searching for notes. "Background: describe your relationship to Midshipman Fourth Class, now Third Class, Whorton."

"Uh, I was her squad leader during Plebe Summer—her first squad leader, you know, first set."

"Any contact with her since then?"

"Not really, I've seen her around a couple of times, coming and going to class. We've said 'hello' on those occasions, nothing more."

"Did you ever make Midshipman Whorton perform a uniform race?"

"Yes . . . heck, we had the whole platoon racing."

"So, you didn't single her out?"

"What do you mean?"

"Did you single her out specifically? Like, make her do it by herself, or embarrass her in front of her classmates? Make her cry?"

"Embarass her? Make her cry?" Durago asked incredulously. "Are you kidding me?"

Antonelli did not respond; he just looked across the table at Durago.

"You're damned right I embarrassed her; I 'singled her out,' to use your term, on more than one occasion, for poor performance and in an effort to motivate her, to try to make her improve. Yes, I did. You and I both have done it millions of times. It was Plebe Summer, for crying out loud!"

"Easy now, classmate, I'm just trying to figure out if a conduct hearing is warranted."

"Riiight," Durago answered sarcastically. "And she did cry. I can't help that."

Antonelli continued questioning Durago. The questions he asked were accusatory in tone, and Durago could tell they were carefully worded to seem damning, especially to anyone who was not familiar with the Plebe indoctrination system. When he sensed Antonelli was finishing, Durago looked at the clock. They had been at it for almost forty minutes.

"Okay, enough of that. Now for the second part . . ."

At this hour, Nimitz was nearly empty. The door was shut during the whole interview, yet Antonelli looked around suspiciously. After verifying that nobody was within earshot, he said, "Listen, this is frustrating for you, I know. But I gotta tell you—be careful. This thing has the potential to be a witch hunt. In fact, I recommend you get a lawyer."

"Are you serious?"

"The battalion office is considering charging people at six-thousand-series offenses."

"Holy shit! They're going to kick people out?!"

"This thing is very political."

"Everything here is political these days. Damn it! I mean, I knew this was serious, but not that serious!"

"It's as bad as it can possibly be. The Whortons have a psychiatrist involved, a lawyer, and there's even been a congressman calling the battalion officer."

"Fuck me."

Durago sat back and ran his hands through his hair, trying to maintain his composure. He was now more than scared. He realized that he was in danger of being railroaded. Antonelli appeared somewhat sympathetic.

Durago regained his composure, "Alright, who else has accusations against them?"

"I can't tell you that."

"Great. Well, what about the results of this interview?"

"The good news, classmate, is that I'm going to recommend that you don't get fried. I don't see a conduct case here. The problem is, my opinion isn't going to hold much weight with Commander Gordon."

"What? What's the deal?"

"He's been on a crusade to fix the Academy since he got here. I am pretty sure he perceives this case as a vehicle to forward some of his agenda."

"Let me guess, he's not a grad."

"Bingo. He was the one who tried to fry the guys who reconned the mules."

"Oh, shit, really? Damn . . ." Durago thought again about Antonelli as a potential source of gouge on the investigation. "So, how do you know all of this stuff?"

"When you live on seven-zero you hear the talk. The company officers say things while mids on battalion staff are around. It's like they forget we're there, or they think we don't know what they're talking about."

"Wait . . . what about the commandant? If there are six thousands brought out, surely his office will know about it."

"The 'dant has been at a conference this week. He's going on leave from there. Apparently, the deputy commandant has some idea of what's going on. But no six thousands have been written yet, so, for now, this is Commander Gordon's show."

Great," Durago said frowning. "Man, you're just full of good news today."

"Hey, if I can help you, I will. Feel free to come and talk with me anytime. I'll give you as much of a read on what's happening as I can."

Durago sighed. "Yeah, okay. Thanks, man. I may take you up on that."

Durago strode quickly out of Nimitz and across the mezzanine in front of Rickover Hall. He turned right and lighted down the steps, headed toward Maury Hall. The legal office, Jan's office, was to the left on the first floor. Even before he met Jan, Durago knew that "Brigade Legal" on 3-0 was a misnomer. The Brigade Legal office supported the commandant and his staff. On the few occasions that the midshipmen needed legal advice, they came to Jan's office. It was an important distinction. The lawyer assigned to help the Brigade of Midshipmen had to be someone who did not fall within the chain of command.

Jan looked up as he entered. Her desk was set up on the back wall so that it was not between her and her clients. She had a nice large leather chair on wheels and a smaller version across from it, just inside the door to the right. On the left side of the room was a credenza with a bookcase. Durago knocked on the open door.

"Good afternoon, ma'am."

"We're alone," Jan replied. "My secretary is gone for the afternoon. How are you?" She looked both concerned and genuinely glad to see him. It lifted his spirits just a little.

"Not good. I just talked to the investigating officer."

"And . . . ?"

"He recommended that I get a lawyer. Not that I've done anything wrong, but because he thinks this could become a *witch hunt*. . . . His words."

"Oh, my. Well, my sense of this thing was correct then, wasn't it? It's good that you've come to see me."

"What should we do?"

"First, don't worry. Like I've said, this is my job. You're in good hands—I'm going to take care of you."

"You sure?"

"I promise. In fact, we'll start right now," Jan motioned to the chair across from her desk. "Have a seat."

Durago sat down in the chair across from Jan. He began to relax.

"Okay, you have to tell me everything you remember about Midshipman . . . what's her name?"

"Whorton."

"Whorton, right. I'm going to record this and take notes."

Jan pulled out a tape recorder from her desk and clicked it on. She then set a legal pad on her lap and uncapped a Waterman. "Midshipman Donald Durago, 20 March '92. Regarding accusations of Midshipman Whorton. Please begin. Again, start when you first met and tell me everything about your relationship with Midshipman Whorton."

"Well, we met on I-Day when I was a second class on the Detail and she was an incoming Plebe. I met her straightaway and she was in my squad . . . "

26

INDUCTION DAY, CLASS OF 1994

July 3, 1990
1020
HALSEY FIELD HOUSE

D urago inspected himself in the mirror to make sure his silver scuba pin—the diver's hooded and masked face with an old-style double-hose regulator—was level with his left breast pocket. There were times when he put it on his uniform without thought. At other times he would notice it in the mirror, or in the reflection of a window, or as he affixed it to his shirt, and it would remind Durago that completing the Navy's scuba diving course in Panama City was the hardest thing he had done since coming to Annapolis. Durago then took one last look at the red nametag above his right pocket that identified him as a member of the Plebe Summer Detail, the midshipmen who would train the incoming Plebes. It represented that he had fulfilled two of the four goals he had set for himself while at the Academy. It provided him a sense of accomplishment, but, now that it was done, it did not seem as impressive or rewarding as he expected it to be.

Well, he thought, *there are two more goals left.*

Durago thought about Induction Day or "I-Day" and Plebe Summer as he walked from sixth wing and past Dahlgren Hall toward Halsey Field House. Now in Annapolis for his second I-Day, he surmised that it was one of the constants at Navy, something that would never change significantly, a first milestone that bonded all grads. He was slightly nervous about being a member of the Plebe Detail. Only the best midshipmen were selected. Puffed up again for a moment, Durago realized that his presence in Annapolis on this day signified that he had come a long way since his own I-Day. He still could not believe that he was about to be a squad leader only two years after he was a struggling Plebe.

Tourists and parents flowed throughout the Yard like schooled fish. As officers or midshipmen approached, they became alert and parted as if a shark were among them. To them, the midshipmen who were about to transform their sons and daughters from civilians to sailors held true mystery. However, the mids' real prey was the incoming class.

Durago smelled such blood in the throng of parents and incoming Plebes milling around outside Halsey Field House. The Naval Academy Band was set up on the lawn across from Halsey, in front of Lejeune. Gleaming in their white uniforms, they played marches—especially *Anchors Aweigh*—throughout the morning to provide the right ambience for the crowd.

Butted up against Annapolis and its harbor, Halsey housed indoor track and basketball. It held a labyrinth of locker rooms, classrooms, squash courts, and offices that were used by a variety of athletic clubs and classes. Durago pushed past the camera crews and reporters in the lobby and made his way into the field house proper. His eyes adjusted to the artificial lights overhead that were humming above the din of I-Day.

Durago found the members of the Golf Company staff near a set of bleachers. The 13th Platoon Commander was Meagan "Penny" Penrock, a star on the women's crew team. Many mids still referred to female rowers as "crewbas," a derivation of the now-illicit term "WUBA" that the Brigade seemed to think an acceptable term of endearment for these athletes. Durago knew her from his naval architecture, or "boats," class. Meagan was a Nordic goddess—svelte, tall, and blonde, with enough bosom that Durago had to force himself to look into her blue eyes whenever they talked. She also had a reputation for being "extremely fucking squared away," as Victor Kolchak put it.

Kolchak, another squad leader, was the old man of the group. He served in the fleet as an aviation mechanic and applied to the Academy three times. He just made the age requirement before arriving for Plebe Summer in 1988. The third squad leader was Midshipman

Second Class Xavier Omerta. Tall and lanky, Omerta was known as a quiet and serious person.

After the first quota of twelve candidates in 13th Platoon sat in the bleachers next to the basketball court, Durago began their long journey.

"Good morning. I'm Midshipman Second Class Durago, your squad leader for the day. All of you will be in Golf Company. The company is split into two platoons, Thirteenth and Fourteenth Platoons. Those platoons will join Thirteenth and Fourteenth Company in August. We live in Bancroft Hall on six-zero and six-one. That's sixth wing, zero deck and first deck, respectively. Remember that if you get lost."

The group stared at him, obviously already confused.

Oh, this is going to be fun, he thought. "By the way, don't get lost. This day is fast paced. Pay attention and don't become separated from the squad. Everyone put on your nametags and form a line on this yellow tape. Now."

The candidates began scrambling. Some moved to the line first, while others fumbled to put nametags on their shirts. After five minutes Durago surveyed the "squad." All of them had seen enough war movies to assume something similar to the position of attention. He went down the rank and noted several discrepancies. There was long hair, weak stomachs, and a dude with an earring. He stopped in front of a thin, pale girl with curly red hair. The girl looked like a red-headed Peppermint Patty. She was slightly smaller than Durago. He looked to her nametag. It was on the wrong side and upside-down.

"Miss, what is your name?"

"Whorton."

"No kidding, huh? Well, then, your nametag must be wrong."

"No."

"No, sir."

"No, sir!"

"Well, Miss Whorton, your nametag is on the wrong side and it's upside-down. Fix it."

"Yes, sir."

"Okay, people, listen up. From now on, you address everyone as 'sir' or 'ma'am.' You will only be allowed six basic responses to a question. They are: 'Yes, sir,' 'No, sir,' 'Aye, aye, sir,' 'I'll find out, sir,' 'No excuse, sir,' or the correct answer to the question. Is that understood?"

"Yes, sir!" the squad tried to answer in unison.

"Okay, next, memorize the six-digit number they gave you when you came in this morning. It's your alpha code. This number is like a social security number here. It will be used for everything from pay to laundry."

He paused to ensure he had everyone's attention. "Okay, let's move out."

The processing through Halsey Field House was relatively uneventful for Durago. He was following his squad like a shepherd with his flock. The Plebes received directions at each station. Corpsmen stabbed them with needles to draw blood, tailors measured them for uniforms, and disbursing clerks processed travel claims. All civilian clothes and articles were tagged, bagged, and thrown onto a flatbed truck, never to be seen again. Durago tried to maintain accountability of the exact location of each squad member so he would not lose one. He studied his notes and realized that five of the twelve Plebes he had today were to be in his squad during the summer.

Like Kolchak, Reginald Mitchell was a prior enlisted sailor from inner-city Detroit. He served as an operations specialist 3rd class for a year before applying for a commission. He spent another year at the Naval Academy Prep School, or "NAPS," to buff up his academics. Gottschalk was at the other end of the spectrum. The seventeen-year-old claimed his flight from Florida to Baltimore was the first plane ride of his life. Then there was Whorton. From the start, she exuded an air that she had no concept of the world around her. *This one is going to be trouble*, thought Durago.

The last task for the incoming Plebes was to try on one set of each uniform to confirm that they fit. Durago watched as his squad tore open packages, pulled pins and tags, and tried to identify uniform items.

"Ah, Mister Gottschalk, that is not a wrestling singlet. It's a woman's bathing suit. I suggest you exchange it."

"Yes, sir."

"Mister Gottschalk . . ."

"Aye, aye, sir."

"Mister Van Zandt, listen to directions. You were ordered to try on one of each article of clothing. I assure you that if the first medium trou in one package fits, all of them will."

After Halsey, the next step was haircuts in the seventh-wing barber shop. Durago first marched his squad to the Golf Company area and instructed them to find their rooms by the nametags on the doors and stow their issue bags.

The next morning, Durago had his first squad instruction period, or "SIP." Some of these sessions were used to pressure the Plebes in a style reminiscent of the basic training or "boot camp" that enlisted members endured. Others were used for coaching or mentoring the Plebes.

"Okay, people, gather 'round. Take a seat on the deck." Durago sat on a chair in the middle of the passageway, and the Plebes plopped down in front of him like first graders at reading time.

"We discussed memorizing your oath of office and 'Message to Garcia' at breakfast. It seems like everyone knows these rates and their meanings. We're going to continue to pick up the pace and add to your required knowledge. One of the most important lessons here at the Academy is teamwork and classmate loyalty. I know you've already begun getting to know your classmates. By noon meal today, you must know all in your squad by name, including their hometown. By evening meal, you must know everyone in the company.

"I want to get to know *you* a little better, as well. So, the second half of this instruction period will be spent writing your own biography. I only need two to five pages. Write about your life until now, your family, what sports and activities you like, and most important, why you decided to come to the U.S. Naval Academy. Questions?"

Durago paused a moment. "None? Good. Mitchell, do you have white works alpha rigged? You know how to set up the neckerchief?"

"Yes, sir."

"Good. Go to your room and bring me one set of each clothing article. We're going to learn how to fold clothes. Gottschalk?"

"Sir?"

"Go get your neckerchief. It's the black scarf-looking thing."

"Aye, aye, sir."

"Fourth Class Regiment, attention to announcements."

A hush fell over King Hall. Each midshipman with his back to the podium performed an about-face so that all hands faced the podium in the center of King Hall's T-shape, the space commonly called "The Anchor."

"Rifle issue for all starboard companies goes tomorrow, starting at oh-seven-hundred. Platoon commanders and above will draw swords starting at fourteen-hundred. There will be a meeting of all company commanders and company officers this evening at nineteen thirty in Chauvenet Hall. Regiment, seats."

Durago sat at the head of the table. To his immediate left, Gottschalk stood by the hot seat with his arm straight out, "requesting to speak." Durago remembered his own time in such a position, and how his poor performance negatively affected not only his life, but the lives of his classmates, as Simpson and Brooks grilled him.

"Gottschalk."

"Sir, request to seat the squad."

"Seat the squad, Mister Gottschalk."

"Squad, seats!"

"Rub-a-dub-dub, bring on the grub!" the squad yelled in unison.

"Cute cheer, Mister Gottschalk."

"Thank you, sir."

"Get another one; I don't like cute."

"Aye, aye, sir."

"What are we having for lunch?"

"Sir, the menu for noon meal is individual pan pizzas, garlic bread, green beans, iced tea, lemonade, assorted cookies, and milk, sir."

"Miss Whorton, who are the members of your squad?"

"Aye, aye, sir," Whorton said in her monotone voice.

Durago had already noticed that when speaking, Whorton produced no inflection at all. He thought she may be doing it on purpose, as if she were afraid her voice was too feminine, or that it was required as part of her Plebedom.

Durago looked past Gottschalk at Whorton. She was looking straight ahead. "Miss Whorton, did you not understand me? What are the names of all of your companymates?"

No answer.

"Miss Whorton?"

"Aye, aye, sir?" Whorton said quizzically as she raised her eyebrows.

"Whoa . . . let's reset," Durago barked. "Whorton, what are your basic responses?"

"'Yes, sir,' 'No, sir,' 'Aye, aye, sir,' 'I'll find out, sir,' 'No excuse, sir,' and the correct answer, sir."

"Great, now we've reviewed day one. Let's turn the page, shall we? Who is in your squad?"

"I'll find out, sir."

"Who's that next to you?"

"I'll find out, sir."

"Earth to Whorton—I've been using his name for the past five minutes."

Whorton did not move.

"Miss Whorton, get with the program. And stop with the voice thing. You don't have to sound like a Speak & Spell."

"Yes, sir."

"How about, 'Aye, aye, sir,' Miss Whorton?"

"How about, aye, aye, sir?" she repeated.

Durago looked at Whorton, dumbfounded. Several of the Plebes were trying to contain their laughter now.

"Squad, pipe down!" Durago yelled. "Miss Whorton, this is not a Jedi mind trick. You just answered your basic responses correctly. Do you know anyone in the squad?"

"No, sir," she responded immediately.

"Have you spent any time trying to memorize them?"

"No, sir."

Durago shook his head in frustration. "Well, you had better figure it out, Miss Whorton." *I wonder if this is what I looked like Plebe Summer, Plebe Year,* he thought. "Let me hear your oath of office."

"I'll find out, sir."

"Whorton, what does 'nine-point-five percent' mean to you?"

She stared blankly into space.

"Anyone?" he looked around the table. "No answer? I'll tell you, and I want everyone to receive and heed what I'm saying. Nine-point-five percent is the acceptance rate of this fine institution. For every one hundred people that applied to your class, ten were accepted. The government, God help us, has selected you to be one of those ten. Get with the program, Whorton, unless you want to become part of the ten percent that doesn't graduate."

"Aye, aye, sir."

"We'll see. Since we're into reviewing day-one rates, Newburg, tell us about 'Message to Garcia.'"

27

Uniform Race

"Plebe ho!"

Durago listened to the twelve Plebes, who were split into four rooms of three, begin scrambling to secure their rooms and enter the passageway. As the Plebes exited their rooms, they chopped in a box shape, making a left- or right-face, then another, hitting the bulkhead next to their room, and ending with an about-face and sounding off. Whorton's room was last, as usual.

"Okay, people, SIP time. Get up to six-one!" Durago's voice was rasping from the strain of motivational yelling and disciplining.

He followed his squad as they chopped up the stairs to 6-1, where their classmates were already in pushup position waiting for them. Kolchak was walking among the Plebes, ensuring that they were all in a satisfactory stance. Omerta was in a one-armed pushup, quietly humming to himself. Durago got on his face between Van Zandt and Tyler.

"What are we going to do today, Mister Kolchak?" he queried.

"I'll tell ya, Mister Durago. Our Plebes have had such shitty uniforms the past two formations that we have to introduce them to our favorite game."

"No, Mister Kolchak, not that . . ."

"Yes, Mister Durago . . . uniform races!"

"Platoon, recover!" called Omerta.

The whole platoon popped to attention. "Beat Army, sir!"

"In order to ensure you know how to properly wear your uniforms, we're going to play a game," said Kolchak. "I want all of you to go back to your rooms and get into white works foxtrot. When you return, you'd better look perfect. You have five minutes. Go!"

The Plebes stood frozen with disbelief.

"Four minutes, fifty-five seconds."

Suddenly a massive traffic jam of Plebes was in the passageway. By the time they cleared out, there was only a minute and a half left.

Eventually, the Plebes began filtering back into the passageway. Most of them at least had the right uniform on—the white Cracker Jack jumper and trousers with a combination cover and shiny corfram shoes. Some brought their neckerchief also; one or two had the wrong shoes, substituting tennis shoes. As they arrived they were inspected by one of the three squad leaders. Omerta was wearing his khakis now, the upperclass uniform equivalent to foxtrot.

When the last Plebe returned, Kolchak looked at his watch. "Eight minutes. Are you people kidding me! You have to be a lot faster than that. Believe me, this exercise has real world applications for you folks. On top of that, many of you are in the wrong uniform!"

"Listen up, people," chimed in Omerta. "Look at me. I casually got into khakis and it only took me three minutes. I had to change everything! You need work! Effort, people!"

"Everyone, on your faces!" called Durago. "Pushups—begin. One, two, three . . ."

"One!"

Durago noticed from the corner of his eye that Whorton still could not keep up with the physical regimen. She lay on her stomach after two pushups, making no effort to continue.

After the reps Durago yelled, "Recover!" He began to stroll down the line of Plebes, scrutinizing each of them. "Okay, let's see if at least *someone* has a squared away uniform." Kolchak and Omerta did the same from the other side of the passageway. When Durago came to Whorton, he shook his head dramatically in disgust.

"Well, Whorton, for starters, you have on the wrong undershirt. On top of that, your uniform is dirty."

Durago noticed that Posner, one of Whorton's roommates, seemed squared away. "Posner, why are you in good shape and Whorton isn't? Are you helping her?"

"Yes, sir."

"Whorton—"

Whorton's bottom lip began to quiver. Tears welled up in her eyes. Durago dropped the volume to a conversational tone. "Whoa,

Whorton, don't you cry on me. You don't rate crying. Come on, now. Don't let this get to you . . . work on it."

Kolchak stepped into his room and blasted his stereo to end the quiet and to create a small lift in the Plebes' morale. He emerged from the room and yelled over the music, "When this song is over, you'd better be back here in summer whites. Go!"

Bodies scrambled yet again. Durago followed his Plebes downstairs to observe their mad scramble. *Why does Whorton seem not to care one day, then she loses it the next?*

When he reached 6-0 he began pacing up and down the passageway. He shouted, "I know what you people are thinking!" His voice became whiny. "'But, sir, I haven't worn this uniform yet. I haven't sized my belt yet. Second and Third Squad don't have to run down a flight of steps.' Well, boo hoo hoo! 'Message to Garcia,' people! You'd better be dressing like you're at your girlfriend's house and her parents just pulled up in the driveway! By the way, children, you *all* are already late!"

Durago mounted the stairs back up to 6-1. He watched as the Plebes scrambled back again and silently observed the other Plebe Detail members correcting each of their charges. Penrock arrived on deck, returning from a meeting with the regimental staff. She was already dressed in summer whites with a sword. Durago thought it was surprising how she could appear feminine, athletic, and military all at once.

"Okay, people," she called out, "evening meal formation in five minutes. Here is your last uniform race. White works alpha—go!"

Again the Plebes ran around like the Keystone Kops. Durago walked up to Penrock. "Penny, this chick, Whorton, needs help."

"Yeah, no kidding."

"No, I'm serious. There's something wrong. I want to talk with the company officer."

"What?"

"Just watch her over the next day or so."

"Okay," Penrock replied.

The next afternoon, the Golf Company Plebes were in Luce Hall attending a class on basic seamanship. Omerta had marched, or 'driven,' them over there, so Durago had some time off. He changed out of his khaki uniform into regulation shorts and a t-shirt. He opened his desk to review the autobiographies that the Plebes had written the day after Induction Day.

"I was a varsity soccer player for four years at Belmont High and was team captain my Senior Year."

"I graduated as valedictorian of my high school class."

"I applied from the fleet and subsequently received orders to NAPS."

"I came to the United States Naval Academy because it is a challenging school and I wanted to serve in the military."

They were all very much the same, except one. Durago realized that it scared him on many levels. When he knocked on Penrock's open door, she was on the phone, an amenity reserved for platoon commanders and above. She hung up quickly.

"Hey, Don. What's up?"

Durago replied with a common Plebe Year response. "Fidelity is up and Obedience is down on my bayonet belt buckle, ma'am."

Penrock laughed.

"Okay, seriously now," Durago said. "Remember what I told you about Whorton?"

"Yes."

"Read this; it's her bio."

"Holy shit, it looks like a third grader wrote it!"

"No kidding. Look at that thing—sometimes she even writes the letter 'e' backwards."

"The tense here is even wrong!"

"I know, I know. Yet she says in there that she got a fifteen hundred on the SAT."

"She's like Rain Man."

Now they both laughed.

"Well, okay. Go see the company officer," Penrock said. "Better take Whorton with you."

The next morning the Plebes had a squad instruction period. Durago called out just as it got started. "Whorton!"

"Yes, sir."

Again, the barely discernable monotone voice. "Fall out and follow me."

Whorton stepped away from the bulkhead and walked over toward Durago.

"I didn't say 'carry on,' Whorton. Chop down the passageway and follow me." She followed him down the stairs to 6-0. They stopped outside the company officer's office.

"Hit a bulkhead right there." Durago walked into the lieutenant's office. The company officer motioned the mid to sit down, and closed the door.

Lieutenant Canavan was a P-3 pilot. He left the cockpit for two years to come to the Academy for some time off from overseas deployments and to pursue a master's degree at Georgetown University.

"Miss Penrock said you would be coming by. What can I do for you, Mister Durago?"

"Sir, I want to talk with you about one of my Plebes, Miss Whorton. This is going to sound crazy, but . . . she doesn't belong here, sir."

"Excuse me?"

"Sir, I seriously think something is wrong with her. I have no idea how she ever made it through the selection process."

"Whoa, slow down. Listen, how bad can she be? We're only one week into this thing, Mister Durago. I understand your desire to ensure this institution only matriculates the best, and some who are not up to our standards are bound to get in, but this is week one! Surely this Plebe under your guidance will come around. Hell, I'd doubt there's a squad out there that doesn't have at least one Plebe who is completely screwed up."

"Sir, this one is beyond."

The lieutenant sat back in his chair. "Okay, mister. Tell me a story."

"Well, sir, she speaks in a monotone. I mean, she can't yell with the other Plebes; she has no inflection. Then she can't follow basic directions. I mean, simple stuff like how to dress on time and wear the uniform. She seems like she's not there all the time, like she can't hear us. When she does seem cognizant, she breaks down."

"What have you done thus far to help her?"

"I've tried to give her some extra instruction. I've talked to her roommates and asked them to be good classmates and help her. But, as you say, we're only one week into this thing."

Durago realized that he did not sound very convincing. "Sir, I would ask that you do two things. First, read this—it's her bio, the ones we had the Plebes write on, like, day two. Second, please talk with her for just a few moments. She's outside right now."

Canavan leaned forward and took the bio from Durago's hand. He sat back again and read it quietly. His face registered surprise. "Okay, send her in. I want you to stand by outside."

"Aye, aye, sir."

Whorton and Canavan had a meeting with the door open. Durago stood ten paces away, out of earshot. After about ten minutes, Whorton chopped out into the hallway, her cover still in her hand.

"Go Navy, sir!"

"Plebe halt!"

She stopped dead in her tracks.

"Whorton, put your cover on when you're in the p-way."

"Yes, sir."

"How about, 'Aye, aye, sir?'"

"How about aye, aye, sir!"

"No, Whorton, what I mean is, the correct response to an order is 'Aye, aye, sir!' This is not hard!"

She stood there, dumbfounded.

"Get out of here."

"He wants to see you, sir," she said before chopping down the hallway.

Durago stepped back into the office. Canavan was on the phone. He looked up as Durago stepped in and spoke to Durago with the phone still to his ear.

"Mister Durago, I will never doubt your judgment again."

"Who are you calling, sir?"

"Ward Hall. Miss Whorton needs a psych eval."

28

WARD HALL

 JULY 10, 1990
1300
BANCROFT HALL, 6-0

The next morning, Kolchak took Whorton to Ward Hall. Durago expected never to see her again. He thought that she would be whisked away to Bethesda, becoming a memory to the squad and her classmates.

After noon meal, Lieutenant Canavan summoned Durago and Penrock to his office. He held several papers in his hand. "I have a report from Ward Hall. It's interesting, to say the least. I am in part quoting the doctor's report. 'Miss Whorton does not deal with the world in the same way that most others do. She cannot handle crowds, loud noises, and she has problems coping with change.'"

He dropped the report on the desk. "There's more. I got access to her application package over in Candidate Guidance. The Blue and Gold officer who interviewed her during the application process wrote, and I quote, 'Not only does this candidate lack the potential to be a successful midshipman and naval officer, she should not be allowed to serve in the military in any capacity.' Unquote."

"Unbelievable," said Penrock.

Durago just shook his head.

"How did she get in here, sir?" Penrock asked.

"That would be a dangerous question for me to answer, Miss Penrock. The point is that she's here. Now we have to deal with her."

"What?!" the two midshipmen exclaimed together.

"That's right. Ward Hall's recommendation is that because Whorton is not a danger to herself or others, she should continue on through Plebe Summer. If we can document performance issues, then we can send her to a performance board."

"Well, that shouldn't be a problem. I've already started, sir," said Durago. "In fact, I may have to buy another notebook before the week is out."

"Fine, show me what you have now and we'll go from there. Listen, folks, I know that this is a leadership challenge. Do your best to train Whorton, and come to me if you need help. Questions?"

"Not now, sir," Penrock said for both of them.

"Dismissed."

Every afternoon from 1400 to 1600 the Plebes had sports. They practiced and played on all levels, from varsity to intramural. The midshipmen on the Detail did not participate, so it gave them a good break. They used the time for their own workouts, to catch up on sleep, or to go on liberty. Durago and Penrock were in the habit of going out in Annapolis during this time.

Durago did not see much of Annapolis during his Plebe Year. He fell in love with the place in his Youngster Summer. Durago liked the colonial seaport feel that the town maintained, which he suspected was two-thirds genuine and one-third affected as a means to draw tourists. There were many pubs and restaurants that vied to be recognized as the best purveyor of seafood, especially crab cake sandwiches. Many people remarked particularly at the number of Irish-themed establishments, like McGarvey's, Riordan's, and O'Brien's. These were interspersed with locally owned coffee houses and t-shirt shops, where anything imaginable was silkscreened or embroidered with "Annapolis" and "Naval Academy." The previous winter Durago went Christmas shopping with Slim, who bought t-shirts for his family with sayings like "I'd rather be in a boat with a drink on the rocks, than in the drink with a boat on the rocks," and "Annapolis: A drinking town with a sailing problem." The red-brick streets gave the whole place a clean and quaint amusement park or movie set feel, but this was counteracted by more than one ship's chandler catering to the whole spectrum of modern day seafarers, from waterman and commercial fisherman to offshore yacht racer and merchant mariner.

All activity centered on Annapolis Harbor, especially the narrow finger jutting into the town, commonly called "Ego Alley." It drew attention because it served as the proverbial runway for boat owners to cruise in slowly, stop, then turn, in order to see and be seen by the jealous crowd. This constant movement of boats of all types and sizes reminded Durago of extras in a dance musical or in the background of a hip hop video—random yet ordered at the same time. Durago had noticed a direct ratio between boat size, age of the captain, size of his waistline, and size of the breasts of his "bow bunnies," women who often acted as if the ritual were more about them than the vessel they reclined upon.

Not far from the corner of Ego Alley, Middleton's Tavern had hosted many of the Founding Fathers when Annapolis was the nation's capital. Durago and Penrock turned their afternoon time off into a ritual, a tradition of enjoying some raw oysters on the half shell. Durago liked to round out the meal with the pub's world-renowned Cuban black bean soup.

Penrock and Durago became closer with each other than with Omerta and Kolchak. Neither of them knew why; they just seemed to understand each other and have a lot in common. Durago saw through Penrock's looks and was inspired by her leadership. She seemed to have an element of wisdom. So, although she only had one more year of experience than he, he looked to her as a mentor. Still, he wondered if after Plebe Summer a romance may develop between the two of them.

They sat down and began to unwind. Penrock sipped her lemonade. "Wow, this is good."

"Especially on a hot day like today."

They spoke about the weather, the food, the people they saw, avoiding shop talk. It was impossible, however, for them to pass twenty minutes without talking about their Plebes. They both realized that being on the Detail was an outstanding leadership experience in a world dominated by academics. Both felt like they were learning more about leadership in these few days on the Detail than they could ever learn in the classroom. And yet, they also felt like glorified camp counselors.

"How is Whorton doing?" Penrock queried.

"She still isn't cutting it. I just don't know what to do with her."

"What do you mean?"

"Well, it's like she's poisoning the rest of my squad. Any little training I give these people is slowed by the fact that I have to review basic shit with Whorton again and again. Time that I could be using to review flag hoists or drill, they're standing around watching me show her how to salute or coaching her through her basic responses."

"What are her classmates doing about it?"

"I suppose they're doing what they can. I know Posner practically dresses her every morning. It's frustrating for them, too. They can't make her memorize rates. It's not about rates, anyway; she simply doesn't have it. You've seen her; Whorton isn't there—she doesn't have a clue."

"So, what are you going to do?"

"Shit on her, document everything she does wrong, and recommend that she goes to a performance board. I never thought I'd be one to say this, but I'll basically, methodically, run her out . . . or at least start her on her way."

"Are you learning anything from her?"

"I've learned that I wouldn't get into an airplane if she were flying it . . . or a car if she were driving. Hell, a bicycle . . ."

"Then you've let her win."

"What?"

Penrock raised her eyebrows at Durago as she sipped her drink. She put it down and looked at him, trying to see if he would get it.

"What?" he asked again.

"The point, Don, is that it requires absolutely no thought or talent, or . . . leadership, to run Whorton out. Didn't you hear what Canavan said? Look, at this stage we could run everyone in our platoon out if we wanted. I could PT all the guys until they ran to their mother's skirts, and you know it. Whorton is here and you have to deal with her."

Penrock slipped another oyster into her mouth. "So," she continued, "you have two choices. One, run Whorton out. Two, train Whorton. Which do you think requires leadership?"

"Uh, two."

"Precisely. Know what I think? I think you're too squared away to just let this one get away. Maybe she has some potential. Be creative, motivate her, make her into the Brigade commander. If you fail, if she still doesn't work out, fine. Know that you did your best. One thing I believe in is the system. She's screwed up, no doubt about it. If the doc is right, then eventually the system will get her. But for now, it's too early to think about that. Just train her."

"I'm not sure I agree with that."

"Why not?"

"Well, for starters, you used the word 'system.' A lot of people use that word around here. They act as if this place is a huge machine. Civilians come in the front door on I-Day, then this place molds them, changes them, turns them into officers . . . or it spits them out. Think about how we talk about it. 'Don't go against the system.' 'The system will fix him eventually.' But you also hear people say, 'Bob spends all his time in the varsity lacrosse locker room so he can avoid the system.' Which demonstrates my belief that there is no system."

"No?"

"No. The Naval Academy is not a system; it's an environment. An environment that some people avoid, and others are able to muck through."

"What do you mean?"

"Look, Pen, we didn't know each other until . . . when? Boats class, right?"

"Yeah."

"I was a Youngster by that time. In fact, hell, it was just last spring. You've seen me as a relatively squared-away guy."

"Oh, please . . ." Penrock said, rolling her eyes.

"No, listen. I was a really screwed up Plebe. It's a long story, but as I reflected on my first year here, I realized that if it weren't for particular personalities, I'd have simply glided through."

"How so?"

"Well, I was a screw-up throughout Plebe Summer, but I endured because I was one of twelve Plebes in a squad. The upperclass would eventually become bored with me and move on, especially with the ratio of four Detailers to almost forty Plebes—one to ten. The numbers obviously change during academic year—"

"Then, three to one."

"Right. So, this continued into the academic year. But if it weren't for a second class flamer named Simpson who kept the heat on, I'd have faded into the woodwork. As a result of him constantly showing how messed up I was, I actually went to a Battalion Performance Board."

"You?!"

"Yes. I even lost Christmas break during Plebe Year."

"Military Performance Winter School?"

"No. Though I learned later that that would have been a possibility for me. I was kept here on restriction because I had piled up a bunch of Form Twos. I had my own version of 'Winter Plebe Summer' with Master Chief Strong."

"Oh, I remember him. I'll bet that was fun," Penrock said sarcastically. "So, now you look back and respect this guy, Simpson."

"No, not exactly—he was a dick. In fact, I've caught myself in dealing with Whorton wondering if I started to become like him. I haven't, but it's made me reel it in. But, in the guy's defense, without him being relentless, I think I'd have simply slid through this whole place."

"Well, I agree with you that some varsity athletes never get it."

"I know. I've heard a guy criticizing one of the football players, saying, 'Dude, you don't go to the Naval Academy, you go to the Naval Academy Athletic Association.'"

"Nice."

"You know that whole Marshall quote."

"Yeah . . . 'I want an officer for a secret and dangerous mission. I want a West Point football player.'"

"Don't get me wrong, I believe that shit. There's a lot of good dudes, and some hooyah chicks, in this place—great varsity athletes, like you, who I know will one day be COs of ships and CNOs of the Navy. I'm just saying that if you want to, you can slip through the cracks. I know, because I think I almost did."

Penrock sat back and pushed her plate forward. "Don, you're a philosopher," she said, almost laughing.

"Huh?"

"Look, I think you're overthinking this. Just remember this—Plebe Summer is for you, too. You accomplish nothing by running her out. You'll only cheat her, yourself, and whoever you think should have had her spot."

"Well, *your* attitude toward her sure has changed."

"So, maybe there is a system; maybe it is an environment. Maybe something bigger is at work. I dunno. I'm merely pointing out that at this point you accomplish nothing by dumping on her. It's bad karma. Do your best to lead; be ready to accept the results."

"Yeah? I dunno," Durago replied skeptically.

"Think of the mission," Penrock said coyly.

"The mission?"

"Of the United States Naval Academy."

"What, am I a Plebe now? Are you kidding me?"

Penrock stared at Durago, making it clear she wanted him to go along.

"To develop midshipmen mentally, morally, and physically in order to create graduates," Durago began.

"Right, but do you really know what it means? You know, we usually focus on the second part, without realizing the implications of 'to develop,' don't we? Do you remember why the Naval Academy was founded?"

"To train midshipmen ashore. Prior to 1845, we followed the British tradition—midshipmen were one step above cabin boy. They were sent to sea aboard ship to learn to become officers. The name 'midshipman' comes from the fact that they were placed literally in the middle of the ship, 'amidships,' so they could call out orders, passing them by voice from stem to stern."

"Yeah, but what about the *Somers*?"

"The what?"

"USS *Somers*. It was an American naval vessel serving in the Atlantic as a small packet. During a voyage to deliver dispatches back in 1842, a midshipman on board by the name of Philip Spencer incited a mutiny—"

"Oh! I remember," Durago exclaimed. "They hung him from the yardarm with a few other mutineers."

"Right. Remember who his father was?"

"SECNAV."

"No, the secretary of war, the Honorable John C. Spencer. Like any pissed-off politician, he called for an investigation into the death of his son. One of the results was a determination that midshipmen should not train at sea. Instead, a naval academy should be established to train them ashore, preparing them for—"

"Yeah, it's coming back to me. Funny, huh? It was probably revolutionary. How many naval officers do you think said, 'This is bullshit. Midshipman Spencer got what he had coming to him. Next thing you know, they'll be . . . I dunno . . .'"

"Letting women serve."

"Ha! You said it," Durago said with a wink.

"I said what you were thinking . . . dick," Penrock said smiling. "My point is that each midshipman develops differently, at different paces. It's for this reason that we have four years here. Don't get me wrong, I think Whorton has issues; I just think at this point we can't replace her, so, let's try to train her."

The two sat in silence for a while as Durago thought about what Penrock said. He felt a little ashamed. His mind went to Washington and to Master Chief Strong, the two mentors who set him on the right track, who made him the midshipman he had become—a mid he was starting to feel was somewhat worthy of his father's sacrifice. *What would they have done? What if they had given up on him?*

"What can I say? You're right," he said finally.

"Always."

29

COACHED

July 13, 1990
0530
Bancroft Hall, 6-0

Durago woke up in a puddle of sweat, typical for a humid summer morning in Bancroft Hall. Unlike his Plebes, he did not have a fan. He was only able to sleep because of his exhaustion after a day of training.

He donned his PT gear and cleaned his room to ensure that it was immaculate. It was very important to him to be an example should one of the twelve Plebes in the squad come around to see him. After his room was sat, he entered the passageway and inspected the squad. They had fallen out for the morning muster.

"Sir, room six-zero-zero-eight all turned out, sir!"

"Very well."

"Sir, room six-zero-one-zero all turned out, sir!"

"Very well."

After the muster he went out to the sixth-wing parking lot to stretch where the platoon began to form up for PT. Penrock was already there.

"Morning, Miss Penrock."

"Good morning, Mister Durago, fine Navy day, isn't it?"

"Yes, Miss Penrock, it is a fine day to be in the Navy."

They exchanged the same banter every morning. The Plebes laughed at the routine. After the platoon was assembled, including the guidon bearer, the platoon commander addressed them with a loud voice. "Ladies and gentlemen, you were not here on time again this morning. I'm sick and tired of having to act as a camp counselor. This is the Naval Academy, not Camp Tecumseh!"

Her voice returned to conversation tone. "Little mistakes are unacceptable. If you do not square yourselves away, we will square you away. Believe me, our corrective methods are not enjoyable. If you doubt me, try me."

Durago noticed that, for once, Whorton and her roommates were not last.

The two upperclass ran the platoon over to the PEP field. Once there, they monitored their charges. The whole class of Plebes performed exercises to develop their cardiovascular fitness under the instruction of Coach Heinz Lenz. Lenz was a legend, the Naval Academy's Jack LaLanne. He was believed to be in his eighties, and he could run any mid into the ground as a warm-up.

Durago walked through the platoon, particularly his squad, giving encouragement, offering pointers on the exercise, and observing his people for health problems. He noted that Whorton was performing pretty well this morning. The kid was sweating a lot, but she seemed to be handling the heat better than she had on previous mornings.

"Okay, Ninety-Four, two round trips! Go at a thirty-second pace!" Lenz commanded.

The Plebes were off on their last set of sprints for the morning. They looked like a herd of frightened antelope, moving so fast that one couldn't pick out any individual member. Durago was running with Newburg.

"Come on, Newburg, last sprint . . . let's push it."

"Aye, aye, sir," the Plebe croaked.

"Don't speak, run."

Suddenly, Durago tripped on something. He got up quickly, for fear of being trampled. He looked back to see that he had tripped on a Plebe. It was Whorton. She was lying on the ground, splayed like she had fallen from the sky without a parachute. Durago reached down and turned her over to face him. Whorton had passed out. Durago picked her up in a fireman's carry and charged through the herding Plebes, heading for the first aid station. At the aid station there were mids with a variety of bumps and bruises, but nothing serious.

"Corpsman, I have a serious problem here!" Durago shouted.

A corpsman came over and saw immediately what had happened. Durago said, "She just passed out."

The corpsman pulled a little vial from his bag and snapped it open in front of Whorton's nose. She began coughing and sputtering. The corpsman then gave her some water and poured some over the Plebe's brow. He looked up at Durago when he saw that Whorton would come around. "What's her name and company?"

"Whorton. She's in Golf Company, Thirteenth Platoon."

"Okay, I'm taking her to medical and we'll call up to your deck to have someone pick her up when she can return to duty."

"Fine. Thanks for your help."

The corpsman did not respond. Without a word, another corpsman came over and the two of them put Whorton on a stretcher and then into an ambulance. They shut the doors and headed for Bancroft Medical.

After returning his Plebes to company area and making sure Penrock would sit with his squad during breakfast, Durago proceeded directly to medical. He walked through the reception area, straight to the emergency rooms. He found Whorton lying on the table in the second one. The Plebe was conscious, and upon seeing Durago she began to get up. She tried to sound off but only emanated a croak before Durago threw up his hands.

"Whoa, Whorton. Relax. How are you doing?"

The Plebe gave the standard answer: "Outstanding, sir."

Durago realized that Whorton might have a little moxie after all.

That afternoon, Whorton was back with the platoon. Durago was tasked by Penrock to march the platoon over to the Chapel to have a welcome-aboard chat with the chaplains. The Plebes all formed up on 6-0 in their white works jumpers and dixie cups. Some were in formation, studying rates from *Reef Points*. Durago centered in front of the platoon to survey that they were all there. Because the Plebes had to report early to the formation, they had time to kill.

"Platoon, atten-hutt!"

The platoon came to attention.

"Report!"

"Sir, First Squad all present."

"Very well."

After receiving the reports of all the Plebe "squad leaders," Durago began to inspect each Plebe. He was extremely critical of each one, and he found at least three things unsat with each one's uniform, until he came to Whorton. He looked the Plebe over slowly three times without saying a word. Whorton was sweating and her lip was quivering. Durago could see that she was trying to look as stern and military as possible—she was actually concentrating on standing there. He noted that her nametag had Brasso in one of the 'Os' and that there were smudges on her cover.

"Whorton?"

"Sir?"

"What is wrong with you?"

"I'll find out, sir?"

"Well, when you do, let me know. You look pretty squared away to me. I cannot find a damned thing wrong with your uniform appearance, and I'm about the toughest second class in the Brigade."

Several members of the squad smirked, especially Posner. Durago knew they were thinking, *We finally did it.*

"You know, Whorton, you were an animal on the PEP field this morning." Durago started to raise his voice in excitement. "Hey, Thirteen, did you see my Plebe Whorton today? She was an animal! Whorton here actually ran herself until she passed out!"

Members of the platoon began smiling and chuckling.

"I mean it. Let me tell ya, Whorton here was running and pushing the edge of the envelope, right?! I guess there's no pussing out for the Class of Ninety-Four!"

"Hooyah!" the platoon barked. By now, Whorton was standing at attention with a pride Durago never saw before.

He continued. "So, Whorton, do you have character? Do you have fight? Have you finally tapped your animal instinct? Let me hear your battle cry!"

"Roar, sir."

"No, I mean it . . . make me proud. Let me hear you bark, girl! I know there's a tiger in there—let it out!"

"Roar!"

"C'mon, bark like a Marine!"

"Oorah, sir!"

Everyone's eyes went wide. Whorton looked like a puppy that had just scared itself with its own yelp. Durago was grinning from ear to ear. "Okay, okay, that's enough, Whorton! You're friiiiightening me! Platoon, right-face!'"

"Cock and drive, sir!"

Three knocks rapped on the door, followed by a shrill voice. "Sir, Midshipman Fourth Class Whorton, request permissions to come aboard."

"Enter," Durago said as he thought, *Did she say "permissions?"*

Whorton stepped inside and stood in the doorway. Durago forgot about her grammar. "Miss Whorton, prop the door open and take off your cover."

There was no look or shame or remorse on her face. *She doesn't even realize it when she forgets basic Plebe procedures,* Durago thought to himself.

"Please sit down, Miss Whorton. Relax for a moment."

The room was quiet. The only sound was a platoon marching outside, singing a cadence that reverberated off of Mother Bancroft.

"Miss Whorton, I have some bad news for you. You're going to go to a performance board before the end of the week."

No reaction.

"Do you understand what I just said?"

"Yes, sir."

"This board may separate you, Miss Whorton. They can kick you out, but I don't think that will happen. What will probably happen is that they'll identify discrepancies in your performance and make recommendations on how you can improve. If you don't improve, a second board will be held during the fall of this year."

Durago paused; still no reaction from Whorton.

"Going to a board is nothing to be ashamed of. Hell, believe it or not even I—"

"They'll never kick me out, sir."

"Excuse me?"

"They will never kick me out, sir."

"Why is that, Miss Whorton?"

"Because I'm a female and I'm going to get good grades. Once they see my grades, my performance won't matter. They'll never kick me out."

Durago was stunned. Whorton had not come up with this idea on her own. Her statement sounded like rehearsed testimony. Somebody coached her.

30

THE DECISION

 MARCH 31, 1992
1530
MAURY HALL

When Durago was finished, Jan continued writing on her notepad for a few moments. He felt better having talked to her. As she continued writing, he was again distracted by her. Her hair was up in order to conform to military standards; her face showed concentration. *She is so pretty,* he thought to himself. He looked again to her legs.

Jan looked up at him, her eyes engaging him through her glasses. She had felt him looking at her, and she smiled. "Anything else?"

"Not that I can think of."

She turned off the tape recorder and closed her notebook. Jan paused a moment before speaking again. "I'm thinking about your dad's friends. The people he served with, went to school with here. Have you contacted any of his classmates?"

"No. I've specifically chosen not to—and please understand me, because this is very personal—I don't want to get in touch with any of them until I actually graduate."

"What? Why?"

Now it was Durago's turn to be silent a moment while he prepared his answer. This was easier with Slim, who did not really need an explanation, just an understanding of the rule. Additionally, he carried the weight of Slim's own issues that were verboten. Durago suspected Jan would need a reason, whether logical, emotional, or both.

"Oh, my gosh," she said suddenly. "You're angry with them. They never reached out to you and your mother, so you're angry with them."

"No, that's not it at all. Remember, my mother had her name changed fairly quickly after my dad died. For all I know, many of his classmates don't know I was born, or they've tried to get in contact with us but couldn't."

Durago paused again. "Jan, it's about me, not them. As you know by now, there were several times during my Plebe Year that I wasn't sure I was going to make it through this place. I can't explain what I was thinking during that period. I sometimes wonder if I was in shock. I know to those around me it appeared as if I didn't care about the Academy, about being a mid. Others thought I was just too lazy to take any action—to either get with the program or quit.

"Then I was introduced—reintroduced, really—to the whole concept of who my father was. I was forced to really see what my father did, what he did with his life. It in turn made me reflect on what I was doing with his sacrifice. I immediately realized that attending a service academy was the one thing he could give me. There were no camping trips, no fishing rods, no throwing a baseball in the front yard after dinner, no driving lessons, no help with my homework—and it wasn't even his life that he gave me. My father didn't die for me. He died for Vietnam, for his compatriots.

"So, the one thing he gave me . . . it's one of the few things that nobody can ever take from me, something that's rarely passed from father to son or daughter. He gave me his honor. My dad died, was recognized with a Medal of Honor, and was able to pass on its benefits to me. I'm never going to earn that medal; I'm only a recipient's son, and I don't ever want his classmates or anyone who knew him to know about my presence here until I make it through this place. To do so, to let them know of my presence and then not make it, would sully the gift, besmirch his name. That's why I remain Donald Durago and haven't changed it to Donald Fitzpatrick."

Jan studied Durago, staring at him in a manner that he could not interpret.

"What?" he finally asked with an accusatory tone.

She frowned, not with resignation, but with sympathy.

"I understand," she said, "I do. So, let me think on this and we'll get together again soon to discuss your case."

Jan got up and moved to her office door. She locked it. Spinning on her heels, she looked at him purposefully and said, "This is not what you think. I've locked the door a moment because I want us to have a very private conversation."

"More private than the one we just had?" Genuine surprise registered in Durago's voice.

"Yes . . . and don't be coy. This is the safest way I can think of doing it without the possibility of drawing unwanted attention."

Durago's shoulders slumped. He had felt like this meeting was bringing them even closer, that he could rely on Jan. But now he sensed he was about to be dumped—again. "Okay, let me guess. Just like spring break, you regret the other night, and you want to make sure we keep this professional from now on?"

Jan looked heartbroken. "Yes, but there's much more to it than that."

Jan's remark removed the last bit of tension in the room. Durago had bared everything, physical and personal, and now he felt hurt that she was going to reject him. He was back to being a kid, a mistake that she needed to fix. He started to wonder if she really cared about him, or if she was helping him simply because it was her job. Maybe he was someone she needed to manage, to keep under control for her career's sake.

Jan walked back to her desk and took her seat. She looked again to make sure she had turned the tape recorder off. Then she faced Durago. "Listen, as I said before, spring break was a total fling. I never had the classic spring break experience, so, for once in my life I let myself go a little wild. You were a pleasant part of that equation. Younger guy . . . cute . . . nice—maybe the fact that you're a mid added to the danger, the spice. But I really figured that was it. Then, when I got back, I was a little—just a little—afraid I'd become the talk of Bancroft Hall."

"I'm not like that. In fact, I haven't even told Slim."

"Good," Jan said with a tone of affirmation in her voice as she held her hands up defensively, "and I think, deep down, I knew that. Maybe that's why I trusted you in the first place. Maybe I sensed you're not the type to kiss and tell.

"Anyway, I thought it was all water under the bridge, but I kept thinking about you. I mean, every day. You know the sex was . . . well . . . it was very, very good."

Durago started to stir.

"And then you rescued me on the bridge. Mentally I was pouring wine and lighting candles before you had the jack out."

Jan stood again and walked to her bookshelf. "Don, we both made a bad decision, and we let it go too far. I don't think what happened in Panama City was in character for either one of us."

Jan looked at Durago and saw agreement. "Then that night," she continued, "when you told me about your Plebe Year, and your father—well, you got under my skin. I think I'm really, really into you. Do you know what I mean?"

"Yeah, I do. I feel the same way. I mean . . . I don't know why, but . . . you should know that I've never been able to tell anyone other than Slim what I told you the other night. I just feel a connection, I guess."

Jan looked at him lovingly. "Don, you're only two months from graduation. I want to help you get through this thing so you can graduate. Then you'll be a commissioned officer, and we can be together without any repercussions."

"So, you don't want to end this," he said, "you just want to wait?"

"I do, I do, Don. I'm really surprised by all this myself, but I do—I want to wait for you, if you're willing to wait for me."

Durago simply replied, "Wow."

"I'm serious. Let's put 'us' aside for a while and focus on getting you through this thing and on to graduation. Okay?"

Durago nodded that he understood. "Yeah, good . . . okay."

Jan looked relieved, while gears started turning in Durago's head, forming plans for a getaway for the two of them during his "basket leave," the thirty days he would have off between graduation and reporting aboard the Surface Warfare Officer's School in Newport, Rhode Island.

Gotta actually graduate first . . .

An hour later, Durago sat at the double desk in the center of his room, staring into space, contemplating his fate. Slim walked in carrying a baseball bat and glove.

"Don, where were you? We needed our star pitcher against Seventeenth Company. Several of us took turns on the mound—"

"Slim, I'm fucked. This whole thing does not look good."

"Oh, that's right, dude, you had your meeting. What did Antonelli say?"

"Not much, but he didn't have to. It's cover-my-ass time and I'm standing alone."

"I'm standing with you, brother."

"I know, I know, but right now I need firepower that the battalion drill officer can't give me. So, I've gone to a lawyer in Mahan on his recommendation."

"He told you to get a lawyer?!"

"They're considering six-thousand-series offenses for this one."

"Holy shit, Don. What the fuck happened between you and this Plebe?"

"Nothing . . . I did everything above board, man. My squad was on six-zero, right down the passage from the battalion officer, for Pete's sake!"

"Well, then, okay . . . don't sweat it," Slim said shrugging his shoulders. "You'll be okay."

"I don't know, man. You know how things can get around here. Sometimes this political correctness stuff runs wild. I'm afraid that Whorton is going to blow things out of proportion, and then it's her word against mine. She's already getting the attention she wants because, in the eyes of Commander Gordon, she's got clout."

Durago repeated Jan's thoughts on bringing his father into the picture. "So, as I walked back from the JAG's office, I briefly, just for a moment, thought about mentioning my father."

"Wow, you sure?" Slim said as he dropped the glove and bat into the closet.

"No—I quickly concluded that I'm not going to play that card. It would be an insult to his memory. Besides, if I pull that I'm no better than she is. So, if I'm going to win, I'm not going to do it that way."

Emboldened by the fact that his roommate breached the subject, Slim said, "Fuck that, man. Fight fire with fire. A six thousand will send you walking."

Durago snapped. "Don't you think I know that?! Don't you get it?! If these fuckers kick me out for this, I don't want to belong!"

"Bullshit, now you're feeling sorry for yourself," Slim said. "You're going to throw all this shit away, everything we've gone through, everything that has become important to you, because some little WUBA's gone crying to her mommy? Remember your dad, man! I know this means more to you—"

"I'll say it one more time, Slim," Durago said as he calmed himself. "I am going to do this the right way. If this goes down badly, well . . . then fuck this place. IHTFP, my man—and I thought I'd almost forgotten that mantra. "

"You're serious?"

"Damn straight."

"Then why the fuck did you bring it up?"

"I dunno," Durago said. "I've not felt like myself lately."

The pair sat in silence for five minutes. Slim got up and opened the blinds. He looked out over the Severn. "Maybe Captain Oberly will tell them about your dad. You know . . . you don't say anything . . . he warns them about bad press."

Durago thought about his Marine company officer for a moment. "Oberly doesn't know, you know that. And don't even think about going to Oberly. Besides, my dad is dead. They would only care if a living recipient were around, to be on television."

"Maybe."

"My dad's heroic death got me in here. I used that opportunity because I was desperate, because I needed it. Now that I'm here, I want to prove that I can do it just like he did, not *because* he did."

Durago looked out the window. "You know how I am about this, Slim, so drop it. I'm sorry I brought it up. I'm just so stressed out, I'm starting to feel desperate."

"Know what, Don? It doesn't matter anyway. This thing is just to appease the Whorton clan. Because you're innocent, you'll walk. I mean, what can they do, manufacture evidence?"

"Yeah, I'm sure you're right."

Oberly decided that it was time to gather some intelligence on the Whorton case. He suspected Durago was innocent, or that there was a misunderstanding between him and Whorton. Oberly had arranged for a meeting with Lieutenant Tripp, the Brigade JAG.

As he walked down 3-1 he encountered Ned Breedon. "Ned, what's up?"

"I just talked with Tripp."

"Yeah? I'm heading there now. How'd it go?"

"Not good. I'm worried that I'm going to lose some of my mids. Apparently, Gordon isn't just spouting off; he really is going after these kids."

"What's the status of the investigation?"

"It's near complete. Tripp believes that there's some very damning evidence."

"Really?"

"Yes, he painted a very negative picture."

"What exactly did he say?"

"I'm not supposed to talk specifics, except with my mids, but it's bad."

"Do you believe any of it?"

"That's the big problem. I believe all of it. I think everything that Whorton claims is true. The issue is perception and perspective."

"She thinks she was harassed—"

"And therefore she was."

"I guess that's the crux of Gordon's point. The indoctrination system can be viewed by the recipient as institutionalized harassment."

"Except we blame the mids, even if they're following midshipman regulations."

Oberly admired the fact that Breedon was so concerned. It would have been easy for him to ignore their plight, work on his master's degree at night, and wait for orders to Department Head School and a billet on an *Aegis* cruiser.

"Well, let me get in there. I need to hear about my company commander."

"Good luck."

"Yeah, we'll talk later."

Oberly pushed open the door that read BRIGADE JUDGE ADVOCATE GENERAL. Inside was a small reception area. The secretary looked up. "Welcome, Captain Oberly. Lieutenant Tripp is waiting for you. Go right in."

"Thanks."

Tripp stood up and extended his hand as soon as Oberly entered. "Welcome. I'm Doug Tripp."

"Bob Oberly. Nice to meet you."

"Please have a seat. Can I get you anything?"

"No, I'm good, thanks."

Oberly sat in the government-issue pleather chair. He had to be careful not to show any disdain for the JAG. He figured Tripp was his exact opposite in the naval service. The lawyer probably never spent a night in the bush, nor a week underway. He looked at Tripp's ribbons. There was no Sea Service Deployment ribbon. Oberly therefore erased any legitimacy from Tripp's two Navy Commendation Medals and his Navy Achievement Medal—decorations that Oberly also lacked, owing to what he perceived as higher standards set by the Corps.

"So, you're interested in Midshipman First Class Durago," Tripp asked.

"Yes, how's it look?"

"Not good. The accusations against him are among the most substantial. He is also the cornerstone of the Whorton complaint because he was the first midshipman in authority. The implication is that all subsequent issues were largely affected by his influence upon her. As a result of his alleged abuse, her perception thereafter was affected. There is even a suggestion that he had such a profound negative effect on her psyche that he rendered her unable to protest when she was violated later."

"Damn it."

"Yes, well . . . he has a lawyer, right?"

"He does; Lieutenant Meyer."

"Good, she's very competent. He's in good hands."

Oberly shifted his weight in the chair and thought for a moment. "I'm interested in hearing your opinions regarding the truth. What do you think really happened? Do you think Whorton is telling the truth about all of this?"

"I think she has a case."

31

DROPPED

Commander Gordon thumbed through a thesaurus looking for an adjective. He was drafting a supplementary fitness report to have entered in his service record. He hoped that his drastic reforms in 3rd Battalion, and possibly a letter from the congressman, would give him a boost to screen for major command at sea.

"Commander, Mister Theo Thurber, that congressional aide, on line one," his secretary called from her desk in the conference room.

He picked up the phone. "Commander Gordon, how may I help you?"

"Commander, this is Theo Thurber. Midshipman Whorton's parents are here in D.C. We would like you to come meet with them and possibly Congressman Adams, if you're available."

"Yes, sir, I am. When is a good time for you?"

"I'm very sorry about the short notice on this. We knew they were coming today, but they just expressed a desire to meet with you directly this morning. Could you come in this afternoon, say around two?"

"I'll be there."

"Great. Naturally, we would like you to be prepared to discuss Miss Whorton's case in detail. I'll patch you through to a secretary who will give you directions."

I'm going to meet Congressman Adams. This could not be better if I scripted it, Gordon thought.

When Durago returned from morning classes, there was a note from Sam Sumlin. "Sums" was a second class linebacker on the football team. He and Durago had been in the same Spanish section the year before.

> Meet me outside King Hall after noon meal.
> Sums.

Sumlin was in 13th Company—Whorton's company. It had to be about her. During the meal, Durago was silent. While the second class grilled the Plebes and the Youngsters joked, he kept looking across the sea of short haircuts and navy blue uniform shirts toward the 13th Company tables. Finally he spotted Sumlin, who looked up, saw Durago, and nodded.

Ten minutes later, Sumlin was sitting on the first bench outside King Hall. He was the type of varsity athlete that Durago respected; he took his role as a midshipman seriously. Durago noted that his uniform was neat and appeared freshly pressed. His massive feet were encased in spit-polished leather shoes, not corframs. His belt buckle and the brim of his cover were both shined with Windex, probably right before noon meal formation. *This guy is what Americans think of when they see Army-Navy football on TV.*

"Sums, what's up?"

"We're in the same boat, buddy—we need to compare notes."

"Finally, someone who can give me the straight story."

"I dunno if I know the whole story, but I'm closer than you are. Whorton's been in my squad the last two years."

"So, that's how you got into this?"

"She's taking down everyone who's ever given her a hard time. Hell, she's even going after my roommate, and he spends his life in MacDonough or at team tables."

"How bad is it?"

"Have you talked to the lawyer?"

"Yeah."

"Well, that's a good start. The long and short of it is this: Whorton as you know, is very fucked up. Her second class, your classmates, ran her ragged her whole Plebe Year. They fried the shit out of her. Ironically, she's actually earned some respect from all of us in Thirteenth Company for not quitting. But she's continued to be a conduct and performance case."

"As a Youngster?"

"Yes, as a Youngster. She misses formations, doesn't show up for watch, misses taps."

"You're kidding me?"

Every time mids leaving King Hall walked by, Sumlin would pause. Durago saw that he was genuinely nervous and felt he could not talk openly about what was happening. As a group of Plebes moved further toward seventh wing, he said quietly, "I know it's all bullshit stuff. If each happened only once or twice, she would be counseled and let go. But people don't have so much sympathy because they think she doesn't belong here. She gets fried because people want her to be identified as a problem child. I mean, you've seen her."

"Yeah, I know what you mean."

"Believe it or not, it's not personal; it's not vindictive. We want to let the system run her out—let it work like it's supposed to."

This comment gave Durago pause. He imagined Simpson having a conversation about running *him* out only three years before. The Naval Academy had evolved much from 1988 to the spring of 1992. The Persian Gulf War had come and gone. In its wake came "total quality leadership," which had arrived with its bedfellow, political correctness. The football player's comment also stirred Durago's theory about the Naval Academy as an environment, not a system.

"Well, Sums, the system—and I really think it's an environment, so let's say the people who set conditions in this environment lean everything toward academics rather than military performance these days."

"I know it, and I know what you're driving at; she gets good grades. Anyway, as you can imagine, she could only last so long. Whorton has been building up demerits all along, and she was looking at a performance board when she got caught drinking in the hall."

"Holy shit, you're kidding me!"

"No."

"Dude, I've broken a few regs in my day. Hell, everyone jumps the wall at one time or another, but drinking in the hall?"

"I know. So she gets fried and goes directly to a performance board."

"That's when the shit hit the fan."

"Precisely. We thought she would lay down. Hell, nobody thinks she's 'there' half the time."

"So then mommy and daddy come into the picture."

"And you can fill in the gaps from there. They use the word 'harassment' and suddenly the administration is doing the dance to keep this thing from ending up in the papers."

"What's going to happen to us?"

"I'll tell you right now what's going to happen. We're going to get hammered and we're going to do time on restriction in Smoke Hall. Whorton's mommy and daddy will be happy, and she'll get moved to another company."

"This sucks."

"I know. BOHICA, right?"

Commander Gordon was shown into a small conference room. The Whortons and a man he guessed was Thurber were already there. The Whortons exuded wealth. She clearly wore expensive jewelry, and they both had Rolexes. Mrs. Whorton styled her copper hair in a tight bun. She was pale and frail, with freckles. She reminded Gordon of the comedian Emo Philips. It was obvious where Midshipman Whorton got her looks. Mr. Whorton was a tomato to Mrs. Whorton's carrot. He was overweight with red cheeks and a nose that revealed he'd had a few martinis over lunch. It also appeared to Gordon that his suit was hand tailored.

Thurber looked very young to be an aide. He was dressed in the D.C. law firm uniform of the day: a grey, three-button suit with red power tie. His shoes looked like shiny leather slippers. *Probably some hotshot Georgetown graduate,* Gordon surmised. He wondered what Thurber's connection was.

Everyone stood and shook Gordon's hand, and Thurber said, "Commander, can I get you a coffee or another refreshment?"

"Coffee would be great, thanks. Black."

After the pleasantries, Thurber asked for a brief on the investigation progress. Gordon wondered where the congressman was. "Maybe I should wait until Congressman Adams gets here . . . so I only have to brief you once."

"Uh, you can begin now. The congressman will be here shortly. We will fill him in on anything that he has questions about."

Thurber pulled out a notebook. As Gordon began his brief, he observed that Thurber was diligently taking copious notes but that the Whortons were not paying very close attention. They were evaluating him, not his progress. He realized that his brief and this meeting were not about content, but his performance. Thurber was probably taking notes out of habit, and to impress upon the Whortons that Adams' office was sincerely concerned with their daughter's plight. *If only the congressman were here, he'd understand,* Gordon thought.

Just as he was finishing, Adams came in. He shook hands all around like he was working a rope line. He invited the Whortons to dinner and promised to discuss the case and anything else they wished to talk about at length. Gordon's only contact was just before the congressman left. "Commander, I really appreciate your help in this matter."

After he left, Mrs. Whorton appeared exasperated. "What's going to happen to our daughter?" she asked.

"What do you mean, Missus Whorton?" Gordon said while trying to appear attentive.

"Is she going to be punished in any way? Is she going to be kicked out?"

No, ma'am. I'm going to see to it that all charges are dropped. She's obviously the victim here."

"That's what I needed to hear. Thank you, Commander Gordon."

Jan listened to the sounds of Eastport: halyards clanging, diesels thrumming, and a boat lift whining just over a U2 melody.

"You want something," Nina said. "I can tell by your voice. You're being antsy."

"Uh, yeah, maybe I am. I do need your counsel."

"Cantler's, then—you're treating me to crabs."

"I knew you were going to say that." Jan looked to the clock on her wall. "It's four o'clock now. Wanna meet there at six?"

The seafood smorgasbord offered at Cantler's had a powerful effect on all who partook of it. A repast unequalled by any other in the Annapolis area allowed the proprietors to forgo the cost of fancy accoutrement: patrons sat on rough-hewn picnic tables covered in brown paper, and yet the restaurant drew in all comers—a great equalizer of class and standing. Jan could not help noticing that even she and Nina were from different strata. Nina Gavilrakis was more like the watermen sitting along the bar. Her dark brown skin matched theirs, and Jan suspected that if her friend continued her life at sea, Nina' skin would become as tough as an elephant's hide, just as theirs did.

Nina nodded toward them. "You know they're not paying the same as everyone else."

"'Course not," Jan agreed, "But then, they brought the catch in, I'm sure."

Throughout the rest of the joint, sitting side by side, were midshipmen and Johnnies, social workers and socialites. Most of them were feasting on the creature that allowed the state to proclaim "Maryland is for Crabs," referring to the *callinectes sapidus*, or "beautiful swimmer, savory." Steamed in Old Bay seasoning, they were brought out by the bushel, the wait staff dumping them in piles in front of the patrons as soon as they emerged from the kettles. The diners grabbed and dissected them with wooden mallets and short-bladed knives. Locals could be identified by the speed with which they pried open the jimmies' candle-shaped armor covering their sexual organs, or pulled the body apart from the pointed shell that encased these aquatic spiders. Tourists were not quite as fast and could be seen smarting as the steam nipped their fingers while they tried to capture as much of the white meat as possible. All enjoyed themselves, lubricated by classic rock and locally brewed beers like National Bohemian or Wild Goose Amber.

Jan and Nina ordered a dozen jumbos to start. The waitress put two pints in front of them. "Keep 'em comin'," Nina said with a smile. After the waitress left, she took a sip. "So, what's up?"

Though many people were close by, Jan could tell that nobody paid any attention to the two women, so she did not think she had to whisper. "I've got a situation, and I need some advice."

"Oh, my . . . you're pregnant," her friend said, leaning in close.

"No, it's not that, thank goodness."

Nina relaxed visibly. "Okay," she said, taking another swig, "well, what? I'm all ears."

Jan was really glad that her friend was still in town. She could confide in Nina, trust that she would keep the matter private, and there was the added benefit that she was not in the Navy. She felt Nina would give her an unbiased opinion. "I'm sort of seeing a midshipman."

"A college guy? Wow . . . a little younger, huh? Okay, what year is he? A senior?"

"He is a senior, a 'Firstie,' they call them. We met during spring break on a scuba diving trip."

"When you went to Panama City."

"Yeah."

"Okay. Well, what does 'sort of seeing' mean? Are you or aren't you?"

"I've kinda put us on a break, but I don't know—I kinda want to keep going . . ."

"Okay, stop. Is he nice?"

"Yes, very . . . and charming, and handsome, with a good sense of humor, and I, uh . . . really appreciate his enthusiasm . . . about everything."

"Yeah . . . and the sex is good, isn't it? I can see it! Damn it! I knew there was something, but I thought it was Tripp."

"Oh, no . . . hell no."

"So . . . ?"

"Yes . . . it is very, very good."

"Okay, great. So, what's the problem? You're not that much older, right? I mean, this is really a generational thing. You're what . . . twenty-six? He's gotta be twenty-one. In ten years, there'll be no difference at all."

"Right, but that's not the issue."

The waitress came and dumped a bunch of crabs on the table. "Anything else, ladies? Ready for that next beer?"

"Yes, thanks," Nina replied as she grabbed her first crab.

Jan quickly surveyed the room again to ensure there was nobody close who looked like they were affiliated with the Academy. Then she talked while Nina methodically separated exoskeleton from meat. Her friend's hands became caked with film from the crabs' innards and Old Bay.

"Until now, we've kept our relationship private and have even put it on hold because it would likely be construed as unprofessional. Normally, the faculty-student relationship is covered by the uniform code of military justice. This stipulates that you can't date someone within your chain of command. Officers can't date enlisted, but mids are considered officers for this purpose. However, there's no rule or regulation that says a member of the faculty or staff can't date midshipmen. So, for example, a nurse stationed at the Academy could theoretically date a mid."

"Okay, so, again . . . what are you worried about?" Nina said, shrugging her shoulders. "What's the big deal?"

"Wait . . . I'm not finished describing the situation," Jan responded with exasperation. "So, I've been thinking about it, and I thought I was in the clear by the letter of the law, though not the intent. I'm not in his chain of command, plus—and this is actually a very important factor—I'm technically not even part of the staff at Navy. I'm posted here from Naval District Washington to support midshipmen, not the Naval Academy staff. That's Tripp's job. But I'm supposed to be able to represent them without bias if needed."

"Okay, so, now I'm really confused," said Nina. "Why are you asking for advice? You're not in his chain of command; you're not even faculty. It's simple—fuck his brains out."

"You always had a way with words."

"I'm a sailor, beeotch. I call 'em like I see 'em."

"Yeah . . .well . . . there's more."

Jan drained her beer, and then started the next one. She sat silently for a while, surveying the room again. Nina was also quiet and simply pressed on with her next crab. Jan listened to the cracks and thunks of crustacean consumption and the laughter of friends having a good time. She wondered if Nina would understand what she was about to say, while realizing again that it was her friend's neutrality that made her so valuable.

"Nina, you have known me as a sailing bum. But the part of me that you don't know as well, the college student, remains. And she's grown into a naval officer and a lawyer."

"I know . . . we talked about this. It's cool. I get it, hon . . . I do."

"Well, that part of me wants to be respected as a lawyer and a naval officer. So, I convinced myself that it was fine, that my understanding of the rules led me to the point where I said to myself, 'We'll be discrete, but we're in bounds. Maybe I can let this go on.' But the other issue is that he needs me as a lawyer—bad. I mean, this is the whole reason I'm assigned here."

"This happens all the time," Nina said. "Recuse yourself."

"Huh?"

"Didn't know I knew that word, did you? '*Recuse* yourself,' I said. Find him another lawyer because you have a conflict of interest, or are too close. Something like that."

"If I do that, then this'll all be out in the open."

"Hmmm . . . I see."

"There's one more subtlety."

"What's that?"

"I'm not actually representing him."

"Okay, now I'm really confused."

"This is why I need you."

"Fuck me . . . I need another beer."

"Nina, right now this is a conduct case, a case of midshipman regulations, not military law. As such, he's not allowed to have representation. I can be there to advise, but not to represent."

"So, is he paying you?"

"No, it doesn't work that way."

"Now it's my turn. Eat and listen," Nina demanded.

Jan motioned to open a crab, but she could not eat and focus, not now.

"Jan, it sounds simple to me. I don't get all the military bullshit, but I get you and why this is important to you. So, you need to follow the rules. But if I know anything about the military, I know this—it's mostly black and white, right?"

"I guess," Jan replied.

"So, are you on the staff or faculty?"

"No."

"Are you his commander, or whatever?"

"Chain of command. No."

"Are you representing him?"

"No."

"And the last one is a lawyer . . . ethical . . . thing. But we all know there are many lawyers who bang their clients, right?"

"Sure."

"It sounds to me like there are three simple rules. You've reviewed all three and realized that you're not in violation of any of them, right? I mean, you're not asking me if I think you're violating rules, are you? No, you're telling me that you're not violating rules. Otherwise, you wouldn't even consider being with this guy."

"Wow, Nina, you're right. This is why I needed you!"

"Exactly. You need me to tell you that it's okay because you're not doing anything wrong. But I also need to tell you that one part of your instinct is right—people *will* judge you if it gets out. So, the real question, the real reason you're about to drop a hundred bucks on a night of hot crabs and cold beers is so I can point out the reason we're here."

"And that is?"

"To tell you that the real issue is weighing your reputation within the Navy against the possibility that by putting your relationship on hold you may lose him. You're trying to decide if you really love him or not."

Jan did not respond, but she knew Nina was right.

"If I were you," Nina said, "I'd work hard to ensure he doesn't forget."

"I know what you mean," Jan replied. Finally, she picked up a crab and started in. "This was so worth it," she said with her mouth half full.

32

STRIBLING

APRIL 2, 1992
1405
STRIBLING WALK

J an left to meet Tripp in his office a little later than expected and found herself on Stribling Walk, heading toward Bancroft Hall, as class was changing. The line of mids going to and coming from Bancroft forced Jan to return innumerable salutes. She wore a serious, almost threatening, look on her face, but she still felt the eyes of several of the mids as they passed. Jan still could not believe that she was involved with one of them. She even found herself straining to find Don's face in the crowd.

Jan's briefcase held the notes from her interviews with each of the midshipmen involved in the Whorton case. She was convinced from the hours that she sat and listened to them that they all were essentially innocent. It was possible that some of them had been a little overzealous in applying the indoctrination system, but none had really broken the rules.

The Yard was blossoming with the continued procession of spring. The grass was emerald green, and flowers added color to the grounds. As Bancroft Hall grew in her vision, Jan saw two Youngsters throw quarters toward Tecumseh's quiver. They both saluted him with their left hands. Jan laughed, recognizing the ritual.

On the other side of T-Court, Jan ascended the stairs of Bancroft Hall and entered the rotunda. She turned to the left, toward the main office and the staff offices on 3-1. Brigade Legal was the last office on the right. She still felt a little nervous about meeting Doug Tripp again. She wanted to salvage some form of professional friend ship. *Friendly yet professional*, she reminded herself before opening Tripp's door.

He looked up as she entered. "Jan, howya doin'? Would you like some coffee?"

"Sure, Tripp, thanks. Uh, things are going well in general. This Whorton case has me concerned, though."

Tripp began pouring two cups of coffee. "I wouldn't fret too much. Cream?"

"Black."

"What are you, a line officer now?" Tripp said as he sat behind his desk.

"Funny," Jan said as she sat across from him. "And actually, I am a sailor. So, where do we stand?"

"Well, in Commander Gordon's view, the Whorton thing is open and shut. These mids all went too far; they overstepped their bounds. Now they're going to pay for it."

"What about the commandant? What does he say about all of this?"

"The commandant is gone for two weeks. He hasn't been briefed yet. I'm briefing the deputy tomorrow." He wrote a note to himself to schedule a meeting with the deputy commandant.

"Tripp, you need to slow this guy, Gordon, down. He's going off half-cocked."

"Look, just because they're being investigated for a six thousand doesn't mean they'll be charged or found guilty. We simply don't want to limit the scope of our investigation."

"That's malarkey and you know it. You guys are trying to appease the girl's family and you're waving the six thousands at them so they feel like their complaints have teeth."

"Who said anything about the girl's parents?"

"Excuse me?"

"Who told you that her parents were in touch with this office or any office in the Yard?"

Jan's throat tightened with regret. She had just made a rookie mistake. Antonelli, the investigating midshipman, had told Durago and a few of her other clients that the issue was being pushed by Whorton's parents and their congressman. None of them had indicated that it was confidential information, yet she should have checked on that fact herself.

"Great," Tripp said. "Well, I guess we have a leak in the battalion office, because I'm the only person in here who knew. Is one of the company officers feeding you information, trying to protect one of his own? I'll bet it's Oberly. He thinks we should drop Durago from the list."

"Let's not go there right now."

"Can we be frank?" Tripp was suggesting to Jan that they talk off the record. They had already learned on two previous occasions that this made their working relationship easier and usually benefited both of them.

"Sure."

"The starting point for these conduct cases is justified. The stories that Whorton has told lead me to believe that the subsequent charges are justified. There's a good case against all of them that they violated the boundaries of the indoctrination system."

"And?"

"And, between you and me, there's no way that these mids drove Whorton to become a conduct case herself. Her problems are her own. Have you seen her or talked to her?"

"No."

"She's a fruit, for sure. I probably agree with everyone, from her company officer down to the Youngsters in her squad, that this chick does not belong in the military."

"Then why are they doing this?"

"Because it's the best way to handle the situation."

"That's where you're wrong. What are you guys afraid of? That Whorton's folks will go to the media?"

"Jan, don't you understand? Have you lost perspective? Negative press has been so damaging recently that it's become an underlying threat in every case like this that we get."

"You think I don't understand? You're the one who's lost it, my friend. Look at the big picture. Why haven't I seen Whorton in my office?"

"Maybe she decided not to seek legal counsel."

"When is her conduct hearing?"

"There won't be one."

"Let me guess: 'All conduct issues in the matter of Midshipman Third Class Whorton have been dropped.'"

"Yes, they have."

"Damn it, Tripp, don't you see? She's already won! Whorton has already gotten what she wanted. She used you guys to buy herself another year at good old USNA."

"Well, I don't know about that. Currently, Miss Whorton is a guest of Bethesda Naval Hospital."

"The psych ward?"

Tripp only gave Jan a knowing look.

"You're kidding me."

"Nope. But her parents and her doctor do think that she'll return. It seems that she has been determined not to be harmful to herself or others."

"Bullshit! What's going to happen when she reaches the fleet? If this girl graduates she's going to be responsible for people's lives, Tripp! She has good grades, doesn't she?"

"Yes."

"How much you wanna bet she service selects aviation? Would you fly with her?"

"I wouldn't get into a car if she were behind the wheel."

"My point exactly. What's she gotta do, kill somebody? How many times are we going to pass this chick off to become someone else's problem?"

"I'm looking out for the best interests of the Academy. We have many challenges before us that you don't see or hear about in your office."

"That's what you all tell yourselves so you can sleep at night. How about doing the right thing, Tripp? Why don't we act like we're officers in the United States Navy?"

"Being an officer sometimes requires compromise. This is a profession fraught with politics."

"I agree, but what I can't get past is that we're losing focus here. The mission of this place is to prepare young men and women to serve as officers in the United States Navy and the United States Marine Corps. Nothing should be allowed to get in front of that mission."

"Jan, some of the folks upstairs are concerned with preserving the institution. They make heady decisions regarding this all the time."

"This institution isn't going to perish. The Academy has been around since, what? Eighteen forty-five? How many of our military leaders, our heroes, have come from here?"

"Tons."

"Exactly. Do you know who's produced the most astronauts?"

"The Naval Academy?"

"Exactly—not MIT, not Stanford—the Academy."

"You're getting pretty worked up about this place for someone from a small women's college in the Midwest."

"Northeast, asshole. Undergrad and law school, both covered with ivy. I'm angry because I've learned a lot about this place in a short period of time. I think I finally get it. After talking to these kids the past week or so, I finally understand what this is all about."

"Well, good for you, Jan," Tripp said sarcastically. "Listen, I have a meeting to get to. Call me tomorrow and we'll talk more."

"You're going to let this thing continue, aren't you? You know Gordon is a maniac, half out of his gourd on this thing. He's wrong, but you're going to go ahead anyway."

"He's a commander, Jan. I'm an office pogue."

"No need to remind me."

A silent moment passed. Jan had to be conciliatory, return this to a modicum of normalcy before she left. "Sorry, Tripp, but you deserved that for the college crack. Look, I'll see you in class tonight?"

"Michelson, eighteen hundred," Tripp said. "Wanna do dinner after?"

"Sure," Jan replied, not meaning it.

Durago was starting to come unglued. He was panicking. He was becoming more and more distracted by his conduct case, and as a result he pitched poorly during the company softball game. He asked to be relieved, but Mole refused. "Dude, nobody else can pitch. I'd rather have you on a bad day than anyone else on the mound. Besides, it's just a company softball game."

Oberly watched the game in silence, knowing what the problem was. He realized the mid was dreadfully worried that he was going to get railroaded out, and Oberly was starting to believe it was a real possibility himself.

Durago decided that he would see Jan after the game. Talking to her would make him feel better. He went straight from intramurals to Jan's office without changing out of his PT gear, which was prohibited in this part of the Yard. *Fuck it, I'm a Firstie. Nobody's gonna say anything.*

When he reached her door, Jan's secretary was closing up. "Uh, is Lieutenant Meyer around?"

"She's not here. Is it urgent?"

"Yes, it is."

The secretary could see that Durago was tense. "She's in her grad school class on the first floor of Michelson."

Durago raced for Michelson Hall. He figured he would ask her to talk for a moment, and maybe she would even skip class and . . . *She'll never go for it. You're supposed to wait until graduation.* He pressed on, following his initial instinct that seeing her would at least calm his nerves somewhat.

The door at the back of the lecture hall squeaked very loudly when Durago opened it. Some of the officers looked back and the professor looked up toward the door. Then, without acknowledging Durago's presence, he continued with his lecture. Durago scanned the class. Half of them were still in uniform, others were in civvies. He recognized one or two former profs and noted that some in the class were company officers. Finally he saw Jan, three rows down on the left side, a few seats in. She did not look at Durago when he walked down the stairs toward her seat.

"Jan," he whispered.

She looked up and motioned for the door. Durago vaulted back up the wide, tiered stairs to the back of the room, then waited outside in the hall.

Jan opened the door and walked toward him. She did not look happy. "Not the smartest thing you've ever done, I'm sure," she said tersely.

"What? I needed to see you."

"You called me 'Jan.'" she said as she crossed her arms over her chest.

"Huh?"

"'Jan'—as in my first name—not 'ma'am' or 'Lieutenant.'"

"Fuck!" Durago responded in scared whisper.

"That is precisely what everyone within earshot is thinking right now, especially Lieutenant Tripp, the man sitting next to me."

"Who's that?"

"The Brigade Legal Officer."

"Oh, shit . . . I'm screwed."

"Now, I'm sure what you have to say is important, but it'll have to come later. Call me at twenty thirty. In the meantime, I have to sit through this lecture and think of what to say to Tripp when he asks me after class why our relationship is so familiar."

"But Jan, I—"

"I told you we have to be careful. Now get out of here."

★★★★★

Back in the lecture hall, Tripp wrote a note to himself.

Mid w/ 14th Co T-shirt

He thought, *Maybe it wasn't Steve after all.*

33

IMPATIENCE

APRIL 2, 1992
2000
BANCROFT HALL, ROOM 7412

Durago could not wait until his watch read 2030. He fidgeted in his room, pretending to study for Slim's sake.

"You okay, man?" Slim asked.

"No."

"Wanna talk about it?"

"No."

Durago was starting to regret not telling his roommate about Jan. It made him feel that he was violating their friendship. It made him wonder, just briefly, about his commitment to her. *How serious is it if I can't tell Slim?* Durago imagined what Slim's reaction would be, and then he remembered why he had not told his roommate. *Slim won't approve. I won't tell him because he'll tell me to walk away, and I don't want to do that.*

At 2015 he made his way down to the battalion phone room. A perpetual line stretched out into the hall. The room had phone booths lining the walls and a bank of phone booths in the center of the room. Almost twenty mids at a time argued with girlfriends, cried to their mothers, or talked with their sponsors. Durago did not know if he was calling his girlfriend or his lawyer.

"Damn," Sumlin said as he fell in behind Durago. "I need to invest in one of those cell phones."

"Hey, Sums."

"Hey, Don, what about you? You don't even have a car, right? You should use some of your career starter loan to buy a cell."

"Car? Cell phone? Only leads to trouble, man . . . and I got trouble enough."

"You speak the truth. So, who ya callin' then?"

"Lieutenant Meyer."

"The JAG? Yeah, she's cool. A total hottie, too."

Durago grinned and nodded in agreement. As he reached the front of the line, a booth opened up. He closed the door to create some privacy. The tiny space smelled of sweat and mint chewing tobacco. He wiped the phone and dialed.

Jan answered on the first ring. "Hello?"

"It's me."

"Good. How are you?"

"I dunno. What did Lieutenant Tripp say?"

"He didn't say anything."

"Is that good or bad?"

"Well, it could mean he didn't catch it, or he may have thought you said 'ma'am' instead of 'Jan,' or he is simply keeping the observation to himself. In any case, there's nothing we can do unless he says something to me about it."

"What will you say?"

"I'll tell him the truth—that I've become too familiar with you in the course of working on this case."

"Oooh, that's good."

"Exactly. By being open about it, I'll remove any suspicion that I was sleeping with you."

"*Was?*"

"Don, we've been over this. I'll admit that I considered changing my mind, but I've reaffirmed that we have to cool it until this thing is over, or until you've graduated, or —"

"Or 'forever.'"

"That's not what I was thinking, dammit. It's just that our timing is terrible."

Durago took a deep breath, inhaling the pungent sweat-mint aroma again. "Normally, Jan, I would protest. But I don't have the strength right now."

"So, what was so important that you needed to see me?"

"I'm really, really scared. I'm scared that they're going to kick me out."

"I'm scared, too. I really am. But we're going to use that to our advantage."

"How?"

"Come to my office tomorrow afternoon. We'll go through every-thing. In the meantime, get some sleep, study, relax. Okay?"

"I don't think I can sleep; I'm too worried."

"You don't need to worry; that's why I'm here. I am going to take care of you."

At 0200, Durago was still wide awake. Slim was snoring soundly. Durago got up and donned jogging clothes. He then slipped out of the hall, jogged across Farragut Field to the Sea Gate, and dove into the water. When he reached *Quantum Meriut*, he noticed the swim ladder was down. In the cockpit, he took off his shoes and hung his wet shirt over the lifeline. He descended into the cabin. Finally, he knocked on the hatch to Jan's cabin.

"Who's there?"

"It's me, Don."

Jan opened the hatch wearing a terry cloth bathrobe over flannel pajamas. "Damn you, Durago," she said as she closed the door behind them.

"Hey, you're the one who put the ladder down," he said.

"That was a simple coincidence. Don, I'm starting to feel like you don't respect me."

"Jan, I need you."

She folded her arms over her chest. "We're not having sex."

"Okay, okay . . . I know . . . I know. That's not what I'm here for. I'm really here because I need someone to help me get through this."

What exactly do you want, then?"

"I don't know. I'm just scared about this whole thing. I'm stressing out, and I still can't sleep."

Jan stood on her tiptoes, put her arms around his neck, and hugged him. Durago returned her embrace. "It's going to be alright," she whispered reassuringly.

"Is it?" he asked.

"Don, sit down," Jan said as she let go. "Wait a minute . . . I'll get my notes."

Durago sat at the table in *Quantum Meriut*'s galley.

"I've developed some key themes, things for you to think about at your board," Jan began. "First, answer all questions clearly, but succinctly. Saying too much will sound like you're bullshitting them. Say too little and it will appear you're hiding information."

"Okay . . . I get it. It's like answering rates."

"Good. Second, when able, point out that Whorton is the only Plebe that has ever accused you of being unprofessional."

"Yeah . . . that's a good point. I don't know when I'll be able to say that, but—"

"Well, for example, emphasize that you treated her the same as all the others, right?"

"Yes, that's true."

"There ya go. Third—and this leverages off the first two—you have always been evaluated as a good leader. It's for this reason that you're now the company commander."

"Wow, that's real good."

"See? So, in summary: clear, succinct answers; Whorton is your only accuser; everyone else says you're great. Got it?"

"I do."

Jan hugged him again as she said, "Don, this *is* serious. I don't want you to think I'm being cavalier about it. But I also want you to try to relax. I don't think they'll kick you out."

"Okay." Durago did feel better. "Thanks, Jan."

"No problem. Now go, before we make another mistake."

Tripp stood on the pier next to *Quantum Meriut*. He could hear talking inside, but he could not make out what was being said. The sound of the hatch opening split the relative quiet on the waterfront, warning him that someone was emerging. Tripp retreated to the anonymity of his car parked in a shadow nearby. As Durago emerged from *QM*, Tripp's suspicions were confirmed. *That's the same mid, and there's only one on the list from Fourteenth Company.*

Durago snapped awake, confused. He sensed the familiar taste of blood in his mouth. His tongue was swelling again. He had been asleep, but he was in a sitting position. He lifted his head from the desk and looked around. He was in class, Political Philosophy. The course was supposed to be an easy "A," an elective that would allow him to relax during his last semester. Unfortunately, the professor announced to the class at the beginning that he derived great pride from ensuring that at least one mid did not graduate on time each year because he assigned a failing grade. Unwittingly, Durago was working toward becoming that mid.

He scanned the room again. The professor was not there. The mids were writing furiously in their little blue test booklets. *Great!* Durago thought to himself. *I'm falling asleep in the middle of tests now.* He looked down at his answer booklet. He had answered the first question and begun the second of five when he apparently had fallen asleep. He looked at the clock. There were twenty minutes left in the period.

At that moment, Jan was on the phone with Tripp.

So, you haven't briefed the deputy commandant?"

"No."

"Why not?"

"I tried to, but he was busy and sent me away."

"Tripp, you idiot! Don't you see that I'm trying to save you some embarrassment? Once you take this above Gordon's head, it'll be over. You need to put this on the dep 'dant's desk before it goes too far. Send an email on NATS, for Pete's sake!"

"You sure you're not trying to get me to do your work for you?"

"Tripp, sometimes you can be as dumb as a post. We agreed to be open on this thing. Yes, it's to the advantage of my client that you go to the commandant's office, but it's also to your advantage. If this thing goes too far, you're the one they'll come gunning for."

"Client?" Tripp said inquisitively, almost with emphasis.

"Huh?"

"Client. You said, 'client.' Aren't there, like, seventeen mids involved in this in some way or another?"

Jan silently cursed herself. She had been thinking only of Durago.

"Yeah, 'clients,' I meant. And only eight have come to my office. Go to the deputy, Tripp." Anyone peering into Jan's office at that moment would have noticed that she was flushed.

Slim arranged to have a meeting with Captain Oberly when he knew Durago would be in class. When the bell rang at the end of his Naval Law class, his book bag was already packed. Slim descended the stairs from the top deck of Luce Hall and quickly zipped over to seventh wing, then started the long climb up to 7-4.

This whole situation reminded Slim of his efforts to defend Durago during their Plebe Year, especially with McDougal. Slim and Durago had not roomed together during Plebe Summer; the incoming class was initially housed alphabetically, but they were both in Gladstone's squad. In the first few days, during the brief moments when the Plebes were able to get to know each other, Slim developed a sense that they were kindred spirits. The biggest factor was that both grew up in boarding schools. Slim knew this said a lot about their home life and family relationships, and that growing up away from one's family built a Holden Caulfield–like streak of independence that many of their classmates may never develop.

Then Slim interpreted what others saw in Durago as a lackadaisical attitude, or that Durago did not care about Navy life, as an inner strength. He recognized that Durago was unfazed, almost nonplussed, by the pressure. No matter how much yelling or screaming was directed at him, Durago simply took it. He had no problem hanging in with the physical demands, so being dropped for pushups or being asked to brace up was unpleasant, but survivable. Slim recognized that this got underneath the skins of most upperclass—as if they had no true power over Durago—which then led to more unwanted attention.

After Plebe Summer, roommates were assigned by the upperclass on the Plebe Summer Detail. Gladstone paired Slim with Durago after talking with Slim about it.

"Warren, you need to help Durago," he said. "He's going to sink fast if he doesn't get his act together soon."

"Aye, aye, sir," Slim responded, thinking, *Durago will be alright.*

Today, Slim still trusted his instincts. Especially after he saw that through Durago's self-realization, his transformation during Plebe Year, his roommate emerged as one of the best leaders in the company—maybe *the* best.

The door to Oberly's office was open, but he was not in.

"Hey, Mate!" Slim called out.

Jeffries, a third class midshipman, poked his head out from the company's wardroom.

"Slim, what's up?"

"Where's the captain?"

"Dunno."

"If you see him, come get me . . . or at least let him know I stopped by."

As Jeffries left the wardroom, Slim stepped in, dropping his book bag and turning on the television. The CNN anchor was talking about the U.S.-led no-fly-zone efforts in Iraq that were part of the Operation Desert Storm postwar operations, followed by plans for U.N. operations in Somalia.

"James, sorry I'm late," Oberly said as he entered the wardroom.

"Good morning, sir. No problem."

"What do you want to talk about? Is it about your roomie?"

"It is, sir."

"I figured. What's up?" Oberly said as he motioned the future Marine to sit.

Slim gathered his thoughts for a moment. He had envisioned having this meeting in the captain's office. "Sir, do you know about Don's parents—about his dad?"

"I do. You're referring to the fact that he's an orphan. I knew that."

"Yes, sir. His dad died before he was born and he was sent to boarding school, so he was never really close with his mom, either. But I really want to talk about his father. Did you know he died in Vietnam? And that he received the Medal of Honor?"

Oberly stood as he said, "No, I . . ."

"Sir, let me show you," Slim said as he stood and pointed to the doorway.

The company officer followed Slim past his office toward the seventh-wing stairwell near the connection with fifth wing. They went down one flight of stairs to 7-3. They stopped outside the first room on the left, 7312.

"Holy shit!" Oberly said when he saw the photograph of Midshipman Donald Fitzpatrick, U.S. Naval Academy Class of 1967. "That photo could be Don!"

"Freaky, ain't it, sir?"

"What was his action?" Oberly said as he leaned in to read the citation. "Wait . . . this says 'Fitzpatrick.'"

"Yes, sir. That's part of what I wanted to talk to you about."

34

PAPERWORK

APRIL 7, 1992
1630
BANCROFT HALL, ROOM 7412

Three hours later, Durago knocked on Oberly's door.

"Enter."

Durago propped the door open, latching it on the catch on the floor. Oberly was wearing a yellow t-shirt with the Marine Corps' eagle, globe, and anchor on the front and a pair of thin, red running shorts. The officer bent over in his chair, tying a pair of running shoes.

"Good afternoon, sir. You wanted to see me?"

"Yes. I've got a tasking for you that I need done by morning quarters formation," said Oberly. He rose from his seat and handed Durago a thick manila envelope that was on the front corner of his desk.

"What is this, sir?"

"The first of your commissioning paperwork," Oberly said. "In here are forms that all the first classes must provide the print shop and the Navy or Marine Corps to ensure the correct spellings for your diploma and commissioning certificate. So, for example, someone might want the certificate to read 'W. T. Door,' while another may prefer 'Water T. Door,' and still another, 'Water Tight Door.' Once you see the forms, it's pretty self-explanatory.'"

Got it, sir."

"Tomorrow morning I want to come in and find these on my desk. Do whatever you need to do to make that happen."

"Aye, aye, sir."

"I'm going to PT now. See you tomorrow," the company officer said as he left his office and headed for the elevator.

Durago sensed Captain Oberly was not telling him something. It was almost as if he were avoiding him. *Does he think my days are numbered?* Durago thought as he walked toward his room. *Is he going to deal with me only when he has to, until he can replace me with one of my Marine Corps–bound classmates?*

Durago dropped his bag on the deck in the room he and Slim shared and opened the package. The forms contained small boxes lined up like a crossword. Specific lines were set for first name (or initial), middle name (or initial), and last name. The diploma paperwork asked for the listing of major. The directions read: "Leave one (1) blank box between each name. Indicate lowercase letters before uppercase letters in surnames with two uppercase letters with a small underline (e.g., McDaniel). Add apostrophes as needed (e.g., O'Shea)."

Durago wondered if Oberly would review the paperwork. Not having an answer, he completed the first form.

Donald Reece Fitzpatrick

The next day, Durago sat at the two-man desk in the room, studying. There was a knock, followed by Oberly entering the room. As Durago rose to his feet, he noted that the company officer had two of the commissioning forms in his hand—undoubtedly his forms. Durago would not be able to avoid the conversation that Oberly was about to have with him.

"What's this about?" Oberly said, tossing Durago's paperwork on the desk and pointing to his name. "Is this some kind of a joke? Some 'Philo T. McGiffin' or 'Salty Sam' Naval Academy bullshit that I'm not previously privy to?"

"No, sir," Durago replied sheepishly.

"Well, what the hell is it?"

"Sir, I think you know my parents are deceased, right?"

"Yes, I do recall that."

"Sir, 'Durago' is my mother's maiden name. I . . . I want to change my name."

Durago paused a moment. He dropped his head and swallowed hard to prevent himself from breaking down. The room fell silent for a second, so devoid of acoustic vibrations that Durago's ears started ringing as if time had stopped. He snapped out of it at the sound of a Plebe chopping outside in the passageway. Durago looked up, sticking his chin forward a little, and with renewed strength said, "I want to change my name to the name of my birth, to my real name. I want to change my name to 'Fitzpatrick.'"

"What about the legal process? Have you looked into that?"

"No, not really, sir. I mean, I researched it or asked once during my Plebe or Youngster Year. I seem to remember it's not that difficult, especially because 'Fitzpatrick' is the name on my birth certificate. It should just be a paperwork drill."

"Durago, or . . . whoever the hell you are . . ." Oberly now said, grinning, "you're not telling me everything, are you?"

"Sir?"

"There's more to this whole name change than meets the eye."

"Damn it, sir!" Durago suddenly yelled. "Slim told you, didn't he?!"

"He did, Don."

"Well . . . excuse me, sir, but that's fucked up. I'm gonna kill him."

Oberly moved to the door, holding up his hands almost defensively in an effort to calm Durago.

"Don, please, calm down. Mister Warren has your best interests in mind. He thinks that your status as the son of a Medal of Honor recipient can significantly help your conduct case. It may even lead to the charges being dropped."

"No, no, no, sir." Durago said, shaking his head with every word.

"Don, you know me by now," Captain Oberly said, cutting him off. "Normally, I wouldn't approve of such politicking—hell, one might even say I'm bad at it; maybe if I'd been more political, I'd be a major already. But, in this case it's warranted. I want you to get a fair shake in this hearing, as fair as what Miss Whorton is getting. In order to do that, we need to present your *whole* case. I want the board to know everything about you."

It was not lost on Durago that Oberly was talking about Commander Gordon. He also realized on a different level that Oberly was comparing him to Whorton. Previously, Durago simply thought that it would be bad press for the son of a Medal of Honor recipient to get the boot. Oberly subtly pointed out that Durago was in the same category as Whorton. A review of his record would show a troubled Plebe Year filled with conduct violations and his battalion performance board. All of this, added to his lineage, would force Gordon to treat Durago as if he were the same as Whorton.

"Sir, that would be very insulting. I don't want to be put in the same category as Whorton. More important, and this is why I'm pissed at Slim, I've purposely downplayed how I got into this place. I'm sure most of my classmates in the company know, but it's not in the forefront of their minds anymore. I had a rough Plebe Year. During that time I decided that I had to earn my way through this place—for me. I can't help that my dad's legacy got me in here, but I want to get through on my own. If you tell the board, respectfully, sir, I'll resign. I'll resign and go to the fleet. My pride, my own personal honor, is more important than a commissioning."

"Son, that is so naïve. I'm sure your father—"

"Captain, don't ever!" Durago screamed as tears welled in his eyes.

"Don, I'm sorry, but you—"

Before Oberly could finish, Durago bolted out of the room. Slim was among the midshipmen walking down the passageway toward the 'back,' the river-view side of 7-4. He noticed Don was upset.

"Don, wait!"

Oberly emerged from their room. "Slim, go after him!"

Slim dropped his books and sprinted after Durago. He followed him down the steps but could not keep up in class uniform, especially uniform shoes. When he reached Santee Basin, he saw Durago running across Farragut Field toward the Sea Gate at full speed. Slim started to jog in that direction. At first he wondered why Durago was heading directly for the stairs leading into the Severn, and then it hit him. *That fucker's going in the water.*

Slim now strolled to the gate, thinking of what he should do next. He wondered if Durago had really flipped out, or if a dip in the Severn was simply a way to blow off steam. As he neared the gate, he saw his roommate in the water making his way in the direction of Eastport, across the entrance to Annapolis Harbor. Slim remembered bay swims in Alligator Bayou and Saint Andrews Bay in Panama City when they were at dive school. Durago always was comfortable in the water. *He sure can swim, like a damned fish.* It would have been pointless to yell or try to call him back. *Where the hell is he going?*

The weather was nice, so there were a number of boats in the harbor. *Is this Wednesday? The Wednesday Night Races?* Durago was not sure and he could not confirm his guess by the mix of sailboats and powerboats around him. Fortunately, it was bright enough and most of the boats seemed to be following their prescribed traffic scheme within the harbor. It quieted somewhat as he crawled into the center of the racetrack pattern where several boats were anchored. Durago paused halfway across and treaded water, looking to where Jan kept *Quantum Meriut*. He could not tell if the ladder was up or down. His Submariner told him it was 1545. *Hell, she may not even be home. Fuck it!*

Slim stood by the Sea Gate, watching his roommate treading in the middle of the channel. He could tell Durago was looking at something, as if he were taking a bearing. *Where are you going, Don? What the hell are you doing?*

He heard Brendan McDougal's voice behind him. "Fucker's gonna get run over."

Turning, Slim saw that his Plebe Year roommate was in PT gear— running shorts and a 'blue rim,' the white uniform PT shirt worn by all midshipmen. The Naval Academy seal was over the left breast, and the sleeves and neck were rimmed with blue, which had turned to mottled purple years ago from the repeated use of government-quality detergent.

"Hey, Brendan," Slim responded as he focused back on Durago. "Nah, he'll be alright. I'm just trying to figure out what he thinks he's doing, where he's going."

"You know how I feel about it, man. Don's never been all there. He's got a chip on his shoulder, an albatross around his neck, chasing demons—pick your metaphor."

"Lit exam?"

"Tomorrow. Anyway, you get my point. Don will never be able to live up to his father, and until he accepts that, he'll never be at peace."

"McDougal," Slim said, turning back toward his classmate, "for the first time in a long time, I think you might be right."

"I am right. Guy's dad was a Medal of Honor recipient, and to make matters worse, he wasn't able to pass on a single thing to the kid. It's a frickin' Shakespearean tragedy."

Slim scanned the water again until he found Durago. "Yeah, well, there's gonna be another tragedy, 'cause when he gets back here I'm gonna kick the shit outta him.

"Fucking dumbass!" he yelled across the water.

"Whoa, calm down, brother. You know, the captain's watching."

"What?"

"Yeah," said McDougal, gesturing over his shoulder. "He's looking down from 7-4 right now. That's why I'm here. He sent me to see what this whole 'jumping in the Severn' thing is about."

"He already knows. It's about Don changing his name."

"No, not that . . . he told me about that. Wild, huh? But I mean, 'Why did Don jump in the river?' Is this some kinda Navy diver thing?"

"I don't know."

"Fucker can swim, though, can't he?"

"Yeah, he sure can."

Durago made his way to the closest set of piers, about one hundred feet from *Quantum Meriut*. The ladder was definitely up. The hatch was closed, and it looked like it was locked. *She's not home.* Holding onto the stern of a Choy Lee for a moment, Durago realized he had calmed down and cooled off a little. He was still angry at Slim's betrayal, but he knew he would have to forgive his friend.

Taking a quick mental bearing, Durago started to swim back toward the *Maine's* foremast. In a few seconds he pumped his arms and legs like a machine, taking quick peeks of his location and progress as he first breathed on one side, then the other. This time, Durago paid no attention to the boats at all. Some bitterness at being found out, at losing the anonymity he thought he had regained, seeped back into his soul. He guessed that Oberly would tell Gordon, and that he would be let off quietly.

Shit! I gotta be the only midshipman who would rather be railroaded than exonerated. Durago realized that Oberly would never understand. Nobody but Slim would ever be able to comprehend his logic. Still, he would somehow have to convince the Marine not to inform Commander Gordon of his status, of his father's history.

The chop increased. Durago bobbed a moment and saw that the waves were reverberating back from the rocks along the seawall. He slowed, anticipating the decrease in depth. As he approached, he felt the bottom. He stood, shimmied up to the steps, and climbed out.

"Let me know when you get your wind back," Slim said as his roommate regained his feet, "'cause I'm about to put a new memorial right here between Triton Light and the *Maine*'s mast. It's gonna be all of your teeth laid out like little headstones on a bronze plaque, with an inscription that reads, 'Here's where Donny Fitzpatrick got his ass kicked.'"

"Who?" Durago queried.

"Donald Fitzpatrick."

"Wow, nobody's ever called me that."

Realizing that he had unwittingly baptized his roommate before the umbilical was cut, Slim dropped his head and swallowed hard with a combination of shame and sadness as his roommate plopped on the granite wall and wept. He sputtered, as if he were trying to hold it in. Slim walked over and put his hand on Durago's shoulder. "It's alright, man. Let it out. Fuck, I'm sorry—I named you before you were ready. Your fucking commissioning name, your baptism, but too early."

"Yeah?" Durago said through held breath. "Maybe not. I wonder if this is my confirmation, right here at the fucking Sea Gate."

"Dude, I'm sorry. I caused this whole thing. I know it wasn't time yet; it just came out."

Durago looked up at Slim. "Nah, it's not your fault . . . and it's not confirmation. I gotta remember my catechism. I've been outta order. It's reconciliation, or maybe more appropriately, 'confession.'"

"What are you talking about?" Slim asked.

"Sit down, Slim. There's something I need to tell you. Something that started during spring break."

When McDougal returned to 7-4, Oberly was still looking out the window toward the Sea Gate.

"Sir, as you can see, Durago's back. They'll be back in a few minutes."

"Looks like Don's really upset."

"Yes, sir. I'm sure this whole conduct case right before graduation is having a stressful impact on him. Don's never handled personal stress very well. Plus, there's the whole thing about his dad, which you now know about. It's a funny thing, sir. Don really doesn't call attention to it. He's like a rich kid who's always dressing down. Heck, I think I'd forgotten about it myself."

Oberly turned away from the window, looked to McDougal, and nodded toward the roommates still sitting on the seawall. "What's up with those two?"

"What? Oh, I get what you mean, sir. Well, they're close. I mean, many roommates here at the Academy become close. They become like man-wives; it's funny how some of them connect. I mean, you ever notice how many opposites there are? How many submariners are rooming with future Marines? Like Moeller and Lagasse. Those guys got together at the end of Plebe Year. Lagasse said to Mole, 'You get me through Physics and I'll get you laid.' If those two went to Dartmouth, they'd be in different worlds. Lagasse would be a frat boy. Mole would be an RA and president of the Theta Tau Society."

"The what?"

"You're proving my point, sir. But, back to Don and Slim; they're actually a lot alike. Both went to boarding school. Don's got no family; Slim's estranged from his. Then there's the whole scuba/*Squid* thing. Those two have been through this shit together, morally, mentally, and physically."

Oberly smiled. "McDougal, you oughta be a chaplain."

"Fuck that, sir. An intel officer—I only wanna know about people so I can manipulate them."

That evening, Durago and Slim met with Captain Oberly together.

"Don," the captain said, "I've decided that I'm not going to 'out' you for three reasons. First, you might get hammered, but I don't think you're gonna get kicked out. Second, we can pull this trump card out at any time. Hell, it may be more powerful if it's revealed at your hearing or after. Third, your roommate here has expressed his regrets for sharing all of this with me, and he made the case that he didn't respect a longstanding understanding between you two—and I should respect your wishes to keep it private. I've decided to do that on one condition."

"Sir?"

"Now, you need to make amends with him."

The roommates looked at each other. "You're right sir, but I already have. We had a long talk out there today, and—"

Oberly raised his hand to stop Durago, "Son, I don't need to hear any more. It's between you two knuckleheads. Let's just get through this hearing, deal with what happens, and get you two to the fleet, okay?"

"Aye, aye, sir."

35

STATEMENT

APRIL 9, 1992
1100
BANCROFT HALL, 7-0

The line for the phone bank moved fairly well. Some nights there may be a homesick Plebe, or a mid arguing loudly with a boyfriend or girlfriend. Without such drama, Durago could not help overhearing a few mundane conversations.

"Yeah, so it looks like I'll pull a 'D' in double-E."

"Mom? Yeah. I found a house for Commissioning Week. It's not far, in Edgewater, Maryland."

A second class Durago recognized vacated one of the phone booths, and Durago slid in. "Ugh," he groaned aloud. As always, the phone booth smelled of body odor and chewing tobacco. Durago left the door open to let some fresh air into the tight space while he called Master Chief Strong. An answering machine picked up.

"You have reached *Strong Diver*," his mentor's voice said. "We are available for scuba diving charters seven days a week, including night dives. Please leave a name, number, number in your party, and the day you would like to dive."

When the recording ended Durago said, "Master Chief, it's Durago."

The phone was picked up. "Hey, sir . . . what's up?"

"Master Chief, I'm calling to ask two things. First, will you come to my graduation?"

"Yes, sir . . . I thought you'd never ask."

"Great, I just got invitations today. I'll send one officially, but . . . you know."

"Hooyah, sir."

"Well, the second thing is, I actually may not graduate. I, uh—"

"What?!"

Durago relayed the whole story to Master Chief Strong, leaving out the details about his continued relationship with Jan. After ten minutes, he finally got to his point. "So, Slim and my company officer think we should somehow make sure the battalion commander knows about my father. They think it'll prevent him maxing me out on the fry. Captain Oberly even suggested that I could, in effect, use the same tactics as Whorton—point to my rough start Plebe Year and suggest that some remnant of my orphan status has led me astray."

"Bullshit."

"That's what I said."

"Sir, you can't say that 'cause it ain't really true . . . is it? As a result, it won't ring true. So, first, let me give a read on this whole thing. First, you said the captain suggested nobody's gonna go down big, right?"

"Right—too close to the end of the year, charges are really bullshit, counterproductive, etcetera."

"I agree. I think—worst-case scenario—you'll get hammered and be on restriction until graduation. More than likely, this is simply to mollify Whorton's parents. They'll have heard there are people getting fried, and they'll be satisfied that someone is gonna pay for what's happened to their kid.

"So, the only reasonable way you can get your father's name in the mix is in your statement to the board. Write something like, you've learned so much in trying to live up to his legacy. That *is* true, will *ring* true, and can have great impact."

"Yeah, I hadn't thought of it that way."

"I think that's what you should do. Don't make it about her; make it about your own growth."

"You don't think it'll be dishonoring to my father."

"Nah . . . the man gave his life for this country; I think his kid deserves a break or two. Besides, we need men like you in the fleet to counteract all the arrogant fuck-ups."

"Thanks, Master Chief."

Durago decided to accept the master chief's advice. He was ready to own his heritage, and he would weave it into his personal statement to the board.

The seventh-wing weight room was like a sauna. Oberly liked coming in during lunch because none of the mids were here. He ignored signs that required him to have a spotter and began his bench-press routine. A decrepit, paint-splattered boom box managed to get a signal from WHFS through a coat hanger and tin foil, drowning any possibility of conversation in the room.

Oberly thought often of the Whorton conduct case. The battalion officer was definitely obsessed. Oberly held on to the hope that the system would bear out truth and justice—for Durago and for Whorton. As he added another plate to the bar, the music stopped. He looked toward the radio. Ned Breedon was standing there in summer whites. "Oberly, we gotta talk about this Whorton thing."

"What's up?" Oberly realized it must be important. Breedon knew how precious his workout time was.

"The commander's going too far."

"I agree, man. So, let's stop him, make him aware of our concerns."

"I just did. I explained to him that I thought Whorton's parents had undue influence over this whole thing."

"What did he say?"

Breedon took off his cover and wiped his brow. He was visibly upset, and Oberly noticed he swallowed hard before speaking. "That he's going to ensure I'm ranked thirty-sixth of thirty-six company officers when the next FITREPs come out."

"Shit." Now Oberly wiped his brow. "You Navy boys sure are fucked up sometimes. I have never seen an organization so hell-bent on eating its young."

"Bobby, I need your help. I need at least two other company officers who agree with me to help me with the commander, or he's going to hang me. Hell, he may anyway, but this witch-hunt has got to stop."

First they went to Lieutenant Santiago, because the 17th Company Officer was a submariner and a Naval Academy grad. His concurrence would be the cornerstone of any argument with Commander Gordon. He would listen to another submariner. Oberly's and Breedon's hopes rested on a guess that Santiago would empathize with the midshipmen involved.

The three of them talked that afternoon on Hospital Point, following a battalion intramural soccer match. Oberly could hear Breedon nearly pleading.

"Manny, he's a little overzealous. We feel like these mids aren't getting a fair shake."

"Fellas, I hear you, but I disagree. The commander has a point."

Oberly shot Breedon a sarcastic look. *You Navy guys . . .* "Were we there when these offenses were committed?"

"Alleged offenses," Breedon added.

"Okay, okay—alleged offenses. Let the system work. Besides, guys, it's already over. The hearing is tomorrow."

"What?!" both Oberly and Breedon exclaimed.

"Didn't you guys hear? Gordon moved the hearing up to tomorrow."

PART IV
THE HEARING

36

INQUISITION

APRIL 10, 1992
1230
KING HALL

Durago walked out of King Hall after lunch and up the stairs into fifth wing. As he crossed the walkway between 5-0 and 7-0, he saw Sumlin.

"How'd it go?"

"Not good. Watch it, man; it was a fucking Inquisition in there."

"What happened?" Durago asked. The outcome of Sumlin's hearing would be indicative of what he could expect.

"Just like I told you—restriction. I'm going to be a Smoke Hall bandito for a long time . . . probably into the summer."

"That sucks, man." Deep down, Durago was happy. Restriction meant retention.

"Fuck it, I was going to go to summer school anyway. The sad part is that I won't get liberty during two-a-days."

"Sorry, man."

"Yeah. Good luck, Durago."

Jan emerged from the battalion office just as Durago arrived. She smiled reassuringly at him. "Hi."

"Ma'am. How's it going?"

"Not good, I'm sorry to say."

"What's happening in there? I just saw Sumlin."

"They've let me go in to review each case after each hearing. Commander Gordon has proved to be everything we expected. I don't know how this is going to pan out for you. Take your time, keep your cool, walk out with your head up when it's over. Okay?"

Durago saw true concern in her eyes. For a brief moment, he thought about their first night together on *Quantum Meriut.* "Okay." It was the first time that Jan's presence didn't make him feel any better. There was a tight, sick feeling in his gut.

Durago noticed that several of Whorton's classmates were gathering in the battalion passageway. They all looked at him knowingly. Van Zandt came over to him. "Good luck, man."

"Thanks, Z."

When Durago entered the battalion office, he saw immediately that everyone else in the room was very casual, like they were not nervous at all. This issue was not nearly as important to the battalion officer and his staff as it was to the accused.

"Midshipman First Class—"

"Sit down, Mister Durago," the battalion officer said, cutting him off. "Mister Durago, this is a hearing to determine if you are guilty of a six-thousand-series offense. The charge is harassment. This office will determine guilt or innocence, and it can recommend lesser charges be brought in addition to or instead of the current charge.

"The board is chaired by myself. The members are Lieutenant Schwartz, Fifteenth Company Officer, and Lieutenant Sinclair, Sixteenth Company Officer, both on my left. On my right are Lieutenant Commander Ferren, Eighteenth Company Officer, and you know Captain Oberly. Captain Oberly will be the board recorder because he's your company officer and is providing the board with a performance evaluation on your behalf."

Gordon stopped to sip his coffee. Durago noted that none of the board members were Academy grads. He felt a cold sweat drip from his armpit, down his side to his waist.

"Additionally, Lieutenant Tripp, Brigade Legal Officer, is in my office to provide legal counsel to the board. I understand you've elected to seek counsel. Therefore, I'm sure you're aware of how this procedure goes. We've read the report of the investigating officer and the written accusations of Miss Whorton. Because she is currently unavailable, you may not question her, but you may read and refute her written testimony. We're going to ask you a series of questions to clarify some issues. You're not allowed to have counsel present, but you may step outside and meet with counsel at any time during the hearing. You may also call any witness on your behalf.

"Any questions?"

"Yes, sir. I was told I could submit a statement on my behalf."

Oberly looked at Durago, knowing exactly what he was driving at. After finally convincing him to discuss his lineage, it would not emerge after all, owing to timing.

"The board was moved up and I was unable to complete one yet."

"You can complete it after and submit it for consideration then." The battalion officer looked over to one of the company officers, a submariner. "Lieutenant Schwartz?"

There was a knock at the door. The commander looked up. "Enter."

It was Jan.

"Yes, Lieutenant?"

"Commander, there's a group of midshipmen here who would like to be recognized as witnesses on Mister Durago's behalf."

"Fine, tell them to wait."

Jan smirked sarcastically. She did not hide her disdain for Commander Gordon. "Sir, there is almost a full company of midshipmen out here. Most undoubtedly are going to miss class—"

"What?!" exclaimed the commander. The company officers around the table dropped their pencils and leaned back in their chairs. Gordon lifted his portly frame and waddled to the door. Durago noticed that his shoes were scuffed and chipped. The commander was far from an example of military bearing. Captain Oberly looked toward Durago, frowning and almost rolling his eyes. The look said, *I know*.

Gordon returned to his seat, a look of disgust on his face. "This is a cute charade, Mister Durago."

"Sir, I didn't—"

"Pick one representative to speak; send the others to class."

Durago got up and went into the passageway. What he saw there put a lump in his throat. It was an overwhelming display.

Three platoons of midshipmen stood in formation. The first was the Class of '94 from 13th Company. Youngsters now, they were the Plebes he trained during Plebe Summer almost two years ago. Mitchell, Gottschalk, Van Zandt—all of them except Whorton. The second platoon was '94 from 14th Company, his company. Next to them were '95, the current Plebes of 14th Company.

"Guys, thanks," he choked weakly. "I . . ."

Mitchell stepped forward. "No problem, Don."

"Uh, they said only one representative . . ." Durago was red with emotion and he was embarrassed that he was displaying it. The mids in formation understood. Most grinned, just now realizing fully the impact of their gesture.

"We already thought of that, Don. I was selected to speak for all of us."

Durago did not have to ask what Mitchell was going to say at the hearing. "Okay, okay. Uh, the rest have to go to class."

"We thought of that, too. Everyone made arrangements with their professors."

Durago looked over toward Jan, standing next to the formation. "Did you know about this, ma'am?"

"No," she beamed. Jan understood.

He turned to go, but then paused. "Someday, when I can pull myself together, I'll ask you guys why."

"You don't need to ask," Mitchell said as he put his arm on Durago's shoulder.

"Give 'em hell, Donny!" shouted someone from the formation.

"I will. And I'll tell you all this: This morning, I was worried. I didn't know what was going to happen at this hearing. Now, thanks to you guys, it doesn't matter. What you have done for me today, out here, means more to me than anything they can do to me in there. So—no matter what the outcome—thank you."

Now several of the mids in formation had red eyes. A few nodded at him as he turned to go back into the battalion conference room.

Back in the room, Durago sat. He noticed immediately that Commander Gordon looked angry. He had pursed lips and his arms were folded over his chest.

Mitchell entered. "Sir, Midshipman Third Class Reginald Mitchell—"

"Did you pick a minority because you thought it would help your case?"

The room was immediately silent. The company officers gazed down at their blank notebooks.

Mitchell broke the silence. "Sir, I could go get a white midshipman if you like, but I was selected to speak on Mister Durago's behalf because I'm the third class company commander for Thirteenth Company, and I was in his squad during his time as a Plebe Summer squad leader."

"Mister Mitchell, I'm sorry. I hope I didn't offend you with that remark."

There was another silence while Mitchell and Gordon stared at each other. Mitchell would not relent. "May I begin my prepared statement, sir?"

"Um, yes . . . continue." Gordon now gazed at Reginald Mitchell as if he were about to deliver the Sermon on the Mount.

"Sir, I represent the third and fourth class midshipmen of Fourteenth Company and the third class midshipmen of Thirteenth Company. The latter group is perhaps the most significant, since we, as companymates and classmates of Midshipman Whorton, were the closest to observe all that transpired between Mister Durago and Miss Whorton.

"We would like to say, first, that we know Mister Durago to be a model midshipman. We consider him to be an example to peers, subordinates, and superiors alike.

"Second, not a single member of the group standing here today has ever observed Mister Durago do anything that can remotely be considered harassment.

"Third, it is the observation of the Class of Ninety-Four in Thirteenth Company that Mister Durago performed in an exemplary manner during our Plebe Summer. He never violated the regulations governing midshipmen indoctrination in either letter or spirit. In fact, those of us who will be on the Plebe Detail this summer, myself included, plan to model our leadership style after Mister Durago."

"Pretty clear to me," blurted Lieutenant Schwartz.

The battalion officer was frowning again. "Thank you, Mister Mitchell," he grumbled. "We appreciate your statement. Unless you have something to add, you and your classmates are dismissed. Send everyone to class."

"Aye, aye, sir."

Mitchell shot Durago another look of support as he left.

37

1-90

APRIL 10, 1992
1400
3RD BATTALION OFFICER'S OFFICE

When the door closed behind Mitchell, Gordon sat back and sighed. He let a moment pass. Durago felt the legitimacy of what just happened disappear in that moment. Finally, Gordon spoke. "Any other witnesses, Mister Durago?"

"No, sir."

"Fine. Lieutenant Schwartz?"

"Mister Durago, did you ever require Midshipman Whorton to change her uniform, run down a flight of stairs, and then change her uniform again?"

"Sir?"

The lieutenant flipped through some papers. "The term here is 'uniform race'?"

"Yes, sir."

"Had you instructed her on how to wear the uniform properly?"

"Sir, that *was* how we instructed the Plebes; we put pressure on them and—"

"Well, it won't be done that way anymore," the commander interrupted again. He turned to Schwartz but spoke as if addressing all the officers in the room.

"See, John, it's just like the Sumlin kid. They've been running amok for too long. This is exactly the kind of behavior that we are to continue to squelch."

Durago's heart sank. *I'm screwed.*

Lieutenant Schwartz began again. "Did you make Whorton conduct this uniform race until she cried?"

"No, sir."

"She didn't cry?"

"I remember the incident you're referring to, sir. She did cry." Durago saw that Gordon looked like he was about to interrupt. "But I didn't do it *until* she cried. We conducted a uniform race. As a result, Whorton did cry, but that wasn't the intent."

"We?" Schwartz inquired.

"Sir, the whole Detail was involved in conducting uniform races more than once."

"You did these with all of the Plebes?"

"Yes, sir," Durago said firmly. "Uniform races, chow calls, physical training, Yard gouge, other rates. Whorton was treated the same as each and every other mid in the platoon, in the company."

A moment passed as Schwartz sifted through papers. Gordon had calmed and was looking out the window. Durago saw Oberly looking to Schwartz. The other company officers seemed to stare into space. Finally, Schwartz asked, "Are you familiar with the directive commonly known as 'one-tack-ninety,' the directive that midshipmen should not touch one another physically?"

"Yes, sir."

"Is it true that you violated this directive by grabbing Midshipman Whorton in a way that violated her personal space, rendered her defenseless, and embarrassed her in front of her classmates?"

"Sir, this is the first I've heard of this accusation. I—"

Captain Oberly spoke for the first time since the hearing began. "Mister Durago, you may consult with counsel outside at any time."

"I would like to do that, sir." He stood up and stepped outside.

Jan was surprised that Durago had emerged so quickly. "Was that amazing, or what?" she said. "I guess Gordon told Mitchell to have everyone leave."

"Yeah."

"What is it?"

"It's over already. I'm sunk before we've even started."

"After that display? You're kidding. What did they say?"

"I violated one-tack-ninety. I touched her."

"Did you?"

"I'm sure I touched her plenty of times. It was Plebe Summer, for Pete's sake."

"You didn't assault her did you?!" his counsel said incredulously.

"Damn it! Now you! Of course not! There are literally hundreds of times mids touch each other. People touch each other! The question is whether or not she found it offensive."

Jan held her hand over her mouth and took a deep breath. "Okay, let's calm down. There's no real legal issue that I can help you with. Here's what I want you to do: go in there and answer all of their questions truthfully."

"Of course."

"No, listen . . . you have got to do this right. I believe you, Don. I believe *in* you. Do the right thing, and you *will* survive this. No matter what the outcome of the board, you will survive it. You said it yourself. What's most important is that your peers know you did nothing wrong."

"Still, I don't want to get kicked out."

"Well, let's plow through this thing. You know the 'dant is going to overturn this whole thing, anyway."

"I hope you're right."

Oberly used Durago's absence as an opportunity to try to persuade Commander Gordon yet again. He knew that if he pushed too hard when Durago was present he would lose. Gordon would not allow himself to lose face.

"Commander, I believe Mister Mitchell's statement should bring an end to this hearing," Oberly said. "There are no accusations by Miss Whorton that have her alone with Mister Durago. Mister Mitchell and his classmates are, in effect, impartial witnesses to all of these events. They have now come forward and stated clearly that no harassment occurred. We should close this board."

"He has a point, sir," Ferren piped in.

"Gentlemen, the United States Navy states that the definition of harassment is based solely on the point of view of the person being harassed. It doesn't matter that anyone else present doesn't see harassment. What's important in this case is that the victim, Miss Whorton, feels she was harassed."

"Then Miss Whorton should have told Mister Durago that she felt that he was harassing her and brought it up with the chain of command."

"Captain, we've been through this. Whorton was afraid of repercussions from the chain of command. That's how it always is in these cases. Look, the point here is not the intention of Mister Durago. I'm sure that he and all the other mids involved thought he was doing right. The point is that the indoctrination system of this place has gone so awry that it's created the perception that the ill behavior that pervades this place is acceptable!"

Oberly shook his head. He looked to his fellow company officers. They would not protest further. They all wanted to finish the day and go home—and Durago was going to pay for it.

The commander finished the board with some closing comments. "Mister Durago, this has been a long afternoon. The board is going to review your testimony and that of Miss Whorton. We will contact you and let you know what the board's decision is. Stand by in your company area."

"Aye, aye, sir."

Durago stepped out of the conference room. Jan was sitting on a chair in the passageway. She looked up.

"I'm going back to company area."

Jan opened her mouth to speak.

"Thank you, Jan. However this turns out, thank you. Right now I need to be alone."

She stepped close to him, closer than a lieutenant would normally stand next to a midshipman. She looked up at him and smiled again. "Call me if you need to talk," she said.

Durago sat in his room in shock. After only five minutes, there was a knock at the door. "Sir, mate of the deck, sir."

"Enter."

"Mister Durago, a phone call just came for you from battalion office. You're wanted in the conference room."

"Thanks."

"Sir, good luck."

"Huh?"

"For what it's worth, sir, the whole company knows this thing is bullshit."

"Thanks, Gant. Carry on."

"Aye, aye, sir."

By the commander's posture and that of the company officers around the table, Durago could see that his demeanor had not changed. He was very succinct. "Mister Durago, this conduct board is going to recommend separation to the Office of the Commandant. There will be another hearing there. In the meantime, you are to begin the process for separation until told otherwise. Any questions?"

Durago jumped to his feet. "Sir, this is all bullshit!"

"Listen here, Durago! You and your kind do not belong here! You are not wanted in my Navy! This place is just a big fraternity to you!"

"Yes, sir—yes it is."

"Well, those days are over, mister! You are now a dinosaur! Do you even know the first thing about the United States Navy?"

"I know enough."

"You're just a midshipman—or were—and a bad one at that!"

"I know what this place has taught me, sir! Like . . . like the Code of Conduct. Can you recite the Code?"

"The what?"

"The Code of Conduct, sir."

Durago saw that all of the officers sitting at the table were dumbfounded. They were shocked by his outburst. He sensed Gordon had no idea what he was talking about. "Sir, the Code of Conduct is a set of articles all servicemen are instructed to know in preparation for the possibility of capture—"

"Don't lecture me, son."

"I'm answering your question, sir. Surely, you know the Code of Conduct. It's one of the most basic—"

"Durago . . ." Oberly interjected.

"No . . . no, sir," Durago replied, looking at his company officer. "I will not be suppressed. My integrity as a midshipman has just been challenged and I'm responding in kind.

"Commander Gordon, what about the oath of office? I know my oath of office—do you, sir?"

"Get out!" Gordon said pointing toward the door.

"I, Donald R. Durago, having been appointed a midshipman in the United States Navy, do solemnly swear that I will support and defend the Constitution of the United States of America against all enemies foreign and domestic—"

"Get out! Get the fuck out of my office!" the commander raged.

"And will bear true faith and allegiance to the same. I take this obligation freely, without any mental reservation or purpose of evasion, and I will well and faithfully discharge the duties of the office on which I am about to enter, so help me God."

Now the commander sat speechless, red with anger, spittle running from the corner of his mouth.

"Commander, your kangaroo court has berated me all afternoon. Hell, for the past few weeks, I've been beat up for doing exactly what I was trained to do by this institution. And quite frankly, I believe in it. You talk to me about harassment. Well, *this court is harassment*! Fuck you, you fat fuck! When you can recite your oath of office, Commander, then you can talk to me about being an officer in the United States Navy!"

The board members sat in stunned silence after Durago left the conference room and crossed the hall to the elevator. Against all regulations, he got on and rode it up to 7-4. Nobody was in sight as he strode to his room and slammed the door.

"Add disrespect to his charges!" Gordon yelled finally.

"Why bother, sir?" asked Sinclair. "We gonna kick him out twice?"

Without knocking, Oberly threw open the door to Durago's room. "Son, that was some performance," he said with disdain. "I hope you're happy. I'll never understand, but it seems to me that you got what you wanted."

"I did not get *anything* I wanted, sir," Durago said with anguish and defeat in his quivering voice. "I'm getting kicked out, for Pete's sake!"

"So, what did you prove? What are you proving? Some bizarre concept of honor? I just don't get it."

"Sir, I've proved that *I* got through this place!" Durago replied, now with more defiance than defeat. "Not you. Not Slim. Not Lieutenant Meyer. And not my father. I've gotten through because of *me*."

"Well, then, maybe you don't really belong here, because nobody, son, *nobody* gets through this place alone."

Oberly slammed the door on his way out. Heading back to his office, he tried to determine whom he was more angry with—Whorton and her parents, for starting this whole charade; Gordon, for kowtowing to them with his false sense of justice; Durago, with his twisted concept of honor; or himself, for his own conciliatory leadership that allowed the whole thing to proceed this far. Reaching his desk, Oberly quickly found the phone number for the commandant's office.

"Commandant Richter's office, this is Petty Officer Goodwin; can I help you sir or ma'am?"

"Goodwin, this is Captain Oberly, Fourteenth Company Officer. I need to meet with the commandant."

At about the same time, Tripp was making a phone call to the U.S. Navy Bureau of Personnel in Federal Office Building Two, a structure that resembled its bigger cousin down the hill, Federal Office Building One—more commonly called "the Pentagon." Although more diminutive in size, the building almost equaled its predecessor in bureaucracy.

"PERS Forty-One, Lieutenant Johanssen speaking; may I help you sir or ma'am."

"Lieutenant Johanssen, this is Lieutenant Doug Tripp at the U.S. Naval Academy. How are you today?"

"Fine, Doug. Call me Carl. How can I help you?"

"Carl, I'm the Brigade Legal Officer here in Annapolis. I'm calling about a midshipman—a former midshipman, really."

"Oh?"

"Yes, Donald Durago. He selected surface warfare in February, but now he will be separated. I wanted to inform you so that you can cancel his orders."

There was silence on the other end of the line. Tripp flexed his hand, making a fist as he sensed Johanssen was wrestling with what he just said. "Carl?"

"Uh, yeah . . . this is a new one for me, Doug. I mean, is there some sort of official paperwork? I mean, we don't just willy-nilly cancel people's orders."

"It's unusual," Tripp replied. "That's why I'm making this call." He unflexed his hand and continued as he had rehearsed three times prior to dialing Johanssen's number.

"You see, Carl, we're about to separate Durago and will either send him to the fleet as an enlisted man, or kick him out altogether and make him pay back his education. Naturally, the former will require orders from an enlisted detailer."

"The quartermaster detailer, right?"

"Exactly, since he's had the requisite navigation classes; or, for the latter, he'll simply get a DD two-fourteen."

"I see where you're going, Doug."

"Yes," Tripp said, admiring his own cleverness. "So, you see, Carl, in any case, Durago will not execute any orders you have written for him. So, I think you'll need to cancel them."

"Well, I won't even have to do that," Johanssen responded. "The orders haven't been written yet. I'll simply take him off my list and fill the need with someone else. There's some shuffling with new commissions, anyway. Always is, I understand."

"I figured as much. So, I'll let you know if we have any others."

"Cool, thanks, Doug. I appreciate you keeping me square. I can imagine a CO being unhappy if a junior officer doesn't show up. I'd be embarrassed, really."

"Glad to help, Carl." *Fuck you, Jan, and fuck you, Durago,* Tripp thought as he put the phone back in its cradle.

38

MASS

APRIL 12, 1992
0955
U.S. NAVAL ACADEMY CHAPEL

As the chaplain sat, Oberly felt his innards begin to reverberate with the massive pipe organ as it joined the choir.

> Eternal Father, strong to save,
> Whose arm hath bound the restless wave,
> Who bidd'st the mighty ocean deep,
> Its own eternal limits keep;
> Oh, hear us when we cry to Thee,
> For those in peril on the sea!

Oberly appreciated that at Annapolis, the Marine Corps was always included in any pomp and circumstance.

> Eternal Father, grant, we pray,
> To all Marines, both night and day,
> The courage, honor, strength, and skill,
> Their land to serve, Thy law fulfill;
> Be thou the shield forevermore
> From every peril to the Corps!
> Ahhhh-men!

With the processional, Oberly watched pockets of people leaving, indentifying each subgroup. Local Annapolitans were preppy—bright-colored sun dresses under hats suitable for the derby, and pastel-colored bow ties over boat shoes without socks. Many of the couples wore matching rings on their left ring fingers, wedding bands curved to the college ring covered with seas, sails, and swords. The tourists were distracted by the chapel's reverent beauty and could not avoid pausing and pointing in awe at the marble, granite, and stained glass. Oberly also noticed the Brigade looked older, wiser, than only six months ago. Most Plebes now had full heads of hair and had long ago lost their deer-in-the-headlights look. The Firsties looked less like midshipmen and more like officers. They exuded a confidence that could only be matched by stars on one's collar and that he knew would be dashed like a mint chocolate chip ice cream cone spilled on the street in front of Storm Brothers' after first contact with their senior enlisted.

The sun started to warm the Yard, and the breeze had died during Mass. Oberly appreciated how, from such a cold start, it could turn into a really beautiful spring day in Annapolis. Then the thought of Durago depressed him. *No, it's more than that*, he thought. *It's because your own days are numbered.*

Oberly had been passed over for promotion for a third and final time. He was convinced it was largely owing to the fact that his peers on the East Coast saw real action in Grenada and Lebanon, while he floated around the Pacific Rim conducting exercises with the Koreans and Japanese. Then he remained at the Naval Academy while most Marines served in Desert Storm and Desert Shield. His record, through no fault of his own, simply could not compete. Within days of graduation, he would begin to process out of the Marine Corps.

He thought of Gordon, Durago, Whorton, and of his own career's demise. *Why are Durago and I to be cast off, while Gordon and Whorton go on?* He hesitated a moment, wondering if he should not plead Durago's case. *Maybe the kid's wishes are best met by letting him go.*

The crowd thinned as mids streamed left toward Bancroft and the civilians turned right in the direction of the superintendent's house, Captain's Row and Gate 1, the school's main portal into downtown Annapolis. Oberly stopped at the commandant's house. Mrs. Richter, the commandant's wife, saw him approach and opened the door as he stepped on the porch.

"Bob, welcome," she said smiling. "We're so glad to have you join us this morning."

Oberly was impressed that she knew his first name. They had met only once before. *Probably got briefed before my arrival; likely looked at my whole damned record.*

"Are you coming from the chapel?"

"Yes, ma'am," he replied, thinking, *Yep, she noted that I'm Catholic.*

"I'm so inspired by Sunday morning services in the chapel, especially in the spring."

"Bob!" the commandant called as he came down the stairs, as if they were long-lost buddies.

"Good morning, sir."

"I hope you're hungry, Bob. We've got a nice spread this morning."

Noticing that his name was used three times in three minutes, Oberly wondered if they repeated it to remind themselves. *Don't be so cynical*, he said to himself while forcing a smile. *They're just trying to be welcoming.*

To be fair, Oberly had no intelligence on the couple, and during their first and only meeting at a garden party, they did seem to be nice folks. Admiral Richter had spent so much time on the road this spring, supporting the Academy's mission in one form or another, that nobody had formed a real opinion of the guy yet. All Oberly knew was that the commandant started his career as an A-7 pilot and transitioned to F-18s when the Corsairs were turned into museum pieces. He would spend another eighteen months at the Academy before heading to command of an air wing. Fabulous Ferren had remembered Richter as an instructor pilot. He had said that the admiral had been popular with his students.

Sitting down, Oberly noticed how attractive the couple was. Both were thin, svelte, and had just a hint of color, as if they had tanned while sailing or had just returned from a trip to Key West. They sat at either end of a small dining room table, with Oberly fitting comfortably between them.

They enjoyed a breakfast of scrambled eggs and sausage, toast, and fruit salad. Oberly drank almost as much coffee as the commandant. When the typical small talk subsided, Mrs. Richter excused herself. "Bob, I have some things to attend to, and I know you and the Admiral need to talk. I'll be sure to see you off."

"Thank you, Missus Richter."

With his wife absent, the admiral got right to business. "So, Bob, I'm certain there's something you want to discuss."

"Yes, sir. It's about one of my midshipmen who will be coming before you this week—Midshipman Lieutenant Durago."

Richter pushed back from the table and canted his chair toward Oberly. "Okay," he said as he relaxed in his chair a little, "let me save you some time. I'm sure you're going to sing Mister Durago's praises, right?"

"Yes, sir."

"Fine. Let me respond by saying I'll accept any such input at face value. My view is more of the overall process. Commander Gordon was clearly following my guidance, but in reviewing this case I can see that these midshipmen may or may not have been overzealous in their dealing with Miss Whorton. If they were overzealous, the responsibility falls on us. We, the officers here at Annapolis, failed to guide them. So, I'm approving each appeal and sending them back to the company officers to handle. I expect you, Bob, to recalibrate Mister Durago. Does that work?"

"Yes, sir, it does."

"Great. Is there anything else we need to address?"

"No, sir."

"Well, then, let's consider this matter closed. Still, I would appreciate it very much if you kept our discussion confidential. When information such as this is shared, rumors grow, things become sensationalized. I'm willing to share the info with you so you can focus on other duties, including how you will handle Durago. Conversely, another day or so of waiting out the appeals process shouldn't hurt the midshipmen at this point—might even be good for them. Do you agree? "

"I understand, sir. Yes, sir."

Mrs. Richter magically appeared as Oberly got up to leave. He shook hands with both of them. "We'll have to have you and your wife, Doreen, over sometime," Mrs. Richter said.

"Thanks, ma'am. We'd like that."

Monday morning had been routine, quiet. Lieutenant Tripp was putting documents in the file drawer and anticipating a long lunch in town, when the phone rang. "Brigade Legal, Lieutenant Tripp, may I help you?" he asked.

"Come see me in my office. Now."

The voice of his immediate superior, the deputy commandant, was curt. Tripp could tell that the commander was pissed off. *What could it be now?* He marched across the rotunda, ignoring the mids who greeted him as they passed. The legal officer wanted to get the latest whipping over with so he could meet his lunch date at Griffin's.

Tripp knocked and entered the office. It was always much quieter in here because of the plush carpet and the soundproofing in the walls.

"Sir, Lieutenant Tripp reporting." He tried to sound formal.

The lieutenant was not invited to sit down. His superior remained seated. "Tripp, you screwed up on this Whorton thing."

"Sir?"

"First, why the hell didn't you tell me that Commander Gordon was running amok on this thing? You know that idiot is blinded by his own agenda. The guy hates this place. I'll bet he tried to get in here and wasn't accepted. Christ, the 'dant leaves for two weeks and Gordon's waving six thousands like he runs the place."

"Sir, I'm just a legal adviser. I—"

"You are the legal adviser to the Commandant of Midshipmen. You should have told Gordon that his charges were a crock, and you should have reported to my office. Gordon walked right into Whorton's trap, and you let him."

"Sir, I merely ensured that Commander Gordon—"

"Stop with the sea lawyer stuff. You screwed up, now you fix it. You're meeting with the commandant in thirty minutes. You'd better have a good plan to make this right."

"Aye, aye, sir."

Tripp went back to his office and called off his date.

39

SENTENCE

Durago strolled through the passageways between 7-4 and 4-1, the same walk he took on Service Selection Night, as if he were willingly walking to his crucifixion. Deep down he knew that he would be retained, but he was not sure he wanted to be. He wondered if the trials of the past few weeks were an omen of things to come. He tried to imagine the advice his father would give him if he were alive today.

Durago desperately wanted to graduate, to graduate into the identity that the Academy had given him. The identity of manhood, discipline, service to country. The identity he almost missed but for the martyrdom of his father. Now that identity seemed unattainable.

Durago gave himself enough time to stroll up to Memorial Hall, to visit his father's name again. He stood underneath the chandelier and turned around, looking at all of the war relics and monuments. What would all the men represented here say if they could speak? He was overwhelmed with confusion and frustration. He felt betrayed.

When he walked into the Brigade conference room, he noted that none of the officers had papers, or forms, or folders in front of them. Gordon was not there. Only the commandant spoke. "Mister Durago, the board and I have reached a decision regarding your appeal. All previous charges are to be sent back to company level for review. I have recommended that they be downgraded to something more appropriate."

The commandant paused as if considering Durago one more time. "I heard about the comments you directed at the board, so, after reviewing your case, I've decided to charge you with disrespect and failure to use good judgment. Your display was uncalled for. I'm awarding you ten days restriction. Any objections?"

"No, sir. Thank you, sir."

"There is one other problem."

"Sir?"

"The Brigade Legal Office was overzealous and began your outprocessing when the battalion officer recommended separation. BUPERS assigned your orders to someone else. You'll receive new orders sometime this week."

Durago struggled to hide his tears. He choked on his words. "Captain, how could they do that?"

The commandant tried to play it down. "Son, it's not as bad as it may seem. If we cannot fix it, you'll have a wide variety of ships to choose from. Where were you going, anyway?"

"To a pre-comm *Aegis* destroyer."

"Oh. Which one?"

"USS *Fitzpatrick*."

40

REUNION

Though the charges had essentially been dropped, losing his father's ship, the icing on the cake of Service Selection Night, made Durago bitter. Captain Oberly again sought to form a protest; Durago did not have any fight left in him. "Fuck it, sir. They probably wouldn't let me serve there anyway once someone made the connection," he said.

Instead, Durago received orders to USS *Laboon*, another *Aegis* pre-comm named for a Naval Academy graduate who was both a Silver Star recipient and a Jesuit priest. Still, when he crossed the stage and accepted his diploma and commission from President George H. W. Bush, Durago had a small moment of inner jubilation—which he quickly suppressed to prevent himself from weeping openly in front of ten thousand people. Then the feeling returned as he tossed his cover into the air with the rest of the United States Naval Academy Class of 1992. His emotions poured out, but now it was shared by other celebrating classmates.

The class parted after hugs and high fives, mixing with the friends and families pouring onto the field. Durago quickly found his only guests, his manufactured family, Jan and Master Chief Strong, both in uniform. An elegant woman in a big hat agreed to take a photo as Strong affixed one shoulder board, and Jan the other. "A proud father and big sister, I'm sure," the woman said as she handed the camera back to Jan.

Durago knew that Slim was wrapped up with his dysfunctional family, packing, and plans for The Basic School in Quantico, the first step of his Marine Corps career, followed by flight school. "Hey, come to the party my folks are having. I'd rather have you there than most of them, anyway," Slim said. "I'll need you to run interference for me, pull me away from uncomfortable conversations."

Durago promised to stop by, but never did. Instead, he drove back to the Academy to retrieve the last of his things from storage and take one last trip to the Sea Gate.

There was a chill in the October afternoon air when Donald Fitzpatrick returned to Navy–Marine Corps Stadium. After the game, he strolled along the perimeter of the parking lot behind the Navy side. He looked at each tent, searching for the numbers that identified each class. Finally, he saw them from about twenty yards away. Signs around the tent proclaimed that it was their twenty-fifth reunion.

The alums were no longer in their prime. Some had thinning hair, others had protruding waistlines, and all were developing crow's feet. Fitzpatrick approached the class tailgater, but then stopped again ten feet from the crowd, not knowing how to proceed. After he stood there for a minute, a group of graduates from the Class of 1967 saw him and recognized him. "Oh, my God . . ." one said.

A second broke from the group and approached Fitzpatrick. His eyes were red. When they met he placed a hand on Fitz's shoulder and studied him. After a moment, tears streamed down his face. "I know who you are," he said.

Within moments, Donald Fitzpatrick had a beer in his hand. He was surrounded by many of his father's classmates, and old tales were retold.

41

BAPTISM

Lieutenant Donald Fitzpatrick drove through the gate onto Naval Base Norfolk. He slowed, looking into the rearview mirror first at the baby in the car seat behind him, then to his college roommate following in a black Ford Mustang.

Turning to his wife in the passenger seat, he said, "How is it that I missed the sports car stage? I'm twenty-seven years old and I drive a station wagon."

"We still have the Jeep," Jan said, smiling at him. "That's cool, right?"

"Yeah, but it's getting old."

"Are you saying I'm old?"

"Older."

They laughed together.

Ten minutes later, Fitzpatrick led his party through the security gate and down Pier 12. He and his college chum walked stride for stride, as if on a drill field. Though of the same grade, Captain James Warren wore the khaki shirt and blue trousers with a blood-red stripe on each leg that marked him as an officer of Marines. Like Fitz, his dive pin was no longer in the primary position above the ribbon on his left breast. It was now superseded by wings of gold spread out from a shield and a fouled anchor. Fitz's own dive pin was on the flap of his breast pocket. "Water wings," also in gold, were above—a destroyer steaming through seas over crossed swords. Fitz was now a qualified surface warfare officer, Warren a naval aviator.

"I can't believe you know how to drive those things," Slim said, nodding at the mass of grey steel in front of them. "You're a regular Bull Halsey."

"And you, you're a regular Pappy Boyington," Fitzpatrick chided.

"Not quite. At least you've got a deployment under your belt. You're a salty sonofabitch. I'm still a nugget."

There was an aircraft carrier to their right, a behemoth of a ship compared to the destroyer they approached; it completely blocked Norfolk's Pier 10.

"Which one is that?" asked Slim.

"*Roosevelt*, the '*TR*.'"

"No shit? That's the boat I qualled on."

The lieutenant remained focused on the ship near the end of the pier. She was port side to, across from *TR*. A bunting of thick red, white, and blue stripe surrounded the lifelines and signal flags ran from the stern to the masthead. From her stern flag pole, a large holiday ensign, the Star-Spangled Banner, danced gently in the breeze.

When most people approached the ship, their eyes were drawn naturally to the radome of the CIWS, or "close-in weapons system." The young naval officer was never distracted by this white protuberance among the muted grey. Instead, he always looked downward, below the missile deck, to a spot even lower than the flight deck. He always looked to the stern, to a name embossed in steel and painted black. The two officers stopped as they neared the stern of the ship and looked to the name. Neither mentioned it or its significance.

Jan pushed a stroller down the pier, Nina in tow. Though they were attending a military affair, Jan had decided to wear a yellow sundress with white accents so she could handle the baby. Besides, she had grown weary of comments about outranking her husband. Nina was dressed similarly, after Jan asked her to forgo a tie-dyed frock.

"Well, let's do this before it gets too hot," said Fitz.

"You go first," Jan commanded.

Continuing down the port side, Fitz now looked up to the ship's crest. In the center was a shield with the bow-on silhouette of a PBR, not unlike the destroyer on Fitz's pin. The Medal of Honor was represented by a light-blue field with white stars across the top edge of the shield. A ribbon along the bottom read "Return with Honor."

"That crest really captures his memory," Slim remarked. "What's the call sign again?"

"'Black Hat,' to note that he was a black beret, a brown-water Navy sailor."

"And your ship again?"

"*Laboon*? It's 'Steel Halo.'"

"For the courageous war hero who became a priest—I get it. You know, the Navy does do some shit right."

Suddenly, a bell rang out twice from the destroyer's quarterdeck followed by a voice booming over the ship's announcement system. "Plankowner, arriving."

"Too cool," said Slim.

An ensign stood watch on the quarterdeck as the officer of the deck, with a second class boatswain's mate as the petty officer of the watch and a seaman as messenger. Fitz saluted the colors aft, then faced the ensign and saluted. "Request permission to come aboard."

"Granted," the officer replied as he returned the salute.

This ceremonial action was repeated with Slim. Fitz looked to his wife, who was stepping carefully, bracing herself on the railing. The baby was asleep in a sling across her chest.

"You good?" he asked.

"I'm fine," she said. "I'm just being extra careful."

Once everyone gathered on the quarterdeck, the ensign said, "The captain, XO, command master chief, and chaplain are all waiting on the foc'sle, sir. The messenger will escort you all there."

The captain and chaplain were both Navy commanders. The chaplain was prepping for the ceremony with the assistance of the command master chief and three other sailors, while the captain welcomed everyone aboard the *Fitzpatrick*. Like Fitz, all were in summer whites. The ribbons on Captain Morris' chest looked like fruit salad. Fitz noticed stars on the CO's sea service ribbon, accounting for seven deployments, and the campaign ribbons for Desert Storm and Desert Shield. "Jan, Don, welcome aboard. How are you today?"

"Great, Captain. Thanks," Fitz replied.

"And thank you, sir, so much, for allowing us to do this today," Jan added.

"Jan, it is an honor," he said with genuine enthusiasm.

Slim stepped up to be introduced.

"Captain Morris," Fitz said, "let me introduce my Academy room-mate, Captain James Warren."

"Welcome aboard, Captain. You know I'm going to ask . . . what is your airframe?"

"Prowlers, sir."

"Ah, yes . . . the electric jet. Unsung heroes of the sky."

"Yes, sir. That's what they tell me. I'm with VMAQ Two in Cherry Point."

"Very good. Well, again, welcome aboard. And this is?"

"My good friend, Nina Gavilrakis," Jan replied.

"Welcome, Nina."

The captain looked over his shoulder and saw that the chaplain's back was still turned as he prepared for the ceremony. "Well, then, I'm going to stand by and let the chaplain do his thing. We'll talk at the reception in the wardroom after."

The forecastle angled upward slightly. Like the rest of the destroyer, it was covered in red-, white-, and blue-striped bunting, and colorful signal flags ran from the masthead to the deck, right in front of the jack—the blue field with fifty stars taken from the national flag that all U.S. Navy ships flew from their bow when in port.

"We could have done it between the gun mount and the VLS," Father Joe suddenly said.

Fitzpatrick turned and saw that the chaplain was now in his vest-ments. On a stand in front of the superstructure, the ship's brass bell sat upended, so that its opening pointed heavenward. The brass shined, almost appearing gold in the morning sun.

"Is it okay to do it here?" the chaplain asked.

"Yes, Father. Right here is good."

"Good, I'm glad. It'll make it easier to return the bell when we're finished."

Father Joe nodded toward Command Master Chief Decker, who in turn pointed to the bell. Two seamen gently lifted a bucket to its edge and poured water into it to just below the lip. Father Joe mur-mured something and made the sign of the cross over the bell. Fitz sensed they were almost ready, as the priest turned to focus on them.

"So, let me introduce myself. I'm Father Joe," he said, extending his hand toward Slim.

"Captain James Warren, Father."

"Oorah."

"Oorah, sir."

"I was with the Marines in the sandbox. Best tour of my career. And you?"

"Nina Gavilrakis, Father."

"Greek?"

"Yes, Father, but I'm Catholic, not Greek Orthodox."

"Please, don't misunderstand. I have a great love for the Greek people, including the Greek Orthodox Church. Lovely tradition. I was stationed at Naval Station Souda Bay, Crete, before this tour.

"Okay . . . let me make sure I have the names correct. Warren?" the priest said, looking to Slim.

"Yes, Father."

"And Nina?"

"Yes."

"And now, the guest of honor—the wee baby. Sleeping are we?"

"Should I wake him?" Jan asked.

"Yes, let's get him up gently, now."

Jan extracted the infant from the sling and handed him to the priest. The baby stirred and opened his eyes.

"Oh, my, there he is," said Father Joe. "Awoken to the day. Now then, are we ready? Good."

Jan, Slim, and Fitz braced themselves for the enormity of the baptismal rite.

"Donald, Jan, what name do you give your son?"

"Donald James Fitzpatrick," they said in unison.

"What do you ask of God's Church for Donald?"

"Baptism," they replied.

At the end of the ceremony, the captain invited everyone involved to the wardroom for coffee and cake. Everyone made pleasant small talk. Fitz thanked the captain and command master chief again for putting forth so much effort. "Sir, again, thank you. My family and I appreciate your willingness to allow our son to be baptized in the ship's bell, and the crew's effort to make it a memorable occasion."

"Don, say no more; the honor is ours," the captain said sincerely. "You know," he added, "I heard you wanted to come here for your first tour. Now that you're qualified, why not come on board for a second divo tour? We could use a good strike officer, or navigator."

"Sir, that would be awesome, but being an honorary plankowner is more than enough. Besides, my career is about to take a more dramatic turn."

"Oh?"

"I've been accepted for lateral transfer to Special Operations."

"EOD, huh?"

"Yes, sir."

"Wow . . . well, good luck."

Just then, the wardroom door opened and a sailor dressed in blue coveralls entered. "Mister Fitzpatrick?"

"Yes?"

"I'm Petty Officer Brose. I was about to engrave the ship's bell. Thought you might like to watch."

"You bet," Fitz replied. "You guys wanna check this out?" he asked.

"You go ahead," Jan said. "I'm gonna start packing up."

"We'll meet you on the quarterdeck," the captain concurred.

As they descended the ladder near the wardroom, Fitzpatrick called out to the sailor in front of him.

"Hey, Brose?"

"Sir?"

"Let's swing by the mess decks."

"No problem, sir."

The space where the destroyer's crew enjoyed their meals looked like a nautical fast food restaurant. Fitz strolled over to the port-side bulkhead to a display of the Medal of Honor citation that he now knew by heart. It also included a five-pointed star, suspended on the flukes of an anchor, below a light-blue ribbon field with a constellation of white stars.

After a brief moment of reflection, the former Donald Durago joined Brose on the forecastle and watched as the sailor etched "8/20/96 Donald James Fitzpatrick" on the inside of the bell belonging to USS *Fitzpatrick*.

About the Author

Stephen Phillips is a 1992 graduate of the U.S. Naval Academy. He began his naval career as a surface warfare officer on board USS *Harlan County* and USS *San Jacinto*. He then applied and was accepted into the Navy's Special Operations community. He subsequently served as an Explosive Ordnance Disposal (EOD) Technician at EOD Mobile Units Six, Eight, and Ten.